KILLING GROUND

The Canadian Civil War

KILLING GROUND

The Canadian Civil War

by Bruce Powe

A CANADIAN

PaperJacks

One of a series of Canadian books
by PaperJacks Ltd.

KILLING GROUND
The Canadian Civil War

Peter Martin Associates edition published in 1968

PaperJacks edition published Nov. 1977

ISBN 0-7701-0052-X
Copyright ©, 1968, by Bruce Powe
All rights reserved. This PaperJacks edition is published by
arrangement with Peter Martin Associates Limited.
Printed in Canada

A WORD FROM THE AUTHOR

When KILLING GROUND first appeared, I described it as a "war game novel", a projection of events based on assumptions which may or may not become valid in actual experience. If some kind of accommodation is not soon reached with Quebec, will Canadians find themselves drifting into the kind of situation that erupted in Ulster, Nigeria, Bangladesh, Lebanon, Cyprus and other places? Are Canadians so virtuous and law-abiding that such a prospect is unthinkable?

This fantasy merely examines that possibility in its most extreme form: the "worst case" for Canada. It is a war game with certain assumptions. Choose your solution.

Some critics have said the story is far too violent and should never have been published. But I hope that it will continue to make a contribution to the solution of Canada's problems in the sense that we avow to one another: "We must never, never allow this to happen."

Over to you.

Bruce Powe
Toronto, October 1977

1

In the course of time there is a blurring of sharp images in the memory leaving what is familiar to every man: the bright peaks that make up what one remembers of his life, far above the murky residue of forgotten events. Even these high points may stay sharp in recall but indistinct at the edges. They may become objects of doubt in one's own mind until a jarring note of some forgotten event or person brings a cold understanding of how protective to one's sanity memory really is.

Even with this awareness of the tricks of recall, I cannot describe my arrival in Montreal on that April day as anything but completely, absolutely idyllic. No amount of clinical insight, nor all the things that happened afterward in swelling breakers of violence and terror, will ever change my secure recollection of that soft morning when I stepped out onto the deck of our liner at dockside and saw pink and orange sunlight in the windows of Montreal's towers.

Sometimes the spring comes to central Canada, into the valley of the St. Lawrence and the land bordered by the Great Lakes, in an envelope of heat that leaves one gasping as the body tries to brake its stiff preparations to meet the sharp winds of fading winter. Such was this April when I returned, happy in reunion with my wife and sons, after two years of more or less continuous absence.

The sea voyage from Britain had helped in its part to ease that mixture of shyness, strain and concealed irritability that occurs when a man and his wife are united again. Our separation especially had not been easy this time with the boys, now in their teens, away at private (or public, if you will) school in the countryside while my wife, Edith, lived in London, not knowing as many people as she thought she did from our previous postings when the idea of following me part way to South Africa had first occurred to us.

They weren't too bad at getting us out of the truce zone either (officially, the United Nations Supervisory Force for the International Demarcation Commission on South Africa) and, every four months or so, some of us would hop an R.A.F. jet to the U.K. if we weren't held up by some local massacre perpetrated by what we called the Kaffir Kommandos on one side or the Afrikaans Assholes on the other. As an employer, the U.N. was always a soft touch. The only thing they were sticky about was careless use of our weaponry and so we learned the interesting technique of talking troublemakers to death while they, wild-eyed and puzzled, gradually let their gun muzzles drop. But even with the generous leave benefits of the U.N. it had been a wearing ordeal for Edith and me, especially for her in a Wimbledon apartment too far from the West End and yet not a full-fledged member of her neighborhood; and for me, the hours of monotonous tension on the brown, faded veldt where often the only splash of colour was the bright blue of our helmets and our jeeps. I felt sure that our own prairies in the west where I had grown up were lush compared to the African veldt and I had dreams of green strips of trees, golden grain and all the rest of it, selectively leaving out the bleak whiteness of winter or the grey curls of dust storms in spring.

Edith was in her bed in our cabin below, cool and asleep in the port of her native city, with that patrician serenity that somehow sets the more inbred English-speaking Montrealer apart from others. In their purest Anglo-Saxon pockets they are—or were—more akin in appearance to the privileged classes of Britain, complete with voice inflections identifiable from, say, the privileged of other cities. They can be seen (or they used to be) in the Ritz, invariably in family groups of glossy young men and women hovering over some obviously wealthy, aged relatives or parents, more the kind of thing you see in the Dorchester or Savoy in London than in the Park Plaza, Westbury or Royal York in Toronto. Even the Empress in Victoria is not quite comparable because the Mont-realers were not tweedy or grey—they wore dark clothes and were ethereal. Edith, for example, has a glowing complexion never in need of makeup and long, honey hair of original hue; even when forced straight back in a clip or bun her hair looks not severe but implies a con-trolled, well-bred turbulence. The assurance that went with her appearance meant that one did not get up at six in the morning to see the sun strike the buildings of the good, old home town.

Our boys, John, fifteen and Steven, thirteen, were also in the sack in their doubledecker bunks in their own cabin, an inside one down the corridor from us. *Their* sleep at this time was the casualness of private school and the strange chemistry of teenagery. I was alone that morning, but content.

We came over on one of those new streamlined single class liners with no funnels or anything else identifiable to the seasoned, class-conscious sea traveler. I stood on what would be the promenade deck on a normal ship about level with the roof of the nearby Customs shed. I could hear and enjoy the sights and noises of the awaken-ing city—the special bustle of North America that I had not sensed in two years. Over the muted rumble of vehicles moving in the narrow streets, I heard the great sound of a diesel locomotive horn and the clear tones of an ambulance or fire engine siren. It seemed to be going towards a flat disk of smoke to my left that, amid the panorama, had flattened out in pancake fashion amid the tall buildings and merged into the bluish haze curtaining the Mountain.

On the concrete pier below, a group of navy-blue Customs men gathered around to receive the flow of passengers. A supervisor talked to them intently, probably in French I thought, as I saw his gestures towards our ship. They would have a fine time with my South African souvenirs, all those bottles of Paarl brandy—the special kind not available outside the Cape—wrapped in laundry and scattered throughout our belongings. What do you have to declare, sir? I declare, by God, that I'm glad to be home and that oughta be good enough for anybody!

I watched the knot of Customs men move in a group away from the white sides of the ship and along the pier past the bow where they stopped. Someone opened the wooden slat gates at the end of the Customs shed, and I looked with interest at a Dodge army truck, canvas-covered and shiny with dark green depot paint, as it whined its way in full low onto the pier. The tailgate clattered down in the morning quiet and I stared as two sections of men, helmeted, armed with FN rifles but awkward and unaccustomed to the activity, jumped in pairs off the back of the truck and lined up across the front of the gate. A sergeant detailed four of them to go on the other side of the wooden gates and it seemed to take him a long time to get across to them what he wanted them to do. The rest were spread around the other approaches to the pier and at the ship's gangways. I watched the two men nearest to me, already uncomfortable in their heavy American-style helmets (a headgear everyone had always hated ever since they had been adopted by our forces). They were awkward at the un-

10

accustomed bite of webbing at their shoulders and bellies and unfamiliar with the heft of a ten-pound rifle. I thought I could make out blue and yellow Supply Service patches on the shoulders of their green bush jackets.

"They look about as dangerous as those Algerians we had," said "J.J." Rousseau, who like all good adjutants, appeared at one's elbow whenever a question began to form. He was actually Paul Urbaine Rousseau, but having decided that "P.U." was not dignified for our adjutant, we called him J.J., of course, for "Jean Jacques." Our Rousseau was no philosopher, however, and somehow with his olive complexion—a touch of Huron, I always suspected—black moustache, flashing teeth and large cigar, he was more in the tradition of a Latin-American junta leader, particularly when in dress uniform. I remember how we once subdued a Shantytown riot by having J.J. pose in bush shirt, fatigues and cigar as a Cuban liaison officer haranguing the natives on an imaginary Marxist theme of non-violence.

"The Algerians could take that lot," I said.

"They had their moments," said J.J. "Remember when they went on the town in Pretoria and kidnapped those Dutch women?" Until he engaged in incomprehensible singsong dialects with a compatriot, one would never guess that he was French-Canadian. It always came as a jar to me, imprisoned by the cold, grammatical high school French of permutations and combinations, to realize that at times he did not have the same thought-processes that I did. Still, I was glad he had gotten up early to see his home town, for he had been silent and wistful staring at the passing shoreline of Quebec in our two days up the St. Lawrence. I suspected he had stayed up all night to get his first glimpse of the yellow clock tower in the harbour and to look across at the islands with their remaining monuments to the more euphoric days of Expo 67 not so many years ago.

He went on, because it was almost our first conversation in three days, "I'll never know why the U.N. sent Algerians to South Africa."

"Politics. The Secretary-General is a tough one, but even he had to concede one contingent from Africa. They were the furthest away, I suppose," I murmured lazily, falling into the soldier's habit of reminiscing while something else was going on under his nose. Every soldier has a touch of the academic in him, maybe as a result of spending so much time in lectures or courses. Or perhaps because he is closer to history than most. I remembered, long ago, standing fresh from Canada at a filthy Korean river called Sami-ch'on, listening raptly to my company commander and the bridging officer having a ringing row about some aspect of the bridge at Nijmegen in the last war while an entire R.C.E. unit stood around awaiting orders. At last, instinctive training stirred itself.

"We'd better find the head man on this computerized tub and see what's up," I said reluctantly.

"I'll check," grinned J.J., and was off. Shortly he came back and led me to the captain's cabin. When we knocked and entered, we walked into a circle of his officers seated and standing, coffee cups in hand while he talked.

"Colonel Hlynka, do come in. I was just going to have someone whistle you up," the captain said, his Tyneside accent subdued by decades of ministering to the needs of passenger cargo. Like all Englishmen, he could not keep an edge of condescension from his voice when he pronounced, what was to him, a foreign name. They must absorb it from the B.B.C. Still moody and introspective, I thought of that dull, brown, little street off Main Street in Vancouver where, as children, we unmercifully persecuted the Price kids, the only English ones on the block. The captain was a classic: ruddy-faced and ageless, the sure mechanics of handling floating hotels absolving him from the stress lines of the more confined and harried landsman.

"We saw the troops and wondered," I said, back in character as the Colonel. An officer handed us coffee and I fished in my tweed jacket for my Players' Mediums.

"Somebody blew up some sort of government building nearby." He looked at notes. "Dorchester and Bishop. Frightful mess," said the captain.

"That," said J.J. frowning, "must be the old C.B.C. building. But they moved out long ago. I haven't a clue what it could be."

"What are your instructions from the port authorities?" I asked.

"All passengers are to remain on board until they establish control at major installations," said the captain. "That explains the troops. They don't expect the delay to be too long."

"Do you have any ideas?" I asked J.J., who always seemed to know what was going on.

J.J. looked strangely upset. "Must be some kind of intensive demonstration," he said. "There was a major federal-provincial meeting planned in Montreal this week. But why the old C.B.C. building, I don't know."

The captain quickly dismissed such vagaries and turned to me. "I would appreciate it if you, as senior officer, would inform all military personnel aboard," he said rather formally. Anything you say may be taken down and used in evidence . . .

"Not all are in our contingent," I said. "Can you give us a list and their billets? Some of them may be getting orders direct."

J.J. automatically took over and I started for the door to wake up my own family with the unwelcome news. The artificial mahogany door thumped and a rating appeared with a subaltern attired in skeleton webbing and green field garb smudged in black. He reeked of smoke.

"Sir, the lieutenant is looking for a Colonel—" said the rating, bogging down on my name in a question mark.

"He's here," said the captain quickly, always passenger-oriented. "Colonel Hlynka."

The youthful lieutenant saluted.

"Sir, General Tremaine asked me to deliver this to you personally and to wait."

I took the envelope. Inside was a scrawled note.

"Alex," it said, "Saw your orders coming through on TWX. Come with bearer if you can and I'll fill you in. Good luck. Budge."

Budgy Tremaine, I thought, opening up the thin paper sheet. He was now acting commander Mobile Command, St. Hubert, with, I suddenly realized, not much to call on. Almost everything was out of the country: on the Rhine to stiffen up what was left of N.A.T.O. after the upset elections in Germany and France, one of the right and the other of the left; in Thailand our new commitments with S.E.A.T.O.; a battalion and assorted troops in South Africa; and heaven knew where else we had little pockets of men. Thinly spread for a small nation.

My message read:

LT. COL. A. N. HLYNKA, OFFICER COMMANDING, CANADIAN CONTINGENT, UNITED NATIONS SPECIAL FORCE ON BOARD S.S. ———. MESSAGE BEGINS. YOU WILL ASSUME COMMAND 3 BN ROYAL CANADIAN REGIMENT IMMEDIATELY REPORT LONDON ONTARIO ACK SOONEST TRAVEL WARRANTS FROM MOBILE COMMAND HQ ST. HUBERT. VICE CHIEF CANADIAN FORCES.

I looked up at J.J. who was watching intently.

"I didn't know the R.C.R.'s had a regular third battalion," I said.

"Neither did I," said J.J., "They must be making one. Their third is militia—the London and Oxford Something-or-others."

"I'm to be C.O.," I told him. "How'd you like to come to London?"

"If this keeps up, I'll never learn French," grinned J.J.

"You go ahead and make the announcements to our people on the ship," I said to J.J. "I've got to go and see the General."

I asked the uneasy young subaltern to wait for me on the dock and to clear my departure from the ship with the Customs and Immigration people. Then I set out down the stairway to our cabin. Even with air conditioning and plastic décor, the corridors trapped hints of the ageless odors of ships: cooking, wax, oil and disinfectant. I made my way to our cabin, paused for a moment along the way at the smaller cabin where the boys presumably were asleep, went on to open the door to our own bedroom and entered.

From the porthole a fuzzy tube of daylight slanted across the bed where Edith stirred, reacting slowly to my faint noises. I stood for a moment in silent admiration, or possibly pride and self-congratulation, I don't know which, in the merging currents of feeling. At 35, her earlier, pale freshness had deepened in colour to a rose gloss. What had been naturally silver tones in her blonde hair were now deeper golds and it lay long, unspoiled and swirled against the rumpled pillow. An idyllic scene, yet I wondered distantly why she slept long into the morning every day as if there were some crushing reluctance to make the climb into consciousness and meet the world, no matter how warm and bright the morning might be.

I didn't know. We always had seemed to be satisfied with each other and, considering the way one gets kicked around in military life, we had spent an amazing amount of time together. That is, until the past four years when I became one of the truce boffins and did my bit in Viet Nam, Nepal and South Africa. That had been a difficult time, far worse I often thought, than the plight of the businessman who spends nights in the office or in travel, yet manages to collapse exhausted at home at least one day a week. There were times in filthy, distant villages when I lapsed into Slav inertia and melancholia that once caused a visiting Russian journalist to say to me: "You're one of us." I had thought, as someone completely a product of North American culture, that those traits which I had seen in my father and grandfather would not affect me. Maybe these things are hereditary, after all.

When Edith and I had our reunions, the scale went the other way. In euphoria, we overindulged ourselves in sex and intimacy on a vast scale made possible at forty by my tough Slav physique and her accumulated needs. In public we laughed and chattered like idiots, for a while anyway. The boys too seemed to enjoy coming out from behind the stone walls of some private school and joining the aura of their reunited and happy parents. But this time it had been different, and now Edith had somehow entered a strange phase of withdrawal in sleep. In fairness, I reminded myself that she wasn't exactly in a coma when it was not yet seven a.m.

With a hand cupped fondly on her satin, bare shoulder I shook gently. The wide, grey eyes opened.

"I've got to go ashore and see Budgy Tremaine," I murmured. "Remember him?"

"When'll you be back?" she whispered.

"Shouldn't be too long. You've got to stay on board anyway. There's been some trouble." I decided not to tell her about my new posting.

Her eyes widened. "What kind of trouble?"

"Not sure yet. I'll find out from Budgy. It seems to be a bombing or something like that."

"Do be careful, darling," she said, and my heart melted. After all that time, when a woman can make you watery on the inside, she is something. We kissed gently and I got up to go.

"Mother and Dad were to meet us," she mentioned.

"I'll phone them, if they haven't already started out," I said.

We looked at each other for a moment. Silently, I

picked up my landing card and passport and left. Outside, I paused again at the boy's door and showing, for once, that I was a true North American father, left it for Edith to tell them. Now I wish that I had, because our lives were never the same again.

2

The young subaltern, I noticed, was a member of the elite Canadian Airborne Regiment. He waited for me on the docks in an incredibly blackened and dirty jeep and, by his glance, I sensed that he would rather I had changed into uniform from my tweed jacket and flannel slacks. The Customs and Immigration men quickly cleared my departure and we started off along the quay.

"Stop at the nearest phone booth," I said.

"Most of them were smashed last night. The phones were pulled out, sir," he replied. We passed the desperately uncomfortable supply types standing guard at the gates. I called to a Customs man talking to them.

"What happens to people coming to meet the boat? We were expecting my wife's parents."

"We should be unloading in a couple of hours," the Customs man said. "The radio and TV have been telling people to stay home, but everyone seems to be coming in to work."

I asked him if he had a phone and, to the obvious irritation of my escort, I went into the small guardhouse at the entrance to the dock. A Corps of Commissioners man moved away from his desk to let me phone. I looked up Edith's parents, the Watsons, in the directory and dialed, but there was no answer after ten rings. The subaltern started up the jeep with a savage jab at the accelerator and away we went, dodging the waterfront normality of huge trailer trucks carrying out intricate manoeuvres in narrow streets and around loading platforms.

"Was there mob violence last night?" I asked, thinking of the phone booths.

"No, sir. It was planned. They just took out the phone booths, that's all. Next week it'll be something else, maybe the Metro."

"It's getting that bad, eh?"

"Yes, sir. It is."

Why was it, I wondered, as I casually studied my driver, that all army people sooner or later acquired that special Anglo-Saxon look. It was almost osmosis, as if a combination of regimental traditions (such as were left), British-type drill, clipped accents and mess routines, seeped into their bones. No amount of army conditioning, however, ever made me look Anglo-Saxon. Through all my years I remained a throwback to the steppes with my black, shiny hair, high cheekbones, V-face and eyes with a touch of the Golden Horde creasing their lids.

Once as a subaltern I did try a moustache, but took it off when everyone called me "Ghengis". Height compensated, in some measure, for my lack of the traditional officer appearance and, as odd as it may seem, there was only one explanation for a relatively successful career. At the start, my hereditary endurance made me a standout in all the obstacle courses, cross-country runs, sports days and all those other strenuous things that are so much a part of army life. That, combined with high marks in almost every course, and reasonable decisiveness in command, pulled me out ahead of many associates with the conventional blonde moustache.

This kid driving my jeep had started a blonde moustache and looked like all subalterns since *Journey's End*. I asked him his name.

"Levine, sir."

I turned away, my lips twitching. The North American variation.

We were on Dorchester driving west along the boulevard, with the high, skinny buildings overshadowing the commuters now beginning to throng the sidewalks. Westbound waves from Central Station clashed and mingled with eastbound waves from Windsor Station. People were obviously disregarding the radio and TV announcements. As we slowed down in the traffic, I studied them.

Along the verges of Dominion Square they waited for lights, briefcase-armed, darkly-dressed and English-speaking. It was difficult, so newly back in North America, to assess the facial expressions, for people of our continent have a tension about them that is different from the Europeans. I tried to relate those anxious, pale faces to the trouble (whatever it was) of the night before and to the warnings amid sixty-second spots, on radio and TV, to stay home. The demands of business had brought them out—anyway, what would they do with their time on an unexpected bonanza of a day without plan? What would they do with all the memos, meetings, dictation and business luncheons blocked out on their desk diaries? Patterns cannot be broken that simply, especially when you have warnings from mellow voices that switch from disaster to selling packaged foods. Which message is the one to believe? These people in their droves obviously had bought the message of normality and had come in on their trains as usual to carry on with the planned day as planned yesterday. Yet, as I looked at their determination to enforce routine, I thought I had seen those faces somewhere else. They were the faces I had seen eighteen months ago when I had first arrived on my U.N. mission in South Africa. They were the faces of Johannesburg.

As we moved on beyond a green light, I thought that there was something missing on the streets of Montreal, and realized that there was an element I had recalled that was sparse and different. The smartly-dressed young office girls, who surpass anything in the world for their combination of sexy clothes, flirty bounce and office colour, were missing. There were hardly any among the dark-suited men along the streets. And then I reflected that most of the office girls were bilingual French-Canadians. They had stayed at home. And I wondered why *they* had stayed and the others had come to work.

Beyond the budding greenery of Canada Square, we passed the Laurentian Hotel on one side and Imperial Bank of Commerce tower on the other, pillars to a sudden curtain behind which was violence and death. A breeze shifted stinking, charred smells in our direction and a thin haze of smoke swirled downward amid the buildings. At Stanley there were six police cars along the curb and a gate of yellow construction barriers with a company's name and "detour" still printed on them. A line of troops stood across the street in front of the construction horses and I noticed that they seemed a little more at home in their gear than the ones on the docks.

A sergeant with Canadian Airborne Regiment patches nodded to the lieutenant and let our jeep through.

Glancing over my shoulder, I noticed that there were few civilians hanging around—either they had been moved on, or perhaps even the sensation-seekers could not bring themselves to come and stare. For this was no ordinary accident or catastrophe that would pass them by.

We drove into increasing smoke and the eery silence of desertion. The stores were all closed. No one was on the streets. As we passed Drummond, I looked up towards St. Catherines and saw the inevitable line of troops and police across the end of the street but there was no one between us and them in the long block. The Y.W.C.A. was deserted, obviously evacuated, and the big, shattered windows at street level yawned on an empty cafeteria. All along the sidewalks the stacks of glass slivers occasionally glittered when sunshine poked through the curls of smoke.

The jeep had slowed to a crawl as Levine carefully eased it over the miniature wooden ramps placed over an enormous spaghetti of fire hoses, themselves damming the sewers and creating rivers of black, oily water. I put on my sunglasses to give some eye protection from the smoke. Bumping past fire trucks and ashen, weary men in shiny, black slickers, we made our way to a debris-ridden parking lot on the south side of Dorchester. Here we entered a cacophony of metallic radio voices amid a cluster of police, fire department and armed forces vehicles gathered tightly together in a square that had been cleared for them out of the rubbble.

I stepped out of the jeep into black, cold water over my ankles and trouser cuffs. The lieutenant, wearing high, laced paratroop boots, grinned as I gingerly picked my way over to the familiar bulk of an HQ signals vehicle. We found Budgy Tremaine, an apparition in slicker, rubber boots and goggles topped by his gold-peaked staff cap. He was writing out something on a yellow signals pad for a waiting corporal who took it and slogged off in double time through the slime. Budgy grinned from a streaked and white face.

"Alex, how nice to see you. Sorry we can't be more hospitable," he said cheerfully.

"What is this? Another crackdown on the strip joints?" I yelled back over the noise of generators and engines.

"Looks more like the breakup, old boy," he said with a grimace.

We came together and shook hands warmly.

"You're looking fit, Alex," he said.

"What in God's name happened?"

"There," he pointed. "Twenty-five dead, another twenty or so seriously injured. All kinds of mucky-mucks from Ottawa and some of the key organizations in Quebec. Wholesale assassination."

I looked across the street, wondering at the ill-sorted victims he had described. I had seen buildings taken apart like that before. It was almost a terrorist trademark the world over. A huge explosion set off mid-way in the structure had blasted out two or three floors, followed by fire that roared through the interior from top to bottom. Now the fire seemed out, but ladder-mounted black figures were pouring massive streams into various levels bringing rivers of water pouring out through the non-existent glass doors and lobby onto the street. In the explosion area the walls had been blown out and the building had been left with only a skeleton midriff of girders with blackened masonry walls above and below the blast area. Three ambulances still stood by on the street, their top red lights twirling angrily.

"Ever see such a mess?" asked Budgy.

"No, not even on the Cape," I answered.

"It's just an opener," said Budgy, ceasing his restless pacing for a moment. We both stared, absorbed by the fears that the shattered building evoked in us.

"Look, let's get the hell out of here," said Budgy. "I've been taking in this bloody smoke since midnight." He called into the big signals caravan and a major, dirty and sweaty from being in the enclosed space, stepped out.

"Bill, this is Colonel Hlynka just back from South Africa," said Budgy. "Anything new?"

"No, sir. We've scraped up everybody we can find. All the hydro stations, waterworks, docks, air terminals, railways, radio and TV stations have something at them." He grinned. "I hope they don't try to take HQ, though."

"We saw an awesome display of power at the docks," I said.

Shannon glanced at a clipboard of notes.

"Chairborne types from the depot," he nodded. "Where'll you be, sir?" he asked Budgy.

"The United Services Institute, I think. Shouldn't be long."

The general stripped off his goggles and slicker and waved to young Levine.

"Come along, Levine," he said.

"Wait a moment, sir," cut in Shannon. He went behind the signals truck where several tough-looking C.A.R. paratroopers were having a coffee break. He came back with a scarfaced corporal who had a Sterling machine carbine slung muzzle down over his shoulder. The corporal heaved himself into the back seat of the jeep.

"Come off it, Bill," muttered Budgy. Shannon smiled, and without another word, ducked back into the caravan. With Levine driving, Budgy in front and myself beside the corporal in the back seat, we started off through the obstacle course of twisting hoses. My blackened and wet feet began to chill. I looked thoughtfully at Budgy's broad, ramrod back, only a slight drooping of the neck showing his fatigue.

It was typical of Budgy, the roaming activist, to take over personally, when perhaps he should have stayed at Mobile Command HQ at St. Hubert. In the forces, however, the activist often can do better than the more reflective soldier—not too different, in a way, from the successful, driving salesman in business who may make more than the vice-president, research, with his Ph.D. After Royal Military College, my higher marks had not counted so much as Budgy's good-humoured and bouncy ability to make instant decisions in a dramatic way. At times, when he was a junior officer, he had been almost a parody of the eternal subaltern and his vibrating salutes sometimes caused audible snickers in the ranks.

Even the way he got his nickname in Korea was in form. Our brigade there (the 25th) had been an odd mixture of veterans and professionals along with the greenest newcomers and, as the war went on, the latter increasingly replaced the former. Among the new officers, a twenty-year old bilingual Montrealer posted to the 2nd Bn. Royal 22nd Regiment (the Vandoos), was Lieutenant

Tremaine. He arrived with fresh, white paratroop wings that today marked us as having obsolete skills. With a batch of replacements he joined the Regiment in the Kowang-San sector on a saddle west of Hill 355 held precariously by a battalion of the 7th U.S. Infantry Regiment.

This occurred at a time when the Chinese, moving from Hill 227, decided to have another try at puncturing the Regiment's expert wiring job out front. Armed with burp guns, heavy matting for getting over the barbed wire and bayonets attached to sticks, the Chinese swarmed in. Instead of shooting, the young soldiers began to gape at the grim forms coming at them through the pre-dawn mists across the melting snow. Then another apparition towered above them on the parapet at their backs. Lieutenant Tremaine, as it developed, had decided to restore morale by pitching grenades over the heads of his men in the slit trenches. With the performance went a refrain.

"No tickee. No washee. No budgee," Tremaine had chanted. Strained faces peered back at him and someone started to laugh.

"No budgee, boys," said a sergeant. "We stay here."

They did, and they also gave the new lieutenant his name.

After Korea, Budgy's career, as was the case with most of us, dragged out in that seemingly endless interval between major and colonel, along with the chilling thought that maybe three rings—or in those days a pip and a crown—would be the end of the line. When I ran into Budgy, he was almost morose, but when I told him of the boredom of peacekeeping with the U.N., he brightened visibly and was thankful for N.A.T.O., assorted courses and minor commands.

There came a time during the late sixties when his incurable optimism became a valued asset. The minority government of the time, before the days of coalition, had embarked on a courageous program of unifying the navy, army and air force into one integrated force—something that a small country like Canada could do well as a pilot study for other allied powers. While most of the support for unification came from the army, who would benefit most from the merger, there were mossbacks, traditionalists and even some officers in dead ends who grumbled about unification as a way of letting off years of accumulated resentment. For them, the adapted badges and uniforms of Britain became idols. It was a time of purge and early retirements. Promotions were rapid for those who knew how to seize the opportunity. As the bilingual, second-in-command of one of the key directorates, Budgy had been quickly tabbed as one of those to help with the bloodletting. The harried men at the top were so glad to have someone carrying out nasty tasks with cheerful enthusiasm, that Budgy had soon made brigadier and more recently, major-general.

He had done well, although in his position, I would have been more concerned about the acting status at Mobile Command. It was a tough time to be going through a trial period. I wondered if he was handling it well and was using some of the intellectual qualities I always suspected he had behind his beaming, increasingly round face.

At Sherbrooke and Drummond the pedestrians could not resist lifting their eyes as Levine swung the jeep across the traffic into the parking lot. We must have looked like something from the depths of the earth with our blackened clothes and dirty, streaked faces. At the top of the long, steep steps to the Institute, we found the door locked. Budgy impatiently rang the bell until an aged soul in shirtsleeves appeared.

"Peters, we need a drink," said Budgy.

"Yes, sir," said the man, quickly letting us in the door like it was a bootleg joint. Instructing the attendant to look after the corporal, as well as us, Budgy led us into the white-tiled washroom on the main floor where we cleaned up. We then adjourned to the small, comfortable gun room by the main entrance where we were served enormous Scotches. Budgy placed the Montreal Gazette, with its big, black headlines about the explosion, on the coffee table for his dirty boots, stretched out his long legs and loosened his collar. I took off my shoes and socks and the old man, hovering in the doorway, offered to dry them out in the kitchen. We gulped our triple Scotches quickly and waited for a second round. Levine primly sipped his first drink in a far corner of the room.

"This is some homecoming for you, Alex," said Budgy at last. "Edith with you?"

"Yes. She and the boys are still on board ship. I appreciate you getting in touch when you have so many other things to do."

"Not at all. Glad to have you back. I had passed on the word to the Chief about the Third R.C.R. appointment. We're activating their third battalion. It's a militia outfit, third battalion, The Royal Regiment of Canada— London and Oxford Fusiliers." He laughed. "You know the local politics of naming militia units."

"I'm a policeman, not a soldier anymore," I said.

"Exactly why I suggested you," said Budgy. "General Bergstrom has sent us glowing reports about your work with the U.N. He says the control system of patrols you set up in South Africa will now become standard U.N. procedure. He says he'll be in touch with you about writing a manual." He smiled. "Once Third R.C.R. is worked into shape you'll be under my command, if my bloody rank ever comes through that is. The battalion is going to need a soldier who is also a policeman. We're going to need a lot of skill combined with muscle to keep the lid on this thing."

"What exactly do you mean by 'this thing'?" I asked finally.

3

From his slumped sprawl, the general looked heavy-lidded at the glass he twirled in his hand. His head was sunk deep into his collar, making rolls of flesh as if there were a shell into which he would soon retreat. The fatigue and whiskey together melted his inner military iron in some kind of silent foundry. He drooped and began a languid soliloquy quite out of character from his usual one-two-three briefings, almost as if he were reviewing his own inner thoughts to himself alone. The subaltern averted his eyes but listened intently. Suddenly, I felt a new respect for my old friend, where before there had been only the rather amused camaraderie from the days when we used to misdirect platoons together.

—Yesterday's radicals; today's conservatives, said the general. The zealots of the past are the senators of today. In Quebec the lineage is a long one and contains many personalities. Papineau, Bourassa, Groulx, Duplessis, Lesage, Johnson; all in their own way attempting to express the feeling of an island of alien people stuck in the northeast corner of North America. Besides the people, there were the movements and parties from Bloc Populaire to the R.I.N. And then latterly the little terrorist groups beginning with the F.L.Q. Out of this long lineage we have the Third Constituent Assembly meeting in Quebec City within the next couple of weeks. It is the third, after Johnson's rather modest effort a few years back.

—There is a difference this time, said the general. The Parti Democratique de Quebec has put together a majority and has formed a government without an election. It was the largest opposition party elected during the last vote and has so dominated the legislature that it has drawn over enough government members to have a majority. The premier is chicken and will not call an election. He has deferred to them and has resigned. The Party is socialist, probably Marxist; is organized into highly-disciplined local cells and is separatist. It will pass a resolution of separation at the Constitutent Assembly come hell or high water. They will use any form of intimidation to get their way. What you saw today was just for openers.

—Just what did I see today? I asked.

—You saw a careful and deliberate mass execution of those who might be suspected of wavering. Evidence of their lack of revolutionary zeal was the fact that they had turned up to listen to a last-minute plea from fellow French-Canadians in the federal government, including the very able and shrewd minister of federal-provincial affairs. Among those present were representatives of the Estates General of the St. Jean Baptiste Society, the Confederation of National Trade Unions, the Quebec Labour Federation and the Catholic Farmers' union plus assorted well-meaning politicians, businessmen and what have you. Just to show you the level of concern, I am told that there were even some from the Order of Jean Talon—La Patente. So how inside can one be?

—Security? I said with accusation in my voice.

—Crawling, said the general. But security in the usual sense becomes a weak reed in a hostile environment where sources dry up and everyone is waiting for a sign one way or the other. In this instance, the signal came from plastic explosives wrapped as electrical insulation around dummy cables in the hollow floorspace under the old studio set up for the conference.

—Won't this have the reverse effect and turn the population against them? I asked.

—The population will go with those who have the leadership, the ability to communicate, the right slogans, and now, a demonstration of purpose. What use are yesterday's radicals if they don't see this and are so uncertain that they are, after all this time, still ready to sit down in wasteful conferences with their enemies?

—In Quebec of all places, I mused, the whiskey affecting my sentimental Slavic temperament. Such fine people with so much on the ball.

—Unexpected? What about South Africa? said the general. Like all English, you don't understand, he went on, himself an Anglo-Montrealer. He stopped and we both laughed, for I thought it funny that I would be so considered. The general looked thoughtful for a while and the young subaltern looked up quickly to see if he was all right.

—The Parti Democratique de Quebec, mused the general. P.D.Q. It all sounds like a rather bad pun. A long string of others behind it, getting more extreme, more impatient, and finally giving up in the face of continual misunderstanding and complacency. I suppose, if one were to sum it all up in hindsight, I would single out three basic areas in which you Anglo-Canadians—or whatever you are—badly misinterpreted what was happening in Quebec.

—Such as? I asked, still wincing at being lumped with all the others and resentful at being blamed for anything.

—Several years ago, said the general; the politician, Levesque—you've heard of him?

—It rings a bell, I said, hoping Budgy would catch the sarcasm. But, as usual he didn't.

—Levesque used to say to English audiences something

to this effect: You think that I am a radical, that the measures I have proposed for Quebec to gain control of its own destiny are too far-reaching and drastic. Yet, you must realize that I am only a middle-aged moderate.

—There is no doubt, went on the general, that many of the Lesage supporters; including many of the brightest people ever to enter public service, shared this view. Literally, they thought that they were jogging slowly along, holding a barrier that kept back the surging mob behind them.

—For a while English Canada believed them and within the ranks of the Liberal Party outside Quebec, especially in Ontario, there was much empathy for what Lesage was trying to do. At one time it was fashionable to be an English *vendu*. His government was regarded by many as the most creative and productive any province had seen in many years. Then came the shock. Lesage was defeated by what appeared to be backlash from the conservative villagers, churchmen and merchants of the boondocks. Among many English people there was a feeling of relief that the brakes had been applied, and Johnson was regarded as someone only going through the motions.

—What they did not see were the currents under the surface. A number of elements came together. For one thing, there was an effect from Expo quite different from what its planners had forecast. Instead of arousing a feeling for Canada, it only served to provide a new confidence in French Canada that it could do things superbly by itself for, in world opinion, the exhibition was a triumph of the culture of French Canada and its style was an integral part of the whole show. De Gaulle only articulated this incipient feeling. At the same time, the more radical groups gradually came to the conclusion that the only route was to organize all the separatist groups into one movement. Those who really believed in Quebec as an independent culture made their own private decisions never again to seek their objectives through the organisms of existing parties, Liberal, Union Nationale or even the N.D.P., which they regarded as being closer to them in ideology, but hopelessly under the thumb of the American labour leaders. English Canada therefore completely misinterpreted the pro-Confederation statements of solidarity that came from the political leaders of the time. For underneath the forces were working that resulted in the P.D.Q. as we know it today.

Through cigarette smoke I squinted and wondered whether to believe him or not.

—The second myth, close to the hearts of the English, went something like this. It was a liberal myth, but had a fatal flaw, said the general. If, it was thought by the English, education and opportunity are opened up for young French-Canadians their ardent nationalism will change with time. Economic opportunity is the bridge between today's radicals and tomorrow's conservatives.

—The student cell groups at the Universities of Laval and Montreal who instigated the separatist demonstrations, the effigy burnings, the pamphleteering and the defacement of monuments, were unusual in that they also had the most dazzling economic opportunities ever possessed by young French-Canadians. They were the New Wave, coming out of university at a time when English or American-dominated firms were frantically searching for French-Canadian executives. Even before this generation started to reach graduation, the English firms were hauling French-Canadians out of the back rooms to become directors, vice-presidents and so-called French Market directors in the front offices. In the same way that firms in the States would put their show Jews or blacks into executive offices, so did the big companies in Quebec look for their window-dressing among the natives. Suddenly everybody tried to become bilingual, as far away as Toronto, but they knew the new executives would still have to do their daily business in English.

The movement in the federal civil service and the Forces was perhaps more genuine. Even so, you never learned French did you, Alex?

—No, I said. Never needed it.

—Typical, said the general scornfully. We have a world where Russians, Indians, Syrians, Swedes and Brazilians know that English is now the common language of commerce and diplomacy. But in Quebec, language was not really the issue. Many Montrealers of my own generation were completely bilingual without one ounce of understanding or sympathy for the people with whom they spoke. Some of them, in fact, used their mastery of French as an ill-disguised expression of contempt for the people of Quebec and a demonstration of their own superiority. Their ability to speak French was self-interpreted as another method of getting their way with rather inferior neighbours. Language is too often not a simple matter of utility and communication, but a political weapon.

—I only speak a few words of Ukrainian, I said sullenly.

—Look at the reason. Ukrainian was a hindrance and not an advantage in your own career and advancement. If you were to break out of the dirt-farmer mould of your ancestors, you had to speak English without any native inflection or accent. Didn't you?

—I suppose so, I muttered.

—In their second major error, continued the general, the English-Canadians combined two sociological disasters. They thought that if they made an effort in language, combined with the opening up of economic opportunity, that the concept of the Quebec Nation would fade. This conclusion resulted from a typically pragmatic idea that is rooted deeply in Anglo-Saxon mentality, North American version. On this continent the dominant forces of society are committed to the business and professional world. Business is not a job. It is a total com-

33

mitment that absorbs the energies of the North American male on a prodigious scale. The lag in social planning and services and the low level of political life in North America is primarily because the most energetic, intelligent and qualified people in Canada and the U.S. have committed themselves utterly to careers in business. Their social obligations are appeased in service clubs, fundraising drives and other community activities. They tend to be contemptuous of politicians, intellectuals, artists, writers, actors, not in any Victorian sense, but in the conviction that those areas of society are for leisure, or entertainment, and not for total commitment. Their real world is in a myriad of private companies. Everything else is escapism and illusion.

—Even those of us in the Forces, I said.

—Especially us. We wouldn't know how to compete in the real world of business, you know, said the general bitterly. That's what they say. Of course, most of them are not true businessmen or entrepreneurs in the meaning of risk-taking or managing capital. The majority of them are employees. Their lives are concerned with moving up to the next notch in the same company. For this privilege they work nights, weekends and holidays—expending all their energies on the development of their own knowledge and efficiency, as well as acquiring the necessary requirements in the field of personal intrigue and, of course, the cultivation of their masters.

—Knowing this to be true, the English-Canadians quite naturally assumed that if opportunities were opened up in business for the rising generation of French-Canadians, the same thing would happen to them. They also would become completely absorbed in giant corporate systems and their energies would be dissipated in the same way as are those of most North Americans. There was one flaw in this theory.

—What was that? I asked.

—They misread the conditioning of Gallic intellect and emotion. As consumers, the French-Canadians have only minor differences from others. They may prefer larger kitchens, drink more wine and soft drinks with meals, stay closer to home and have somewhat different colour preferences. But no significant differences. The market research of the big companies showed this and led them to the conclusion that they were dealing with people not really different from themselves. They were wrong.

—In what way? I asked.

—You mean, said the general with a grin, how do they differ that much from you with your unique ethnic background? Not the same.

—I don't see how . . ., I said irritably.

—We are talking about a subculture concentrated in a geographical area, with firmly established values. A culture that has been steeped in the need to codify the basis of society. This is why the French Canadians used to talk of some mythical "compact of two races" that was supposed to have taken place at Confederation. The "associate state" concept of some years back was based on the assumption that all relationships between Quebec and the rest of Canada could be finely codified. They prefer a formal, clearly defined system on paper, rather than the shambling, pragmatic Anglo-Saxon way of governing. This mentality, and the search for a codified ideology, led them into all kinds of paths, from fascism to Marxism. In this search many of them developed close connections with kindred souls in Latin America, especially when France lost interest in any cultural bridge after the demise of Gaullism.

—They looked south. Far south. An affinity was developed between some of the founders of the P.D.Q. and those who were to lead the well-organized revolutionary movements in South America. Carpentier, their deputy leader, even fought in Venezuela. Now this has proved to be a useful connection. Three weeks ago, we are told, two Panamanian ore carriers unloaded heavy arms at Sept Isles. They had stopped off in Cuba.

—Didn't anybody try to stop them? I asked.

—We heard about it afterwards. The C.I.A. doesn't catch everything in Cuba and our Coast Guard had no particular reason to stop two ore carriers. We don't know exactly what came in, but whatever it is, it's been dispersed by now.

—Can't you find the stuff?

—Up in that country once the shipment has been split up? Something more than just one shipment is bothering us though.

—What's that?

—Our usual sources of information are drying up. They're apparently afraid to keep in touch with us and we're having increasing difficulty getting reliable intelligence. That worries me more than anything else. It means someone is getting control and it's risky to keep in touch with us.

The general frowned and looked at his watch.

—What was the third factor you mentioned? I asked.

—The Coalition in Ottawa, said the general, venturing into the forbidden halls of politics. It was formed out of the stalemates of the sixties in high hopes that a strong majority would have the voting strength to deal with our national problems. All it did was to transfer the bitter partisan warfare to the caucus chambers instead of out in the open. It takes a long time to weld together old political adversaries. You've seen it in the U.N. agencies and commissions even with its new lease on life. I can't get any goddam decisions out of anybody.

Budgy glared at me and at Levine who immediately got to his feet.

"Let's get back," he growled, once more the general.

"I'll take a cab back to the ship," I said.

Our aged retainer appeared from the kitchen with my shoes and socks followed by a somewhat glassy-eyed corporal. I shook my head free of the whiskey fumes as we stepped out of the hushed, gloomy hallway into the glare of the morning sun.

"So it's all coming apart at the seams," I muttered.

"Not if I can help it," said Budgy.

He pulled the peak of his cap down low on his forehead just as the assassin's bullet, fired upward from the bottom of the steps, slammed accurately into the middle of his face. A reddish shower sprayed a cloud before my eyes. Below me I saw the youngster in a white shirt and black suit swinging the muzzle of his .45 towards me.

4

A bright droplet of blood shimmered on the wiry strands of my jacket lapel, quivered on the dark green and rolled down, losing itself in the woolen cloth. Above the gun I saw the white face and glazed, liquid brown eyes of the kid. For a second or two we stared, before I jumped and he fired. Behind me, on my rolling plunge down the stairs, I heard glass shattering. My hands reached for the pillars of the balustrade and in a painful wrench I pulled myself to a halt spread-eagled stupidly near the assassin. My head was facing upward taking in the blurred figure of Levine, his 9 mm. Browning out of his holster and lurching rapidly in his hand, the explosions echoing in the street amid the traffic noises. Painfully, I twisted my neck past the remnants of Budgy's skull just beside me and saw one of Levine's shots catch a beautifully groomed elderly woman, who had started to back up in tiny, mincing steps from what she had seen.

The woman said "Oh," sat down on the sidewalk and rolled slowly onto her side, twitching her nylon legs. Levine fired again, hitting the roof of a passing car with a metallic whack.

By this time the assassin had gone from my vision to somewhere along the sidewalk. I pulled myself shakily to my feet and hung onto the lower part of the railing looking easterly along Sherbrooke. Along the curb a gray car was picking up speed, its two curbside doors open. The black-suited youngster, in long leaps, had reached the back door of the car and was stretching out a hand to another arm grasping outward from the back seat, when I heard the familiar blurred staccato of a submachine gun. Our C.A.R. corporal, stolidly planted at the base of the steps, his stance leaning correctly and exactly into the braced pose described in our manuals, his left hand grasped correctly in grip around the stock in front of the magazine, coolly fired in bursts of five. He would be counting seven bursts of five in his magazine. The kid trying to get into the car didn't touch the hand groping for him. Three slugs expertly placed, as if he were a cardboard silhouette on a fifty-yard range, took off most of his head in a explosion of scarlet debris. A pivotal half-turn on his heel and the corporal gave the same careful hosing to the driver of the car in its mounting speed towards him. The doors of the car never closed. In a wild shattering of glass and tearing of rubber, its doors flying open like grotesque wings, the car swung across the traffic towards the Berkeley Hotel where the first spring sidewalk tables had been placed. Glancing off a delivery truck, the gray car leaped over the curb and landed in a splatter of wood and glass amid the outdoor cafe. I saw a silver spoon arch high into the air on some orbit of its own. The corporal kept on firing, hit the driver of a Volkswagen who put both hands over his face and weaved across in our direction, smashing into a car on our side of the street.

"Corporal!" I yelled, jumping after him.

The C.A.R. man turned when I grabbed the muzzle of his gun and forced it downward. For a moment I looked into flat, yellow killer's eyes until he slowly relaxed, let his arm drop and clicked the magazine off his gun. By this time, Lieutenant Levine was across the street, actually leaping over the crumpled hood of a stopped car.

In the wreckage of tables, chairs and the wooden fencing that surrounded the sidewalk cafe, he stretched into the back seat of the gray car and pulled out the man who was there. Levine held him up by his lapels with his left hand, placed the Browning automatic between the man's eyes and blew his skull off.

I grabbed Levine by the arm and swung him around.

"How're we going to interrogate him now?" I shouted.

With an infinite weariness, Levine let his arm drop. He looked at the wreckage and slowly turned to me.

"It was worth it, sir," he said quietly.

Worth it. I looked at the cost scattered around us, the crumpled killer car amid the splintered wooden remnants of the sidewalk café. In the street, the cars were piled up at odd distorted angles in a curious, ominous silence in contrast to the usual lively traffic battleground that was Montreal. The people who slowly emerged from the stalled mass of vehicles and from the doorways of buildings moved in subdued groups towards the focal points of the violence. Some gathered around us at the hotel; others at the Volkswagen with its dead driver and some around the body of the woman curled up neatly on the sidewalk. Grim-faced Montreal cops, in their floppy hats, guns drawn, started to move in, breaking the strange silence with their guttural orders to clear the crowds. I looked over their approaching heads to across the street where Budgy Tremaine's body lay, large and impressive even in death, on the steps of the Club. At the top of the steps stood the old man, Peters, rigid and fragile in front of the broken glass in the door. The old man looked around him and dabbed at his eyes with a handkerchief. In the morning sunlight it showed as a tiny patch of fluttering white.

5

London—Ontario, that is—had never grabbed me.

As the two-engined JetStar slipped westward out of Downsview, me the only passenger, a true V.I.P. in solitary splendour in the plush little transport, I looked out through the haze at the vast runway of the Macdonald-Cartier Freeway, or 401, or whatever they called it, and wondered at the bitterness with which I took up the posting to the Royal Canadian Regiment. London, that haven of Ontario complacency, was only part of it. The inner rage and sadness of Montreal and all it implied; leaving Edith and the boys in that uneasy, crisis-ridden environment with her parents, even though I knew they were in the shaded protection of Westmount, all weighed on my mind. And now, in the lonely privilege of the Jet-Star, not knowing what seat I should occupy and still keep some dignity, I studied the widening green patches of land as we drew away from Toronto.

Semi-soldiers, halfass hussars, truncated troopers: they were all alike. Professional soldiers were no good at police work. Even without a tropical climate, they tended to get mouldy at the fringes and lose their hard edge. They start out all right: brass polished, discipline up and a new job to do. But months of semi-crisis, with civilian temptations, U.N. switches in policy and complete isolation from home take their toll. I thought of my hopeless efforts to get Canadian beer for my troops in South Africa. Eventually they sent out three entertainers from some C.B.C. program we'd never heard of, including one fairy guitar player and two somewhat faded "stars" who gave recitations on the inner meaning of life in pear-shaped Rosedale accents. I remembered the night after when six troopers from the Hussars deserted and we picked them up in Durban a week later. Others gave more trouble.

To police one's own country would be even worse, far more tense, needing tighter discipline than the lack of involvement in a foreign land. I had seen a disturbing sign that afternoon. There had been a three-hour delay while I waited for my plane and I had been the luncheon guest of the Downsview C.O., an air arm colonel. We had talked about the Quebec crisis.

"I'll show you something," he said. In his staff car we drove the short distance south on Keele, east on Wilson to Dufferin. He pulled across the traffic into a parking lot at the Denison Armouries, one of the supermarket efforts built some years ago. All it needed was "99 cents off" signs in its broad glass windows to attract the house-wives. We went in through the glass doors, now guarded by newly-mobilized militiamen from the Horse Guards who were surrounded by an awestruck group of little kids. Inside, in the echoing drill hall, there was a hollow rumble of voices. I stared at several snaking lines of men shuffling to tables where officers and N.C.O.'s questioned them and filled in forms.

"You may get some of these," said the Downsview C.O.

"There must be three hundred or more," I said, feeling chilly inside.

"Every day. More on weekends."

"Are we taking them? I didn't know quotas were opened up."

"Not yet. All they can do is take names, give medicals and make up lists. Want to take your pick?"

Unskilled city kids mostly, I thought, and the youth of our urban civilization make lousy soldiers, too accustomed as they are to the plush seating of convertibles, the controlled atmosphere of indoor life and, above all, a lack of any feel for black nights alone in a hole in the ground. Some had a talent for things mechanical, but nothing compared to the inbred engine awareness of the farm lad with his instinctive sureness for fixing everything and his affinity for wind, climate and earth. But with less than a quarter of the population living in rural areas, there was a decreasing source of sturdy peasant stock to fill the ranks.

As I looked at the current crop, I hoped my own origin in farm and coal mine did not distort my judgment of these hopefuls. Largely, they tended to be sportshirted, their clothes stretched with fat or hanging on fleshless bones; they were acned in face, long and rather grubby in hair. A few wore jackets and ties, but these were a minority, for those with good jobs would not be likely to apply, and anyway, these days they tended to get married at eighteen or nineteen. These standing in line were what used to be called the "dropouts". Out of what had they dropped to gather in their pungent masses in the armouries? What did they think they were getting into? I asked one of them—a reedy, long-nosed kid with hair that left grease marks on a white and yellow sports shirt.

"If we're going to kill Frogs, I wanna be in on it."

I gave him a long stare and sought another, wearing a checked sports jacket.

"Wildcat strike at the plant, sir," he said. "I decided to get out."

I noted that he called me "sir", and took interest.

"Have you heard about the trouble in Quebec?"

"Yes, sir. I'd rather go somewheres overseas."

I hauled him out of the line and turned him over to a

lieutenant for priority enrollment. Maybe there was some hope, I mused, taking a last glance at the grubby throng.

Would there be more of them awaiting me in London in their pimply-faced droves? One of the troubles of being a Regular Force man for so long, and an officer at that, was one's isolation from the civilian masses, but perhaps no more so than the business executive whose cycle was office, club and suburb. I tried to think when I had last seen recruits in such a raw stage and decided that I never actually had. Even the newest platoon I had ever handled while a subaltern with 25 Brigade had, on reflection, been scrubbed, haircutted, pressed and shined by the N.C.O.'s before exposing a sensitive two-pipper to such scruff. I left the armouries in disgust.

The pilot captain, observing the courtesies, came back from the flight deck and finally located me amid the empty seats.

"Sorry, sir," he said. "This was such a short hop I didn't lay on a steward or coffee."

"That's all right," I waved. "I suppose we're almost there."

Just after he returned to take the controls, the JetStar began to skid down the other side of the shallow arc it had made in the sky and we came into London. At the side of the two-storey glass-enclosed terminal—Department of Transport model, Grade "B" airport—I saw three black staff cars and seven green-clad figures, all wearing vizored regimental hats: my welcoming committee.

Seeing their shining brass and leather, I momentarily regretted that the emotional backwash of the events in Montreal had discouraged any thoughts of dressing up for the occasion. I had on my old, rather stained hat and was wearing my cold weather serge greens with their blue and white U.N. patches still at the shoulder. It being mid-afternoon, my black beard would be starting to show on the jawline. They gathered around, young, trim and smart. We would soon be on a first name basis, but now they were just Major This and Captain That representing Alpha, Bravo, Charlie, Delta and Support companies of the Third Battalion. The first one to be sized up was the adjutant.

"Captain Rhodes, sir."

"Do I have to call you Dusty?"

"No, sir," he grinned. "My name is Sebastian."

"We'll call you Dusty," I said and everyone laughed.

I missed J.J., who had, in an awkward and painful conversation for us both, expressed a need to return to his own with the Royal 22e at Valcartier. Two years was a long time to have the same adjutant cum executive vice-president. Unlike the way I felt, after the grime and tension of South Africa, these men looked fresh and untried. Yet I was grateful that they were professionals, obviously not short-term commissions. I noticed three of them didn't even have moustaches. My new adjutant, Rhodes, was thin-faced, about 31 and wore plastic-rimmed glasses that emphasized his shrewd eyes.

"Sir, there was a long distance call from Montreal," he said when the others had gone back to their cars and we were about to get into mine. "I think it was your wife."

I appreciated his discretion.

"Let the others go on," I said. "I'll phone from here."

Rhodes gave me a pink phone slip with the operator's number on it and I went into the terminal where the manager gave me an empty office. The number was Edith's parents in Westmount. Mrs. Watson came on the line in her annoying, upper class Montreal accent and I was somewhat abrupt in asking for my wife, harbouring a thin resentment that they had persuaded her and the boys to stay with them until I was "settled". Even my insistent arguments that we would have the C.O.'s quarters in London, furnishings optional, had failed to persuade her parents that Edith should leave the nest. Now I wondered what had happened and my voice was edgy. I wished they weren't in Montreal.

"Edith? What's up?"

"You needn't bite my head off, darling," came her cool voice. I pictured her by the phone. At mid-afternoon she would be wearing a sweater, tweed skirt, pearls and loafers. Edith never wore slacks—thank goodness.

"Didn't mean to," I said more softly. "Just got off the plane and the adjutant told me you had called."

"You're in London?"

"Yes, just got in, complete with reception committee. When are you coming?"

"Well, actually, darling . . ."

"—I wish you'd get out of Montreal. Especially with the boys."

"That's what I wanted to tell you, Alex," she said calmly. "Mum and Dad want us to go up to the cottage for a couple of weeks."

I choked in silence.

"A couple of weeks?" I said finally.

"Yes, darling. As you said, it does make sense to get out of Montreal. There's an awful air about this place now; it isn't the same at all. Besides, they're predicting an early heat wave."

"When're you coming here?" I demanded.

She was patient. "I really don't know what to do about Mum and Dad. So I thought if we went up to the cottage for a while, we might have a better chance to see what's going to happen and be outside Montreal. Don't you think that makes sense?"

"I suppose," I said at last.

"Don't be like that, dear. It's just that I don't know what to do about Mum and Dad . . ." Her voice quavered.

I relented. "When are you going?"

"Tomorrow."

"It's a fair drive isn't it?'

"Just under a hundred miles, I think."

"They have a phone, haven't they?"

"Yes. It's through LaBelle, a rural line, two ring four."

"What's that little place where you pick up the mail? The place with the funny name."

"Notre Dame des Pistoles."

"A good name for the times. Any box number?"

"Mum says it's 257."

"Okay," I sighed. "Don't be too long, Edith."

"Give me time to sort things out," she said very softly. "Do write often. I suppose you'll be terribly busy."

"I expect so. There won't be many free weekends. First chance I get I'll pinch a plane and get over to the Mont Tremblant field. You could pick me up there and we could shack up in one of the ski chalets—just the two of us."

"Sounds wonderful, darling. See you."

"Are the boys there?"

"No. They're out somewhere."

"Keep an eye on them. Don't let them wander far."

"Yes, darling. Bye."

I sat for a moment and stared out at the deserted airfield; the JetStar had left for Downsview.

I thought again of that day in Montreal. It had been dusk when a staff car from St. Hubert had brought me to the cool, tree-shaded street in Westmount where I rejoined Edith at her parents' home. Only an unusual twitch of curtains in some windows betrayed anything out of the ordinary, although I did notice that no one was out cutting, clipping or weeding in the still, balmy evening. A pinkish haze softened the lines of the leafing trees, deceptively picturesque because I knew it was only a drifting of smoke from more sinister things downtown.

After the assassination of Budgy, the day had been one of strained interrogation and conferences. At some point between the question period from a couple of young R.C.M.P. men, who looked like advertising types, and a senior officer from the Montreal police, who almost hypnotized me with the grandeur of his uniform, I had managed to find time to phone the ship and instruct Edith to take the boys to her parents. Then one of our own, a captain from Intelligence, respectfully interrogated me and a sullen Levine, followed by a special inquisition from the Associate Minister of National Defence, who had been in Montreal catching up on his law practice or something.

All I could think of was Budgy's dead hulk sprawled on the steps of the Club; all I could hear was the careful chop-chop of the corporal's submachine gun and the tearing of automobile metal echoing in the street.

I had a long session with the new C.O. of Mobile Command, a lieutenant-general named Douglas, who appeared off the end of some organization chart in Ottawa in that overlapping stream of people and command that makes the armed forces a living organism. Douglas was a new face from the air arm. I wondered, under the circumstances, why they hadn't replaced Budgy with another soldier. The problems ahead would be on the ground. However, Douglas made a good attempt at discussing my takeover of the 3rd R.C.R.

"You may have to whip them into shape sooner than you expected," he pointed out, as I sagged, half listening in his commandeered room in the Ritz.

"In that case, I'd better get them up to Borden. The facilities around London are lousy," I said.

"All right," said the young general. "Let me know when you've had a look at things."

"We can give them concentrated range work at Borden. It's good for night work. Is The Street still there?"

"The Street?" the airman asked blankly.

"They used to have a complete main street at the Combat Arms School. Not just false fronts—brick, masonry, everything for town clearing," I said. "Special Warfare Div. used to run it."

48

"I'll check that out for you," nodded the general, making a note.

"I'll need some good Provost instructors; specialists in riots, mobs, traffic control," I went on. "We might use some special instructors for training on rescue work."

The general took some more notes as I played back my South African folklore. Even the room in the Ritz had been similar to the one in Johannesburg where the regular tremors of the city shifting on its thin crust over the mines had at first startled me.

Now, as I drove out of the London airport with my new adjutant, I started on him. I turned to Rhodes as the sun caught his large R.C.R. badge in a glittering silver star.

"I'm sorry I missed Colonel McKay," I told him. "He's an old friend of mine."

"He left last week, sir. Went back to Second Battalion in Germany," said Rhodes.

"Had he, or have you, received any special word on the syllabus?"

"No, sir. The men have just completed their first month basic. The usual stuff."

"How are they doing?"

"Very well, sir. Of 856 all ranks, only about a hundred are completely green. The others are militiamen, some of them with a fair amount of summer time and special courses. All our officers and N.C.O.'s are from First or Second Battalion plus some other units."

"Sounds like a good start. We'll have all companies complete their T.O.E.T.'s next week," I said, communicating in the jargon we all understood. T.O.E.T.'s are tests of elementary training. "I want to get the whole unit up to Borden within two weeks for special training."

"Yes, sir," said Rhodes, trying not to gulp.

"Are they up to it?"

Rhodes made a thin smile. "I think it's what they need."

We drove west on Oxford Street, away from the airport past the line of gray, beige and yellow factory buildings, unsooted in the clean air of the western Ontario plain. London emerged discreetly from the odorous, fertile black fields now tinged with green. In the midst of such opulent land, the Londoners carried on their commerce never very far from the soil with a sureness of spirit quite different from the jittery inhabitants of larger centres. To me, as a westerner, London was everything we had been taught to detest about Ontario. The divine right to Victorian prosperity and a willingness to support a true establishment of a wealthy few was the thread that bound them together in their spotless, unspoiled little city. In a way, I supposed, they were an anachronism, really more rural than urban. In Toronto or Montreal the managerial class and the professionals in entertainment and the arts had long since swamped the tight grip of the few wealthy families. What London needed, I thought, was an infusion of Hamilton steelworkers, a drove of Sudbury hardrock miners and some of the characters I had grown up with in the Coal Branch. As local commander of the armed forces, I would confine all troops to barracks and let these other types loot and rape the town. Or, if China ever invaded us, we would place large directional arrows from the Arctic Circle to Ontario with signs reading: "Take London first . . . please."

Not really fair, I reflected. Now, as senior officer in the area I would be on the periphery of the establishment, and might even have the occasional lunch at the London Club or the Hunt. Last time, some years ago, I had been there for six weeks on a logistics course at the Central Ordnance Depot on Highbury Avenue and had found it a dreary, unfriendly town, fully up to everything I had heard about it. There had been a girl, though, and there wasn't anything dreary about her. A bouncy, lively brunette with an hourglass figure; she had sort of drifted into my arms, so to speak, after her escort had passed out at a Mess party. What was her name? Agnes Something. I couldn't think of it, but wondered where she was now.

We came through the gates into Wolseley Barracks, our own little city of white-painted buildings, immaculate squares and rectangles, whitewashed stones and artificially manicured grass, confirming our ordered lives. A quarter guard was drawn up at battalion H.Q. In two gleaming lines they stood, their green uniforms pressed razor-sharp and hanging correctly over spotless boots. Brass shone, cap badges reflected silver and oiled FN's were an exact line of shimmering blue metal. An impressive, fleeting moment. For the first time I felt I was back home, secure in our ordered cocoon of ritual.

In the next few days I grudgingly admitted to myself that having the family away was not such a bad idea. Working around the clock, I was able to intensify the pace of training and make us partially ready . . . ready for what? I cleared the matter of moving to Borden, fifty miles north of Toronto, and had a yelling session on the phone with the Directorate in Ottawa telling them I'd land the unit in Borden in two weeks even if they had to live in the open. I dispatched an advance party to look things over. A few "O" groups were sufficient to get the officers with me. I got to know the R.S.M. Mr. Wilson, one of the new breed: slight, wiry and bright. We immediately liked each other. In the cavernous recreation centre, I addressed the troops on the function of the modern soldier in keeping peace and good order in troubled times whether abroad or at home.

At Ipperwash on Lake Huron, I started them prematurely on company exercises. As I expected, their field signals were erratic. I sent urgent word to Barriefield for more signals instructors. They were somewhat chaotic in their handling of the M-113 armoured personnel carriers, and not until an eighteen-year-old private got crushed under a tread, did they get the drift of moving in and out of the vehicles without falling flat on their faces. They were nervous when I made them take extra time with grenades and the adapter on their FN rifles, but they were not bad with the FN itself on the ranges where our ex-militiamen did quite well. I told the range instructors to intensify accuracy.

"Chances are they'll have to be careful where they do their shooting," I told them.

I started classes for other ranks in elementary French. Most of the Ontario boys, fortunately, had some French from their public school. I made sure we had detailed maps of all the major Quebec cities and arranged for special evening lectures on the areas of the province for the officers. Amid all this, I made several futile attempts to call Edith and somehow never seemed to get beyond an operator in LaBelle who vainly tried to get through to the operator in Notre Dame des Pistoles, a female who obviously did not comprehend French, let alone English. Between phone calls, I wrote letters and received only one in return, an extended account of water skiing from our oldest boy, Johnny. I cursed the mails and assumed that the army, in its wisdom, was still forwarding all letters to South Africa.

Instead of using the C.O.'s house, I took two rooms in the single officers' quarters. I was wrestling with a new syllabus on my second Saturday night in London, when my standing order to the switchboard finally paid off. The operator's efforts every four hours to reach the little village in Quebec had at last resulted in a connection of sorts. Over what seemed to be background noises of a boiler factory, a minor riot and a thunderstorm, I heard Edith's voice faintly.

"Come out of the water so I can hear you," I yelled.

"Alex, is that you?" came her distant voice.

Then I lost her. Two French operators began arguing with each other and the line went dead. I sat fuming while my base operator tried again. In the silence I could hear the muffled sounds of the Saturday night Mess party warming up across the way. My officers needed a blowout after ten days of my acid and nagging regime, I thought. I listened to a small combo tuning their instruments. The stack of papers piled on the desk stared back and I made a few notations and arrows to fix up the movement order to Borden. At last I changed into a suit and white shirt and went downstairs.

The R.C.R. Mess is a very pleasant one, with large, modern rooms and French doors opening out onto a terrace and garden, complete with a couple of pieces of white statuary. At the bar, I joined a couple of company commanders and their wives. Rhodes tapped me on the shoulder.

"This lady says she knows you, sir," he said.

I turned from the bar. There was no doubt, even after all these years and my difficulty with last names. It was Agnes.

6

From the balcony of the apartment just off Richmond Street, I looked out on the buildings of the university campus. In the muggy dawn their gray stone lines swam in a ground mist that was a textured green from the lawns. The morning was unseasonably warm in an opulent softness that measured my mood as I leaned on the railing and inhaled the damp air with its hint of sharp chemicals from the fields not too far away. At this time on a Sunday the city was wrapped in a silence so absolute that a robin's call was a welcome sign of life. The university, almost English in appearance except for the buildings being so far apart, slept; its academic year almost completed. The ground mist hid the bridge and river which gave out faint noises from swollen currents created by the spring runoff.

There were two doors on the long balcony, one for the living room and the other for the bedroom where Agnes, tousled and lovely, slept. I smoked one of her cigarettes, a long tasteless filter of some kind which I didn't need, and sipped a cup of instant, black coffee I had made in her kitchen. Somewhat fuzzy from the liquor and passion of the night before, I welcomed the blunting of my edginess.

Through the open door, Agnes called sleepily.

"Alex, are you there?"

"Out here, darling. The morning is beautiful."

She appeared at my side hugging a negligee around her. I put an arm over her shoulder and we looked in silence at the first sun rays giving silver light to the streaks of haze low among the trees.

"I had such a good time," she said. "I'm so glad you came."

"So am I." And I was. Remorse had not yet set in, but it soon did while Agnes and I were avidly eating poached eggs and toast in the small kitchen.

"Agnes," I said, with an edge in my voice I didn't mean, "What is your last name, anyway?"

She stiffened.

"Which one?"

"Well, both."

She paused and tried to toss it off.

"My maiden name was Daley when you first knew me. My married name is Ellsworth."

"Where's your husband?" something made me say.

"I don't know and I don't care. Oh, Alex, you've just spoiled a perfectly good time." She got up and left the little table, her face drawn and her brown eyes dull with disappointment. I tried to follow her into her bedroom but she closed the door. I called her a few times, found the door was locked and went back onto the balcony. She had closed the bedroom door to the terrace and had drawn the curtains. I dressed except for my jacket, found the latter thrown over a living room chair and slipped it on.

"Agnes," I called softly at her door. "I'm going now. I have work to do."

There was no sound. I let myself out of the apartment and took the automatic elevator downstairs. Without knowing or caring how far it was to Wolseley Barracks, I started to walk south on Richmond Street towards Oxford along silent, tree-shaded avenues.

The night before, as I had turned from the bar towards her, the ingredients began to come together for one of those explosions of tension for which the off-duty military life is geared. With two quick Scotches I began to appreciate the music, the chatter, the gleaming, bare shoulders of the women. At such times the Mess takes on the warmth and comfort it was intended to, but seldom does convey. I felt the pressure building up.

"The Rhodes invited me to come with them," Agnes had said, her wavy, black hair, brown eyes and smooth olive skin giving her a more finished and glossy look than when I had last seen her.

"I'm glad they did," I said.

As I turned to the bar to order a drink for her, I was shocked at the lust that stared back at me from the mirror. My face, thinner than usual, was muddy under its tan and there was an urgency in the eyes that was almost frightening. The effect, I supposed, of endless days driving others hard; of absence from a recently reunited family; of the fears of what we might be preparing for. So there she was, her rich skin shining in a low-cut, black dress, her lips red and full and her eyes on mine. She was ready too. Not far along in the course of the evening, Agnes and I were doing a solo demonstration of such vintage dances as the twist, to the hilarious approval of the junior officers. Some time afterward in a taxi, with cool, wet night breezes coming through the open windows, I held her tightly, silently. At her apartment, we hardly waited until the door closed, and as I slowly unveiled her magnificent body, I realized how long it had been since I had enjoyed a woman so full and shapely. Edith was trim; and my mistress in Durban, Dorothy, had been a pale and willowy English type, who in her thirties, still looked great bikini-clad on the white beaches. Agnes never would look right in a bikini; her large breasts and buttocks were the kind that women in North America packed away, unappreciated, into various fabric and plastic straitjackets until someone liberated them. Whether it was the result of a long separation from her husband, or the glowing continuation of the party, or my intensity of need, she was responsive in a way that was almost overwhelming. My lips on her long nipples aroused wild gasps that changed to rasping cries when my tongue caressed the firm skin of her thighs.

It was dawn when we awoke to make love again, this time more slowly and with a harmonious tenderness that must take many couples years to reach. Afterwards, half asleep again, she stirred and said: "You are such a savage."

Awake, while she nestled warmly down into the covers and fell into a deep sleep, I had twitched restlessly and then had gotten up, washed and, dressed in shirt and trousers, had gone to the balcony.

Such a savage. Was she being astute or were they just sleepy words after love? She may have sensed something in my intensity which she could only describe in that way. But I knew she was right. I had seen it all again too clearly in the mirror in the Mess that night, and it was this realization that made me fear the future more than anything else. The many years of discipline had created the controlled, professional officer, hard but considerate. And it had not been often that the veneer cracked to let out that viciousness the soldier sooner or later has to contend with. The strain of peacekeeping in the world had not brought it out, for that left a sense of non-involvement. One was more of a judge among litigants than a participant. And, anyway, the foolish national or ideological fine points that brought about our presence in the first place, seemed ludicrous at close range. Sadness for the human spirit was more likely to be our dominant emotion and, as a result, my own melancholia was more common than any outburst of raging energy.

But J. J. Rousseau, my friend and confidant, knew. For he had seen my one lapse in Capetown. After it had happened, I also realized that J.J. himself recognized it because he was much the same—an alley cat fighter from the east end of Montreal who had grown a protective shell of suavity. J.J. and I had been alone in a jeep taking an ill-advised short cut in daylight through the infamous District Six. Two stupid Salvation Army girls, obviously not South Africans, had slipped past the barricades and were distributing oranges and chocolate bars to some of the kids. The inevitable had happened. A half dozen locals had pushed the women and kids out of the way and had the two Salvation Army girls backed up against the rippled tin wall of a shanty. Very carefully they had used their long knives to split open the girls' uniforms from top to hem. They were just starting to complete the process when we arrived on the scene. As a parting shot, one of the shantymen slipped his knife into the tallest girl's breast and sliced off the nipple.

We had to fire our Sterlings over their heads and the rounds clanged into the corrugated metal. The one who had done the damage ran among rubble-strewn spaces amid the shacks, but I saw him slip behind a gunny sack curtain. I came cautiously to the doorway, poked my Sterling through and started firing. When I was finished I had killed four cute little black kids and their mother. The slasher had only been wounded in the arm. As he came out, his hands over his head, I gave him five rounds in the groin. J.J., who had been covering me, watched with great interest, and as I turned towards him, I saw him nod slightly with an odd glint in his eyes. No one, least of all ourselves or the Capetown police, ever made out a report on the incident. But J.J. and I understood each other better after that.

I could attribute such actions to no particular factor. A psychologist might say there were certain elements of harshness in my childhood, but others had suffered homes that were far more stultifying and tense than my own, even though our material standing was lower than many others. Most of the time we were not desperately poor or deprived, although the mine layoffs, and then later my father's injuries, hit us at times. My father didn't begin as a miner, though.

My first memories are of us living on my grandfather's farm, a short distance from Cooking Lake, a few miles east of Edmonton. My father had lost his own farm near Vegreville and we had arrived to live with my grandfather in his tiny, white frame house on an acreage he had bought from a veteran of the first war. There were a number of Soldier Settlement Board farms in the area, not many of them successful. For someone of Ukrainian origin, my grandfather had strayed fairly far afield, beyond our accepted enclave in the more easterly parts of the province. Today, of course, our people are more evenly distributed, but at that time it was a matter of moving into an area that was predominantly first generation English or Canadians of Ontario origin. I never liked the latter. The English farmers at least aroused a certain sympathy in their pathetic and helpless stubbornness. I can't recall any of them who were any good at farming, yet in common with us, they had a deep urge to have their own land.

Once, when I was seven or eight, my grandfather, a classic peasant from the steppes with shaven head and long, drooping, dirty blonde moustaches, took me with him on an errand of charity. We visited an English family barely surviving on a scrubby acreage, typical of the area, with small islands of fertile earth surrounded by muskeg. The swampy land was good only for blueberries. The roads were dry that summer, caked into smooth, silvery tracks with weeds growing in the raised mounds in the middle. My grandfather had a Model A that easily cleared the dyke of hard mud in the centre of the track. The chokecherry bushes, the willows and birches grew so close to the edge that they brushed and scraped against the high frame of the old car. The people we visited,

Jones was their name I am sure, lived in an unbelievable cabin of hewn logs. Not a small one, but a rambling succession of rooms, the uneven floors covered with the mail order linoleum you saw at every farm. The barn was of unpainted planking, shiny with weathering. Flies from a nearby manure pile somehow got into the house in droves. The whole place had a high, musky smell, not entirely unattractive.

The five girls in the family lined up in dirty, loose fitting cottons to greet us. My grandfather, after grave inquiries about the health of everyone, handed the thin, leathery Mrs. Jones our kettle of *pyrohy*. Mr. Jones, equally thin, joined us and insisted we have tea. Their eight-year old daughter told me I must come blueberry picking with them sometime. Eventually we left. On the way back, down the packed mud trail and its buzzing insects, my grandfather remembered that he had forgotten his briar pipe. As we drove back into the straw-littered yard, we saw Mr. Jones tipping our blue kettle of *pyrohy* into the pig trough. My grandfather recovered his pipe and we never went back.

Shortly after, my father got a job and we moved away to the Coal Branch not far from Edson. I had enjoyed our stay at my grandfather's and missed him. I remembered the evenings when he would sing sad songs to the accompaniment of an ancient *tsymbaly*, although just before we moved we got a radio and my father would yell at him to shut up. Another enjoyment had been the aeroplanes. The farm was only a short walk overland through paths and brush from Cooking Lake, a low, leech-ridden slough that had a special glamour because it was the floatplane base for Edmonton. Often, over our house, we saw the floatplanes of the bush pilots coming and going from the north. Of all the aircraft, the great Junkers appealed to me most, with their all-metal bodies and the noise they made as they took off in flashing twin sprays. By slogging our way around the lake to the wharf, we could see the planes come and go and sense the pulse of the north country.

A brother of my father's was a pit boss at one of the coal mines in Foothills and found a slot for him. We went west on a C.N.R. train in a coach that had stiff, leather-covered seats with high backs. A film of soot crept under the windows and added an acrid smell to the vinegar stench of the nearby toilet. I sat beside my father across the aisle from my mother and three older sisters, all of whom were light-coloured, ash blondes. My father was dark and understandably somewhat brooding. He had lost his farm and had suffered the indignity of bringing his family to live with his father. Because I was the only boy, after three daughters, he always showed great patience and affection for me. Later, when we were settled in Foothills, and he had his self-respect back again, he took me fishing or hunting bush gophers and squirrels with a .22.

In those days, one changed from the transcontinental at Edson and took a short, mixed freight equipped with two reddish, wooden coaches in front of the caboose. Up the valley of the Embarras River, the railway line wound through the hills and broadened out into spurs where the coal trucks were lined up. At Coalspur the line branched out to Mercoal, Luscar, Leyland, Cadomin and Mountain Park on the one hand and to Sterco and Foothills on the other. Foothills, now a ghost town, as is the whole valley, at that time was scattered in an unruly way on the hillsides. Further down the valley began the headwaters of the Pembina River. My Uncle Steve had found us a three-room, unpainted house on the side of a hill, not far from where they had just built a new community hall. For two years my father was in and out of the mines as my uncle placed him wherever he could. The beginning of war brought a new demand for coal. Wages began to inch upwards. We painted the house a dull yellow, a painted house being a status symbol in a mining camp.

There were mostly Poles and Italians in the mines, with a few midget-like Welshmen thrown in. All of them fought us Ukrainians, especially the Poles, who outnumbered us. A Finnish kid named Maki, from a woods family, not miners, taught me how to use a knife, although most of the time it was fists and feet. But when my father had his leg crushed in a rockfall, they fed us for two or three months, took up a collection to pay our rent, and the Polish boys at school gave me a baseball mitt. Well-connected Uncle Steve found my father, now hampered by a game leg, a job as a timekeeper with a construction outfit in Vancouver. We moved to a little, brown-shingled house off Main Street where wood or sawdust fuel was stacked up at curbside. I did well at high school and had decided to go on. This led to my first real quarrel with my father. For him, the suspicions of his ancestors exerted such influence that he was incapable of expressing a political thought. He only grumbled or choked when local politicians were mentioned and, ordinarily, his only comment on world news was a scowl or a slight grin. I was therefore shaken and upset when he erupted over my acceptance by the Royal Military College.

"The war is over and you want to start getting ready for the next one?" he suddenly yelled at me, scaring me out of ten years' growth. We had been sitting in our tiny kitchen, and through the screen door I had been gazing out at our two pear trees shading the long, feathery grass and feeling content and pleased at the R.M.C. thing. I jumped and looked up at his strangely flashing eyes.

"You know who they will want to fight next," he shouted. "You know who it will be."

"Who?"

"Our own people in the Soviet Union. They're getting ready for it now."

"The Russians are our own people?" I asked, trying sarcasm.

"What choice will Ukraine have?" he yelled. "What choice has Ukraine ever had? They'll toe the line and they'll fight. And you want to get ready to fight our own?"

"I don't intend to fight anybody if I can help it," I said mildly. "Next time there won't be a Ukraine or a Canada or anything. All this means is a way to get some higher education—"

"Higher education. In the army?" he snorted.

"Okay," I began to shout at last, "Where's the money for me to go university? Show me the money and I won't go to R.M.C."

He threw up his hands and seemed to subside.

"There isn't any. You know it," he said with a sadness that reached far down. "But the army. Is there no other way?"

"No. There is no other way, father," I said, my throat stiff.

"You'll end up killing somebody," he went on. He paused. "We're bad for that kind of thing. We have some Cossack."

I laughed, breaking the tension.

"You're talking fairytales," I said. "All we're doing is getting me an education at government expense. Nothing more; nothing less."

His eyes were damp.

"I guess you're right, Alex." He clapped me on the shoulder and called to my mother to make us some tea.

Now, as I walked through the gates into Wolseley Barracks, I wondered. My father may have been right.

The empty quarters were dark and bleak within drawn curtains. In the lonely stillness, I heard my phone ringing, muffled behind the closed door. It was still ringing by the time I had reached the top of the stairs and unlocked the door. I wondered if it was Agnes.

"Sir, it's long distance. I think your wife has finally made a connection," the base operator told me.

"Edith, we got through at last," I said in a mixture of relief and guilt.

Her voice was faint but clear.

"It took you so long to answer. Where were you?"

"Out for a walk. Just came in the door," I said, a trifle hoarsely. "How is everybody?"

"Oh, we're all fine. The weather's been gorgeous and the boys send their love." She paused and spoke again very distinctly and carefully. "Alex, do you have any information on what's going on?"

"You mean where you are?"

"Yes."

"Nothing special in that area," I said, beginning to worry. "Have you seen anything?"

"It's very hard to describe. There's nothing startling I can explain in itself. Just a series of little things that are beginning to seem rather strange. Like yesterday."

"What happened, darling?"

"All of the cottagers along our part of the lake were visited by a couple of officers from the Quebec Provincial Police. They were very polite, but it seems they asked everybody the same questions—"

I stiffened.

"Speak up, Edith. I can hardly hear you. What did they ask?"

"Well, what they wanted to know—"

The line went dead.

7

By noon I had tossed an empty package of Players onto the untouched papers, gaping inertly for attention, and sat down to rest. I had paced myself into a state of exhaustion. Across the arms of a chair I had draped an aerial navigation chart as if it would somehow lift me from London to the airfield at Mont Tremblant. While waiting for the base operator to try and make the connection again, I had tried to think about aircraft and where to get one. Not being an operational commander, as yet, I didn't have even an L-19 at my disposal. I thought of phoning up the hospitable C.O. of Downsview for an aircraft, faking some mysterious mission, but I didn't have much hope that he would produce one without checking up the line. A private charter from London airport was out of the question because my pay hadn't yet come through and there wasn't a bean in the bank, nor had I taken the time to establish an overdraft with my local friendly banker. Still, a colonel should have a good credit rating among the local people and on a Sunday no one could phone a bank about the state of my account. I had decided to try a charter on credit and was looking up the yellow pages in the directory when the phone rang. Thankfully, I heard the operator say it was long distance, but it was not Edith. The rather dry, high voice of a man came on.

"Colonel Hlynka, sorry to bother you on a Sunday. This is John Douglas calling." It took me a moment to realize he was the new commander of Mobile Command, the young airman I had met in Montreal.

"Did you have anything planned for this afternoon?" he went on.

"No, sir," I answered, not accustomed to such politeness.

"Good. I'd like to see you. How'd it be if I drop in around 1330?"

"Fine, sir. I'll meet you at the airport.'

"Good," he repeated. "Don't lay on anything, by the way. I just want to brief you personally on a couple of things." The dry, casual voice was finished and we hung up.

At one I was at the airport, having dredged up my staff car and a duty driver out of the Motor Pool. The antiseptic terminal building was echoing and deserted. A silver two-seater Tutor came in low at about 400 m.p.h., pulled up and landed away out on a runway. Looking more like somebody's weekend hobby, the little plane rolled up to the terminal and cut off engines with a quick whine. Douglas, who had been flying it, had another airman with him. They both walked like football players, laden with padding and carrying helmets. It was evident that Douglas didn't have much time for flying any more because he was chattering away to the other man about the technical details of their flight from St. Hubert. As they peeled off their flight suits, I noticed they were wearing their old R.C.A.F. blues.

At the barracks, Douglas and I went up to my rooms. No one apparently had noticed their arrival and the station was still enveloped in its Sunday hibernation. The other airman, a captain, went off to the kitchen to get something to eat. I arranged for coffee to be sent up.

Douglas looked around the small sitting room with its littered papers and maps.

"You've been busy," he said. He was about five years younger than me, slight and blonde. The airmen always looked as if they lacked substance, somehow. Possibly it was just that they didn't get the physical weathering that the soldier acquires over many years out on the ground. "How's it shaping up?" he went on.

"We're going full tilt," I said. "Give us a month or two a' Borden and I'll have them in reasonable shape."

"I hope everybody' cooperating," he said. It was a question.

"Training Command still resents me reporting directly to you. They've been a bit slow on some things. Otherwise, okay."

"Do you want to give me a list?"

"I think we can handle them," I said. "The main thing I want is to nail down full cooperation at Borden."

"You may never get there," said Douglas quietly. I stared and let him go on. "That's what I wanted to see you about." He got up and looked at some old R.C.R. photos above the fireplace. "By the end of this week we're going to have it right in our laps. I don't think any of us are quite sure what the government's policy is or secession," he said to the picture.

I told him about Edith's phone call, hinting strongly I was anxious to get her out of there. If Douglas got the message, he didn't show it. He jammed his hands in his pockets and paced.

"That fits the pattern," he said. "We're getting reports from all over the province. They're building the climate for the Third Constituent Assembly."

"Including the business in Montreal," I said bitterly.

"Everyone seems to be intimidated. Lefebvre, Carpentier and the P.D.Q. are ready to get their way. What's more they've set the date."

When he said that, I felt bleak and empty. I began to

see implications for my green unit and started to worry about some kind of preventive move that might prematurely involve us. I began to probe for some other explanation.

"Is there any chance that the assassinations in Montreal were not them?" I asked. "Possibly some other group entirely?"

"Not a chance," said Douglas. "The assassins were members of the P.D.Q. Legion, their paramilitary branch. The ones we got had the fleur-de-lis tattoo on their arms and the R.C.M.P. identified them all right. No," he said grimly, "There's no doubt what's facing us. Lefebvre has called the Constituent Assembly for a week Thursday. From what we know, the Secession Resolution will go through the first day without a peep from anybody. On Friday the new nation will be proclaimed. It's going to be that fast."

I suppose I was not alone in trying to absorb the magnitude of what was about to happen. I had difficulty forming a mental picture of how it would take place and how the traditions of almost two and a half centuries could suddenly be made obsolete. How would it take form, I mused, in the towns and villages along the great river that formed the spine of the new country? On Friday morning, would they awaken early? Perhaps it would be more like a Sunday. Along a twisting street that was also the main highway through the village, the people would emerge from their homes, crammed close to the edge of the road. Echoing deep peals from the church would bring them out and, in their best clothes, they would walk or drive to the church, the sun glinting on its steeple like a sword thrust into the sky. On the broad steps of the church they would gather in quiet, nervous talk and cluster around the local P.D.Q. members in their new-found power. At each end of the main street there might be a police car, perhaps Q.P.P. or local police, the only signs of anything unusual or military. Soon, the people would enter the church, damp and cool at that time of the morning, to celebrate an early mass and to hear a white-faced priest tell them it was a time of trial for all Christians when everyone must be steadfast, calm and do his duty. If he supported secession, the priest might say some words about freedom after two centuries. Throughout the morning, some stores would be open and there would be heavy buying of canned goods and flour . . . just in case.

At noon, there might be a ceremony at the town hall, with the local Papal Zouaves band and the lowering of the blood red maple leaf flag and the raising of the blue and white flag with the fleur-de-lys in each corner to cheers or maybe an unbelieving silence. The school children, having heard what it was all about in their classes from cautious nuns or the secular teachers who mostly supported secession, would gather in a hollow square, shortest in front, tallest at the rear, to see the change of flags. They might be amused while the local council decided what to do with the maple leaf flag once it was held like something hot in their hands, until an impatient P.D.Q. man would snap at them: "Burn it!" They would burn it to some cheers from the young P.D.Q. supporters, but an awed silence from most. And the children would go home, happy to have a day off in unseasonably warm weather and the prospect of running in bare feet along the mud flats of the river. While the women went home, the men might gather at the local tavern. In the mayor's office, the local P.D.Q. leader would drop in for a chat. He would tell the mayor that, in view of the tense situation and until the emergency period had passed, it might be a good idea if the mayor and council agreed to let the P.D.Q. organization make all decisions regarding law, order and security—just for awhile. The mayor would agree. That evening the streets would be patrolled by the P.D.Q. Legion, young men with blue and white armbands and rifles, proudly nursing smarting arms with fresh fleur-de-lys tattoos signifying that they had been sworn in and had taken the oath. In their homes, the families would gather around their TV sets, for once eschewing the stronger signals of the U.S. stations across the border, to listen in French and see the events of the day on the Quebec network. They would wait in anticipation. What could they expect? I asked General Douglas.

"Who knows? The Cabinet and caucus are still arguing," he said. "As nearly as we can make out, opinions vary from immediate and strong intervention, to a minimum position."

"What is that?"

"It has three basic elements," said Douglas. "In its simplest form: access for all navigation on the St. Lawrence and the Seaway; free railway and highway connections from the Maritimes to Ontario; the granting of a free city status to Montreal because of its large English-speaking population. According to our reports, that's about the position we can expect the government to take; assuming, of course, protection of lives and property. I don't think they feel that they can completely prevent secession without a civil war."

"Do you know if they have conveyed this position to Lefebvre and Carpentier?"

"Yes, they have. Privately, of course. I doubt if they will accept those terms."

"Not accept them? Surely they're too reasonable for the rest of the country to accept. I can't see some of the other provinces going along with an offer like that. If Lefebvre turns down that offer, the rest of the country will pressure the government into taking the obvious course."

"Exactly," said Douglas. "That's why I'm here. I think it's going to happen." He paused to light a cigarette and I borrowed one from him. "The Coalition can't afford to pull back too far. So we've got our orders."

"This should be interesting," I said nastily.

"Very," he said. "I am to take all steps necessary to cope with a possible emergency. This is to be done without provocation, repeat, without provocation, within Quebec. No extra troops or equipment are to be moved into the province from outside, but we may take any steps necessary to organize existing forces outside the province into concentration areas near the borders in the event that they are required to protect property and lives. There is to be no mobilization of militia in Quebec. All permanent installations and forces within the province are to be placed on the alert and issued with ammunition and emergency rations. All leaves are cancelled."

"No mobilization of militia in Quebec?"

"We can't take the risk. There are about 8,000 of them in fourteen infantry units, three armour, three artillery, two engineers and one signals unit. We now know that the P.D.Q. has been infiltrating the militia to get training and to set up cells. Some of them have already taken it on their own to guard the armouries. We're trying to figure out a way to pry them loose without setting something off."

"Oh."

"This brings me to your position," he said. "Let me sketch in my intentions."

My intentions, I thought. My troops; my plan. All senior officers were the same in their possessiveness and I suppose I was no exception. In the shoulder board club they all knew it was their names that would be attached to whatever operation they devised. The game was General So-and-So's brilliant tactic, or his lack of decision or blunder in a critical moment, when it might not be him at all, but a tank commander who strayed off line, or a company of green troops who didn't hold, or an artillery officer who called it wrong and fired short. And those in business held us in contempt, I reflected, because, instead of scarce capital, we dealt in the allocation of scarce humans.

"All 1 can do at this stage," went on Douglas, "Is build up the perimeter with what we've got here at home. You'll get an official briefing later on the disposition of units, but you can quess what we've got to work with."

"Not much," I said.

"Right," the general said. "So we're concentrating air transport at Trenton and Gagetown. We've made arrangements with the provincial governments for a vehicle park on the New Brunswick border and a bigger one at the Long Sault, here in Ontario. I'm moving every wheeled and tracked vehicle I can find into these areas where they'll stay under canvas and I've set up a separate field command structure to handle them. The largest concentration will be at the Long Sault." He was referring to the provincial park created by the flooding of the Seaway, only about thirty miles from the Quebec border. It consisted of islands linked together in a ten-mile chain of causeways and was suitably placed near the 401 and Route 20 superhighways leading to the Montreal area.

"Now, as to your unit," said Douglas. "The plain fact is I can't give you battalion airlift out of Borden. I can clear some billet space at Trenton so you'll be right on the spot for a sudden move. I wanted to get your opinion."

I thought for a moment.

"What can you give me at Borden? For instance, could you guarantee some Buffaloes?"

"Yes, but only a flight of three at any one time. Our commitments elsewhere don't permit any more. So we could lift you only a company at a time."

I looked out of the window at the deserted roadway rimmed by whitewashed stones. A lone figure in coveralls, on some kind of fatigue detail, shambled towards the Mess. I turned from the window.

"If you can guarantee the flight of Buffaloes, I'd still prefer Borden," I told him. "First, at Trenton, we'd have no training space and we'd have to double up with the Guards down at Picton. Secondly, at Borden there is the space and the facilities to do something with them in a short time; for example, we have the staff of Combat Arms School. Thirdly, with the kind of time you're talk-about, they won't be ready for battalion movements any-way. I'd sooner move them piecemeal by companies and take the risk."

Douglas absorbed this information.

"The alternative I've been thinking about is to move training elements of P.P.C.L.I. from Edmonton and into Trenton," he said.

"Well, surely they're in better shape than we are?"

"Not a great deal," frowned Douglas.

"Yes, but their officers and N.C.O.'s have worked to-gether for a long time. Mine haven't," I argued.

Douglas nodded, and his young face looked tired. At last, I exploded irritably.

"Come on, sir," I said. "Can't you bring anybody back from overseas? Any of them are in a helluva lot better shape than we are."

"I know, I know," said Douglas, as if he had often answered that question. "The decision of the government, for the time being anyway, is not to make a public display of urgency or panic. We've just taken on our new com-mitments with SEATO and there are a lot of implications to the international situation if we pulled out of NATO at this point. And, as far as South Africa goes, you know how conscious our people are of our standing with the U.N. We've been the ones who've pushed for U.N. inter-vention; now we've got to live with it. The same holds for the supervision of elections in Viet Nam. We can't take Second Vandoos out of there."

I grinned sourly. "I've got about five years of my life to prove it."

Douglas stood up.

"I have some other calls I want to get in this afternoon. I'll let you know my decision in the morning," he said.

On the way back to the airport, I toyed with the idea of asking Douglas for permission to fly to Mont Tremblant and almost had the nerve to ask him if he could drop me off there. On seeing his grim, pale face, however, I decided that it wouldn't be a welcome suggestion. Somehow, I would have to figure out something else. Instead, in our last few minutes in the staff car, I probed for more information.

"What have you actually got inside Quebec?" I asked.

"The government hasn't been completely stupid," he said, in an offhand way that conveyed the feelings of the general staff better than anything he had revealed all day. I could picture the Chief saying to his Minister or the Cabinet, words to the effect that if such-and such was to be the policy, the forces would do the best they could, but would not take responsibility for guaranteeing peace and order. The Minister (and/or Cabinet) would look hunched and worried, exchange furrowed glances and decide, all things considered, that would have to be the policy until the situation in Quebec became more definite one way or the other. "We have turned over the three anti-missile bases in Quebec to the Americans," Douglas was saying, "which, in effect, neutralizes them. This has all been done by airlift without public knowledge, except that we have leaked it to Lefebvre and company so they won't try anything at those bases. I sent all our personnel from the bases to Ottawa. They're no use to me for keeping order on the ground."

"What have we got at Valcartier and St. Hubert?" I asked.

"Only training units and service troops," he said. "At Valcartier only two companies of Vandoos; 2nd Battalion is with the U.N. in Viet Nam and the First is with NATO, along with the Third in its anti-tank role. There's

74

an experimental ground-to-air missile unit at Valcartier and a recce squadron. At St. Hubert, I have a reinforcement unit of the Canadian Airborne and assorted service troops, but at the moment, they're scattered all over Montreal on guard duty."

"Do you feel the city is battened down, then?"

"No, not by a long shot. Why?"

"I was just thinking about our training syllabus. The cities are the key points, aren't they?"

We were at the airport, and Douglas was already zipping himself into his shiny flight suit. He pulled his collar together and swung his helmet back and forth. The captain, who had been with him, was already in the cockpit of the little jet and doing whatever it is that makes up their strange ritual with all the dials. The young general turned his eyes, already farsighted in anticipation of flight.

"The streets are where this whole thing will be decided," he said slowly. "And there are a lot of narrow streets in those Quebec towns. Quite a lot."

He scowled at the thought, then shook hands and restlessly was off in his little jet.

8

There is nothing like its first full scale move to size up a battalion's mental state. When orders came from Mobile Command on Monday to move to Borden immediately, if not sooner, I unleashed a reign of terror in Third R.C.R. Impossible objectives were set and I was pleased to see that most of them were met. My unit was glad to get moving, shown by occasional expressions of interest on the tanned, deadpan faces of the young soldiers. Somehow we made it in three days after a shambling and disorganized trek of men and vehicles in something resembling convoys. Despite a tendency for the new drivers to get a bit unnerved by the civilian traffic, dodging among the lorries with that livid impatience of the Ontario motorist, the convoys more or less stayed on schedule and all arrived in Borden, except for one truck that ended up in Hamilton. Its driver had a girl friend there, we found out later. The main body of the troops who went to Borden in the mixed train of ancient coaches and flatcars, that carried the tracked vehicles, arrived in good spirits and, for the most part, sober. Before leaving London, I phoned Agnes at her apartment and when there was no answer never called again.

With the pressure of time we put them to work with a tight syllabus, long hours and everything double time. The

N.C.O.'s and junior officers began to learn economy of words and motion. I noticed the signs of team work in their street training where I watched them closely whenever I could get away from the desk.

Over the years innumerable troops had taxed their imagination to give The Street a name, including inspirations such as "Red Light Square," "Peking Place," and "Parliament Hill". But as long as I could remember, it remained simply The Street. A stranger wandering ten miles out of Borden, amid the low, tan sand dunes, would come across what appeared to be a ghost town transplanted from Colorado or Nevada. Instead of weathered timber, he would find solid concrete shells, one or two of them four storeys high, separated by a forty-foot, paved road, sidewalks and rather battered street lights. Most of the time, the doors swung creaking in the wind while the windows gaped bleakly with no glass. Ripples of sand drifted in ridges along the curbs and the doorways and along the concrete walls that were chipped and grooved with the marks of battle. This was The Street where we tried to take our city boys for the most part, who had just been reconditioned to get a feel of the land, and show them a different view of the urban life.

When an infantryman has been taught to use earth—to dig in it, hide amid its growth, use it to move unseen and to master its eery shadows at night—he must be trained all over again for street fighting. Once his affection for the earth has been rekindled, he will look upon city streets fearfully. Even though he may have lived all his years indoors and on pavement, these once comfortable surroundings take on strange and terrifying aspects when he comes to them as a soldier. For there is no place to burrow; no place to creep or crawl; no protection from night, only black and sharp lines where the human form stands out in silhouette, vulnerable and awkward against walls where steel can ricochet and splinters fly. His whole instinct is to hug against walls, look up at windows above him, and sprint like a madman from one sheltering pool of shadow to another. He runs and he may panic. So we had to give him new insight and teach him how to use the contours of buildings cruelly and ruthlessly, without regard for the aesthetic values of a cathedral or the pity of a nursing home.

They didn't do too badly, those youngsters so new to the game. We started them out on basic principles, showing how to work together cross-covering the street and moving in parallel up opposite sides. We showed them the elements of room clearing and how to get up on top and work down through a building, floor by floor. Then we started adding the subtle bits, like having the C.A.S. instructors concealed in alcoves while the trainees came in upper windows with grappling irons and ropes. As they started down through the building, the instructors would come in from above with thunderflashes and scare them out of their wits with the shattering blasts those tubes of gunpowder can make in small rooms. We added other diversions, such as real snipers who took potshots over their heads with live ammunition. And, just when a section thought it was getting pretty good, the instructors would slip chicken wire screens slightly back from the windows, so that the training grenades would bounce back. This was always a good test of agility for the thrower and, to their credit, only about a dozen suffered burns from not moving fast enough or scrapes and sprains from rolling ungracefully for cover.

For variety, we gave them riots. One company would act, in baying realism, as an irate mob attacking a tear-gas armed platoon drawn up across the street. There were a few minor injuries in these encounters, too, but it was good for them. Final workouts included night sessions, showing them how to use shadows, and we had some run-throughs with vehicles. We taught them how to get out of a truck fast in a street ambush involving molotov cocktails and how to work with armoured cars under crossfire from the turrets. I often watched them, the wind whipping sharp grains of sand into my face, eyes protected by tinted goggles from the summer glare. When they came back for a break and cold drink of water, I gave them encouragement and always stopped by the U.A.S. to survey the bruises, scrapes and burns. There was a sense of exhileration mounting in the battalion as the pace was stepped up, but it was tempered in the evening when we gathered in the mess to watch the interminable TV specials dissecting the crisis in Quebec. At such times a faint depression enveloped us all, for we knew what our daily exercises were all about.

The news was not encouraging. A strange, shocked silence had followed the Separation Resolution, as it was commonly called, passed unanimously by the Third Constituent Assembly in Quebec's graceful, bright legislative chamber. The Prime Minister of Canada, at 45 a victim of twenty years of politics, his urbane, businessman features empty of any emotion or determination, told us he was flying personally to Quebec to see the premier. As it turned out, shown in grainy, raw photography on the TV screen, they wouldn't let him off his plane at Quebec City. He was given a jeering sendoff by the Quebec Provincial Police and a ragtag group of armed P.D.Q. legionnaires. Again the P.M. appeared on the screens, the media cult that had pushed him to the top leaking its ethos in a cool so detached it could no longer cope with the need for more primitive and rough words.

"The bland leading the bland," grunted my adjutant, Rhodes, causing snickers with his treading on forbidden political ground.

"The poor bastard has the Coalition to look after," said someone defensively. "He's got to hold the government together."

"What government?" said somebody.

" 'A government can get along without an army, but an army cannot get along without a government,' " quoted Rhodes, being the soldier-academic; "Marshal Foch."

Realizing that they had stepped beyond the bounds of casual Mess chatter, my officers lapsed into silence. Someone got up and turned the channel to an American station, but we could not escape. Tumbling to the story developing next door, the U.S. networks had sent up film crews and commentators who invariably mispronounced the names of the Canadian personalities. Lefebvre, as I recall, came out as something like "Lefeeber."

"I hope they never come to my name," I said, and my officers guffawed.

Later that night we saw our Prime Minister in Washington. The news commentators, in puzzled tones, tried to speculate on the purpose of the trip—External Affairs having told them it was just for "friendly discussions on matters of mutual concern"—but we knew what he was there for.

"He's trying to get First or Second Brigade off the hook," said one of my company commanders.

"What's the betting?" I asked. The majority predicted a pullout in SEATO, a recent commitment. Third Brigade was not a factor because some of its elements had gone to NATO and others to U.N. work in South Africa and elsewhere.

"The States calls the shots in SEATO," said one of my majors. "But in NATO we'd lose face with several allies."

"Is that what they give you in staff college?" someone asked sarcastically.

"You'll never find out."

"If the Commies are smart," said our pundit, Rhodes, "they'll put the pressure on First Brigade in Thailand. They'll try to keep us in there, making it easier for this Quebec thing to stick. It'll be nice for them to have a neutral nation straddling the St. Lawrence and the approaches to Hudson Bay."

"Not that simple," said a major. "You're talking about Chinese policy. The Soviets might approach it from another angle entirely."

I didn't pay much attention to what the major said, but some time later in much different surroundings, I remembered his words.

As the argument began to degenerate, I got up and started out of the room. These days I found it increasingly difficult to sit still for long. On the way out, the station padre, who had been listening in obvious discomfort, got up and followed me. He was young and darkly intense. He called himself Father Miller, and he was not a Catholic so he must have been High Anglican. We stood wordlessly for a while and contemplated the night. Across the parade square, yellow rectangles showed the barracks windows. A jukebox pounded a heavy bass over a weedy treble through the screen doors of the Sergeants' Mess. Two men on patrol could be heard, but not seen, their steel heel plates clashing somewhere on asphalt. The base commander, a full colonel, had laid on security with live rounds up the spout. In view of the newness of the troops, everyone made a point of always wearing his uniform at night. It was safer that way. Otherwise the night was peaceful, with crickets making sounds in the grass and the soft Ontario air almost tropical in its humid stillness.

It was not a good setting for warlike thoughts, but I couldn't avoid them. The Buffalo turbojet transports were coming in tomorrow and we'd start some exercises at the airfield to time the troops' entry and exit until they could do it without tripping all over their gear. I wished I could fly, and thought I would have to take the time to find a congenial pilot around the station who would take me into Mont Tremblant.

Since Separation Day there had been complete silence from the cottage. Telephone, telegraph and even ordinary mail apparently had disappeared in Quebec except for the Montreal area. Every day, at some critical point in a briefing or while doing paper work at my desk, I turned off while my mind probed horrible and imaginary fates for my family. In more tranquil moments, I assured myself that, at worst, Edith, the boys and her parents were only isolated in relative comfort and better off to be outside Montreal. The sunny days on the lake would help to blunt their anxieties. The Watsons had been going to the lake for over twenty years; the villagers knew them well and were helpful and warm. Still, I wanted to see them and get them out. And I remembered what Edith had tried to tell me about the visits of the provincial police.

"It's peaceful out here," said the young padre at last.

I began to feel a rising irritation. Every night he had sat in silence in the Mess, listening with flickering eyes to our blood-thirsty and obscene talk. Father Miller did not seem to belong with the religious military, customarily older men who could swear and drink with the troops better than the N.C.O.'s. I didn't want to have any accusing spectre around while I drove my men to fitness for their violent work.

"You don't think it was peaceful in there," I said shortly.

He was too new or too intense to take the usual way out and dismiss it all with a hearty laugh of the kind that they must specially teach padres in the forces. Instead, he hunched his shoulders and looked down the front of his green uniform with its black buttons.

"I have seen civil war in other countries," he said.

"So've I."

"It's almost impossible to preserve any kind of values in a civil war," he went on.

"We're not in one yet."

"For all practical purposes we are."

"The government may let them go."

"Do you really think so?"

"No," I turned on him. "Look, if you have something on your mind, say it."

His large eyes darted and jumped. "I have made a point of observing some of your training," he said slowly. "I can't help feeling that you're getting them ready to make war on civilians."

"Only those who have guns or get in our way," I said, breathing deeply. "What do you expect us to do?"

"It's just so different from the kind of situation one would expect from a country whose main role is peace-keeping," he said a bit pitifully. I softened and began to understand what was bothering him. He had probably regretted his enlistment the moment we had taken on the fighting role in Thailand, and now he found himself locked into an organization readying itself for the most sleazy jobs of all: war against its own people. This realization came too slowly to me, however, to prevent my switching into a bluff colonel role. I clapped him on the shoulder, causing him to jump and recoil at the same time. The young padre didn't like being touched.

"Be my guest," I said. "Feel free to make what contacts you like with my men. You may attend any of our exercises or activities, and you can talk to them anytime you want."

The young padre looked at me in horrified distaste, and without a word, walked away rapidly.

The next morning a tropical monsoon of sorts swept in from Georgian Bay with such ferocity that we relented and moved the drenched troops indoors where we substituted some basic French for the usual V.D. lectures given at such times. After a morning of cleaning up paperwork and a taut "O" group on results to date, I called in my Intelligence Officer. Over the noon hour we devised a hasty *kriegsspiel* for the officers, using a blackboard sketch of downtown Montreal and myself and the I.O. as Control. He had quickly run off the scenario on a ditto machine and we had a useful session, with one team as us and another a resistance group of P.D.Q. legionnaires defending Dominion Square. There was much hilarity about the strategic nature of well-known bars and hotels. It was during this uproar, concerning the capture of a bar with all its topless waitresses, that our young padre appeared again, slipping into the back of the room like a gaunt shadow. It bothered me that his presence only spurred on my officers to suggesting excesses that made the Mongols in Budapest seem like the Y.M.C.A. But I made no move or sign as Father Miller, his face blotched, turned and left the room.

My final encounter with our suffering priest occurred during exercises with the Buffalo. I use the singular, because to my rage, only one aircraft showed up. The pilot, an older and unflappable captain, told me he didn't know anything about other aircraft. I burnt up the wires to St. Hubert and was told we had been allocated one Buffalo for training purposes; others would be assigned when needed. I seethed at the cutback in training that would result. With three of those aircraft (41 men apiece) I could lay on company exercises. Now it had to be by platoons in a long, drawn-out process that had me simmering on the tarmac a couple of days later, as I watched Number Three Platoon of Delta Company go around for the fourth time in a vain attempt to sort itself out.

The olive-green turboprop, almost defying gravity with its slow approach, its engines whining in the thick, heavy air, came in with tail up in its distinctive style. The old smoothy at the controls brought it in like a cargo of eggs on velvet. For the fourth time I set my stopwatch. Three Platoon was to hit the enemy at the edge of the field while the imaginary balance of the company landed at the other corners and worked around it. As the engines cut out with slow bass notes, Three Platoon came out like old women, weary and hot in helmets and gear. They handled their weapons like apprentice plumbers.

"Get Captain Davidson over here," I yelled to my runner. I turned to my taut-faced R.S.M., who looked more thin and wiry than ever.

"Mr. Wilson, what the hell's the matter with your N.C.O.'s in Delta?"

"Same question just occurred to me sir," he said and was off.

Captain Davidson, a good-looking blonde man in his late twenties, came up with an outward show of purpose, which was about all he could do under the circumstances. I walked away from the inevitable claque of runners, signallers, and others watching the show, followed by Davidson. Our short walk brought us unintentionally within earshot of Father Miller, who had been standing alone, away from the group. This made me turn it on more than I had intended, something I immediately regretted for both men, but somehow couldn't seem to avoid doing.

"Mr. Davidson," I said with deadly formality. "You've got to find ten minutes. You've got to work those men until they've picked up ten minutes. You have just caused the massacre of my entire battalion because you can't get their ass off that plane. And I want you to put that entire bloody platoon through their Basic again in three days so that they know one end of their weapons from the other. You get out there and teach them to move and how to kill fast, or by God, I'll find somebody who can!"

Davidson glanced resentfully at the padre who could not help hearing us.

"Yes, sir."

"Keep at it and we'll talk about it tonight," I said a little more kindly.

Davidson jogged away, undoubtedly regretting the day he had joined the militia for its social life, and now found himself in an environment where the efficiency of the executive was not enough. He lacked the streak of coarseness that makes the good officer, as distinct from the businessman. He left the field, carrying his helmet like a lineman coming off at the end of the first quarter.

"Did you mean what you said?" asked Father Miller, moving up.

"Yes," I said and walked away from him. I don't know if that had done it, but the next day he disappeared from the station. Some time later, I heard that he had deserted the army and had joined a Quaker ship delivering medical supplies and food to the Communist insurgents in Thailand. I always thought it odd that he would do that when it was apparent that suffering was to become the lot of many of our own people at home.

I had watched him stride towards his jeep that day and vowed to myself that the next time we met, I would try and be a little more considerate. But there was not much time for such luxuries. I turned my attention to the Buffalo moving down the runway again. A jeep motor cut across the sound of the turboprops and Rhodes, looking clean and unsweaty, sought me out. He handed me a yellow message form and saluted.

"Orders, sir," he said.

I felt my heart sink. The yellow paper fluttered in my hand from the backwash of the Buffalo as it turned around into the wind and sent a flurry of dust across the field.

"It's only you, sir," he said quickly, apparently reading my face.

"Me?"

"Yes, sir. You're to be at C.F.H.Q. at 0900 tomorrow. A conference of some sort."

Ottawa. I wondered what Ottawa wanted.

9

Ottawa was not exactly an armed camp, but there were signs of a clampdown. The base at Uplands, where we landed, had sentries, mostly inside doorways where the public couldn't see them. I noticed several R.C.M.P. cars at the civilian air terminal. From my staff car, one of several waiting in a line for arrivals, I noticed an unusual number of Ontario Provincial Police cruising around, as if they had been moved up to border areas. I assumed that no one was worrying any more about jurisdiction on federal or provincial roads in the National Capital District.

It was 0830. I had left Borden at 0600 in a single-engined L-19 Bird Dog, the fragile-looking little high-wing monoplane that did more jobs for us than anything else. It was a slow trip and I had taken the Bird Dog over the two-seater jet the base commander had offered. I had a germ of an idea, depending on how long the conference took, and the plan involved a flexible aircraft and a short day at H.Q.

As we drove into the city along Bronson Avenue, I pondered, as do all visitors, the strange contrasts of the capital. The wide roadway took us over the green, land-scaped banks of the Rideau, past the adjoining recreational centre for easing the libidos of the civil servants, large pool and playing fields on the east side. On the west was the Carleton University campus that always seemed to be dug up for what was apparently a hundred-year plan of expansion. Further on, another bridge took us over the National Capital Commission Driveway. On the left stretched Dow's Lake, glittering in the morning sun. Beyond was Carling Avenue, and I reflected that everything in Ottawa seemed to be named after beer. Below, to our right, the Driveway curved in its magnificent framework of trees and flowerbeds, the unseasonable heat having wilted the last banks of Dutch tulips. Almost immediately the street became a clutter of overhead wiring and dark, dingy, brick dwellings relieved only by the glass facade of the occasional apartment building. Once we had gone through the Queensway underpass, the landscape became even more depressing. A few commercial buildings, followed by rows of old brick or dirty frame row houses, lined the street. At the north end of Bronson we came over the ridge dropping down to Wellington Street and the enormous pile of glass and concrete in LeBreton Flats. This was Canadian Forces Headquarters.

Beyond the E. B. Eddy buildings at the Chaudiere Bridge, I could see the spires of Hull and the purple, hazy mounds of the Gatineau hills forming an artificial-looking backdrop to the whole scene. I wondered if, in fact, the Ottawa River would now become a boundary between two nations and what would happen to all those people in Hull, French-speaking for the most part, who worked in the government offices in Ottawa. Perhaps they would go on much as before. Otherwise there would be one hell of an unemployment problem on the Quebec side of the river. But those who made nations these days didn't seem to worry much about such things.

A rather thin ring of barbed wire and a detachment of Canadian Guards from Petawawa barred the approaches to C.F.H.Q. I produced my I.D. card and made a critical mental note that the Guards would be a lot more useful as sentries if they weren't wearing their British-style peaked caps with the vizors that came down low over the eyebrow. I could never understand how they could see anything. Inside the large foyer, with its impressive inlays of regimental emblems, I was taken by a young guardsman to the bank of elevators. We went down two levels where I knew the Ops rooms were, although I had never been in them in the new buildings. Along some pastel green corridors, cool with air conditioning, we came to a small anteroom. A staff captain checked my credentials and marked me off on a list.

"Just in time, sir. Go right in," he said.

I stepped through open doors into a conference room that would hold about a hundred people. In the front rows I counted about thirty officers wearing a colourful variety of shoulder patches. There was a low rumble of their voices, a subdued, tense kind of sound. I noticed some of them sat silently, lost in thought.

My peers, I thought, glancing at sleeves. Half colonels and up. Unit commanders for the most part. Some brigadiers and a major-general or two from the various branches. As I edged into a seat in the third row, some familiar faces looked up and nodded greetings, acquaintances I hadn't seen for years.

"You don't look right without your U.N. badges, Alex," grinned "Pearly" Gates, C.O. of the newly-formed Third Black Watch, Gagetown.

"Better than looking half-dressed in kilts," I said. "How's your mob doing?"

He looked at the ceiling. "I'll get ulcers, yet. Do you sometimes get the feeling that modern youth is awkward and slow-witted?"

"All I can say, is I hope we never have to use them."

"Don't count on it," said Gates cheerfully.

An entourage of officers came down the aisle and we all stood up, each one of us trying to identify the faces that gathered over the shoulder boards and decorations.

One man stood out. He was taller than the others, well over six foot three. He had craggy, Scottish features with Roman nose, busy, prominent eyebrows and a long, thin mouth. This was our top soldier, General A. D. Mac-Lennan, Chief of the Defence Staff. I thanked our luck that he was an army man and not a sailor or airman. Beside him, Douglas, commander of Mobile Command, looked youthful and unfinished. MacLennan didn't waste any time and spoke quickly in a surprisingly light, tenor voice, but then again, generals don't have to develop their voices by shouting at people.

"Gentlemen," he began, "this is an unusual conference, but these are unusual times that will require extraordinary initiative and at the same time, careful restraint, on the part of each one of you. You are the unit commanders of our forces assigned to Mobile Command in Quebec and its periphery. Others of you represent support formations, training establishments and the directorates. With me here is the Vice-Chief, the Deputy Chiefs and heads of Maritime Command, Air Defence Command, Training Command, Air Transport Command, and Materiel Command."

The whole works, I thought, and squinted in anticipation. I felt Gates beside me lean forward. A thin colonel, who looked vaguely familiar, placed papers on the lectern and clicked on the reading light. His movements were quick and jerky and he sort of skipped backwards on his heels and lost himself in the phalanx of brass hats. Mac-Lennan transformed himself into a professor, with heavy, half-moon reading glasses on his impressive nose. The lights in the room were dimmed. Curtains pulled away from an enormous wall map of Canada, outlined in fluorescent green against a black gridded background. MacLennan began to talk in his dry, high voice. I thought it was like a scene out of the old "crisis" movies we still saw sometimes on late TV, like "Fail Safe" or "Dr.

Strangelove". Somehow they didn't seem so funny now.

"I assume I don't need to remind you that what you hear today is top secret. You will not receive any papers except for your own orders, which will be issued and in your hands by tomorrow. You are not to take any notes, nor convey anything of what I have said to your staff, unless for any reason, you are to be replaced. In such a case, we will arrange for the briefing.

"What you are going to hear today is an outline of our strategic thinking. We will then go into some detail on how your forces will be deployed under each eventuality that may occur. Those of you who have done a stint at NATO or SEATO headquarters will be familiar with this kind of briefing. But there are two basic differences. First, we have never before had to consider such matters in our own country. Secondly, unlike NATO, this is not a theoretical discussion, but an actual consideration of alternatives that now face us. I should point out that the objectives and situation estimate are those of the Canadian government and therefore of the Canadian Forces." He peered down at his papers and read quickly.

"Basic objectives are: (1) To maintain Canada as a complete political entity, including Quebec, and to persuade the people of Quebec to abandon the regime produced by the Third Constituent Assembly. (2) To protect all Canadian citizens in Quebec and other parts of Canada, from any harassment, threat to safety or loss of property. (3) To safeguard all federal government installations in the province of Quebec and to protect all vital facilities and services in Quebec and other parts of Canada. (4) To prevent civil war, i.e. war between the Canadian Forces and any organizations or forces owing allegiance to the Third Constituent Assembly, beyond minimum steps required to preserve order."

Somebody in the darkened room began a mirthless laugh, and a couple of others followed with snorts. Mac-

Lennan looked up quickly and glared over the room. I could have sworn he gave a slight shrug of his shoulders. In any event he said nothing and resumed his reading.

"Immediate objective is to re-establish and maintain *status quo ante* the Third Constituent Assembly and Provisional Government. It must be made clear to the Provisional Government that the Government of Canada cannot remain indifferent to any moves in Quebec actually to assume political control of the province.

"Immediate actions: (1) The appearance of armed irregular forces owing allegiance to the Provisional Government (the so-called 'P.D.Q. Legion') makes it imperative that they be disarmed. (2) While no action has been taken, it is assumed that there will be a move to occupy all key installations in the province of Quebec by the irregular forces, local police forces, Quebec Provincial Police, and possibly some militia units, acting under direction of the Provisional Government.

"International actions: (1) It is evident that the Chinese Peoples' Republic and Cuba are supplying arms to the Provisional Government. The Canadian government will issue notes to both powers implying trade sanctions on Cuban sugar and a cessation of grain deliveries to the Chinese Peoples' Republic. Canadian naval forces and the Coast Guard will be deployed in the Gulf of St. Lawrence and the St. Lawrence River to protect lives and property in ports and to search all incoming vessels destined for Quebec ports. Patrols will be established by air and sea in Hudson Bay. All foreign powers will be notified of the search provisions. (2) No special action will be taken at the United Nations, except to advise the Security Council on a confidential basis of the suspected foreign arms shipments which, if not controlled, could be the subject of a formal protest by the Canadian government. (3) The United States will be kept fully informed on a confidential basis. It will be recommended to the United States that border travel into Quebec be curtailed, that their customs and immigration personnel be increased at Quebec border points and that they consider asking the appropriate governors to increase State Police detachments at the border points. The Canadian government will urge the United States not to place troops or military forces at the border at this time. (4) The Canadian government will make representations to the South East Asia Treaty Organization for the temporary withdrawal of elements of First Canadian Infantry Brigade. No representations will be made to NATO or the United Nations at this time."

General MacLennan paused and lifted off his half glasses.

"The last point is of particular importance to us, gentlemen. We are going to have to make do with the forces we now have on hand in Canada for several weeks at least. That is why I wanted you to hear this document and fully appreciate what it means to each one of you. Now I shall go on to read you the section entitled 'Contingency Actions'. As you must realize, I am reading only relevant sections of the document and not the whole thing." He cleared his throat and continued.

"The following contingency plans apply to the immediate situation: (1) Favourable. If the Provisional Government does not take any further action, and if there is no evidence of popular support in Quebec, the Canadian Forces and R.C.M.P. will disarm all irregular forces and police forces and arrest the leaders of the Provisional Government. (2) Less favourable. If the Provisional Government is only partially successful in establishing control over a small section of the province, likely the immediate Quebec City area, the Saguenay Valley and the South Shore from Lévis to Rivière du Loup (based on Intelligence Reports of the main areas of support) the Canadian Forces and the R.C.M.P. will occupy all major installations from Montreal to Lévis and prepare to take full military action against the territory occupied by the

Provisional Government. (3) Serious contingency. If the above is accompanied by demonstrations of support in Trois Rivières, Lévis, Montreal, the South Shore and Sherbrooke, and attempts to occupy vital installations, the Canadian Forces and R.C.M.P. will give priority to securing the Montreal area, including the South Shore to the United States border. (4) Worst contingency. If the Provisional Government is able to establish control of all major centres in Quebec, the Canadian Forces and R.C.M.P. will retain St. Hubert and Dorval at all costs and prepare for offensive action on the arrival of elements of First Brigade. At that time, the reinforcement situation will have to be reassessed."

The tall general stood in silence for a moment, twirling his glasses. Beside me, Pearly Gates exhaled noisily. There was much shuffling and scraping and clearing of throats.

"Now, gentlemen, if you will turn your attention to the map, I will show you how our forces will be deployed to meet each contingency unit by unit. Before I go on, are there any questions?"

As I suspected, Pearly Gates was first on his feet, as he always had been at staff college.

"Sir, what contingency do you anticipate immediately?" he asked.

Everybody knew Pearly Gates, including the Chief.

"The most likely is an attempt by the Provisional Government to take over all vital installations. We expect this within the next few days."

A brigadier I didn't recognize stood up slowly and diffidently cleared his throat.

"Sir, may I ask a question about the political aspects of the paper?"

"Go ahead, George."

"Thank you, sir. It seems to me that one contingency has been overlooked in the paper. There is no mention of the possibility that they—the government of Canada—

might negotiate for the recognition of the Provisional Government under certain conditions. I think we've all heard rumours of this: Montreal to become a free port, and all that."

Having been through many similar sessions in various parts of the world, I knew a plant when I saw one. I waited anxiously for the answer. The Chief had a glint in his eye as he replied.

"The Minister tells us that it is his understanding from his Cabinet colleagues that this is no longer under consideration."

That was a message that got through. Most of us must have known why the question had been planted. In effect, what must have happened was that an activist group of the Cabinet had decided to act, probably with the tacit support of the P.M., but not necessarily with unanimity or complete backing of them all.

For us, it meant that we were acting in partial independence, subject to sudden change or reversal if we stepped far enough out of line to arouse an opposing pacificist faction. It was not a good climate in which to work, and I think all of us sensed a hollow note in the firm statements of the strategic estimate. It would be harder, I reflected, on some of those who had not been on the international circuit with the U.N.

There were no further questions.

The Chief turned us over to Lieutenant-General Douglas who went into vast detail on the disposition of forces in relation to each of the contingencies mentioned in the estimate. Little squares, triangles and arrows popped up all over the map in windows of red, blue and white, moving from the perimeter of Quebec into its vitals, step by step. I followed the tiny piece of geometry that had been labelled 3 R.C.R., and was relieved to see that they fully understood the readiness of my rawboned, awkward kids. We were to settle in on the international airport at Dorval and extend our control out of there to cover the western part of the island. I would have a reconnaisance squadron, signals, engineers and some Civil Defence units along with powers to commandeer all vehicles, aircraft and rolling stock. Overseas flights already were being diverted to Ottawa or Toronto International Airport to reduce traffic at Dorval, but domestic and U.S. flights were continuing. The next map overlays showed 3 R.C.R. moving through Montreal along the North Shore Autoroute towards Trois Rivières. The final positioning revealed us as tested troops taking part in the final assault in an as-yet-unformed brigade striking towards Quebec City itself.

At noon the meeting broke up for drinks and a buffet lunch in one of the underground rooms. I sought out the C.O. of 8th Canadian Hussars (the Plugs, i.e. the P.L.D.G, i.e. The Princess Louise Dragoon Guards). In the Canadian ground force, the smaller the unit the longer its name. According to the briefing this armoured recce unit was to give me a squadron at Dorval. The Plugs' C.O. was younger than me, dark with a black moustache. We didn't know each other, so we sparred carefully over our cold plate and Scotch.

"You're at the Long Sault?" I asked.

"Yeah. Bloody awful, but anyway the weather's warm. The rain damned near washed us out last week."

"How're your people?"

"Oh, fine. We're short of vehicles, so I've cut out the fat. What we've got left is good. How about yours?"

"They're coming along considering how long they've been in. About all they've had is an intensified basic."

"Well," said the black moustache. "I thought I'd assign a squadron of Commandos to you. That'd be two troops of six Commandos each. I may need my heavier stuff for a straight fighting role."

"Good," I agreed. A fast, wheeled vehicle with two 50-calibre m.g.'s, the Commando can carry eleven men. In addition to their scouting role, they would give me capacity to move nearly a company under armour plate at speeds up to 60 m.p.h. We arranged liaison, but I was destined never to see the cars.

My watch said 1.30 p.m. The others were still standing around, chatting. I began to fidget, and when I saw General Douglas off to one side alone for a moment, I cut him out of the pack.

"If there's nothing else, sir, I'd like to get back," I said.

"Sure, go ahead," said Douglas in his offhand manner. "I'll be in touch. I'll see you get your Buffaloes for the move to Dorval. We're setting up billets in hangers on the west side of the field. Send in your advance party as soon as you can."

"Tomorrow all right?"

"Yes, that's fine."

I phoned the Mess at Uplands and unearthed my pilot, a Lieutenant Campbell, and told him I was on my way. At an almost unseemly run for the casual, indoor waddle of C.F.H.Q., I shot out of the mausoleum into my temporary staff car. On the way to Uplands I stopped at a pay phone and made a quick long distance call. Within twenty minutes I was back at Uplands and sprinting towards the little Bird Dog with a bewildered and somewhat stout Lieutenant Campbell puffing along behind. At the aircraft, I paused and looked at him with what I hoped was a steely, commanding gaze.

"I have a special assignment," I said. "We're not going back to Borden for a few hours."

"Where're we going, sir?"

"Do you know the airstrip at Hawkesbury?"

"Hawkesbury?"

As he slowly reached for the map, I dived into the L-19 and emerged with a small travel bag. I had soon peeled off my uniform and had put on sports shirt, slacks and windbreaker. Campbell looked slightly adrift as he watched me take my 9 mm. Browning automatic from the bag. I stuck the pistol into my waistband and put two extra clips in the jacket pockets.

I could hardly blame Campbell for gaping. After all, Hawkesbury is fifty miles east of Ottawa.

10

Albert (Ab) Tremblay was waiting for me at the Hawkesbury airstrip, which is on the plateau between the Trans-
Canada Highway and the ridge of hills that must have
marked the south bank of the Ottawa River in prehistoric
times. An old biplane, four gliders and a Piper Cub stood
near a weathered shed where we rolled up to Tremblay's
pickup truck.

If central casting searched Quebec for a native stereo-
type they could not have come up with a better choice
than Ab Tremblay. Find a French Canadian for that
lumberjack part, they might say, complete with gravel
voice, big chest; someone who looks good in a checkered
shirt and a tuque. He should have a big laugh. Ab had all
of these; he was big, paunchy, red-haired and had a
lantern jaw under a sweeping, hooked nose. His voice
even had an appropriate throaty rasp, but the occasional
expletive of "by gar" that one might expect from such a
combination never came. Ab spoke perfect English and
educated French. Now he shook my hand warmly and
boomed a greeting that echoed off the wall of the shed.
While he was doing this, his grey eyes took in the military
colours of the L-19 and the green uniform of the pilot.

"Alex, you son of a gun!" He clasped my smaller hand
in his two big ones.

"Where can we talk, Ab?" I muttered quickly before Lieut. Campbell came over.

"Come on back to the place," he said without changing a beam in his welcome. "I knew you'd phoned for a reason." He raised his voice to its normal roar as Campbell joined us. I introduced them.

"How long are you in for?"

"I have a special job to do, Ab," I said for Campbell's benefit. "We probably won't get away till dawn."

My pilot looked startled and threw an anxious glance at his plane.

"Move it over with the others and immobilize it," said Tremblay, abruptly becoming an officer again. "Tether it and we'll put tarps on to cover the markings."

As Campbell still looked worried, he added: "The Provincial Police come by the field every hour or so. The whole town's lousy with them because we're a border point, I suppose." He clapped Campbell on the shoulder. "I'll fix you up with a room. You'd better take off your uniform jacket and lid."

We worked a few minutes to secure the aircraft. With the three of us in the front seat of his pickup, Tremblay drove a short distance to a service road where we joined the Trans-Canada for a couple of miles. A discreet yellow and green highway sign told us to keep right for a service centre. This was Ab's place, a North American wayside inn with its expanse of asphalt, square gasoline pumps, restaurant and motel. It was something he had always told me he was going to do in his hometown when he retired from the army. I was glad he had made it. The last time we had seen each other had been over two years ago in Kashmir. He had been a major.

"Be thankful you missed South Africa," I told him.

"More civilized than Kashmir, wasn't it?" he said. He looked worried for a moment. "Any word of them calling up people like myself?"

"Not likely in your case. You know why."

He thought for a few seconds and then his eyes blazed. "Has it gone that far? No French Canadians?"

"They haven't activated any of the militia units in Quebec. But they're pulling some militia into new permanent force battalions in the rest of Canada. I'm commanding one of them: Third R.C.R. What are your own feelings?" I asked. I didn't have any time to waste.

"You know, for Christ's sake," said Ab. "I'm Ontario French."

We got the puzzled Campbell settled in his motel room with TV, magazines, beer and sandwiches. Ab phoned the Provincial Police and told them that the extra plane at the field belonged to a visiting friend of his and would they keep an eye on it during their hourly checks. At the rear of the motel office, Ab had built a bungalow, joined onto the main unit by an enclosed passageway. It was a comfortable three-bedroom house with picture windows looking down the slope over the outskirts of Hawkesbury and a bright, blue glint of the Ottawa River beyond. His three children were at school and his wife, Marie, was in town shopping. We sat alone in his living room in the loneliest of all silences that envelops an empty house in midafternoon.

"Edith, the boys and her parents are at the cottage near Notre Dame des Pistoles," I opened. "I figure it's not more than eighty miles from here, if that. I want to bring them out."

Ab looked at me for a long time and blew clouds of smoke from an old, hook-stemmed briar.

"How do you propose to do it?" His voice was cold.

"If you'll let me have your pickup, I'll make it all right."

"You don't speak French. You'd never get through."

"Get through what?"

"Montebello and all the villages north are crawling with those P.D.Q. Legion bums," he said. "They're not so open down this way because there are a lot of English around. They'll make a move sooner or later, but they already control the villages up there.'

My mouth felt dry.

"All the more reason I've got to get through," I said. "How do you know all this?"

"I go back and forth all the time. I've got a cottage up there, and I do some business with the locals. They know me, but you wouldn't have a chance."

"What's happened to the English-speaking cottagers up there?"

"Nothing much. They just haven't come up this year, that's all. Anyone who did would be nuts." He looked embarrassed when he realized what he had said.

"Can you phone from here?"

"Nope. No calls over the border. Only authorized calls allowed inside Quebec. They have effective control of the telephone system."

"Montreal is still open," I told him. "Every day I've been phoning and sending telegrams to Edith's parents in Westmount. There hasn't been any answer, so they must still be at the cottage."

Ab frowned. "I don't see why they would stay. It's only a short drive down to the Ontario border. When'd you last talk to them?"

"It must be over two weeks now. Edith said then that the Q.P.P. were nosing around."

Ab got up and lumbered over to the picture window where he surveyed the peaceful town below us.

"Well, I don't see where any harm will come to them. Those kids with the armbands do a lot of swaggering and talking, but I haven't heard of any really bad incidents."

"You've heard of some, though?"

He waved his arm. "Some roughing up and a few scraps. But I don't think . . ."

My voice cracked. "I've got to find them, Ab."

From the window he turned and looked at me steadily.

In the kitchen, the refrigerator vibrated and began to hum. A tap dripped somewhere.

"I'll take you," he said at last.

There was no point in pretending to protest, for that was what I had been counting on without having the courage to admit it to myself. All I did was to stand up and shake his hand. We started almost immediately in his new pickup truck, which only had the name "Tremblay" painted on the door. Before we left he armed himself with a .38 and put an old Winchester 30/30 behind the seat. In his garage he took some Quebec licence plates out of a strongbox, and replaced his blue and white Ontario plates on the truck.

"We're going beyond my usual stamping grounds," he explained. "Let me do all the talking. You pretend to start talking and I'll interrupt as if you can't get a word in. Do a lot of nodding and shrugging."

We came off the Trans-Canada into Hawkesbury. Across the river on the Quebec side the hills, spotted with black smudges of evergreens, filled up the horizon. Ab drove east on Hawkesbury's narrow main street with its clutter of stores, bilingual signs and gold-painted parking meters. At John Street we turned north to the bridge that would take us to the Quebec side. Beyond the Presbyterian Church at the approaches to the bridge were two Ontario Provincial Police cars. Ab waved to them; the cops nodded back; we drove up onto the two-lane bridge, its steel girders for some reason painted a bright green. On the other side were two Quebec Provincial Police cars; Ab waved to them in the same way and they made gestures for him to go on through.

"They all know me," he said.

Turning west at the base of the hills, marked by the jagged teeth of coniferous trees above us, we moved west on Route 8, past the narrow strip farms which gave the highway the appearance of a continuous village. There wasn't much traffic. At Calumet, the highway by-pass moved in closer to the ridge, bulging with trees and rock that came to the road's edge and, as we pulled around the village I could see out in the river, the C.I.P. mill with its black tower and single stack. On our left, the railway line followed the highway. We crossed the Rouge River, with its rapids upstream and log boom across the mouth where it joined the Ottawa. All along the road there were signs of almost uninterrupted settlement, but we saw few people. The motels and motor courts, which looked like something out of the thirties, were unoccupied and there were no signs of activity in Pointe-au-Chêne or Fasset. Sun shone on tin roofs; no one could be seen around the frame houses that hugged the roadside. We crossed the Salmon River bridge and entered Montebello. As we came in on the main street, I tensed and touched Ab's arm. Along the sidewalk, gathered in a cluster outside a building identified as The Commercial Hotel, was a group of armed P.D.Q. legionnaires, most of them carrying rifles slung across their white shirts. They seemed to be debating whether or not they would go back into the hotel for more beer, or some such argument, judging by the waving of arms.

"Don't worry about them," said Ab. "This is a sort of headquarters town for the Legion in the area."

The youngsters on the sidewalk didn't look at us as we crawled past. At the single-storey, red brick post office building, I noticed the maple leaf flag had been replaced by the blue and white standard of Quebec. On the south side of the street, a heavily wooded area came into view.

"Isn't that the Seigniory Club property?" I asked.

"Yeah," said Ab. "The P.D.Q. has taken it over as a headquarters. That's why you see them around."

I sat forward tensely and fingered the pistol in my belt until Ab turned right onto Route 57 which turns north before coming to the Club entrance. We crossed the railway tracks and pulled away from the town towards the hills. I looked at the road leading into the golf course and to the exclusive cottage area on the Club's property, a vast enclosure of elaborate summer homes, more like an enclave of *dachas* for members of the Politburo.

"Kind of a posh place for a headquarters, isn't it?" I said. "You mean they just took it over from the C.P.R.?"

"Well, there's more to it than that," Ab said. "Remember, the Seigniory Club site has great historical significance for them. It was the home of Louis Joseph Papineau. After he came home from exile in Paris and then retired from politics completely, he lived in the manor house which is still on the grounds. It's all very symbolic."

"You mean the Papineau who led the rebellion in 1837?"

"The same. The Provisional Government has nationalized the site and declared it an historical shrine. In the meantime, they're using the Log Chateau as a district headquarters."

"What the hell are we doing so close to it?"

"Who would expect us. We'll soon be well away from it."

A low-key country, Canada historically has tended to have rather mild rebellions or the occasional riot, rather than convulsive revolutions. The one that Papineau had led in 1837 in Lower Canada, to achieve much the same goals of popular representation and legislative democracy as the simultaneous outburst in Upper Canada (Ontario), came close to being a revolutionary effort. There had been several bloody clashes with British troops and militia, with the climax at St. Eustache just north of Montreal, where they fought it out from behind stone fences. Papineau had become far more of a symbol to French Canada than had William Lyon Mackenzie to the settlers in Ontario. And now, as if they had formed a Poetic Justice Department, the Provisional Government had taken over that exclusive haven of the English-speaking establishment and turned the Seigniory Club back to the ancestors of those who had fought at Papineau's side. A nice, imaginative gesture, I thought with some sympathy.

The highway climbed gradually upward to an inner plateau of thinly-soiled farms where the earth was an anaemic, silvery grey. The hills had pulled back into a brooding circle as if they were waiting to move back in at any time and crush the defiant farmers. As we travelled further north, the country became more rolling again. We passed quickly through a couple of small settlements, where I noticed the kids hanging around the general store. For the most part they wore dungarees, white shirts with blue and white armbands, and some wore blue sashes which seemed to complete their uniforms. A few of them carried pistols, but most had rifles. Oddly enough, there were no roadblocks, and while we got a few stares and turned heads, no one made a move to stop us. Ab's Quebec plates and his cheerful waves seemed to give us passage for the time being.

"When we get to a town of any size, I'd like to try and phone ahead," I said.

Tremblay looked across at me, started to argue and fell into a scowling silence. A few miles further on, we came over a knoll and down into what should have been a picturesque village backed against a small, oblong lake. Like many Quebec villages, its natural location was marred by ugly houses crammed against the roadside, made even more grotesque by yellow, pink or green paint or patently artificial siding, supposed to look like stone, but fooling no one. A short sidewalk marked the beginning of the main street where a few stores had been created out of the same, high-peaked design as the houses, complete with front porches in some cases. Ab Tremblay swung the truck over to the curb and angle-parked it beside a bright-red convertible, some ten years old.

"I know the telephone operator here," he said. "You stay here and don't speak to anybody."

From the notebook in my pocket I gave him the number of the cottage, and sat back in the heat as he went into the building. The street was deserted. A few souped-up old cars were angle-parked at the only brick building in town, the Hotel Champlain, but there was no one outside in the mid-afternoon sun. The screen door of the telephone office slammed again, and I saw Ab standing on the step arguing with a man inside. The man stepped out of the shadows, and I saw that he was one of the armed kids. He had a stripped-down sporting version of a Lee-Enfield rifle slung over his shoulder and was waving his arms a lot. By taking a few steps away with each burst of words, Ab was making his way back to the pickup. Remembering my instructions, I waved and grinned at the armed kid. He looked up and couldn't resist nodding. From inside the little telephone office, a woman came out onto the street. She was a petite, dark woman of about forty with a fine, trim waist and shapely breasts pushing against a filmy, white blouse.

"Chic, even in the boondocks," I thought.

The woman brushed past the guard and followed Ab as he got back into the truck. Her dark, brown eyes looked in at him fondly as he sat behind the wheel, and she said something to him very quietly. Ab nodded and kissed her on the cheek. While the P.D.Q. kid watched, he slowly backed out the truck and we started up the street.

"What was that all about?" I asked.

"The kid wouldn't let me make the call," he said. "But Monique told me to go use the pay phone at the hotel and she'd just put the call through without him knowing the difference."

"Monique seems to have a thing for you."

"We've had our moments."

Tremblay angle-parked the pickup beside half a dozen garishly painted older cars outside the hotel.

"You wait here," he said.

"No, I'm coming in. If you get through, I want to talk to them."

He saw it was useless. "You talk only if I tell you!" he repeated.

The entrance to the hotel was at the corner of the building. There was a small lobby with cracked, leather armchairs, a dark-wooded stairway leading to the second floor, and off the main lobby a darkened bar with plain wooden chairs and tables. Through the doorway, I could see several kids drinking beer and playing the pinball machines. I noticed their rifles, assorted models, stacked in the passageway. Two old men occupied the chairs in the lobby and there was no one behind the desk.

The pay phone was attached to the wall, a shelf underneath and two plastic dividers on either side to make some semblance of a booth. Ab put in his dime and started to mutter instructions to the operator. I stood at right angles to him, back to the open doorway of the bar to act as a shield. The receiver to his ear, Ab turned and made a face at the ceiling. He was waiting. There were some more mutterings, and he picked up the four quarters I had placed on the shelf and put them into the telephone. Each coin made a shattering clang as it dropped into the black box. I leaned forward and reached out a hand to pick up the receiver. Ab waved me away, and I craned to hear what was happening in the subdued torrent of French he kept up. Something cold and round jammed into the back of my neck. Without turning around, I knew only too well what it was.

"What are you guys trying to do?" whispered a gravelly voice in my ear. I had enough sense not to jump.

"*Excusez*," I mumbled. "*La téléphone*"—

Ab snapped his head around. A rifle barrel passed across my shoulder and stopped, almost touching his ear.

Tremblay, still holding the receiver, launched into rapid French, in which I picked up the words "*ma mama et mon père*". The rifle barrel moved closer and rested against his neck. Ab looked through me and slowly put the receiver onto its hook. The quarters clashed down into the return cup. A hand reached past him and scooped them up. Ab turned around slowly, angrily and didn't put up his hands. Somebody took my shoulder and spun me around.

We were looking at four youngsters who might have been termed handsome if they hadn't tried to grow beards and let their hair grow down to their shoulders. They all wore dirty, white short-sleeved shirts with the blue and white armbands pinned up high near the shoulder. The main armament in these parts seemed to be old, stripped-down Lee-Enfields, and we now looked into four of these. Ab began shouting at them, and they shouted back, drawing in the rest of the contingent from the bar. Two of the armbands moved outside and started to go through the pickup. They emerged with Tremblay's old 30/30 which was waved up and down in sight of those in the hotel, the way Indians in movies give signals from hilltops. I looked into their young faces and saw the flashes of excitement they had probably been waiting for. Another smaller kid, not more than seventeen, ran upstairs two at a time.

Ab started to do a strange thing. He reached into his hip pocket, took out his wallet and nodded at me to do the same. I paused, because this would be fatal. His Ontario driver's licence and my Canadian Forces I.D. card would finish us. Then I understood why. He was stalling, even with the risk of the cards in our wallets, to prevent a search that would take our pistols away. One of the young legionnaires took the wallet and put his rifle down to leaf through it. Another tucked his rifle muzzle down under his armpit to look at mine. I began to think. Ab wasn't in too bad shape because he had a .38 with one in the chamber. But my Browning, heavy in the waistband under my jacket, had the safety on and no round in the chamber. You don't walk around with a cocked, loaded pistol in your belt unless you want to take the risk of shooting off something vital should the trigger get a sudden jar. On the other hand, I looked over the Lee-Enfields around us and noticed that most of them had their safeties on. I made a silent wager that most of them would not have a round in the breech.

Down the stairs, in the slow march of one in command, came a thin, narrow-shouldered man in his late twenties. He wore a spotless white tunic which had a high collar, navy blue boards with gold stripes on his shoulders. His armband was sewn on neatly and he wore navy blue trousers. He was unarmed. The group around us stood back and handed him our wallets. The thin, transparent face, with its fine skeletal jaw, turned to each of us and looked us over through big, brown eyes. There was a glint of dedication about him of the kind one used to see in young priests in Quebec. He was one of the new priests, I thought.

"And what is a colonel" (he pronounced it "coal-ah-nell") "of the Canadian armed forces doing in our little village?" he asked softly, looking at me.

I shrugged and grinned.

"And we have one of our own compatriots, no doubt a *vendu* from Ontario," he went on, sizing up Ab in deep bitterness. I had seen little men like that before, and knew what we would be in for. I was not disappointed.

"Our hotel lobby is hardly the place to continue this conversation," he said. "Let us adjourn to some other place. As it is such a hot day, I think the basement would be much cooler."

Ab spoke to him in machine gun French, of which I didn't catch a word. The slight young man regarded him so contemptuously that he was moved to reply in English.

"You might have gotten away with it," he said. "Perhaps you do have a place here. But your colonel friend here somehow doesn't fit with what you say. Are you trying to tell me that he is going fishing—that he can take leave at a time like this? We shall also be most interested in who it was you were trying to call. We still have not dug out all our traitors."

His fine features set and white, he turned to give orders. Three of his men walked down the hall, opened a door and disappeared downstairs. That left about five of them. The little man moved away from us and the others spread out to let him past. I had seen men move fast before, but nothing to equal Ab Tremblay. In one sweeping motion he had brought his knee up into the balls of the man nearest him and at the same time snapped off two thunderous shots at their leader. I saw a large black and red hole in the back of the little man's neck; his body teetered for a moment before it clattered forward through the open doorway and down the cellar steps. I used my shoulder in order to release both hands for work on the Browning. The steel muzzle of the nearest rifle ripped my jacket and flesh as I jammed upwards against the closest man. After what seemed a century of fumbling with the Browning, I got a grip on its slide action and got it pointed outward. I started shooting fast into white shirts and faces so close that the muzzle hardly seemed to have cleared my waistband. In the narrow hallway the inexperienced youngsters couldn't get their old, heavy rifles into action. One in the doorway to the bar got off two wild shots, frantically working the bolt until Ab split his face in two with a .38 slug.

"Get the car going. I'll hold them," I yelled at Ab.

While I backed towards the door, he ran, backed up the truck and started moving down the street. One of the old men in the lobby tried to get in my way as I sprinted through the door. I pushed him down the concrete steps and his skull cracked like a hollow piece of china on the sidewalk. By this time, the legionnaires, such as were left, had caught their second wind and .303 steel jackets were cracking past my head into the thin metal panelling of the truck. With the door swinging open and me sprawled on the seat, feet sticking out into the street, we lurched southward.

"The other way," I managed to gasp. "North!"

"Are you crazy?" Ab shouted. "We'd get cut off."

I struggled to a sitting position and had just slammed the door shut when I saw a kneeling figure in the doorway of the telephone office.

"On your left!" I yelled.

We were now directly opposite the young guard who, only a few feet away, had his rifle leading us precisely and dead on. At that distance he couldn't miss. I stared, stiff with aftershock. Behind the guard appeared a small white figure, sort of floating out of the door of the telephone office. The guard was pushed, sprawling forward into the street. His rifle exploded harmlessly somewhere. Out of our side window, I saw Ab's friend Monique wave and go back into the telephone office.

"Hate to think what they'll do to her," I said.

Ab nodded. "She's a good kid." But he didn't stop. "Get in the back and cover the rear," he said.

With much grunting and effort, I crawled up over the back seat and opened the panel into the back of the truck. I lurched along the floor in the semi-darkness and looked out the small square windows at the rear. Two of the brightly-painted convertibles were already pulling away from the hotel.

"They're coming," I told Ab and knocked the glass out of the two small windows to clear a field of fire. Over a hill, just south of town, Ab swung the pickup off the paved highway onto a gravel sideroad. The dust, you idiot, I thought to myself. There were sudden bumps and trees scraping against the metal. We were in a thick bush of some kind, behind a shallow knoll. Around us was a stand of tall pines.

"They could still catch us," said Ab. "It's all we can do. Stand by."

Silence fell inside our truck. The metal in the engine pinged and crackled as it cooled. A few mosquitoes slipped in through the open windows and began to go after my torn shoulder where I held a padded handkerchief tightly. I eased up on the handkerchief long enough to put a full clip into the Browning. Their double-barrel carburetors spluttering, the old convertibles shot by on the paved highway, not too far away. When their roar had faded, Ab started to back the truck out to the gravel road.

"Shouldn't we wait for night?" I asked.

"They'll be back," he said. "I want to get as far as we can before the roadblocks are up. I know these sideroads and we'll just have to take our chance on the dust."

"Wait," I said. The now familiar motorboat sound of a split muffler came back again and slowed its throbbing beat on the highway. I eased out onto the trail behind us and moved through the bush to the edge of the gravel road. From a screen of bushes, I could see the brightly painted glimmer of one of the old convertibles creeping along the gravel surface, its wheels noisily squeezing out large stones. I ran back to Tremblay.

"Better move the truck further in," I said. "They'll see us."

"They will anyway," he said. "We'll have to take them."

I tried to think of arguments, but in the pressure of survival they didn't come. Running, I realized, was not good enough. We had to stay mobile. To settle for going on foot through the bush would lead us to ultimate capture or at least many suffering days of slow going. Ab waved me to cover on one side of the track, while he jumped into foliage on the other. I crouched amid willows breathing, as I thought, like a steam engine at the insects who began to take notice.

In its slow passage the convertible crunched past the opening to the trail, stopped and backed up. It turned into the grassy track and I heard young voices mount excitedly when they saw the truck. With springs and shocks creaking on the uneven track, the convertible, decorated in blue and white diagonal stripes, moved past us and stopped. The kid beside the driver was sitting up on the top of the front seat, the muzzle of his old Lee-Enfield pointed towards our truck. Ab had the easiest shot. He fired upward twice and caught the boy just below his shoulder blades. The youngster jumped up off the back of the seat and tumbled, gurgling and rasping, over the side of the car. The other kid was faster and came out of the door on his side, rolling for cover. He landed in the tall grass cradling his rifle and the last thing he saw was me crouching over him. I shot him mercifully between the eyes and turned my head away quickly. It was so easy that I almost felt ashamed. There was a fourth shot as Ab finished off the first kid who was suffering and making awful noises. A slight breeze caught the tall pine trees around us in a swishing hiss of disapproval for what we had done. Ab and I stood for a while, our pistols weighing down our watery arms. As usual, Ab was the first to move.

"Take the other kid's shirt and armband if you can," he said, his voice so throaty it was almost inaudible. "I can't use this one's shirt, but I'll take his armband. Let's put the bodies in the front seat of the pickup."

When the two youngsters were sitting up in the pickup, their sightless eyes looking upward, Ab got behind the wheel of the convertible and backed it out to the edge of the grassy track. He threw the two Lee-Enfields into the back seat. I sat beside him, trying to catch my breath.

"I'll be back," he said and got out again. He moved

quickly along the trail until he was out of sight around the curve in the track and the slight rise that hid the pickup from view. I could hear the scraping of metal and a hammer hitting a spike. There was a pause; Ab came running back down the trail, jumped into the car and we started off along the gravel road towards the highway. Behind us, a sheet of flame was beginning to spread through the underbrush.

"Keep our forests green," I said.

"When they eventually find the truck, they'll think we're in it," said Ab. He had poked a hole in the pickup's gas tank and set fire to the pool.

"It's a pretty bloody awful thing to do," I said, looking back. "I mean the forest fire."

"Great diversion though," said Ab, managing a grin. "Everyone in the area soon will be up here to fight it, while we just slip south."

Whether he had accumulated such energy and nerve during his retirement, or whether he had always been this way unknown to me, was something I was to think about later. I wondered if there was any way I could arrange for him to be reactivated in the forces again, especially when I thought of my own hesitations and the bad judgment that had gotten us into this mess in the first place. It was difficult to say whether it was raw courage or a wild foolishness that brought us out onto the paved highway again. Ab drove south about seventy, his blue armband draped conspicuously over the side of the door. Both of us wore our sunglasses. We passed a couple of garish, souped-up sedans going north, and waved to them. Over my shoulder I could see a blue smudge begining to grow on the horizon behind us.

Along the way, we noticed that the loungers had disappeared from the porches and in front of the general stores and that their cars had evidently gone with them. Without incident, we came over the hill into Montebello, but as we approached the highway intersection, we noticed a Q.P.P. roadblock covering both Routes 8 and 57. It was not easy to resist shrinking down into the seat. Ab drove right up to the cops standing on the road, stopped and engaged in one of those rapid exchanges in French that might as well have been Chinese as far as I was concerned. There didn't seem to be any argument about our identity. Rather, it was a dispute about where we were going. Ab kept pointing east on Route 8, and the Q.P.P. men kept gesturing towards the Seigniory Club. At last, sensing that he had reached his limit wihout attracting any more attention, Ab came back to the car; we drove slowly west on Route 8 for a short distance and turned into the gate of Seigniory Club.

"We have to report here and join the search for us," said Ab. "A big sweep is being organized. When it starts, we'll get away."

"Christ," I muttered.

At the end of the paved driveway, we emerged into a colourful mass of parked cars that had all the appearance of an enormous secondhand lot specializing in souped-up models for delinquents. Most of them had blue and white pennants drooping from aerials. Some kind of an attendant or guide waved us towards the entrance to the main building. The structure, called the "Log Chateau", was a four-storey, rather forbidding pile of blackened cedar logs. It had been built in a rush over forty years ago for the times when even the wealthy travelled by train. It was a reflection of that kind of architecture known unofficially as "1930 baroque" which can be seen scattered around in rather unlikely places throughout North America. The main characteristic of the style is that the architects of the day were suddenly unable to cope with all the dirt-cheap labour and inexpensive materials, so they used both lavishly without quite knowing where it was all going to end.

Inside this quaint monument, we stepped into a huge central foyer built around a stone fireplace that towered

116

off into the dark rafters. Tiers of log-railed balconies surrounded this central area, with its chesterfields and deep chairs now occupied by white-shirted youngsters. The vast, carpeted floorspace was filled by legionnaires, standing and looking up silently at a point in the balcony above them. In the gloom of this large amphitheatre, made even more dim by our wearing of sunglasses, we could make out several figures at the railing above. All of them were dressed in what I assumed was the officers' garb of the Legion: white tunic, high collar and rank shown on navy blue shoulder boards. Using a loudhailer, a man with more gold on him than the others was haranguing them in a harsh, high-pitched voice, made even more shrill by the instrument. Smoke from a hundred cigarettes, of the pungent, imitation-French variety, gathered in the dome of the rafters and trapped stuffy, fetid air down below. The place wasn't very exclusive any more.

Activity began on the balcony, and the ear-splitting harangue stopped. The dignitaries moved in together like a large, white flower closing up its petals. They emerged from their huddle and the harsh-voiced one took up the loudhailer again to spit out bursts of speech laced with a shrill urgency. Ab and I had stationed ourselves carefully at the back of the mob near the entrance. We were far enough back for me to risk whispering to him in English: "What's up?"

"The forest fire up north," muttered Ab, giving a fair imitation of a stiff-lipped convict in the movies. "It's already reached the village; both sides of the street are burning. We're all to get going and help put it out."

I thought of our wallets and identification lying somewhere in the basement of the hotel near the body of the Legion officer Ab had shot. With luck the fire might destroy the evidence of our identity.

All of the faces in the room seemed to turn towards me at once. I didn't have time to ask Ab what had been said and had visions of our corpses hanging from the big, black rafters. The faces started to break around us and I realized that everyone was running for their cars outside. Ab poked me on the arm and we joined the grim-faced throng. The parking area echoed with slamming doors and the roar of special muffler attachments filled the air with acrid, blue exhaust. Our car was parked on the east side of the curling rink, now a barracks, and to reach it we had to dodge among those already starting to move. Soon the inevitable happened. After a couple of cars had squeezed out onto the driveway, the rest of them came together, more or less at the same time, from various directions. There was a traffic jam. Everyone started yelling at each other and blasting his horn. A couple of sweating officers tried to sort out the mess and, as we were on the fringes, waved us on through. As we drove out at the head of a lineup, passing an immobilized clump of cars on the turf of the children's playground, someone started to shout at us. We could hear the voice clearly over all the other sound.

"Kids from the village," Ab said. "They recognize the car and the fact that we don't belong in it."

I pulled out my automatic and checked the slide action. Ab placed his .38 on the seat where I could get at it. All we could do was follow the cars in front of us towards the gate. From the big side mirror on my side, I could see the other car was still hemmed in by others. One of the kids was jumping over the side and running down the road. We belted out of the gate still in line. The Q.P.P. cops at the roadblock waved us on through in the only direction we could go. We were heading north again.

"We'll cut out just ahead," said Ab. "Stand by."

Ahead of us, the cars were beginning to string out as they picked up speed. In the mirror, I could see the bright colours of others coming up the road. Only about a quarter of a mile after we had crossed the railway tracks, Ab slammed on the brakes and swung to the right in a spray of dust onto a gravel road. Our wake spumed a fine, brownish smokescreen.

"There's someone behind us," I told Ab.

"How many?"

"I can see only one. It must be the kids who saw us on the way out."

In a series of sharp turns, Ab cut towards the Montebello railway station, turned with squealing tires onto a road that took us belting past the Church of Notre Dame de Bonsecours. Another screeching whirl and we were back onto Route 8 going west. At the town hall, Ab turned left and I saw that we were heading towards the river. The car skidded to a halt on the ferry dock. The ferry was gone.

"You didn't really expect—" I snarled.

"There'll be a boat around here somewhere," said Ab. He backed the car sideways across the dock and leaped out. "Hold them off," he growled.

From the highway, a yellow and green convertible came into view, approaching cautiously as if the kids suspected what had happened to their friends. The car stopped. Lying flat behind a rear tire of our car, a Lee-Enfield cradled painfully in my injured left arm, I followed them over the sights. I held fire as long as I could, because I knew that shots would bring in the police from the roadblock and the remainder of the legionnaires now pouring out of the Seigniory Club grounds.

"Found one," called Ab. "Come on." I heard a motor turn over with the infuriating reluctance that somebody must build into outboards in order to help fill up leisure time on weekends. Two whiteshirts were moving at a snail pace on either side of the road. They weren't anxious to tangle with us and one kept looking over his shoulder, as if he was thinking of going back for help. My injured left arm, carrying the weight of the rifle, began to shake. At the end of the dock the motor at last began to buzz in neutral.

"Come on," repeated Ab.

A couple of minutes grace would make all the difference, I reasoned. We needed that time to get clear. I let my arm down, raised it up again, and through a wobbling sight, lined up a whiteshirt, now crouching uselessly behind a small shrub. The rifle jumped and I saw dust spray beside the kid. I lowered my arm to work the bolt, and got off another shot that must have gone over his head. It was evident that I wasn't going to hit anything, so I put down the rifle, knelt behind the car, and fired off the clip in the Browning as fast as it would go. No harm was done, but much dust was kicked up. The kids, bent uselessly as inexperienced troops sometimes do, ran back towards the highway. At that point I turned and ran to the boat, a small fibre glass job with a broad beam and a rounded bow. I flopped down in front of Ab, who jerked the lever around to full throttle.

It seemed only seconds before the olive uniforms of the Q.P.P. and some whiteshirts were blended at the end of the dock. Ab kept full throttle, tilting us back in the water in a wide, sweeping wake that curled out on either side. Shots began to crack and sizzle into the water. I turned around, knees up and resting my aching left arm across them, balanced Ab's .38 pointing high. I emptied the cylinder in rapid fire, the pistol jumping all over the place. As if I had been using a machine gun, everyone on the dock flopped, but I knew no one could have been hit. They kept trying. The more dangerous crack of a Lee-Enfield sent me rolling to the bottom of the boat, and a steel slug tore a groove in the fibre glass.

I heard Ab say "Oh."

Slowly I looked up, ignoring the snapping things in the air overhead. A red stain was spreading through Ab's shirt, but he still sat whitefaced, holding onto the tiller of the outboard. My move towards him was stopped by a plunk and a rip that brought a geyser of water bubbling up from the keel. I tore off my jacket and stuffed it into

120

the hole as another geyser erupted by my hand. I tore off my shoulder bandage, made of two handkerchieves knotted together, and rammed them into the leak with pink, frothy bubbles. More shots sang and skipped across the water, but when I next looked up, Ab had steered us up to the wharf at Lefaivre on the Ontario side of the river. Aroused by the shooting, the entire population seemed to be gathered on the dock, and helping hands dragged us out of the boat. Two Ontario Provincial Police started asking us questions as we wavered, breathing heavily, on the edge of the dock. I gave a false name, but Ab gave his, then fainted. The O.P.P. men didn't waste any more time and said they'd get us to Hawkesbury and a doctor.

As I turned to leave the wharf, I looked across the river. In the gathering dusk, a red glow showed on the horizon from behind the line of hills. But the sun doesn't set in the north. I hoped they would get the fire out before it spread too far, like towards the cottage where my family were virtually prisoners far inside hostile territory.

11

THE COMMISSIONER: Colonel Rousseau, up to the time you have mentioned, would you have described yourself as a loyal member of the Canadian Armed Forces?

COLONEL PAUL URBAINE ROUSSEAU: Yes, sir. I would say so.

THE COMMISSIONER: I don't want to dwell on the point needlessly, but it does have a bearing on the way in which the events came about. At precisely what point were you a loyal officer of the Canadian Armed Forces and the next moment not a loyal officer?

COL. ROUSSEAU: With respect, sir, I don't think that is quite an accurate description . . .

THE COMMISSIONER: How else would you describe it?

COL. ROUSSEAU: Sir, I think perhaps you are attaching too much importance to what happened to me. After all, I was only a captain in the Canadian Armed Forces. And I don't know whether my experience was typical or not.

122

THE COMMISSIONER: We suspect otherwise, Colonel Rousseau. You had a significant part in the events we are investigating and we are interested in tracing the motives and personal emotions of those of you who assumed leadership and responsibility for your actions. You had just returned to the country, hadn't you?

COL. ROUSSEAU: Yes, sir. I had been in South Africa for over a year with our United Nations contingent.

MR. LARKIN: Did you get any ideas while you were in South Africa?

COL. ROUSSEAU: I'm not sure that I follow you, sir.

MR. LARKIN: What you saw there . . . did that inspire you?

COL. ROUSSEAU: No sir. On the contrary, I was appalled by what I saw in South Africa.

MR. LARKIN: But you were quite prepared to aid and abet the same kind of thing in your own country?

COL. ROUSSEAU: Somehow I didn't think it would develop into that kind of thing here.

MR. LARKIN: What did you expect? That it would be a tea party?

THE COMMISSIONER: Come, Mr. Larkin. It is precisely that line of questioning we are trying to avoid. Let us go back to the point where Colonel Rousseau became involved in the events in which we are interested. You say then, Colonel Rousseau, that you entertained no thoughts of disloyalty when you arrived back in Canada?

COL. ROUSSEAU: I began to get concerned when we arrived in Montreal at the time of the unrest and the assassinations.

THE COMMISSIONER: Disturbed in what way? Were you sympathetic?

COL. ROUSSEAU: Not exactly sympathetic, sir. It's hard to describe. My emotions were upset because it seemed to me that my own people had gone a long way on a certain course of action. I couldn't see any turning back, and I wondered what I would do.

THE COMMISSIONER: So what did you do?

COL. ROUSSEAU: I decided the only place to be was with my own people, so I asked to be posted to the Royal 22e Regiment, the Vandoos.

MR. LARKIN: With the idea that they would rebel?

COL. ROUSSEAU: No, sir. Not with any such idea. I felt that regardless of what happened, I would be among my own people speaking my own language. I didn't know then what the Vandoos might do, but at least I would have compatriots to talk to. I wouldn't be isolated among others who didn't understand us or who might mistrust me because of my racial background and language.

THE COMMISSIONER: You were then posted to the Royal 22nd at Valcartier?

COL. ROUSSEAU: Yes, sir, after a short stay at St. Hubert waiting for my posting.

THE COMMISSIONER: Would you describe what happened when you went to Valcartier?

COL. ROUSSEAU: I flew to Quebec in one of our Hercules transports, which I understood was to pick up weapons and other equipment from the regional ordnance depot before they got into the wrong hands. At any rate, the aircraft was empty, except for myself. As soon as we landed at the field an armed party of militia came on board and made the crew and myself prisoners. Somehow the word had not gotten through to St. Hubert that they had taken over. When they had checked my identification and established that I was

French-speaking, they took me to the Forces Base at Valcartier. There it was evident that the entire place had just been taken over by local militia groups; they were all over the area, wearing blue and white armbands over their regular uniforms. I assumed that headquarters, holding units and the Citadel detachments of the Vandoos had been put in the bag . . .

THE COMMISSIONER: You mean taken prisoner?

COL. ROUSSEAU: That's right, sir. There was no sign of any fighting or damage, however. Anyway, they took me to the C.O.'s quarters on the base, where I was interviewed by General Drouin. He informed me that he had been named Commander-in-Chief of the Armed Forces of the Provisional Government, and gave me a fairly lengthy explanation of what had happened.

THE COMMISSIONER: Did you know who this so-called General Drouin was?

COL. ROUSSEAU: I remembered his name. I knew he had been a senior officer in the Canadian Forces, and I recalled seeing something about his retirement.

MR. LARKIN: He was another one who came back from Africa with ideas . . . Nigeria.

THE COMMISSIONER: Did he try to persuade you to join his forces?

COL. ROUSSEAU: I suppose that was the idea, but he just seemed to assume that I would. He seemed to convey a sort of tacit understanding that, when we were asked to do our duty for our own people, we would do it.

THE COMMISSIONER: By duty, you mean rebellion?

COL. ROUSSEAU: That's the point, sir. He didn't mention rebellion. A rebellion is against something. The feeling, which he expressed very ably, was not negative . . . rather the opposite. He spoke about the positive knowledge of having been reborn as a free and independent people, and how our nation would be bigger and more powerful than many new countries throughout the world. He was very upbeat and convincing. He said there was an urgent need for officers with a regular force background and that he would give me the rank of colonel and important responsibilities right away.

MR. LARKIN: And, of course, you couldn't resist that.

THE COMMISSIONER: Did you have any doubts?

COL. ROUSSEAU: Naturally, sir. But they were very clever about it all. General Drouin . . .

MR. LARKIN: He was only a brigadier-general with us.

COL. ROUSSEAU: . . . General Drouin asked me to join him and his officers at lunch, which I did. We went over to the Mess. When I got there I was greeted by the other officers—mostly militia—as if I was a celebrity. Their spirit and infectious good humour was hard to resist. Before I knew it, I was one of them.

THE COMMISSIONER: That brings us to your own activities. Can you describe the kind of operation you then organized?

COL. ROUSSEAU: Things moved pretty fast. The next day I was placed in command of a special assault group of about a hundred men who had already been selected personally by General Drouin along with N.C.O.'s and junior officers. Most of them were militia people with fairly advanced training, drawn mainly from Les Voltigeurs de Québec, Le Régiment de la Chaudière, Les Fusiliers du St. Laurent, Le Régiment de Joliette, Le Régiment du Saguenay, and others who had been quietly pulled into the Quebec area. He had picked the best men he could. When I joined them, they were already off in a far corner of the training area where they had started rehearsals. We were not allowed contact with anyone else.

MR. LARKIN: Rehearsals? Did you think it was some kind of stage play?

COL. ROUSSEAU: Not too different, sir. We had plans of our target buildings which we laid out in exact size in white tapes on the ground. I would have preferred to work from replicas, but there wasn't time.

MR. LARKIN: You had no doubts you would get there?

COL. ROUSSEAU: Before I took over, they had planned to go by road. I recommended that we cut back our numbers and use the Hercules transport if they could find aircrew. This we were able to do without too much trouble—although they were civilians, not airmen. In the meantime, I drove my group hard, beginning every day at 0630 . . .

THE COMMISSIONER: I don't think this hearing is too interested in details of the training. We're more concerned with what happened afterwards.

MR. LARKIN: Just a moment here. I have a question about your training.

COL. ROUSSEAU: Yes, sir?

MR. LARKIN: Or rather, your briefing. What did they tell you about prisoners?

COL. ROUSSEAU: Prisoners, sir?

MR. LARKIN: You know what prisoners are, don't you? What were you told to do with prisoners?

COL. ROUSSEAU: I'm not aware that we were told anything about prisoners, sir.

MR. LARKIN: If you weren't given instructions about prisoners, how do you explain the atrocities that followed?

Col. Rousseau: If you're referring to the incident in the hangar, sir, I . . .

Mr. Larkin: Incident, he calls it.

Col. Rousseau: . . . I was not there. I had left with most of my assault group to carry out our second task. There were no special instructions given to the detail we left. I believe it was an accident . . .

Mr. Larkin: The witness is taxing our patience, Mr. Chairman.

The Commissioner: It seems to me the colonel should be given an opportunity to tell his story as he recalls the events. Perhaps we can come back to the incident that is concerning Mr. Larkin later in the proceedings. Colonel Rousseau, it does seem to me that you had an extraordinarily short training period. Two weeks doesn't seem like a sufficient time for an operation of that magnitude.

Col. Rousseau: The officers and men were the pick of the militia regiments. They were semi-professionals. Two weeks was the best we could do.

The Commissioner: Moving on to the operation itself, it began on June 15th, didn't it?

Col. Rousseau: Yes, sir. At 0630, we boarded the transport. I had crammed in ninety men with their equipment, so it was really a tight fit. They had only one day's cold rations and the ammunition they could carry. We were counting on surprise and on picking up extra supplies at the base.

The Commissioner: You had no heavy equipment with you, then?

Col. Rousseau: Only light infantry weapons, sir. We had our FN rifles, the FN-C2, Sterlings, grenades and two Carl Gustaf rocket launchers. That's all. Anyway, it took us some time to get sorted out on the aircraft, and we were behind schedule on takeoff. We took an easterly course from Quebec.

THE COMMISSIONER: An easterly course?

COL. ROUSSEAU: The plan was to take a wide swing east from Quebec City to the U.S. border and come in from the northeast. When we arrived over St. Hubert, we were to tell them that we were a contingent of Black Watch from Gagetown.

THE COMMISSIONER: And nobody caught on? You would think they would be more alert.

COL. ROUSSEAU: I don't blame them for that, sir. There were all kinds of troop contingents passing in and out of St. Hubert at the time. Even though we weren't down on any filed flight plan, they let us land.

MR. LARKIN: Without interference?

COL. ROUSSEAU: While we were circling over St. Hubert, I listened in on the talk between our pilot and the control tower. Our pilot spoke perfect English with no accent. There was no problem. The air controller said he had no flight plan and couldn't authorize the landing. Our pilot, of course, launched into a tirade and told them he had filed one and couldn't understand why Gagetown hadn't told him. He suggested that he get the duty officer from Mobile Command, which the air controller did. The duty officer, who was a captain, seemed uncertain. I also speak English without an accent . . .

MR. LARKIN: Too well, obviously.

COL. ROUSSEAU: . . . And told him I was a Major Graham of the Black Watch bringing in a contingent for a stopover on its way to Trenton.

MR. LARKIN: Why were you so explicit in saying that?

Col. Rousseau: We had found out that the Canadian government's policy was, at the time, not to move troops into Quebec from outside unless absolutely necessary. If I had said we were being posted to St. Hubert, or anything like that, he would have been suspicious. I reasoned he wouldn't suspect a stopover. He didn't, and we landed and taxied right up to the headquarters area.

The Commissioner: You mean to say that the duty officer even then didn't arrange for Provost or someone to cover your arrival, just in case? Didn't he notice your shoulder patches when you got off?

Col. Rousseau: We had anticipated that, sir. We knew we would need time to deplane the troops. So we didn't have any regimental patches, and we were wearing helmets. The duty officer was there to meet us, and I got off first to talk to him while our boys got formed up. He didn't seem to notice anything unusual until it was too late.

The Commissioner: Colonel Rousseau, do you think Mobile Command Headquarters was negligent?

Col. Rousseau: That's difficult to say, sir. It's hard to condemn them. They were in a peculiar position dealing with a crisis at home; we had all been conditioned to think of our role as being international, or at the worst, defence of our own country against an outside invader. No, I can't blame that duty officer. At that time, everyone was having difficulty making the mental transition. Also, remember they did have security details to prevent an attack from outside the perimeter of the base. We had a tough firefight with the guards at the gates. That's where both sides had the most casualties. It was just that they didn't expect anything to drop down smack in the middle of the base.

Mr. Larkin: Plunk.

Col. Rousseau: Exactly, sir.

THE COMMISSIONER: According to all the reports in my possession, you then moved very smartly.

COL. ROUSSEAU: I hope you'll excuse me if I express some pride in the operation.

MR. LARKIN: Pride—in murder?

COL. ROUSSEAU: To us, it was warfare, sir. We did try to keep casualties on both sides to a minimum, and I think we did because of the surprise element. When I gave the signal, our assault group took off exactly as planned and with a speed that impressed even me. The first casualty was the duty captain, I'm afraid. He reached for his sidearm, despite my warnings, and I had to shoot him with my machine carbine. The assault group had three main tasks. The first section, which I led, was responsible for securing the headquarters buildings. The second struck for the gates to knock out the armed security force. And the third was to clean up the service areas, the civilians and the air force.

THE COMMISSIONER: Would you describe in some detail what happened in your attack on the headquarters building and the tragic consequences?

COL. ROUSSEAU: We had little trouble taking care of the guards—unfortunately we had to kill most of them. Once inside the main building it wasn't too difficult. The men on duty in the various offices, radio rooms and operations rooms were not armed. The radios and telephones were knocked out very quickly; we had a local group cutting lines outside the base. As far as I know, no messages got out

THE COMMISSIONER: That's correct. Some garbled messages did get out by radio, but they soon stopped.

COL. ROUSSEAU: Well, it was a big base and we really had to scramble to keep the lid on it. Fortunately, most of them just couldn't believe it was happening. There was confusion, too, because our uniforms were the same.

MR. LARKIN: I want to hear about General Douglas, Mr. Chairman. The witness seems to be stalling.

COL. ROUSSEAU: My main task was to destroy the central operations centre and capture General Douglas and his staff. The first thing I had to decide was where I would find the general. I took a gamble on him being at the operations centre. I sent a lieutenant and several men down the corridor to the general's office and his personal staff area. With another group, I headed towards the operations centre. At this point, we ran into some opposition. Two guards with Sterlings, covered by an intersection of corridors, pinned us down and I lost three men right on the spot. But we had momentum. I told my men to keep running. Two of them got off grenades around the corners, which finished the opposition. We were moving so fast that myself and four men ran through the gap in the steel door of the operations centre, just as it was being closed. If they had managed to close the place up, our operation could have turned into a siege. So it was just by the skin of our teeth that we got through that door. As it was, they closed it behind us. We shot the men on the door and reopened it.

THE COMMISSIONER: You must have been considerably outnumbered in that room.

COL. ROUSSEAU: We were, sir. I guess there must have been about thirty officers and men there. But again, most of them were unarmed; only one or two had their sidearms with them. A couple of guards had Sterlings and killed two of my men before we got them. It was a melee in a confined space, jammed with radio, teletype and office equipment. Some of the officers tried to use chairs and anything handy to stop us, but we did our best to subdue them with rifle butts and keep the shooting to a minimum. While this was going on, in an awful clatter of sound and shouts, I saw General Douglas behind a large desk. He looked very rigid and cool standing there. I grabbed our company sergeant major and headed around the debris towards him. General Douglas was holding a red telephone to his ear in his left hand and had a Browning pistol in his right. When he saw us coming towards him, he took a chance in the crowded room and fired. He got C.S.M. Vezinas in the chest, and he went down beside me.

As nearly as I can recall, I shouted to General Douglas to drop his gun and surrender. I could hardly hear his reply in all the confusion, but I think it was something like "Not to traitors, I won't". He then shot at me and the round clipped the collar of my field jacket. I called to him again. He still continued firing and his second shot ricochetted off the side of my helmet, knocking me off balance behind a metal desk. I crawled under the opening in the desk, and for a moment debated what to do. Then I pulled my way through to the other side of the desk and rolled to one side. As I looked up, I saw him only a few feet away, still tall and straight, trying to get a shot at me. His next one ploughed into the desktop just an inch or two from my head. I called out once more and shot him.

THE COMMISSIONER: In other words, he shot at you three times before you replied?

COL. ROUSSEAU: Of that, I'm sure, sir. I kept his pistol and turned it over to H.Q. as evidence. There were only three rounds gone in the clip.

MR. LARKIN: Tell us in more detail how you shot him.

COL. ROUSSEAU: Lying on the floor between desks, and partly under one, was hardly a good spot to get away an accurate shot. I had intended to clip him in the shoulder or arm if I could. If there was any mistake on my part, this was it. I thought I had pushed down the single shot button on the Sterling, but in the excitement I guess I hadn't done it. Instead of firing single shots my machine carbine let off a burst that caught him in the shoulder and went right across his face. He went down without a sound.

THE COMMISSIONER: Was he dead then?

COL. ROUSSEAU: Instantly, sir. There wasn't any opportunity to give first aid. The death of General Douglas seemed to end the resistance in the operations centre. We were able to line up everybody and destroy the equipment in the room. Things quietened down so quickly that I was able to send most of my own assault group off to help the team that was still fighting with the security forces at the perimeter. This turned the fighting, and the base was in our control.

THE COMMISSIONER: What were your instructions at that point?

COL. ROUSSEAU: We were to contact the Provisional Government representatives in Montreal and advise them the objective had been taken. Our orders were to take over all the trucks we could, two men to a vehicle, load them with arms, ammunition, field rations and P.O.L. . . .

MR. LARKIN: What's that?

COL. ROUSSEAU: Petrol, oil and lubricants, sir. We were then to mark our vehicles with Provisional Government colours and start out as soon as we could. We were able to take the Trans-Canada Highway north from St. Hubert, follow the expressway to the Laurentian Autoroute, and rendezvous with an advance party at the General Motors plant at St. Therese. From there we were to go on to our second operation.

THE COMMISSIONER: I think everyone here knows what that was. We'll come to it later on. As far as your action against Mobile Command at St. Hubert was concerned, is it correct to say that you were only to knock it out as an operating headquarters, loot it of all supplies and get out? You never intended to hold it?

COL. ROUSSEAU: No, sir. It was never our intention to hold it against counterattack. We assumed correctly that it would be easy to take, especially when most of the troops normally stationed there were scattered all over the Montreal area doing guard duty. We were under no illusions that we could have held the place against a determined counterattack by say, the Canadian Airborne Regiment. After all, there were only ninety of us, not counting casualties. As soon as I had informed Montreal of our success, the whole place was swarming with P.D.Q. legionnaires . . .

MR. LARKIN: You hadn't used the legionnaires up to this point?

COL. ROUSSEAU: No, sir. We didn't think too much of them. However, I got them to help us load up our trucks and left them with instructions to completely destroy the base and then get out too. They seemed quite enthusiastic at the prospect.

MR. LARKIN: Hold on. This is hardly a time for flippancy. You seem to have given us a clue about the prisoners. Were you explicit about the prisoners when you left the legionnaires in charge of the base? You say you told them to destroy everything? Did that include people?

COL. ROUSSEAU: No, no. I had left ten men with three FN-C2's to guard the prisoners, once they were all rounded up and assembled in an empty hangar. Even though I couldn't spare them, we left our men in charge of the prisoners so that they wouldn't be left in the hands of the legionnaires.

THE COMMISSIONER: What was to ultimately happen to the prisoners?

COL. ROUSSEAU: We were to turn them over to the Provincial Police. This did happen.

MR. LARKIN: Yes, and they were interned in temporary camps under appalling conditions. Tell us what happened at the hangars.

COL. ROUSSEAU: With respect, sir, I can't. I wasn't there. By that time we had moved out with our convoy. One of the last things I did was to check with Lieutenant Hurtubise in charge of the prisoners at the hangar. Everything seemed under control. The C2's were set up on improvised platforms, and the prisoners were all seated on the hangar floor. There was a mob of them, all right, at least a couple of thousand servicemen and civilians.

MR. LARKIN: I'll rephrase the question. What is your understanding of what happened?

COL. ROUSSEAU: Do I have to answer, sir? It's all hearsay.

THE COMMISSIONER: We want to hear your version.

COL. ROUSSEAU: I heard it from our men when they rejoined us at St. Therese. Apparently, after they had set fire to all the buildings at the base, the mob of legionnaires was pretty worked up. Some of them came to the hangar and wanted to burn it down too with the prisoners inside. Lieutenant Hurtubise had to move a couple of his machine guns to the outside of the hangar to keep them off. Evidently, some of the prisoners inside either got panicky or saw it as an opportunity and made a break for the doors. They were shot by the guards on the platforms.

MR. LARKIN: How many?

COL. ROUSSEAU: As far as I know, sir, about twenty were wounded and three killed. At least, that's what I heard. Lieutenant Hurtubise then ordered his men to fire over the heads of the mob outside the hangar and dispersed them. Before long, a large contingent of Quebec Provincial Police and Montreal Police arrived to take over the prisoners. At which point our men left.

THE COMMISSIONER: Thank you, Colonel Rousseau. We appreciate having your version. Now, it's almost four o'clock and I would like to adjourn this hearing for today. We will continue with other witnesses tomorrow and will probably call you back when we come to other aspects of the military

136

operations. Before we break up for today, however, I want to ask you about your knowledge of the civilian disorders that coincided with your attack on St. Hubert. Was it your understanding that these were planned?

COL. ROUSSEAU: Again, only through hearsay, sir. They were never mentioned in any of the briefings we received before or after our attack on St. Hubert. There seemed to be an unofficial idea among us all that St. Jean Baptiste Day on June 24th was some kind of a target date for accomplishing all objectives leading to independence.

THE COMMISSIONER: What you say is interesting, because there is little doubt that the whole series of events was planned as a package.

COL. ROUSSEAU: I would have no way of knowing the political strategy, sir.

MR. LARKIN: Is that what you call organized mayhem?

THE COMMISSIONER: We'll bear in mind that you are speaking from secondhand information, but, at the same time, you mean to say, that you were not aware that the P.D.Q. leaders had organized massive riots starting in the East End of Montreal to sweep the non-French population westward off the island?

COL. ROUSSEAU: Not until afterwards, sir. I was too busy getting my troops to St. Therese.

THE COMMISSIONER: Didn't you see any sign of these riots as you drove across the island?

COL. ROUSSEAU: We had Q.P.P. escort all the way. They cleared a lane on the expressway for us. We saw a lot of traffic trying to get onto the expressways, but this was to be expected once word got around about our attack on St. Hubert. I can't say we really paid that much attention, sir. All I wanted to do was to get my men to St. Therese as soon as possible.

MR. LARKIN: You're a strange witness to events, Colonel Rousseau. Here you go with a gang of rebels to take a major military base, and you don't know what happens to the prisoners you take. You don't even seem to have any knowledge of the strategy of which you were a vital part. Did you not realize that the key problem facing the Provisional Government was to get control of the Montreal area—that they were determined it would belong to them and not become a free port? And didn't you know that the plan was for you to take St. Hubert, which would be a signal for massive civilian outbreaks organized by the P.D.Q. to drive the non-French population off the island? If Montreal was thus purified, there would be no justification for it becoming a free port. It would be an integral part of the new nation. Were you not aware of these things?

COL. ROUSSEAU: At the time, no sir, I wasn't.

12

A giant foot had kicked the anthill of Montreal. Standing behind the pilot and copilot in our Buffalo transport, I looked down through the haze at tiny cars bulging the highways like a diagram of blocked blood vessels. On either side in line I could see the other two Buffaloes, their wings rising and falling like ours in the alternating updrafts of misty heat from the land and colder currents from the broad surface of the river. Our course took us in a wide circle over the railway yards where the brown lines of box cars were marked by sluggish bulbs of burning freight. On the concrete aprons of Dorval airport, several planes, one of them a big jet, sprawled, broken-winged infernos of flame and greasy smoke.

We had arrived too late.

I leaned toward the pilot's ear. "I was afraid of this. They should've moved us sooner."

He was defensive. "Sorry, Colonel Hlynka. We only got our orders yesterday."

"I'm not blaming you," I said shortly.

"We've been going like crazy," he grumbled. "Our squadron's in Thailand, y'know."

"Nothing on the radio, yet?" I asked. The pilot shook his head.

There wouldn't be any answer, I knew, and it made

me sick. If we had been on the ground we could have held the airport open, at least until our ground forces struggled through the plugged roads from the Ontario border; or we would have had the field under control for air transport to get in. Now we were going to fight for it. The government had held us back too long. That the reins were on Mobile Command had been evident to me in the days following my return to Borden, the morning after my personal warfare on the Quebec border. I had slipped back by dawn with a set-faced and disapproving pilot, a throbbing arm and a nagging conscience for Ab Tremblay, now in the Hawkesbury hospital with a hole in his shoulder. The orders that came in from General Douglas told me to send my advance party to Dorval in the Buffalo transport, which would then be detached from my unit for more urgent requirements. No mention was made of moving the main body of the battalion to the airport to carry out the role assigned to us. The advance party was sent off, and I was left at Borden with no orders or aircraft.

On the morning of June 15th, we started to hear the radio and TV reports of explosions and fires on the south shore of the St. Lawrence in the direction of St. Hubert, and when the Mobile Command telex suddenly became silent, we feared the worst. By evening we had given up trying to reach our advance party by phone and sat around listening to the stories coming in about large-scale riots and mob violence in the city of Montreal. We tried to get through to Ottawa for orders, but the only reply was to stand by. All we could do was put the troops into battle order with rations and ammunition and confine them to barracks. At two in the morning, while I was dozing on the cot I had set up in my H.Q., the call finally came through directly from Ottawa to move the battalion into Dorval as soon as air transport arrived. I had the entire battalion at the Borden airstrip by the time three Buffaloes winked in out of the dark. When I found out that these were the only aircraft we were going to get, I left the battalion with my new second-in-command, an able major from the Combat Arms School, grabbed R.S.M. Wilson and hopped aboard with Alpha Company.

Now, as we circled, I turned to Wilson who was leaning bird-like and taut over the shoulder of the copilot. A lieutenant, with the unfinished features of a baby food label, stood between us. The Alpha Company commander, Major Young, and his 2-I.C., were in the other two planes.

"We've got to go in for a closer look, Mr. Wilson," I said, and turned to the pilot. "Have the others maintain altitude and circle. We're going down to have a look and we'll rejoin them. Are the seats in this bucket armoured?"

The pilot looked startled.

"No, sir."

"Mr. Wilson, tell the men to sit on their packs. They could get a bullet up their ass."

"Yes, sir."

He went back into the plane. The lieutenant hung around unsure, but I didn't have time any more for the care and feeding of the young. Wobbling in the uneven air, we banked sharply over grey water and came in low over the Dorval shopping centre, its parking lot now a petrified maelstrom of cars in a strangely vivid whirlpool of colour.

"Go right around the terminal building as low as you can," I told the pilot. He gulped and nodded.

A glance from the flight deck told me the story. The six-lane highway had solidified into the ultimate in traffic jams, with the median strip and ditches blocked by the overflow of those who had pulled out to get around it all. The side streets and even lawns sprouted a mosaic of useless vehicles at all angles. In the yards and along the sides of the road were the people from Outremont, Mount Royal, Westmount, Côte-St.-Luc, Montreal West, St. Pierre, Lachine, from downtown apartments, town houses and grey stone rooming houses—all of them swept up in a science-fiction horror that made one expect to see a gigantic dinosaur or monster of some kind looming up from the eastern horizon. Clusters of refugees sat around campfires in deserted suburban yards, adding little grey streams of smoke to the haze. Others, mostly with children, sat by the roadsides, and in a long, wavering line, burdened with suitcases, packs and children on their shoulders, moved like sleepwalkers among the stalled hulks of the cars. They were trudging towards the airport. There were no trains in sight and I could see why. Where the railway grade dips into a cut parallel to the highway, a coach straddled the line at a stricken angle.

In the open land around the airport buildings, from the circular Hilton to the parking lot, they were gathered in their thousands, waiting, prone, crouching or standing in fearful knots. Our low descent over them brought white faces looking up and some hopeful waves. In the immobile crowds I noticed sudden little whirls and opening up of gaps in places where they were packed so tightly you couldn't see the ground. In the parking lot I saw them kneeling behind cars or lying flat. On the roof of the terminal building I could see distinctly a group of white-shirted legionnaires prancing and running up and down and firing into the crowd now and again. My imagination heard their laughter.

A sharp banking of the Buffalo brought us alongside the long terminal building over the burning and wrecked planes in what was normally the passenger loading zone. Now the whiteshirts turned their attention to us, running in some kind of weird ballet along with us, stopping to shoot amid long leaps across the roof.

"No sign of life from the control tower," said the pilot.

"Let's get out of here," I said.

A shot sighed through the aluminium behind me and clanked into something on the other side of the aircraft. The young lieutenant lurched into the cabin as we heeled over to evade the shooting.

"Casualty, sir," he said, whitefaced.

"Who?"

"One of the men, sir," he said.

"Rejoin the other aircraft and I'll give orders," I told the pilot. In the cabin one of the kids was doubled up, half sprawled onto the floor. R.S.M. Wilson and a sergeant were gently straightening him out and laying him down. He had red bubbles on his lips. I looked at the others and felt encouraged. Except for a flickering of their eyes, they had kept their faces blank. In the semigloom their brick-red, weathered skin was tight over facebones without any fat. Some of them didn't even look at the dying boy. Most chewed gum slowly, alone with their own thoughts. R.S.M. Wilson looked up at me and shook his head. I went back to the flight deck and saw that we were up with the other planes. We had to move now and as I took one more look at the layout of the airport buildings, I made up my mind. The radio-navigator at his console gave me the mike.

I told them: "Number One aircraft will land at the east end of the main terminal building; Number Two at the west. Attack immediately and clear the enemy out of the buildings. I will land behind the second row of departure lounges you see just north of the main terminal. There's a tunnel under the apron into the main building. We'll try to get in that way. R.T. between platoons only if you're in trouble. Officers "O" Group in control tower in about thirty minutes. Move fast: don't stop for anything. Good luck."

In wild tilts, the Buffaloes dropped down onto the runways and darted in at speeds that I hoped would throw off the whiteshirts at the terminal. The planes looked like scorpions, tails up, attacking a big, grey box.

"Get them out fast," I told R.S.M. Wilson.

Swaying and hanging on as if he was a passenger on a subway car out of control, Wilson shouted his orders back to the forty N.C.O.'s and men bumping against each other. I had let the other two planes go in ahead of us to draw the whiteshirts. The first one had reached the north end of the terminal building going in as if it was about to take off. Playing his turbo-props like some kind of musical instrument, the pilot swung the plane around in a screeching circle so that its hatch faced away from the buildings. I saw figures tumbling out and running. One or two dropped. The other Buffalo skidded to a stop dead on at the west end of the building. They got out their troops by placing two men with FN's in the cockpit. Crouching beside the pilot and copilot, they had knocked out the windscreens and were firing into the buildings as they rolled up.

These fleeting images passed from my sight as we touched down and, in what seemed only seconds, were heading full tilt at our low, one-storey building. Two men fired at us from kneeling positions on the roof. Another one on the ground came running, apparently trying to get off a molotov cocktail or grenade. He disappeared in a flashing red spray as our pilot quickly swung the plane around and caught him with a starboard prop squealing in reverse pitch. With the aircraft still moving slowly, R.S.M. Wilson jumped out, his men rolling after him. It didn't take him long to get six of his people boosted up onto the roof. The two whiteshirts were cut down and their bodies kicked off onto the concrete apron. I got out and ran past the men making their way through the jagged glass remnants of the big waiting room windows where, not so long ago, airline passengers had waited in that peculiar quarantine just before a flight is boarded.

"Here it is, sir," called the young lieutenant, who had outdistanced us all.

Under a sign that said "Gates 31-40" he pointed downward to a short flight of about twenty steps. An escalator, normally moving upward, was silent and still. The long corridor that stretched in front of us was a black tunnel, carpeted by two lines of moving sidewalks, now immobile. The power was off.

"We can't stop now," I told R.S.M. Wilson who came up unsweating and cool. "We'll have to take a chance on it being boobytrapped or an ambush."

"There weren't any others in this wing," he said. "They won't expect us from here."

I sent the young lieutenant off first—he was the most expendable—with a corporal and five men. The others, now waiting their turn for the word to go down the dark corridor, began to talk to each other in low, slurred monotones. Their voices rumbled and echoed in the empty cavern ahead of us. They were now soldiers talking about their first action and trying to show each other they weren't excited.

"See that fucking Frog get it with the fucking prop.'

"The guy on the roof with a fucking Mossberg .22. Used to hunt fucking groundhogs with one."

"Get that, eh? Taking us on with a fucking .22.'

"They can killya good as anything."

"When I got that fucking Frog on the roof he musta jumped six feet."

"Same guy I got. You got him in the fucking head and I got him in the balls."

"No wonder he fucking well jumped."

"Can it," snarled R.S.M. Wilson. Their voices died away against the walls, and we heard the footsteps coming towards us. It was one of the men who had gone up with the lieutenant.

"It's all clear, so far," he said. An echoing clatter of rifle fire came down the tunnel.

"It won't be for long," I said. "Let's move."

"No shooting unless we tell you," said Wilson to the platoon, "Watch for civilians."

With Wilson and myself leading, we started off down the corridor on the rubber tracks of the non-moving sidewalk, a monument to the erroneous calculations of the terminal designers as to how far human beings can walk to an airplane. In its stalled state the rubber floor sank around the rollers causing us all to lurch from side to side as if the building was heaving. We came into brightening light again from the stairway at the end of the corridor. We had crossed under the apron. Behind us, slipping and cursing, their boots making an unholy thunder, came our men. At the top of the stairs, the lieutenant and the men with him were crouched behind the shelter of a three-foot masonry divider that hid the steps from the main concourse. They were sprawled with heads down, and as we came up to them, slugs tore grooves in the blue wall of the stairwell and whined off in sprays of stone chips. I threw myself down on the stairs beside the lieutenant.

"I told you to keep moving," I snapped at him.

"Just a minute, sir." He grabbed my sleeve. "Take a look."

From the steps, I raised up on my knees to look out at floor level. Whoever was shooting at us paused to let me take a look.

"Holy Christ," I murmured.

In the silence after the shooting there was a rising sound, as if a gigantic wind had begun to sweep through the shattered windows of the terminal building. The floor was covered with people; hundreds of them stretched flat, toe to toe, head to head; children and women were cradled with rings made by the arms of their men. They were all jammed together amid broken glass, strewn baggage and upturned furniture in green and yellow leatherette. The mass moved as one organism and heads were raised slowly to peer around. I looked, only a few feet away, into the eyes of an elderly man, staring at me with a shocked glaze. The wind-like sound was a long, low moan that rose from them in a mournful chorale. They were swimmers seeking air.

"At least they're alive," I said, and slipped back down the stairs. "You were right to wait for orders," I told the subaltern. R.S.M. Wilson and his N.C.O.'s gathered around me, waiting as they always do for the officer to think it out. Above us, in the concourse, children began to cry and individual adult voices could be made out shouting to one another. There was a rip of sound from a submachine gun, followed by silence.

"You there. You soldiers down there," came a voice. "Come on out with your hands up, or we let them have it. All of them."

The voice was that of a woman. It came from the ticket counters partially hidden by narrow, square pillars and a telephone booth.

"We've got to open up the airfield regardless of the cost," I told those who had gathered around. "Remember, I take the responsibility for what happens." I looked at them. We could hear rapid shooting not too far away at the opposite ends of the buildings and it sounded as though Major Young was having a fair shoot-out with the whiteshirts. I hoped the rest of Alpha was making progress, but couldn't take the chance of waiting for them. At last I said: "I'm going out to get them. If I make it, follow. We'll do the best we can for the civilians."

"I'll go with you sir," said R.S.M. Wilson. "I'll pick up a couple of good men." The subaltern and the other N.C.O.'s wanted to come too, but I told them they had to stay to handle the troops. Wilson went down the line of men crouched in the tunnel and hauled out three tough-looking lance-corporals. We took off our helmets and crawled slowly up the stairs. I ventured a peep over the edge.

"I see you," she screamed. "Come on out with your hands up."

I saw her. Gorgeous in a short, black leather skirt and a white blouse with sharp vee in front, she was a brunette.

Her long, wavy hair was held in place by a blue and white headband. She was sitting on the SAS ticket counter, her legs crossed where a Sterling rested, pointing straight at us. There were others. I caught a quick glimpse of young men standing openly in front of the counter, facing us and grinning. Another woman seemed to be lying sideways on the top of the next counter. She was smoking a cigarette and waving a Sterling loosely in our direction. She must have been doped to the eyebrows. Between us and them was a carpet of people on their bellies

"Be careful to shoot high," I murmured to Wilson and the three lance-jacks. They nodded and double checked their weapons. "No grenades," I added, then made a motion with my hand.

From out of the stairwell we came running, two Sterlings and three FN's on automatic and fired by experts as soon as we had cleared our field of fire over the heads of the mob on the floor. We used the pillars, with their black marble facings, the way we would normally use trees. I don't think the kids in the whiteshirts expected us. The gorgeous doll on the counter looked down at the red remnants of her beautiful breasts and toppled backward off her perch. One of the lance-jacks to my right jumped in the air and fell backwards over an upturned chromium-trimmed chair. Beneath our feet, people started to groan and roll out of the way; some of them ran crouching and stumbling over each other to get clear. Somebody's hand crunched under my heavy boot as I ran forward. Only a few yards from them our professional training began to tell. They had been shooting wildly and had lost time rolling over behind the ticket counters for protection, where, of course, there was none. My men, seeing them do this, shot under the counters, the high-powered FN slugs easily tearing through the wood and the bright travel posters.

Perhaps because she was on some kind of pills, the

other girl on the counter stayed where she was and started to shriek like a banshee to rally the young men collapsing around her. She used a mixture of French and English, of which I caught only the latter.

"Kill them. Kill them all," she screeched.

"Drop it, honey," yelled back R.S.M. Wilson.

For the first time, she seemed to remember that she had a gun in her hand. She fired a low burst from her Sterling, catching a male civilian who had been desperately crawling on his hands and knees out of the line of fire. Wilson hesitated. I knew I had to take the responsibility.

I ducked a spray of 9 mm. fire from her wavering gun. Her clip would soon be empty, but a lot could happen in those few seconds. She was much closer than the cardboard silhouttes we used on the range, and my five-round burst got her in the face. With her head hanging by a thread, her body slipped off the counter onto a horrified child.

"Sorry," I muttered. "Sorry."

From the Air Canada section under the TV monitors came more wild shooting. A group of whiteshirts came around the corner firing blindly. By that time, the troops behind us had started to flood up the stairway and into the concourse. After a quick exchange of shots, the young legionnaires started to run back along the long line of counters at the main entrance. The civilians on the floor began to stir when they saw how things were going. I saw one man reach up, grab one of the running kids by the ankle and bring him down. A woman on the floor beside him stuck her finger into his eyes, and they grabbed his rifle.

"Stay down," I shouted. "Everybody stay down."

A knot of the whiteshirts came running and jumping back towards us, and I saw the green uniforms of our men coming from the west end of the building to link up with us. About twenty of the young legionnaires, trapped between us, put down their assorted rifles and raised their hands.

"Come on, let's get upstairs," I said to Wilson.

He followed me back to the main lounge where we made our way past the smashed remnants of the coffee counter and restaurant to the stairs. The whole building seemed to reek with cordite. Now people were beginning to sit up. Some plucked at our greenclad legs as we went by.

"Thank God, you're here," someone said. I paused and looked down at a young housewife, her face dirty and tearstained.

"It'll be all right now," I told her. R.S.M. Wilson's ordinarily tense features were transparent, and I saw the twitch in his eyelid. "We'd better keep going," I said hoarsely.

Followed by a corporal and a section of men, we threaded our way among people now getting stiffly up on to their feet. In the upstairs bar, another subultern from Alpha was in control. There were a dozen young legionnaires standing under guard, their hands on their heads. The lieutenant was sitting in a comfortable lounge chair holding a baby on his lap. He started to get up when he saw me.

"Never mind, father," I said to him. "Have we got the control tower?"

"Yes, sir. Major Young is up there, sir."

We made our way along some corridors and up more stairs to the bright daylight of the control tower. Its green-tinted windows had been obliterated and the whole place was a junkyard of smashed equipment and a spaghetti of coloured wires. Major Young and his second-in-command, Captain Johnson, were waiting calmly for my arrival. They had found an air controller and a couple of maintenance men who had been locked up in an office somewhere in the building.

"How soon?" I asked, nodding towards the men burrowing in the complex of useless machines.

"They don't know," said the major. "They have to get the emergency plant on before we can get any power."

"Is anyone working on that?"

"A crew just left to get on it. This is the airport manager."

I turned to the Department of Transport man, an ashen-faced civil servant in his forties. He had an overnight growth of grey stubble, and his shirt was soaked with sweat.

"We've got to get the power on," I told him. "We're sitting here on this little, airtight island with no way of moving reinforcements in or evacuating these people. That's number one. When can you start moving those wrecks out on the apron?"

He told me they were doing their best on the power. He would round up what maintenance men he could and volunteers to move the wrecks.

"Where's our aircrew?" I asked Young.

"Here, sir." The air force captain who was senior man on our three Buffaloes came into the room, out of puff from the stairs.

"Take our casualties and some women with babies and get back to Borden for the rest of the battalion," I told him. "Radio C.F.H.Q. to send in every plane they can find. Troops should bring their own rations. Tell them we've got at least a couple of hundred thousand displaced persons to get off the island."

"More like five hundred thousand before we're finished," Major Young said.

"And," I said to the pilot as he started down the stairs, "Tell them we haven't got any power, navigation aids or radio. Daylight flights only, till they hear from us."

The three of us, Young, Johnson and myself, had our "O" group. We decided to send a fighting patrol of twenty men west along the railway to try to link up with our ground forces; a recce patrol of six men was sent up to Canadair to find out if the Cartierville airport was service-able and to check on the traffic jam on Metropolitan Boulevard. Another patrol was sent out to have a look at the Aeroport Hilton hotel. Others were already out look-ing for our advance party in the buildings and hangers on the west side of the field. We pondered our casualties; they had been high, with five killed and twelve wounded.

"It was mainly the close quarters in the east wing," Major Young said. "We were blasting at each other only a few feet apart."

My hands fumbled with a cigarette and I looked out of the glassless windows. Our Buffaloes were turned around, and I saw some of our men leading a line of women with infants out to them.

"So it starts," I murmured in black anger.

R.S.M. Wilson reappeared in the doorway and saluted. He looked about as white and shaky as I felt.

"Sir," he said. "I've just come from the V.I.P. lounge."

"Good," I said. "Did you find any?"

He looked hurt. "Would you come with me, sir?"

"Sure," I said, staring at him. "What's the trouble?"

He wouldn't say anything more. I followed him along office corridors, now silent and empty. Our boots echoed. I thought we could move some of the refugees with kids into the unoccupied offices. He took me down a short flight of stairs to the V.I.P. lounge where, under normal conditions, the men suffering the pressures of being at the top were sheltered from the stifling presence of the masses. Ordinarily it must have been a pleasant room. There was a small bar with only three or four yellow-covered stools, several of those standard airport leatherette couches that must keep some factory somewhere going full tilt, and a deep blue carpet. The amber-coloured drapes were closed, giving the room a rusty glow.

Under the guns of our men, a dozen half-dressed men

stood with their noses to the mural on the wall, their hands in classical surrender, clasped on their heads. Around the room, on the couches and chairs, were about fifteen young women, also half-dressed. Some of them were sobbing; others stared dully at our entrance.

"They were having some fun, sir," said Wilson. "One of the women is dead."

I looked down at a waxen-faced blonde on the blue carpet, her features bruised and bloody. She was naked. I turned to one of the women who, of all things, was crying and reading a Fortune magazine from a nearby magazine rack. She wasn't really reading the magazine— just flipping the pages over and over.

"Can you talk?" I asked her gently. She looked up, nodded and carefully closed the magazine as if some librarian were watching.

"They just came and took us out of the crowds," she said. "My baby's down there somewhere."

"Someone help her to find her child," I told Wilson. He detailed a corporal to take her out.

Primly avoiding the shapely, half-naked women sitting around the room, I made my way over to the prisoners against the wall. They exuded the stale aura of booze vastly consumed and stolen cigars chainsmoked. In appearance they seemed different from the good-looking kids we had shot down in the attack on the terminal. These were older men, hairy with beefy shoulders and big bellies. There were one or two younger ones, squat on bandy legs.

"You've come a long way across town for all this," I said.

They didn't say anything. One of them with no pants on, turned his head sideways and spat on the floor near my foot. I looked downward through a red haze and thought of these men and Edith and other women we knew who lived in Montreal.

"Is there a washroom here?" I asked Wilson.

"Just over there, sir," said Wilson pointing.

"Put them in it," I said. I looked at the floor while my men herded them into the washroom. One of the prisoners laughed at me as he went by and said something in French. When they were all in the washroom, I turned to the R.S.M.

"How's your grenade supply?"

He grinned for the first time that day. I turned to the women and spoke in my best imitation of a kindly tourist guide.

"Now, ladies, if you will get dressed and accompany me, we'll make you as comfortable as possible in some other place. We should have medical attention for you before the day is out."

One of them, with magnificent breasts still bared but badly scratched, looked up from an armchair and then over at the washroom. She watched R.S.M. Wilson unhooking a grenade from his webbing.

"I'd like to stay," she said.

13

The office I occupied on the southeast corner of the terminal building had belonged to someone named Blake who, judging from the files still on his desk, had a lot to do with electrical engineering problems around the place. I wished he was still there. His wife and two children beamed at me from a standup frame beside the green desk blotter; there was a large metal ashtray with the name of an engineering firm on it, a mechanical calendar in the shape of an eight-ball that didn't seem to be working (March 28), a marble-based desk set with two ball point pens in holders on either side of a gold clock that had stopped running (4.30). I tried out the pens, and they didn't work either. The dog tags from my five dead soldiers were lined up in a neat row on the desk. The swivel chair creaked as I leaned back and sized up the prisoner one of our sergeants now delivered.

The prisoner was wearing one of those white, high-necked tunics denoting the officer class in the P.D.Q. Legion. He seemed almost like a twin of the one that Ab Tremblay had killed in the village north of Montebello. Thin, fine-featured with a characteristic pointed jaw and pale skin, he stood before me in quiet dignity, despite the hands tied behind his back. The brown eyes shone.

"He won't speak English, sir," said the sergeant.

"Where'd you catch him?" I asked.

"On the roof of the Hilton. He had a transmitter."

"Did you get it?"

"No, sir. He kicked it over the side."

I looked up at the almost fragile-looking prisoner. His only motion was the bobbing of a sharp adam's apple in his thin neck. I wished I had my Intelligence Officer with me, but he was still in Borden with the rest of the battalion. I was lousy at interrogations and detested them.

"Your name, rank and serial number, if any," I opened. No answer.

"I'm giving you the opportunity of becoming a military prisoner," I said. "I hope you take advantage of it. It may help those kids of yours that we've got."

A stare.

"I hope you take responsibility for them," I went on, "because I intend to see that you do. If you give grass and guns to kids, you shouldn't be surprised if we have to shoot them."

The eyes widened.

"Those were two very lovely girls—turned on till they squeaked—but magnificent just the same. I was sorry to have to kill them. They had a right to a much better life."

He was on the verge of saying something. His lips were beginning to rub.

"Presumably you are responsible for instructing them to carry out atrocities against women and children," I continued. "I felt badly about those girls and some of the other nice kids of yours we had to shoot—about twenty of them, I think. Just high-spirited youth carried away by slogans, I suppose. But," I said, "when they turn into rapists and murderers, they get what's coming to them."

His voice was a low bass, coming out deeply from a narrow chest.

"My legionnaires wouldn't do that," he said in accented English. "They're good boys. You're lying."

"I'll bring in some of the victims if you want to see

156

them," I said. "Anyway, it doesn't matter much. Your kids have no military status and won't be treated as prisoners."

"They are part of an organized military formation," he said stiffly.

"Okay. Give."

"I am Captain Sarto Levesque of the Amable Daunais Brigade of the Legion of the Provisional Government."

"Who do you report to?"

"Brigade headquarters."

"Where's that?"

No answer.

"Who's your superior?"

No answer.

"Where is your headquarters?"

No answer.

"How many men are there in the brigade and where are they? What weapons do they have? What are your orders?"

No answer. I slammed my open palm down on the desk making a loud crack in the still room. I got up and looked out of the window at the mobs of refugees still waiting for the airlift to begin. I singled out a young man seated crosslegged, cradling a baby and almost enveloped by two other kids holding onto his shirt. He was looking up at the sky and didn't move. Around him, as far as the eye could see, were the refugees, looking suddenly shabby and dishevelled the way refugees always do. Some were still in their night clothes. The overnight collapse of their affluent society made them even more pitiful than the inured peasants of other lands. This is in my own country, I said again to myself, a pulse hammering in my neck. My own country. I turned to the pale, effete prisoner.

"We have about forty of your men prisoners," I told him. "We could turn them loose in that mob out there."

"You wouldn't do that. They're just boys," he said finally.

I sat down and sighed.

"No, I guess not." I smiled at him and he appeared to relax his thin shoulders. "Undo his hands." The sergeant looked at me as if I had flipped and cut the ropes with his bayonet. I gave the Legion captain a cigarette and told him to sit down, which he did quickly, showing that his knees had been getting a bit watery.

"You tell me where your headquarters are and I'll look after all of your people well," I told him. "I'll put you on the first aircraft that comes in and send you to a proper camp. I imagine there will soon be a prisoner exchange anyway."

He smiled through blue smoke. He was getting his confidence back.

"If you don't," I said quietly. "I'll bring in each one of those boys, one by one, and castrate him in front of you. Then we'll do you."

The Legion captain looked at me, went green and threw up on the floor. I told the sergeant to get somebody to clean it up.

"I'll give you until tomorrow morning to think it over," I said. "Then we'll start."

I got up, told the sergeant to keep him under heavy guard in a nearby storeroom and left, the stench of the place almost turning my stomach too. I went up to the control tower to find Major Young.

"How's our prisoner doing?" he asked.

"Feeling a bit shaky at the moment," I grinned. "I've given him till tomorrow morning to make up his mind. He knows where his headquarters are in Montreal, but that isn't much use until we get some reinforcements and some helicopters in here. Any of the radio equipment working yet?"

"No, I'm afraid not. They're having trouble."

"I hope they get something working soon. We can't go on much longer like this."

A thunderclap of jets announced that the rest of the

country finally had wakened up and were coming to have a look. Out of the glassless window frames, I could see a flight of Voodoos banking low over the field, flashing around in an impressive manner.

"Fat lot of good they are," grumbled Young.

"We can use them," I said. "Wave them in. I'm going down on the field."

After much waving of Canadian flags and whatnot, the Voodoos eventually got the message and three of them landed while the others circled. They stopped far out from the terminal building. I drove out to them in an Air Canada jeep and met an air force major who greeted me with a levelled automatic. He looked young, well-rested and clean in a shiny flight suit. I told him who I was and asked him where they had come from.

"Oh, we got out of Bagotville yesterday," he said. "We had to leave our ground crew behind. Uplands suggested we pop in here to see if we could lend support. Any targets for us?" he asked hopefully.

"All I need is your radio," I said wearily. I was tired of people always looking for targets. "I need D.R.'s. Despatch riders. Get off to every base you can find and tell them we've got a refugee problem like they've never seen before. Leave one aircraft here to circle and act as radio control till we get the tower going."

Somewhat chastened at their mundane role, the shiny-suited ones took off again in smoky blasts of noise. I drove back across a vast expanse of concrete, feeling like an ant on a sidewalk. It wasn't even noon, I realized. In the brightening haze, now starting to lift off, I looked across at the distant hangars and wondered if one of them might contain a small helicopter. But I didn't have a pilot. Next on my list was a visit to that quiet street in Westmount where Edith's parents had their home. Supposing they had left the cottage and had returned to the city? Was this why I hadn't been able to reach them? If they had returned to town, maybe they had been caught up in the human waves that swept through Montreal the night before. They might even be among the thousands of aimless people who now carpeted every patch of ground as far as the eye could see.

I began to feel a little better when a patrol showed up with our advance party, five Mounties, several Customs men and other airport employees who had been held prisoner in the Timmins hangar on the west side of the field. Their guards had fled without firing a shot. While we were all shaking hands and grinning like idiots, we had another arrival from civilization.

A fast, five-passenger Bell Iroquois whirled in low from the east. It came down perilously close to a couple of the wrecked aircraft on the apron. Just to make sure, I had a section of men around it with FN's levelled. When the rotor sputtered to a stop, the first man out of the open hatch was an immaculate figure in pressed summer greens, shoulder boards and a long, malacca cane in his hand. He paused on the concrete, took a handkerchief from his sleeve and brushed at his nose. Four other men, a major, a captain and two staff sergeants, all equally nattily dressed, joined him. None was armed.

The tall, immaculate creature had, as I feared, a blonde moustache and flat, grey eyes. His appraisal of me was something less than contemptuous. Understandably so. Hatless, my bush-shirt open down my chest, sweaty and with a machine carbine slung around my neck, I must have looked like a Congo mercenary.

"I'm de Gruchy," he said. "I'm taking over operations in the Montreal sector. We'll have to operate out of here for the time being." He was a brigadier-general.

"Hlynka, Third R.C.R.," I told him. "I'm responsible for securing Dorval and Cartierville, sir."

"I know." He looked around slowly and sniffed. "Rather a mess. You haven't gotten very far, I see."

"No, sir," I said, withdrawing into a hostile sulk. The old problem was coming back. The thing I always had difficulty controlling. I had never learned how to charm my superiors—and that is half the game in the army or anywhere else. Instead, the good old Hlynka rule-of-thumb, developed through long practice over the years, was the higher the rank the more insolent you got. It was not a success formula.

"I shall need quarters for myself and my staff when they get here. We should be near the communications centre." He whacked the side of his leg with the cane and looked around some more.

"The place is jammed with refugees, sir. We haven't got the tower working yet," I said.

"We shall have to get things moving then, shan't we?" He said with an increasingly disapproving stare.

On our way into the terminal building, he deigned to tell me they had picked up radio reports in French that General Douglas had been killed and St. Hubert overrun. On his way in he had taken a pass over the south shore, but had found St. Hubert burning, with whiteshirts on the ground taking potshots at them. I began to gather my wits and gave him a more organized briefing, including our special prisoner.

"Oh?" he said, affecting surprise that we had been able to do anything. "I should like to have a chat with him."

I decided to get the prisoner myself and give him some more psychological warfare on the way. At the windowless storeroom the two guards looked heavy-lidded in the steaming corridor, the temperature in the nineties without air-conditioning. I started to tell them to open up, when I noticed something under the door. It was a quarter-inch wide scarlet worm moving from under the door slowly across the floor.

"Open up," I yelled.

In the dark, bare storeroom, I could sense the story in the sharp smell of fresh blood. Captain Sarto Levesque sat motionless and staring against the wall, his arms hanging loosely, leaking blood from slit wrists. He was wheezing badly and I could see from the mess on the floor that we were too late.

"Where did you get it?" I shouted at Levesque.

There was no response except a feeble twitch of one hand, and I saw the half razor blade gleaming blue in the blood. He probably had it sewn into a seam somewhere. Anyway, there was nothing we could do. His eyes were beginning to glaze.

When I reported back to de Gruchy, his disdain held no bounds.

"He should have been watched every minute," he said in icy anger. "Our first prisoner of any rank. We don't know a damned thing about them: how they're organized, how many troops they've got, their arms, their plans— nothing. He might have helped us shorten the rebellion." He looked through me for awhile. "I expect you have other things to do, Colonel Hlynka."

On the way downstairs an idea partly cleared away the red mist of anger. I found R.S.M. Wilson supervising the removal of the little legionnaire's corpse.

"Go find the general's pilot and tell him to stand by," I said. "The general has given me a special assignment. Collect some grenades." The R.S.M. nodded and was off in his usual quick, hopping gait.

When I had sent the advance party to Dorval, I had included my batman, Hinch, to set up quarters for me. A grey-haired oldtimer, Hinch had been liberated with the advance party and now appeared, complete with a valise of my clothing he had kept with him. A master scrounger, he had already found a cot and was setting it up in my confiscated office. Somewhere he had found water and disinfectant and cleaned up the place. From my valise I dug out my gold-braided regimental hat. Hinch looked at me disapprovingly and started to unpack a set of summer greens.

"No time for that now," I told him.

Wearing my staff hat I detached a couple of men with FN's to come with me, and headed for the baggage store-room where the legionnaire prisoners were held. They were not crowded, but the room was windowless and with air-conditioning off, it was rank with human heat and sweaty fear. The prisoners were mostly sitting in rubbery poses around the walls. Three guards with Sterlings faced them, even though each legionnaire had his hands tied behind him. The captives were young, good-looking kids with white, worried faces.

"I have a message from Captain Levesque," I said in English. "He is our captive and has asked to see the senior N.C.O."

There was a shuffling of legs, but no answer.

"Because of the intervention of Captain Levesque, you will be treated as prisoners of war," I said. "If it hadn't been for him, we had planned to shoot all of you."

"If we're prisoners of war, untie us," said a voice. It belonged to one of the few hefty kids. He had a dark beard beginning to show through, and must have been in his mid-twenties.

"Are you the senior N.C.O.?" I asked.

"Sergeant Laliberté of the Amable Daunais Brigade, sir. Captain Levesque will vouch for me."

"Very well." I turned to the corporal in charge. "As soon as we have gone, untie the prisoners." I made a face at the corporal and he got it. "Now, Sergeant Laliberté, if you will come with me. I'll also need two of your N.C.O.'s."

The man sized me up, sighed and picked two of his men. He looked fairly tough. I didn't know if it was going to work or not.

"As we'll be walking. I'll have to keep your hands tied, Sergeant," I said.

Still not sure, but anxious to help his men, the swarthy N.C.O. came out into the hall with the two others he had selected. With my two guards I took him straight outside to the helicopter where R.S.M. Wilson waited beside the general's pilot.

"Get in," I said.

The Legion N.C.O. realized too late that he had been taken, but the guards dragged him and his two men into the helicopter.

"Tie their feet," I told the guards. When that was done, I told the pilot. "Okay, let's go out over the river." He looked a bit uncertain, but did as he was told. The helicopter lifted in its peculiar sway and took us past the control tower where startled, white faces peered up. I hoped the control tower radio equipment was still not working. It wasn't. I told the pilot to go out well over Lake St. Louis, away from the refugee crowds, and lift up to about 3,000 feet.

"Now," I said to the Legion sergeant, wriggling his bonds. "Where're your headquarters?"

He swore at me in French barely audible above the noise of the helicopter.

"Open the door," I told R.S.M. Wilson, who slid back the panel.

"Your headquarters," I said. "You understand me. Where are they?"

He clamped his big, square jaw shut and closed his eyes. We kicked out the first kid and watched him go down in what seemed like slow spirals, his white shirt showing up against the green surface of the water.

"Your headquarters," I repeated. Eyes closed, he moved his head from side to side and muttered silently to himself; I didn't know if they were prayers or whether he had snapped. The second kid screamed something in adenoidal French as we heaved him out. I didn't feel much like watching him.

"Let's go get some more," I said to R.S.M. Wilson.

The pilot, absorbed in the intense attention that helicopter flying requires, looked straight ahead, sweat pouring off his face. He banked the helicopter, almost throwing me out of the open door. Maybe on purpose, I thought, and in some ways I didn't blame him. We started back towards the terminal building. The remaining prisoner raised his head, streaks of tears running into the black whisker stubble.

"They were last at the Etienne Brulé Motel on Upper Lachine Road," he said.

"You've just saved the lives of your men," I nodded. R.S.M. Wilson picked him up by the scruff of the neck and hauled him towards the open door. Laliberté's head swung loosely.

"Wait," I said. I studied the two of them for a moment. "Would you like to live?" He managed a nod. I would have done the same, hanging onto any thread that prevented the final darkness.

"Guide us to the motel and I'll leave you there unharmed," I told him. This time I meant it, and I think he sensed that I did. It did involve a certain risk for us, but he would have problems of his own with his own people explaining why he had helped us. The main disadvantage was that he might give some propaganda punches to the Provisional Government—heaving prisoners out of a bird. On the other hand, maybe it was time they began to realize that terror is a two-edged sword.

We followed the river into thickening smoke that hung over the western part of Montreal in a greyish-blue mass of still, humid air. Only dimly could we see the outlines of buildings on the shoreline.

"About here," shouted Laliberté.

The pilot, with hostile glares at me over his shoulder, droped the fast Bell down through the thick haze and we found ourselves over an arterial street choked with abandoned, stalled cars. There were no people in sight. Along the cluttered strip of motels, gas stations, drive-ins, and small businesses there was rubbish piled deep, as if there had been a garbage strike for a year. Everything had been looted thoroughly and smashed. Our prisoner peered over the side and would have pointed if his hands had been free. Instead, he moved his head to one side. Just above the power and telephone wires, we slipped along Upper Lachine, eyes squinting to see a familiar landmark through the smoke, not helped at all by the occasional building smoldering untended and adding its own greasy smoke to the acrid layer.

"Just ahead," the prisoner told us.

A big sign, that in normal times would have been competing in flashing lights with all the others nearby, loomed out of the blur. I made out the word "Brulé" supported by the outline of a steel skeleton. The motel had two stories and was made of buff brick.

"We can't land on the roof, sir," the pilot told me. "The sign is too big."

"Use the parking lot by the main entrance," I said.

We whirled in low around the big sign. I turned to Sergeant Laliberté, tore off his blue and white armband and pinned it on my own sleeve. I took off my regimental hat and threw it on the floor.

"You're going to take us in," I told Laliberté. "You will ask to see the brigadier. I know enough French to tell if you try anything. As soon as we have the brigadier, you're free to go. Okay?"

He thought about it, because it was an extra I hadn't mentioned in the deal. His hatred was a live thing floating in big, brown eyes. At last he nodded. R.S.M. Wilson reluctantly cut his hands and feet free with a commando knife he carried low on his right thigh. Over the edge of the buff-coloured motel, I could see the parking lot. Signal trucks, probably stolen from the Canadian Forces, told me it was still their headquarters. There were three stubby, brown vehicles clustered near the concrete canopy over the main doorway with lines snaking out of them into the building. Four or five motorcycles were lined up, upright on their stands.

"Lean out and wave," I said to Laliberté.

At the open door of the helicopter, he crouched, pumping his arm at a couple of legionnaires who came out of the motel and looked up. Laliberté pointed downwards, and they signalled to him to bring the helicopter in near the signal trucks. In my throat, the hard pressure began to ease. There was hardly anyone around. Their headquarters in the field were not much different from ours: a skeleton command post with a minimum of people around, except those with specific jobs or others waiting for orders and resting up. Knowing the field headquarters psychology, I had counted on this, but I hadn't known if it would work with a para-military organization like the Legion. Seemingly, it did.

The helicopter landed, churning up a whirlpool of paper debris. This flurry of garbage kept the men at the motel entrance away from us and gave us time to get out of the bird with Laliberté in front of me, the muzzle of my Sterling aimed casually at his back. Two tired looking kids in dirty white shirts, and with pistols in leather holsters, sized up Laliberté's white shirt and my armband.

"Tell them you're bringing an urgent message for the brigadier from Captain Levesque at Dorval. The helicopter is one you captured when you took the airport," I told him.

Apparently, Laliberté did what he was told. The exhausted kids, neither of them yet in his twenties, took us through the lobby to the dining room. Every chair and sofa in the lobby was occupied by a sleeping man, curled up in stained white shirts. I noticed their weapons; this group seemed to be armed with Chicom K-50's that had the straight clips and wire butts. I hoped they stayed asleep. The dining room, being used as the brigade's communications centre, was hardly a hive of activity. Two signallers in earphones at the end of the cables from the trucks outside were trying to stay awake at paper-strewn tables. A bleary-eyed officer in one of the high-necked white tunics watched our entry into the room, but didn't get up. The only people wide awake were four gorgeous, dark-haired girls in tight-fitting white blouses, who seemed to be playing a game of cards of some kind. I noted small pistols at their belts and kept an eye on them. Was ever a rebellion fought with so many beautiful women around? It was almost enough to make one defect, and I allowed a grudging sense of admiration for insurrection conducted with such style.

Laliberté spoke to the ashen-faced officer in the high collar. He argued wearily, then nodded and pointed towards an open door. The four girls stopped playing cards and watched us with bright, suspicious eyes. I felt a sudden pang of fear when I realized that we still had our blue and gold R.C.R. patches on our shoulders. All I could do was grin and nod at them as we left the room. The prospect of having to shoot any more attractive women made me edgy. Laliberté led us along the carpeted hallway, done in a hideous, wavy design of purple and green, to a corner suite. Through the doors I could see more men sprawled on the beds in the rooms.

Outside the closed door of the suite another kid was sitting in a deep armchair, his head on his chest and his Soviet-style assault gun resting crosswise on the arms of the chair. He looked up, heavy-lidded and nodded to Laliberté, who pushed open the door and walked into the suite. Because the air-conditioning was off, the windows were open to the smoky haze that drifted into the room. Two girls in the inevitable white blouses were curled up asleep on the couches while a small transistor radio unheeded poured out tinny messages in rapid French. We headed straight for the bedroom.

Two double beds had been pushed together, one of them occupied by a big, curly-haired man with a beard, and the other by two girls, bare olive shoulders showing above the single sheet that wrapped them. R.S.M. Wilson moved quickly to where the two girls were dozing and covered them with his machine carbine. I shook the sleeping man, who snapped awake with a speed that made me jump. He sat up, his matted, hairy chest emerging from the dank sheet. Laliberté spoke quietly and urgently to him in French, but he hardly needed to, because the brigadier got the message. I jammed the cold muzzle of my Sterling into his bare belly and told him to get dressed. The girls began to sit up and lifted beautiful naked bodies out of the sheet to stare wide-eyed at us. R.S.M. Wilson motioned to them to disappear under the sheet again, which they did. He drew the sheet up over their heads.

There was a door leading directly outside from the bedroom leading to the parking lot. R.S.M. Wilson tied up the girls inside their sheet with towels, and we started out of the motel without having to run the gauntlet again inside the building. The brigadier in his high-collared tunic and starred shoulder boards, looked frantically around him as we led him back to the helicopter, but he didn't say a word. He was tired, and probably his mind wasn't as clear as it might have been. From his stale breath it was evident that he had been drinking before his roll in the hay and sleep. Trying for the spoils of victory too soon, I thought, as we made our way past the humming signal trucks to the helicopter. Even the two guards under the canopy only watched dully as we clambered on board, and the pilot revved up the rotors.

"Goodbye, Laliberté," I said. "And thanks."

We pushed him forward out of the door and lifted off with that quick sway of a turbo-prop bird. Laliberté ran for the door of the motel, shouting and waving his arms. R.S.M. Wilson, always on the ball, quickly heaved two grenades at the signals trucks, but we moved up too fast through the smoke to see the results.

"That should wake them up," he grinned.

"Let's make sure that never happens to us," I said grimly. "I want wide-awake security at all times."

Aside from a half-hearted dash to the door of the helicopter, our prisoner gave little trouble after Wilson had tied him down to a bucket seat. He was slowly beginning to wake up, and the enormity of what had happened to him began to come home. He closed his eyes, worked his beard and groaned softly to himself. Over Dorval our pilot told us the control tower was on, and as we circled the terminal, we could see several jet transports with airline markings unloading troops and equipment. The refugees were now in motion, forming long, snaking lines leading through the terminal building and around it. The airlift had begun, and the crunch was about to start.

"Bring us in close to the terminal," I told the pilot. When he looked at me now, it was with a new respect. Maybe he wouldn't talk.

We came down in a space near the terminal building, scattering a lineup of refugees. I took off my fleur-de-lys armband. We hustled the brigadier upstairs to the control tower past gaping troops and civilians, including some reporters who started to trail after us shouting questions. I ignored them, silently envying their ability to get priority transportation anywhere, any time. The control tower was now an uproar of activity, with metallic voices exchanging messages and a clutter of smartly-dressed staff officers surrounding a table where de Gruchy stood. We pushed our way past them all. I saluted, having put on the regimental hat.

"A replacement, sir," I said. "The officer commanding the Amable Daunais Brigade of the Provisional Government forces."

From behind the map-littered table, de Gruchy looked up in enraged contempt.

"You took my helicopter," he said. "Are you some kind of pirate, Colonel Hlynka?"

"You wanted someone to shorten the war, sir," I said. "Here he is."

"One thing that will shorten the war, Colonel Hlynka," said de Gruchy, "is if you are nowhere near it." One of his staff officers laughed. Brigadier-General de Gruchy looked at the prisoner. "I must apologize to you for any mistreatment you have received at the hands of this officer. You are a prisoner-of-war and will be given every consideration."

The Legion brigadier nodded and looked at me smugly. My own senior stared at me and tapped the table with a map protractor.

"Going to throw him back, sir?" I asked, and then knew I had gone too far. Beads of moisture stood out on de Gruchy's high forehead. He swallowed hard and bent the map protractor in two. His head was down, and he spoke through a stiff jaw.

"Colonel Hlynka," he said. "You are relieved of your command immediately. Go to your quarters until you receive further orders."

I saluted in dismissal and left without a word. Outside in the hallway, I thanked R.S.M. Wilson and told him to give his new C.O. his best effort and cooperation.

"They'll bring you back, sir," he said, saluted and left in his quick way.

In the upper areas of the terminal, sealed off from the sweltering mobs below, there was a strange quiet. Voices from the control tower and from various offices along the hall rumbled distantly, as phones, radios and complex equipment of various kinds brought life back to Dorval. I walked along the empty corridor, passing open doors where shirtsleeved men were working to restore normality. Against the subdued background, I heard my own footsteps. The black depression that had been skulking around the edges of my consciousness now struck like some big, shadowy bird of prey.

14

If you have ever noticed, you seldom see a senior army officer who is short and ugly. There may be hidden psychological reasons for this in the selection procedure, which might make a good study theme for an undergraduate Freudian, but I think the explanation is simple enough. When you start out as a junior officer, you are judged essentially on three things: man management (you've got to look like a born commander); cheerfulness to all concerned, and physical stamina (when everyone else is pooped, you have to come along and stir up N.C.O.'s and men alike to new heights of effort). Getting off on the right foot as an officer is mostly an athletic business, because the things you have to learn are simple and require little mental effort. The mental effort comes later when you've passed the first barrier and your personnel reports say that you are "cheerful, with definite leadership possibilities". Later you have to use your head a little more: getting good marks on the academic courses, developing judgment on the details of handling your N.C.O.'s and men, and learning how to handle your superiors. I had always done well in everything but the latter.

The army remained my career because I found over the years that its physical activity, combined with the massive grind of regular procedures, helped to level out the ups and downs of my own emotional cycles. The routines dampened even the most restless soul, yet were demanding enough in detail and accuracy to prevent complete deterioration in times of melancholy. These long intervals of moving paper and placing men on the organization chessboards, however, in my case served to build up a latent store of energy waiting for the spark to fire it. It had happened before, but not with the intensity I had felt during the events of the past few weeks. Now it remained to be seen how they would react to what I had done. The scale could tip either way, depending on how they wanted to fight this war.

Alone with my thoughts, I reflected that perhaps I had been away too long on the international scene, away from the de Gruchys and the other successful ones who had grasped the fine points of how to use the system. They knew, better than me, how to judge timing, where the pressure points were to move things at the right moment, and exactly in the degree needed to get what they wanted. These things were important. As an army, we had not been in action for over twenty years—the Thailand commitment being very recent—and no one had been able to prove himself and create a record in action. Those who knew their office politics were in the forefront; we were more civil servants than we were soldiers.

Only relatively few of us, who had made an uncomfortable and lonely bed in U.N. peacekeeping, had to improvise with decisions on the spot, and the drawback to that was our isolation. Leave was the only time when we could catch up on who was moving up, who was not, and why. Our daily lives were spent in stinking villages, on backroads amid troops who might not speak our language, and under commanders who might be Canadian, but more than likely were Indian, Swedish, Yugoslav or Irish. We dealt with local politicians directly. When some terrorist group got out of line, we moved in without waiting for

173

orders from anyone. Sometimes in our blue-painted jeeps, our U.N. flag waving at the end of a high aerial like an incongruous splash of washing, we would drive between lines of opposing forces who were firing at each other. Most of our actions were hastily devised, unorthodox and unreported to our multi-nation masters until we had carried them out. Such speed was necessary if the blue flag was to have any meaning at all.

South Africa had been bad, because one could come out of hell-holes like Jo'burg, or dust-choking chases through scrub, and pass into the serene, secure British environment of Durban. We grasped at time in Durban to unwind. I remember a party once, up on The Berea overlooking Durban, when J.J. Rousseau, myself and a couple of other Canadian officers sat out in a magnificent garden, draped by willowy English girls who tried to kid us out of our long silences. But the day before, after a panic call from one of our F.D.L.'s, we had hit a raiding party of Kaffir Kommandos who had caught some Afrikaans refugees. We had to shoot the raiders, and their victims as well, to put them out of their misery.

Away from the army mainstream too long, with the U.N. too long, absent from my own land too long, and a naive stranger now when it came to understanding its problems and the forces that were starting to tear Confederation apart. But mad. A churning rage that they could have let this happen to our country—a country that I often thought was only truly appreciated by those who had to spend any length of time away from it. Was there no place left in the world for men who could compromise, talk with reason and calm or, at least, a feeling of goodwill? Did everybody have to be a wild-eyed supporter of some goddam Cause?

I knew where there might be a bottle. Downstairs, I walked along a corridor to the V.I.P. room. A single guard covering the hallway nodded, saluted and accompanied me to the door of the lounge.

"They've removed the bodies, sir," he whispered in a conspiratorial tone. Obviously, R.S.M. Wilson had read the riot act.

"What bodies?" I asked.

The young soldier grinned and nodded. "I get you, sir. There's someone still in there, sir," he added.

"Who?"

"One of the women, sir. She insisted on staying."

I paused, and wondered if I should go in.

"All right," I said. "I'll be out in a minute."

The private stayed outside as I pushed the glass doors and went in. Mercifully, the amber curtains were still drawn and the place was in subdued gloom with only a faint light trying to get through the drapes. On one of the sofas the figure of a woman was curled up, the way women often do in repose, her feet tucked under her. At first I thought she was asleep until I saw that her eyes were wide open staring at the carpeted floor. She had long, streaked blonde hair and wore a black skirt with a white waiter's jacket as a blouse. On a closer look, I remembered her as one of the women we had rescued from the fun-loving legionnaires. I recalled her sitting in the same place with her big, bare breasts and the scratches on them. She gave no sign that she had noticed me. I looked around the room.

The door of the washroom hung askew, emitting from within a heavy, pungent odor of blood and shattered flesh. They had removed the debris from R.S.M. Wilson's grenades, I thought, but there probably hadn't been enough water to clean up the place properly. Quickly, I moved behind the bar. My boys had removed almost everything from the shelves. Below the bar counter, I found a door and inside, after kicking in the flimsy lock, a small stock of full bottles. I grabbed the first one, vodka, and grinned at myself for the sure racial instinct. I found a couple of unbroken glasses, two bottles of tonic water and a bag to put them in. I started back towards the door. The girl on the couch suddenly looked up and let out a little gasp.

"Don't worry," I said. "I'm from the army. I was here before."

She uncoiled her legs and shook her long hair.

"You must think I'm nuts," she murmured.

I didn't say anything but stopped to watch her.

"They didn't finish with me," she said with an attempt at a laugh. "It was just . . . when I saw the mobs downstairs . . . After all I'd been through, I just wanted a quiet place for a while . . . Seems ghoulish, but . . ." She looked up. "I haven't flipped. I just wanted to be alone for awhile . . ."

I stood in front of her, feeling foolish with the clinking paper bag in my arm.

"Why don't you let me take you away from all this?" I asked. "I've just liberated some booze and need a change of scenery as much as you do."

She actually laughed. I suppose it was relief at the intrusion of clumsy normalcy—the pickup. In the gloom I saw her stand up. At the door I told the guard that the lady was leaving but not to let anyone else in until it was properly washed up. I made a mental note to remind R.S.M. Wilson of this but then remembered that I no longer had any responsibilities. The girl padded beside me in low-heeled loafers, her head down. Inside my temporary office, I found my batman, Hinch, sitting behind the desk looking worried. He stood up when I came in.

"Sir, I've been told to report to the brigadier as a runner," Hinch said. It was a question.

"That's all right, Hinch," I said. "I'm unemployed for the moment. You go ahead. Thanks for everything."

We hadn't been together long, so there wasn't any sentiment involved, if there ever is any sentiment with oldtimers like Hinch. He put on a beret, saluted smartly and left. I locked the door and opened the window to let in some air but closed the venetian blinds. The girl looked tense.

176

"Relax," I smiled at her. "Colonels aren't supposed to drink where the taxpayers can see them. Like one?"

She nodded and sat stiffly on the cot. I noticed Hinch had scrounged a couple of packs of haversack rations which he had placed on the desk.

"We can have something to eat," I said. "You get it ready and I'll pour."

She busied herself discovering the mysteries of the small tins and plastic bags packed so scientifically into the dark-brown, waxed boxes no larger than bricks. We had a couple of drinks and ate, then had a few more vodkas and warm tonic. I smoked about ten cigarettes in rapid succession, even though I only had one small pack of Players left. Feeling half human again, I sat in the armchair, my feet on the desk. She lay in the cot on her hip, beginning to loosen up. Her blue eyes began to take on life.

"I still don't know what happened in Montreal last night," I told her. "What caused the panic?"

Her name was Anna, not Ann or Anne. She was Finnish from the Lakehead where doors were left unlocked and where a neighbour, with some long-imagined slight, once tried to kill her father with an axe. At an early age she was labelled as being well-stacked which resulted in her being ardently pursued by a horde of slurred-voiced young men who became even more slurred with massive intakes of foul-smelling beer or cheap rye, and sometimes both.

"I could find no one who looked or dressed or talked in a civilized way like the men on TV or in the movies," she said, smiling and twirling her glass. "Much less a man who read a book or wanted anything more than to get into me."

Through heavy-lidded eyes, I wondered how many had.

"I suppose," she sighed, "it's the eternal problem of every small town girl. The able, attractive males leave early, as soon as they've got their high school. They clear out for university or the jobs they can find in the big cities. We who are left are the pawed. An evening out builds up tension to the inevitable wrestling match, made even worse by the revival of cigar-smoking among the kids. Also, the small town boy gets fat much earlier."

At my guffaw, she started to giggle quietly.

"Like so many others, I got out," she said. "Why Montreal? I don't know. Some of my girlfriends went to Winnipeg. We were Winnipeg's hinterland, not Ontario's. I had been there. It always seemed to me to be an oddly flat place. There's an edge missing. Perhaps because it is so landlocked, it's lost its purpose in life. Land doesn't mean much any more, but space does. Anyway, I had no urge to lock myself up in an aging ghost town in the middle of the continent. The action is around the edges."

She was good therapy. My warmth must have shown in my face, because she continued.

"Toronto? They called it swinging. I went there for a long weekend to stay with some girlfriends. There didn't seem to be any men, or at least they didn't know many. The big offices are murder, they told me, mostly married men who spar and hint. They're poison. We went to movies, so I decided to go to Montreal."

"Why not New York?"

"After seeing the loneliness of the girls in Toronto, I was scared. When I got to Montreal my pattern wasn't too different at first. I roomed with three other girls in a two-bedroom apartment off Cote des Neiges. Every night I hated myself for drifting into the habits of female apartment living: the occasional date, but no affairs; the discussion of said dates among one's room mates; the sitting around in slacks and curlers; the tensions over the use of the john; the endless chatter about intimate female problems.

"Of course, we met no French. From a distance I admired some of them. They were better-looking and had more style than the others. But around the office I found

178

some were cry-babies and whiners. Others, though, had great pride which my English friends told me was fairly recent and something they were glad to see, even though they knew they (the English) would suffer for it over time.

"I started out as a typist in an architect's office who did well enough to make the move into Place Bonaventure. When we moved, I asked to be let out of the back room to become the receptionist, even though my French is lousy. My boss, Arthur, agreed but told me to fix up my hair and get a better wardrobe. Even though I did the overflow typing, I took up knitting to occupy my time at the desk. Soon afterwards—God, it's only three months ago—I met André. A client, married, about forty, he was at once the kind of man we most often talked about as our ideal during our hen sessions at the apartment. In that strange Montreal atmosphere—at least in his circle—where one is admired for having a fine mistress, he took me to the best places to show off to his friends who would nod and smile with approval. He got me an apartment on Sherbrooke Street just across from the Seminary—you know, where the towers are. I continued at my job. My boss approved the arrangement with a simple warning not to allow the inevitable breakup to occur in a way that would lose his client. Which was fair enough." She shrugged.

"André had a big house full of kids somewhere near Rosemere, so he had lots of excuses to stay in town during the week. The weekends were lonely but I didn't mind too much. For the first time I was happy. I didn't know or care anything about the crisis. I remember one day when one of our young draftsmen wore one of those blue and white armbands around the office. Everybody made such fun of him that he left and never came back."

She paused and frowned at the memories that came to her. A low-flying jet transport shook the windows. I must have looked up.

"Airlift's getting under way," I said.

"I don't want them to lift me anywhere," Anna said sulkily. "There's no place I want to go."

"Where's André now?" I asked. She brushed back her long hair and clenched her jaw to prevent it from trembling, as if it would set up a chain reaction that would shake her apart.

"Last night," she went on, "was not one of André's nights in town. Anyway, he had been in Quebec City all day on business. About nine, while I was washing my hair and listening to records, Bartok I think, I heard the key in the lock. It was André, looking terrible. He told me to pack a small bag and get out. He'd take me to the airport. It was over that quickly, I thought, and began to raise a fuss to find out why.

" 'It's not that,' he told me. 'Don't you ever watch TV or listen to the radio?'

"He told me about La Fontaine Park, clogged with crowds spilling over into the surrounding streets and the grounds of the Normal School. He said the orators and sound trucks were working them up and there were organized cadres of whiteshirts standing by to lead them. He told me he was getting me out.

"La Fontaine Park is at least two miles from my apartment. I asked him how did he know they would come in our direction and anyway, wouldn't the police stop them? He began to get red and impatient. He said nobody was trying to stop them; there were no police anywhere near La Fontaine Park, nor were barricades being set up. The Westmount police were calling around at doors, getting people to move out while they could. There was no sign of troops, except the guards at the various buildings and they weren't going to stop anything for very long. He switched on the radio and told me I knew enough French to get the drift but the announcers were so excited, I could make out almost nothing. I heard St. Hubert mentioned several times and when they cut in the orators in La Fontaine Park, I picked up the chants of *'au l'ouest, au l'ouest,'* rising in a bellow of thousands over the thin voices of those who egged them on.

"That apartment meant so much to me that I must have stood rooted in disbelief, because the next thing I heard was André's voice, screaming in competition over the radio. And in French. I realized then how frightened he was. In the bedroom I threw some things into a small bag, got dressed and took one last look around the place. Then the lights went out.

" 'Phase Two,' André had said in English.

"I had wondered what he meant, especially when I saw him take a small flashlight out of his pocket. Then I realized that he must have known about it and I remembered that he had been in Quebec City earlier that day. Possibly, he had heard about it there."

Anna's voice began to get lower and the pauses longer. I had difficulty hearing her over the almost constant noise of aircraft.

"We ran down the dark backstairs, bumping against other shadowy figures," she said. "No one seemed to talk and all you could hear was the fast shuffle and clack of feet on the stairs and gaspy breathing. It was weird. We made our way down six floors onto the street. I saw that Sherbrooke was a slow-moving mass of cars from curb to curb, all going west. There were a few eastbound cars and buses stopped and abandoned, while the tide flowed around them to the west. André's car miraculously was still at the curb and hadn't been stolen or pushed up onto the boulevard out of the way, as they were now doing to clear an extra lane.

"At that time," she went on, "Traffic was still moving. We were almost at the Atwater corner, only a matter of a couple of blocks, when everything came to a stop. We could see it ahead, like daylight in all the headlights pointing in the same direction."

She shuddered and asked for a cigarette. I got up and lurched against the desk. I lit her cigarette, looked down at her and debated whether it was time to sit on the cot beside her. Instead, I turned and went back to the office chair. She gave me a grateful look.

"The whiteshirts had set up roadblocks at Atwater, and were searching cars. But they were letting most of them go through. Oddly enough, there wasn't much shooting at that time. Mainly because the men in the cars just seemed to want to get themselves and their families out, I suppose. Anyway, there wasn't any resistance or street-fighting going on; everyone seemed strangely passive about it all. When our turn came at the roadblock and we got to the whiteshirts, André made a dreadful mistake. He spoke to them in French. Only then did I understand that's what they were looking for. They saw at once that I wasn't French and tried to be gallant about it.

" 'It is the *vendus* we are after,' one of them told me. 'The English and the Jews can go and good riddance. But we want the *vendus*.'

"André leaped out of the car and started running past a group of men and women gathered under guard on the sidewalk. Some of the whiteshirts started to run after him, and to my horror, I saw André turn with a small gun in his hand. I heard a couple of pop-pops and one of the whiteshirts fell. The rest of them seemed to swarm in on André like a bunch of white ants. The last I saw of him, he was hanging head down from one of those modern, curved lamp posts that look like a piece of sculpture. They had slit his throat and some of them had given him a push so that he swung back and forth like a pendulum, spraying drops of blood all over the cars lined up on the street. I started screaming, and a big whiteshirt hauled me out of the car and carried me across the intersection through the crowds and the cars to a bus. He dumped me down on a seat in the bus, which seemed to be full of sobbing women and children. The whiteshirt said something in French to the driver and we started off along Sherbrooke in the creeping traffic. It was then I realized fully what they were trying to do. They were forcing us all—the English-speaking ones, I mean—off the island. All they wanted was for us to get off and they had organized one great big push to do it.

"I don't know," she said, "how long it took us to go up and down countless side-streets and roads, with long waits in between. Once, when we stopped, a local mob of some kind rocked the bus and threw bricks through the windows until some whiteshirts with guns pushed them back and let us go on. I didn't care. I had lost André."

"When did you finally get to Dorval?" I asked her.

"I'm not sure. I think it was almost dawn, about five a.m. We must have been about the last bus to make it, because everything seemed to be bogging down."

"And then?"

"When we got off the bus near the terminal building, there was this reception committee of thugs to pick out the best-looking ones. God, I'm glad you did what you did to them." Her voice trailed off. She didn't seem to hear the growing din of aircraft engines in the gathering dusk. "I'm tired," she said, put her head down and was asleep. I covered her up, poured another vodka and resumed my place, feet up on the desk.

I tried to understand. I couldn't relate the French-speaking people I knew to what had happened. None of them could belong to the grim-faced, but strangely frail kids I had seen in the whiteshirts—the Legion that was to be the main force to secure independence. Nor could I see others taking it, either submitting in fear like her André, or if they were English, not fighting back. Every Canadian had a rifle or shotgun in his home. Why weren't they being used? I supposed that the first and most human reaction was to put themselves and their families first. Get out alive if you could, for there was still the rest of the country to take you in. Better to leave now and organize the counterattack later.

Above all, I could not comprehend the forces that had brought it all about. Over a period of years, I recalled, there had been a gradual, almost imperceptible, escalation. Centennial year, back in 1967, instead of being a unifying force for the country, had degenerated into a series of unseemly squabbles, from the top level, concerning such things as de Gaulle's visit, and from the villages, like the places where the separatist elements had stopped Centennial celebrations and no one locally had had the guts to fight back. The separatists tested the climate and found the moderates had no muscle. And even the moderates had to share much of the blame. Expressions like "two nations" became ingrained in everybody's conversation. The moderates said they looked at Confederation in a different way from the rest of Canada and they talked about a different kind of relationship to be worked out within the federal system. But they did not see where this was leading them, for to deny the concept of a nation at all was to lead to the position of the separatists. It could go nowhere else.

The rest of the country remained bewildered and now, with a civil war on their doorstep, were still not quite sure what to do. They had tried to understand as never before in our history. More people had tried to learn French without the remotest hope of ever doing so when they had no chance to use it. There was more exchange of students and learners, no more effective than the "cultural" exchanges between East and West during the sixties. There were commissions, investigations, seminars and conferences, all to no avail. And with this fact facing them at home, our government had launched costly ventures in the Pacific.

Militancy and hard, organizational ability were hardly

their attributes, if one looked at the French-Canadian in business, government or the armed forces. Some had flair and dash; I thought of the crop of bright, young financiers who had emerged in Quebec. Others were erudite, careful executives, professional types or senior civil servants and officers. On balance, though, there was lacking the hardness that so features the successful in the North American environment. Perhaps their sense of gaiety was too strong.

One time Edith and I—where was she now?—had been guests of J.J. Rousseau at the Quebec Winter Carnival after he had become one of the rare French-Canadians to divorce his wife. He had to go through the humiliation of a parliamentary bill and all that. It didn't help his army career very much and he didn't get the kind of help he should have had from his own at senior levels.

We were among several hundred guests who had crammed onto the ferry boat, chartered by some tycoon, to go out into the river and view the bateau races across to Levis. Stacks of ice in the channel did not deter them and soon the entire, whooping, laughing crowd, their women beautifully slap-dash drunk, stood on deck and cheered the icebreaker ploughing to our rescue. As the icebreaker peeled aside the thick crust on the river, our boat lurched in odd directions, crunching into the ice until I thought the hull would crack. The icebreaker almost gave up ever getting us back. Out of curiosity, I went up to the wheelhouse and found the helmsman, the captain and most of the crew doubled up with laughter, each taking a drunken turn at trying to straighten out the boat. They invited me to take the wheel and I was so loaded I almost took the ferry boat right up onto the ice. And we all collapsed with laughter, our breath steaming the glass windows of the wheelhouse. Could these same people carry out a revolution and civil war to its ultimate conclusion? Those days were a millennium away from me now.

I must have dozed, because I fell off the unknown Mr.

Blake's office chair with a crash, an empty glass still clutched in my hand. The room was in darkness, split at intervals by flashes from a searchlight sweeping the buildings and grounds, probably looking for infiltrators or snipers. When I untangled myself on the floor, I saw the pale figure of the girl, Anna, standing over me.

"It must be uncomfortable there," she said, laughing. "There's room on the cot."

She had recovered.

15

With something akin to a laundry list, except that it was labelled "Itinerary", I made my way from office to office in C.F.H.Q. on what would be called the executive floor in a big corporation. It seemed everybody wanted to talk to me. Even though the press reports and the TV footage from Dorval had made me into something of an unofficial celebrity—*Daring Colonel Nabs Rebel General*—I knew the army pros would regard me in a somewhat dimmer light. Besides, there was de Gruchy's bad report, which was brought out strongly in my first interview with the Vice Chief and the Director of Personnel, both Lieutenant-Generals.

On my second day in Ottawa, I had reported in from my quarters in an apartment on the rocky escarpment above Wellington Street, looking across into the windows of the skyscraper known as "Hellyer's Tower", named after the dynamic defence minister of the pre-Coalition days. When the new C.F.H.Q. had been built to replace the wooden firetrap on Cartier Square, where a match could have ended any war effort, it had been found that a Russian spy could sit all day on a balcony across Wellington Street and watch every movement through binoculars. The offending apartment building had been expropriated and was now used as quarters for military personnel.

In freshly-pressed summer greens, I had delivered my written report and sat without expression, I hoped, while the two generals poured quiet invective at me from moustached lips. In closing my ears I had noticed a pair of shears on the desk, and wondered if they were going to cut off my rings and buttons on the spot. Inside an insulating layer of indifference, I listened dimly to their voices and was grateful to the girl, Anna, for rescuing me from the oncoming depressive state that had threatened. After two days at Dorval with no duties, enjoying her company and helping her look after kids and refugees, I began to fight back against the black self pity, mainly through the awareness that others were much worse off than I.

Anna had not been upset when the word finally came from de Gruchy. We had one more great roll in the hay on the rather shaky cot and she went back to comforting kids and parents who were still lined up waiting to get out. A spontaneous, cheering sendoff by the Third R.C.R., organized and conducted by the Acting C.O., Major Young, was recorded by the avid news media people now underfoot everywhere. I had kept silent but they had sniffed out the story from my officers and N.C.O.'s. Some even took pictures of a livid de Gruchy peering down from the control tower. An Air Canada DC-9, crammed with kids, mothers and me, made the mercifully short run to Uplands.

As I half listened to the brass taking me apart, I was thankful that no one at the top had yet latched onto the incident in the V.I.P. washroom, nor the way in which we had carried out our interrogation of the whiteshirts to get our information for the "daring raid". Sooner or later, somebody would get a skinful and talk, and the word "atrocity" would become a two-way street. Still, I supposed, most people would feel it was a small return for what had happened to many thousands of others in Montreal.

The long monotoned duet had stopped. I shook myself mentally and opened the shutters on my eyes. The generals had me fixed in an identical steady gaze. The Vice Chief got up.

"Well, must be off. Good luck, Hlynka." He startled me by shaking hands, and left. There was a humorous twitch at his mouth as he handed me the laundry list.

"These interviews will keep you busy for the next day or two. Let me know if you need anything."

He directed me to the first office, and left me wondering at the quick change in climate. They had stopped far short of the limit. I was not court-martialled, not cashiered, not dismissed—just left mysteriously with a long list of senior officers, apparently burning with impatience to talk to me or to listen to my opinions. I began to wonder what they had in mind. On the nineteenth floor of the tower housing the Defence Staff, I passed through a series of interviews, mostly with brigadier-generals who presided over what used to be known as the "directorates". The Deputy Chief Plans, the Deputy Chief Operations, the Director General of Operational Research, the Director General Land Forces, all had their innings and wanted to know my opinions and recommendations on everything that touched their responsibilities, arising out of my experience with Third R.C.R. When it came to his turn, the Director of General Intelligence touched on a subject I dreaded. He was an air arm brigadier-general, who looked more like a smooth-faced diplomat.

"Our monitors have picked up French broadcasts accusing you by name—badly mispronounced, I should say—of carrying out certain atrocities," the D.G.I. said.

"Like what, sir?"

"Like taking several prisoners up in a bird and kicking them out."

"I know the source of that, sir," I said earnestly. "It's the legionnaire sergeant we turned loose. He had to save his skin with his own people. I guess I shouldn't have kept my word with him."

"Just how did you get him to talk?"

"We did threaten to throw him out, and that made him talk. Obviously, we didn't go through with it."

"Unfortunately, because of everything that's going on, we haven't been able to carry out thorough interrogation of your officers and N.C.O.'s," said the D.G.I. regretfully. "They all seem to have the same story, and it doesn't add up." He riffled through some papers and looked up with a case-dismissed expression on his face.

"Sooner or later," he said, "somebody may have to try and put this country back together again. The fewer incidents of this kind in the future, the better." Again, an almost lecturing tone about the future, as if I still had one. "If this business starts to get much more coverage, we have to put you on TV. But that's up to the Information types."

"I'd rather not, if we can avoid it, sir."

"Oh, I think you'd be quite plausible on TV," said the D.G.I. with heavy irony.

On the third day, I made it to the twentieth floor and was ushered into the presence of the Military Assistant to the Chief of the Defence Staff. A lieutenant colonel, he soon revealed that he had been a close friend of Budgy Tremaine, and that we had met once years back at a party at Budgy's house when we all shared Ottawa postings. I didn't remember him from those days, but recalled his presence during the strategy briefing we had received a short while back in some bygone age. The MA/CDS, as he would appear on the establishment charts, was about my vintage, had once been lean, but was getting a bit soft around the jawline. He didn't have a moustache. His thick, dark hair was neatly shaved in a crewcut so short that his skull looked like a burnt-out forest on a pink landscape. The triangular identification block on his desk said "Lieut. Col. E. F. Mason" and he introduced himself as Ted Mason.

"I remember your wife, I believe," he said, and I wondered how much was from memory and how much from the files. "Most attractive. What was her name again?"

"Edith."

"Yes, that's right. And you have two boys? I trust they are all well?"

"I don't know." I told him that they were missing.

"I'm sorry," he said. "Susan is missing too, you know."

"Budgy's widow? She stayed in Montreal?"

"Afraid so. It's a mess all over. There are a lot of missing relatives and dependents. That's not much consolation, is it?"

"No."

"All we can do is get the fighting over with as quickly as possible. That's the only way things will get sorted out."

I decided to broach the subject.

"Actually, I had hoped maybe this . . . layoff would give me a day or two to go look for my family. They're not in Montreal, as far as I know. They're in a summer place up near Labelle."

The curtain came down.

"Not likely, I'm afraid," he said. "The main thing is to bring this rebellion to a quick conclusion. After that, we can all go our separate ways." His face was hard and set. "Sorry," he added, not showing it. He looked away for a moment, got up and pulled down a map of Montreal on the wall. He picked up some aerial recce photos and threw them at me.

"We have a plan from the officer commanding Montreal sector," he said, meaning de Gruchy and his staff. "They think we should establish control of the roads— the expressways. The city would then be divided up into watertight compartments. But look at the roads. They're still packed with worthless scrap iron."

"That's right." I didn't have to see the photos.

"Even in the heyday of the evacuation theories of Civil Defence, I don't think anyone fully comprehended what would happen. The refugee in the affluent society takes to his car. No North American city has ever been through this before." He stopped musing. "Anyway, it's my feeling that it'll take too long to clear the roads."

"There doesn't seem to be much choice. The roads are the only way to slice up the island. I suppose the alternative has been studied . . ."

"Several have," Mason snapped defensively. "What one do you mean?"

"Use helicopters and airborne to get control of the bridges. Bring in some light naval craft and blockade the island. Start starving them out. At the same time, go ahead with clearing the roads but keep them penned up on the island."

Mason frowned and paced a bit.

"You know the problem. We're too thin on the ground until we can get some forces back from overseas. God knows how long that will take if the government wants to go on trying to downplay the rebellion with our allies. What I'm afraid of, is getting our limited forces tied up in street-fighting in Montreal. What do you think of the capacity of the irregulars to fight?"

"Might as well face it. Once we start off the main roads into the narrow streets, we'll be in for a long haul." I grinned. "Two things Montreal has got is lots of bottles and gasoline to put in them. They'd shower molotov cocktails from every window. The trouble is, the longer we put it off, the better armed they'll be. I mentioned the imported weapons in my report."

"Now you're coming to the point," said Mason. "We've got to move quickly before they really start receiving military aid. Even with our blockade, the stuff is still getting through; the coastline is just too vast to prevent it. The centre of government is at Quebec City. Some of us feel that it must be our prime objective and the hell with Montreal. If we take Quebec City we've hit their core and split them in two."

"It makes sense if that's what the government wants to do."

"If they don't there'll be a new government. Public opinion now won't let them waffle." I wondered if he meant that the military would make sure that "public opinion" was enforced. Mason pulled down another map, this time of Quebec City and district.

"In plain military terms," he said, "The Provisional Government is weak—for the time being. All they have is a series of militia units organized into loose assault forces, one of which knocked out St. Hubert and is still in the Montreal area somewhere. Our information is that they're hauling in everybody they can with military experience. A bunch of cadets from the Collège Militaire at St. Jean have gone to Valcartier to be subalterns. So they're moving."

"What about their weapons?"

"No air force, except for a couple of transports they snitched. They didn't get any jets at Bagotville or St. Hubert. So they are vulnerable on that score and I don't see any way for the Chinese or Cubans to deliver many aircraft to them."

"They seem to have lots of whiteshirts around."

"Yes. Recruiting is going on as fast as they can produce armbands and collect rifles. There are already twelve so-called 'brigades' of from two to ten thousand men each, all over the country." He laughed. "They've named the brigades after the martyrs of 1839—the men who were executed following the so-called Second Rebellion in Lower Canada. There's the Joseph-Narcisse Cardinal Brigade, the Chevalier de Lorimer Brigade, the Joseph Duquette Brigade and so on."

I wasn't too interested in his knowledge of history, and rubbed restlessly in my chair.

"No, their fighting capacity isn't much at this stage, except to keep the towns and cities under the thumb of the Provisional Government and the Party. Everybody seems to be scared of them. If we wait too long they might become a serious fighting force." He stopped. "You look annoyed."

"I am," I said and got up to pace the room. "For years we've preached the gospel of mobility. Mobility and more mobility! We have Mobile Command here and Mobile Force in Europe and Mobile Brigade in Thailand and Mobile Reserve at home. Where the hell's all this mobility now? We're acting as if this is some kind of goddam Riel Rebellion or something. Why the hell can't we flatten them in about ten days?"

It was Mason's turn to flop down in his chair while he watched me pace.

"Not that easy," he sighed at last. "There're a lot of complications. You know about some of them. There are others you probably haven't heard about." He wrinkled his forehead. "We're having a little internal struggle; as it were: discussion; it's about the tactics and strategy of how to use what we've got available."

I whirled around after studying on the wall a rather appropriate etching of Batoche. In the watercoloured panorama, a lot of little wooden figures were scattered over a parklike setting. Neat balloons of smoke came from their rifles.

"Why does everybody want to talk to me?" I demanded. "I don't see where anything I have to offer is . . ."

"We have to improvise and do it fast," said Mason. He got up and looked out the window at the Gatineau hills in their blue haze. "Some of us have been looking at your record and comparing it to one or two other people we could pull back from overseas. You've done well so far in a situation that requires speed and imagination. Third R.C.R. was whipped into shape in record time and they did well. But your escapades leave something . . ." He stopped and beckoned to me to come to the window. "For God's sake, look! What the hell?"

Even in our sealed high tower we could hear the muted popping of small arms fire and the faint rip of machine guns. A deafening metallic bong showered us in glass from the heavy-paned window. A hailstorm of masonry chunks plunged past the window, some bouncing into the room. We threw ourselves face down on each side of the window and glass ripped our clothing, but left us intact except for some painful, bleeding scratches. I was the first up and looked far down at the miniature green figures running through the flimsy barbed-wire barricades. Through the gaping window I could clearly hear the next familiar thud of a Carl Gustaf launcher.

"Down!" I said to Mason as he was moving to the window. "They've got launchers."

"It's a raid?" he asked into the carpet.

"Yeah, and it's not whiteshirts," I told him. "They must be militia and they're trying to get some rockets into the top floors. We'd better get out of here."

He looked across the floor at me, his face streaked with small bleeding cuts.

"The Chief is away," he murmured. "Thank God."

Another rocket struck the roof above us bringing down plaster and the light fixture on the ceiling. From the open window small arms fire echoed louder and I heard the muffled crack of grenades. Mason reached up to the desk, tried the phone and dropped it.

"Dead," he said. "They must've got the communications centre."

"Any weapons around here?" I asked. My heart sank as he slowly shook his head.

"Not even a pistol," he said. "Everything's in the stores in the basement." Mason got up and slapped at the dust on his uniform. "Let's do what we can."

I followed him out into the smoke-filled corridor where there was a yammer of voices from shadows that ran back and forth in the murk. Some women employees were gasping in high-pitched hysteria.

"The stairs," said Mason.

We pushed past the blundering forms and a group of civilians with white handkerchieves clasped to their faces. The civilians were standing in a clump while one of them vainly pushed elevator buttons. At the end of the corridor we looked down the fire stairs at the smoke billowing up at us. A group of senior officers, identified by their shoulder boards, stood uncertainly.

"What'll we do, throw inkbottles?" a brigadier-general asked.

"Who's got an inkbottle?" said another. "All I've got is a ballpoint pen."

They looked around anxiously at Mason. Even though he was their junior in rank, he was from the Chief's office.

"Old Man's away, anyway," Mason told them. "All phones out?"

They nodded.

"Anybody got weapons?"

They exchanged glances and shook their heads.

"It'll be some catch if they get up to this floor," said Mason. "All the top people in the Defence Staff." He looked over his shoulder and thought. "The only way they can get up here is on these stairs. Grab every piece of furniture you can, and block the stairs—heavy desks, everything. Clear out every office. You'll just have to take a chance on the place burning down, but it's supposed to be fireproof."

"The smoke's already bad, Ted," complained a watery-eyed brigadier-general.

"Your job, sir, is to avoid capture even if you roast alive," snarled Mason. "Come on, Hlynka, let's go down and see what we can do."

With handkerchiefs tied over our noses, we made our way down the stairs, holding onto the railing. Some officers and civilians were gasping for air at the windows. Further

196

down, the smoke began to thin out. Instead, we smelt the acrid stench of explosives. Some shouting began to echo up the stairwell. On the seventeenth floor we paused as a machine carbine ripped not too far below us. Mason signalled to try the floor. We ran along a corridor that had open doors and employees crouched under the desks in the offices.

"Anybody here got a gun?" yelled Mason.

There was a rumble of "no sirs". We went back to the stairs and clattered down to the next floor to a large room, a secretarial pool of some kind, where there were terrified women cowering under desks.

"Stay calm and sell your honour dearly!" shouted Mason in a slapdash attempt to keep up morale.

"After all those stairs?" I muttered.

"You don't know the French," said Mason.

The exchange struck me as ludicrous and I began to laugh behind my handkerchief. Anyway, I was beginning to wonder what we were going to do when we did meet up with the raiders and it struck me that Ted Mason himself would make a fair catch or target for assassination. But he was off down the next flight of stairs before I could hold him back. At the fourteenth floor, with sounds of shooting and grenade blasts much closer, we ran into two M.P.'s pelting down the corridor towards us, their pistols out of white, blancoed holsters. We pushed down our handkerchiefs and yelled our identification.

"Give us your sidearms," said Mason. "We've got to go below."

"You can't do very much, sir. It's bloody murder down there," said an M.P., a pug-nosed lance-jack.

"They're going floor by floor and tossing grenades into every room," said the other, his eyes shifting.

"What are you two doing here?" demanded Mason.

"Tryin' to find some help and weapons," said one of the M.P.'s.

"We got something, sir," said the other, waving for us

to follow. The floor belonged to Operational Research and in a closet one of the M.P.'s had found a metal box of training grenades. These have a plastic cover, a ribbon instead of a cotter pin, and one ballbearing that the explosion might bounce off walls in a confined space.

"Whoever kept these around should be put on charge," said Mason. "But bless him now." We hauled the metal case to the stairwell.

"There are senior officers upstairs. They'd be a prize catch for the raiding party," Mason told the M.P.'s. "Go up with them and hold out till your last grenade is gone. Now, give us your sidearms."

The M.P.'s studied us, debated silently for a few interminable seconds, and handed over their Browning automatics with extra clips. We left them, both knowing they couldn't hold out long against launchers. Still, heaving plastic grenades down a narrow stairwell might slow up the attackers if they were beginning to lose steam from running up so many steps. We began to meet civilians, officers and soldiers panting upwards away from the noise and smoke below.

"Gather on this floor and stay here," Mason told them. "On the floors above there are men with orders to throw grenades if anyone comes near them."

A frightened, stammering grey-haired major, who was probably regretting he had opted for an extension of service, offered to stand on the stairway to direct traffic onto that floor. I saw that it was the twelfth. We were getting close to a maelstrom of explosions, voices tearing out their vocal cords and the blast of FN's in small spaces. The Browning felt small and insignificant in my slippery hand. I wasn't sure what we were supposed to be doing but shared Mason's need to do something, just for the sake of it. The stairs were empty now, except for two huddled figures in green uniforms groaning in pain. We stepped over them, now moving more carefully.

"If we lose touch," said Mason, "do what you can to

organize some resistance. Get some messages out. Tell them to put an airstrike all around us."

"Right," I nodded.

On opposite sides of the stairwell we made our way down to another landing. Where it angled into a reverse flight of steps, we paused, then continued to the next floor. One of those odd silences that often occur in the middle of an action caused us to stop. For a brief moment the explosions stopped and only a low wail of voices came upward. An FN on the floor we were now approaching blasted three rounds in rapid succession. Someone along the hall screamed, choked and had no more to say. Hobnailed boots clashed on the floor and two grimy figures in green field uniforms and brown, wool stocking caps, pushed open the swinging doors and stopped to get their breath. Each man cradled an FN like a hunting rifle. I saw the blue and white armbands against green denim. The two men were close to us in an unguarded lapse not expecting to run into anyone armed. Almost like conducting an execution, we fired fast at close range. Even with pistols, we got each in the head.

"That feels better," I said, as I picked up an FN and bandolier.

"Gives you that secure feeling, doesn't it?" grinned Mason.

Along the corridor on that floor we found what the two raiders had been shooting at. A grey-haired private with crew cut and three good conduct stripes on his sleeve lay dead in an office doorway. In his hand he held an indoor range model of the old Lee Enfield, the kind that had been rebored as a single shot .22. Out of curiosity, I pulled the bolt open. There was no round in the breech.

Below us the muffled reports of shooting began again. As we came out onto the stairwell, a brown woollen cap bobbed up and yelled something in French to those behind him. Before he could step back, I squeezed off a burst from the FN on automatic, holding it tightly against

199

the hip. It jumped and a cascade of empty brass casings bounced musically on the stairs. I got him and he fell back. Another woolcap, who tried to run up with a 36 grenade, was hit by Mason and collapsed on the stairs. His grenade rolled off the edge of the step down into the stairwell, its toffee-square steel cover bouncing noisily. The grenade blew, and some men coming up from below suddenly stopped shouting to each other. The chink and crack of flying splinters subsided. We picked ourselves up from the landing, nodded to each other and started down again. The stairwell reeked with fumes and burnt flesh.

At the next landing we moved slowly towards another reversed flight of stairs. Five bodies were scattered along them in limp disarray, just rags of scorched cloth. We picked our way around them, being careful not to lose our footing on the slippery steps. In the curls of blue smoke a figure below us lurched out from a corridor and stood firmly in the middle of the landing. He was holding an FN that had a bulge on the end of an extended muzzle. I heard the crack of the launching cartridge and glanced at Mason to see if he knew what to do.

"Run down!" I shouted, pointing.

The grenade arched high over our heads as we jumped, half fell in painfully slow seconds to get away from it. Above and behind us I heard the grenade clang against something and start bouncing back down the stairs. Mason, with longer legs and faster reflexes, had bounded into the startled militiaman with the grenade adapter, bowled him over and was gone from sight. The concussion hit me. I must have dived, or possibly was thrown, upwards and went through the glass doors on the next landing like a torpedo. The FN spun somewhere out of reach. A heavy hand squeezed at the back of my skull, making a distorted world of shimmering forms and odd bursts of light. It wasn't entirely unpleasant. After what seemed a week, I found my face pressed against the cold tile floor staring transfixed at a waving reflection of myself in a pool of blood. I wondered idly if it was my own.

I sensed that one of my arms was curving nearby and stretched every foolish nerve to make it move. I must have grunted or groaned. A pair of brown issue boots came into view, seemingly with a life of their own. Watching me. I tried to say something to the boots.

Life was not so tenuous that I couldn't recognize the cold chill of a gun muzzle against the back of my neck. There wasn't much to be thankful for, except that a nervous system already half dead left no emotion, but an odd euphoria of the kind one gets on the night before a holiday starts, swept over me.

A voice, distant and foreign, said something to the gun barrel, which was withdrawn. A boot caught me under the armpit, bringing alive dormant muscles and nerves into a unified, aching howl. I was lifted over onto my back and tried to achieve vision. Green forms, white blurs of armbands, faces. A face.

"J.J.," I tried to say. So slight was the grasp of reality that I might have been delirious. But if I was able enough to think that I was off my rocker, then it must mean I couldn't really be gone. Whatever it was, spirit, guts or survival, I strained to pull together wits, impulses, sanity into a narrow tunnel. Through that tunnel—a reverse telescope—I saw clearly the well-known face, the moustache, the eyes. Together they had a healthy, three-dimensional realism. His features were sweaty and streaked; he wore no headgear and the eyes blinked, either in compassion or indecision or just surprise. I didn't know.

"J.J., you son of a bitch," I said. I think I said it. Certainly I thought it before passing out.

16

The old air force station at Rockcliffe, now Materiel Command, is on one of a series of broad, rocky steps that lead from the ridge of the old Montreal Road down to the Ottawa River. A steep road cuts through the heavily treed slope, with a couple of large ranch-style houses on either side, and the station begins at the bottom. At the entrance there is a small guardhouse and a pole barrier that has no practical purpose, for the station is military in name only.

In the mornings a stream of civilians and servicemen arrive in their cars to make their way slowly along winding roads, cluttered with children on their way to school from the P.M.Q.'s. It is a little suburbia with washing on the line and, during the day, housewives in shorts decorate the backyards and wheel around their pre-school tax exemptions. It is a factory town, dominated by the massive acreages and buildings of the Command; a shift town governed by time clocks and bells. It is also a museum. A yellow line on the road takes one to the old hangars filled with full-sized collectors' items of our aerial history: Spitfires, Camels, Moths, Cornells, and CF-100's. The airstrip itself is seldom used any more and ancient guns of past wars look helplessly over the field. Rockcliffe is many things, but military it is not.

For this I was thankful. From my hospital window I

watched the daily routine in its casual, slow-paced normality. It was a reassuring view confirming one's sanity when a throbbing head and dizziness might cause doubts. Why I drew the frame, clapboard hospital, I never knew. Those of us who were casualties of the now famous "Ottawa Raid" had been eventually shunted off to any available bed in the Ottawa area—in accordance with our rank, of course. As one of field rank, I rated a private room, which provided an opportunity for contemplation and gathering raw, jarred nerves together for the next round. That there would be a next round—and an escalated one—was certain.

Coming out of my drug-induced stupor, the first thing I had heard was the rip of jets going north, low across the Ottawa River. They were CF-5's, and sometimes during the day I could hear hollow explosions echoing in the hills. At night the helicopters went over sputtering like Model T's in the dark. From my window I sometimes saw the blue searchlight beams probing downward on the other side of the river. Day and night they were hitting anything that moved.

Those first days were fuzzy and painful. The doctor was too busy to tell me anything much, but a nurse, with short, streaked hair, golden-brown pancake makeup and an air of assuming that she'd be in bed with me when the time came, sat down and told me all about it. Possible mild concussion from a crack on the head, face lacerations from glass cuts, one of the cheeks requiring stitches, and a cluster of nasty little grenade fragments in the back of the thigh and calf of my left leg. She said I would live. Depending on their findings with regard to my headbone, I should soon be up and around. They were anxious to start physical therapy on the legs. Once the cotton wool inside my head and flashes of nausea occurred less frequently, I began to get lonely, but they kept the door closed and there were no visitors. The nurse told me they had orders not to let the casualties talk to each other or outsiders until security had a chance to interview everyone. They took their time in coming. In the meantime we weren't allowed any newspapers, radio or TV. When my head was clear, I read some Penguin spy stories.

Instead of a D.G.I. man, my first visitor was Ted Mason. Aside from a big bandaid on his forehead and an Elastoplast bandage around his left hand he was all right. His normally intense face was even tighter with fatigue, the skin drawn tightly over the high cheekbones. Strain had sucked away all flesh colour from his face, and his eyes were deep in big, shadowy craters. He was dog-tired from pulling the pieces back together again, and I wondered why he had taken the time to come and see me. I asked him.

"After all we've been through, I wanted to see how you were," he said sarcastically.

I told him he could have found that out on the phone.

"I like to think that you and I helped to save the day," he said. He outlined how he had somehow made his way to the basement of C.F.H.Q. and slipped out of the building to a confectionery store on Wellington street, of all things, from where he had called down an airstrike.

"Did the raiding party get to the top floor?"

He sighed. "No. We were lucky. They made one try after we had slowed them up, but the M.P.'s with their grenades kept them back until I got the airstrike laid on. They got the hell out when that started." He said the airstrike had been pretty indiscriminate and there had been casualties on both sides. I told him about listening to all the aerial activity going north.

"That assault group is finished as a fighting unit," Mason said. "Some of them will infiltrate back to Montreal and Quebec, but it'll be tough. We're hitting anything that moves on the roads. We sent in a company of Guards out of Petawawa in birds and they caught the rearguard at Kazabazua. Nasty little fight, I'm told. We've got about twenty-five prisoners."

"Okay. How'd they do it?"

"Cars."

"You mean, automobiles?"

"Right. That's why they rendezvoused at the G.M. plant in St. Therese. It was quite well planned," he said grudgingly. I grinned. All the rubes had done was knock out C.F.H.Q.

"All right, it was well planned," admitted Mason without grace. "Local whiteshirts had closed up the plant at St. Therese, put complete security around it. The group that hit us is the same bunch that took St. Hubert. They left St. Hubert, went to St. Therese where they got some brand-new cars off the lot. They put five men each and their equipment into separate cars. They wore civilian jackets and hats. There was a complicated route plan and timing schedule, using different roads to get to Hull. Most of them went up through St. Adele and down Route 8, all travelling individually."

"Not in convoy?"

"No, no. Singly or in pairs, at different times of the day and night. How'd you like to plan that one—about fifteen cars altogether plus a tank truck for emergencies, travelling all that distance without being detected and then regrouping in Hull?"

"It's offbeat," I agreed. "I don't see how they avoided being seen by someone. It's mostly English up the Gatineau."

"No one was expecting it. They didn't stop anywhere for gas, and had cold rations with them. The Q.P.P. were in on the deal, and arranged the whole infiltration plan through Hull and the assembly area at the Chaudière Bridge."

"You didn't grab a guy named J. J. Rousseau, did you?" I asked bitterly.

Mason stared at me. "No, but we know who he is. He headed up the whole effort and the French prisoners refer to themselves as being in 'Assault Group Rousseau'. Why?"

"He used to be my adjutant in South Africa," I muttered. We pondered the perfidy of man. "How's the Chief?" I asked.

"Still flying six feet off the ground. We've set up in Uplands. Lost a lot of good staff people."

We lit up cigarettes again and he squinted at me through the smoke.

"The M.O. says you're coming along fine," he said at last.

"So what?"

"Do what you can to speed things up," said Ted Mason. "We want to talk to you soonest." He went to the door and his driver came in with a stack of newspapers and a small, black transistor radio.

"D.G.I. will be in for their report," he said at the door. "We'll be in touch."

"Wait a minute," I said. "How did the raiding party ever expect to get back?"

"I don't think they did," said Mason. "What price glory?"

"Christ," I murmured.

I started to leaf through the papers, some of them four days old. The news stories of the action itself were sketchy enough to show signs of censorship and a clampdown on any interviews. There were a lot of photos taken at a distance with telephoto lens. Closeup shots were obviously handouts from the Department, showing nurses ministering to those wounded in the "savage attack". There were no pictures of bodies; I supposed they had been kept or taken inside and moved out in closed vehicles. Most of the news stories were paraphrased official despatches which didn't add much to my knowledge. There were photos of some prisoners.

A noon edition of that day's paper—it was a Thursday —was somehow on the bottom of the pile. Big square headlines told of the resignation of the prime minister, but not the government. An announcement of his successor was expected almost immediately. I thought about the youngish, bland man who had been so calm on TV. It was tough heading up a Coalition. The censorship didn't seem to apply to the editorial pages. I turned to one in an Ottawa paper to catch some deep thinking and flipped on the transistor radio to hear more about the P.M. The station I got had a woman telling housewives how to budget in view of rising prices brought about by the dislocation of traffic in the Seaway and rail and road traffic through Quebec.

"Many imported items from the Caribbean and overseas will have to be diverted to New England ports," she was saying, "and we may not see maple syrup for a long time."

"Nor pea soup," I said.

"And there may be a shortage of certain canned items, such as pea soup," she went on. I turned to the C.B.C. A woman with a bass voice was reading David Copperfield to shut-ins. Another station was engrossed with the current jangle of tunes labelled as "Number Ten", "Number 23" and so on. The final station I could reach had a commentator rasping in gravelly whisky tones the thesis that tactical nuclear weapons should be dropped on Montreal and Quebec. I switched off the set and turned to the vast expanse of ten-point print on the editorial page.

The full-page editorial began in that peculiar wave of sportsmanship that occasionally inspires editorial writers when the object of their attack has disappeared from the scene. They congratulated the ex-prime minister for having the courage and sense to resign, and pointed out that, while they hadn't always agreed with him—an understatement—they wished him well. I skipped several passages along this line and found some interesting thoughts further along.

"The daring raid on Ottawa, following so soon on the

planned outbreaks in Montreal, raises some intriguing questions. Just what are the Rebels" (the writer would give them a capital "R", but no Provisional Government stuff) "trying to accomplish? What message is the rest of Canada, the United States and the world, supposed to get from these apparently senseless acts of violence?

"Let us examine first what they didn't do. In Montreal, for example, there were many horrifying instances of atrocities and personal violence, but it is evident there was no wholesale massacre of defenceless civilians. This would have been easy to do. Nothing could have stopped them, least of all our own splay-footed armed forces. On balance, the Rebels acted with restraint. In the near future, there undoubtedly will be bloodshed and fighting in Montreal, assuming, that is, that our armed forces, who occupy the western portion of the island, ever get around to organizing some kind of counterattack. Armed men on both sides will perish. But the question remains, why did the Rebels act in the way that they did?

"Similarly, in the Ottawa raid," went on the editorial writer, "There were many things they didn't do. With great daring and ingenuity, and little hope of ever getting back to their home base, an assault group of French-speaking militia carried out a raid that for all practical purposes knocked out Canadian Forces Headquarters, including many key staff personnel, the entire elaborate communications system and countless records and files and left the headquarters, designed for more genteel days, unfit for habitation. However, they did not attack the Parliament Buildings, nor any other government building; nor did they attempt to kidnap or assassinate any member of the government, M.P. or civil servant. They weren't after funds, for they ignored the Mint, the Bank of Canada and the banknote manufacturing plants in the west end. They did nothing to encourage the French-speaking population of Ottawa to revolt, and as far as is known, left no pamphlets. In very efficient fashion, they carried out their raid and then vanished.

"If one studies other recent events, there seems to be a relationship. Where, to name one, did the rebels block the Seaway? They sank ships at the Beauharnois locks. Now-where else. There have been no raids, no sabotage, no agitation at any other point in Canada. What are they trying to tell us?

"To us, the answer seems relatively simple. They are trying to establish a recognized border, and by displays of military strength and mass expulsions, to demonstrate to Canada and the United States that they are physically capable of maintaining their border. It should be obvious to the new prime minister that if the Rebels continue to make points in this fashion, they will have convinced everyone that they are a *de facto*, viable nation. Then what do we do?"

Indeed, I thought, what do we do? Invade New England to find an outlet to the Atlantic? My reflections were cut short by the arrival of the nurse with the tan pancake complexion. She had changed her role to that of a brisk harridan, ordering me out for a stepped up schedule of leg exercises and massage. Mason must have spoken to her.

"We'll have you out of here in no time," she said cheerfully.

That was what I was afraid of.

The next day an Intelligence man in civvies, who introduced himself curtly by his last name only, came in with a clipboard and a ballpoint pen. I suspected maybe they were short of men and had sent an N.C.O. or junior officer in civvies so as not to embarrass either party. This was confirmed when he called me "sir" throughout the interview.

After all this activity, a lonely weekend followed. We were still not allowed to fraternize with our fellow patients, and except for some grunting conversations with other victims in the exercise room, had no one to talk to. I listened to a cold rain drumming against the windows and memorized from the radio the top thirty-five tunes on the hit parade. Sometimes I wiped the condensation from the window and tried to look across the river. It would be cold out there for the surviving raiders on the run, but at least the planes would be grounded. I thought of those planes and their targets. Would they shoot up houses—or cottages along a lake? And what of the raiders themselves, streaming through the tracks in the bush heading eastward? Would Edith find rough, unshaven men appearing like Indians at the cottage, and growling demands for food? What would they do when she answered in English or at least, in French with a bad English accent? Or, was she no longer there?

I paced the room and kicked at the bed.

On Monday the quasi-military routine of the Rockcliffe station began at full strength again, the civilian employees apparently having had the weekend off as if there were no emergency of any kind. The rain had gone, but when I opened the window, a cold, sixty-degree wind blasted into the room. At noon a private arrived with my clothing from the apartment I had briefly occupied on Wellington Street. Not much longer now.

Around four-thirty in the afternoon, I was dozing on the bed when the pancake nurse opened the door.

"They want you for a conference. We've agreed to let you go for a couple of hours," she said.

"Fine," I said, glad to get out of the place even for a short break.

I was easing gingerly into unfamiliar clothing when I caught a glimpse of a large man in summer greens standing in the doorway. I finished getting into my trousers, thankful that much of the stiffness in my legs had eased, and did a double take. The man in the doorway was grinning.

"What in God's name . . ." I said.

He put a big finger to his lips and in so doing winced from a stiff shoulder.

"Been thinking about you," he said quietly. "Thought maybe you'd like to take an aeroplane ride. Have a look around a lake?"

I stopped buttoning my shirt and laughed.

"I'll be damned," I told Ab Tremblay.

17

East of the Chaudière Falls, where the Ottawa is pinched together as if the E. B. Eddy company had done it on purpose, the river quickly broadens out again, absorbs the big log booms coming down the Gatineau, and rolls on containing gunk and effluvia from the towns and industry on its banks. On the north shore the land is low, swampy and slummy in comparison to the heights on the south bank that smirk with the residence of the British High Commissioner, the National Research Council, the French Embassy and the Prime Minister's residence. Beyond is Rockcliffe Park itself, and just below the hill leading down from the park is a flat tableland where there is some kind of a club with tennis courts, boats and a dock where private floatplanes are tied up. This was where Ab Tremblay drove me in a Ford sedan, black enough to look official. Nobody seemed to notice that it didn't have official khaki and white number plates.

"Just got to thinking, after all that time lying around," Ab told me. "Thought you must be going out of your skull trying to do a job and worrying about them."

"I got you into a mess," I said. "I owe you a lot, among numerous other things, my life."

"I wouldn't do it if I didn't want to," Ab said simply. He had lost weight and his skin was saggy with a greyish tinge slow to go away. He told me that no bones had been broken in his shoulder, but that he had it taped up like a mummy. "When I heard your name on TV," he went on, "And some of the crazy things you were doing, I made up my mind. I decided I'd haul you out on a second try the first chance I got, before you developed into a raving S.S. type or something."

"It wasn't quite that bad," I said. "How'd you find me?"

"From the casualty lists in the Ottawa papers," he said. "I dusted off my old uniform and made a couple of phone calls. They aren't very sharp, yet."

"And Marie?"

"Told her the only way I could get to see you was in uniform. She wasn't too impressed."

We came to the floatplane dock. A short distance away, the hillside was a yellow splash of flowers, but it was too late for tulips and I didn't know what they were. An equally brilliant yellow Cessna swung muted and lazy at the dock. Suspiciously new-looking paint said it belonged to "Department of Lands and Forests, Ontario, Province of Opportunity".

"You didn't . . ."

"Oh, no," said Ab. "We just painted it. You have to be official to get anywhere these days."

A man, who had been pacing around on the dock as if he wished he had some tires to kick, came towards us. He wore faded blue jeans, a leather jacket and had a shock of black hair, long sideburns and a neatly trimmed goatee. All he needed was a big sign on his back with "Angels" or some such name. A smaller crest was sewn on the front of his jacket and I made the connection. It had the name "Marc's Lodge, Hunting and Fishing" in a faded circle of letters.

"This is Marc Bedard," said Ab. "It's his plane. He flew down and I drove. Make out all right?"

"Got buzzed a couple times," said Marc, shaking hands with me. "The yellow paint was a good idea." They spoke in English which in itself was a sort of commentary as to why we had a rebellion in the first place.

"Marc's an old friend," explained Ab. "He likes this kind of thing."

I wasn't too sure. Marc kept darting glances in all directions.

"Let's go," he said. As he turned away from us, pulled the plane over and got in, Ab answered what must have been the question on my face.

"He owes me a favour," he said.

"Must be some favour," I muttered.

While pulling myself up into the cabin, I looked down and saw a red canoe complete with outboard strapped to a pontoon. The man must know the bush, I thought. While Marc warmed up the engine and taxied slowly out into the river, Ab and I bent over some 1:50,000 Ordnance maps he had taped together in a long strip, covering the last few miles of our journey.

"Isn't this it? Ab asked, jabbing at a large, jagged blue patch among a cluster of others on the pale, green paper.

"Yes," I said. "Your landmark is the microwave tower on the hill about five miles to the south. Line up with the tower and you're over the lake."

"Where should we touch down?"

"On the west side, I think. It's almost unpopulated. High cliffs and deep water. There's an inlet where we could put the plane and take the canoe across to the cottage."

"Is the lake rough?"

"Not particularly. Normally, we wouldn't have any trouble. But you and I are a bit crocked to take a canoe that far," I grinned.

"That's what the outboard's for," said Ab. "You think you can find the cottage?"

"Oh, sure, once we're on the lake," I said. "But shouldn't we wait for dusk?"

"Marc is nervous about taking off in the dark."

The pilot, overhearing us, nodded unhappily. We lapsed into silence as the engine revved up and we slapped the water in the takeoff. Marc took the plane in a wide arc to the southwest. I raised eyebrows at Ab.

"We're going to clear with Uplands," he shouted with a wink.

I watched in fascination as our freshly-painted yellow Cessna wobbled around the tower at Uplands and Marc cleared himself as a Forestry plane. He told them we were looking for another Forestry plane believed to be down near Mont Tremblant and vicinity.

"Tell those madmen in the jets about us," he said to the tower.

The tower didn't think the trip was a good idea and they were probably wondering what an Ontario plane was doing on the Quebec side of the river.

"Call Queen's Park if you want," said Marc truculently.

Reluctantly, the tower gave clearance, having decided they couldn't very well ask us to land and file a flight plan when we had only pontoons. They told Marc they would give him clearance only for six hours, after which he had to answer to the jets or check in again. Following the exchange with authority, we curved away across the city again, our backs now to the sun. It was five thirty, and we had a good look at the normalcy of the traffic below. The city was a mass of fluffy, green trees, and occasionally the sun flashed on the metal roof of a church. We followed the river for a while before moving north. A CF-5, just to see for himself, slipped past, cut in his burners and went straight up. We heaved on light updrafts. Beyond the Ottawa, the narrow fingers of farmland soon were swallowed in the rock, bush and water of the Shield country. Only strips and pockets of land showed through the sea of grey granite and the dark green or blue masses of timber.

"Our forest fire," I asked. "How far did it go?"

"Not too far. Rains put it out a couple of days later," shouted Ab. "The local radio has been screaming sabotage."

"They're right."

I watched Ab peel off his tight-fitting uniform and put on a rough, red wool plaid jacket. He pointed to another one on the floor and made signs. I began to feel a bit fuzzy, as if I had dropped into a private little air pocket of my own. I nodded loosely, and stared out of the window. There were some pressures behind my eyes, distorting the focus like heat waves rising from the ground. My eyes closed.

The spring I had met Edith in Kingston had ended a bloody winter for me in my last year at R.M.C. My first years had been all right, running about fifth in class backed up by favourable reports from summer stints at Petawawa and Currie Barracks. In that last year the privileges of being in senior year had served to bring out an accumulating sense of resentment at all the guff we had to put up with. There was no doubt that the physical outdoor life of the army made it the home I would choose, that is, if I could ever reconcile myself to the garbage and gaiters of ceremonials, funny-looking dress uniforms and the phony mannerisms of mess life. This problem of adjustment wavered on a fine line.

There was, to begin with, an outburst of violent horseplay, not entirely of my own doing, but aided and abetted by a carton of thunderflashes I had brought back from the P.P.C.L.I. that summer. I kept them in my locker until we had built up a good simmering feud with those in the barrack room one floor down. One cold November night we raided them, running along the broad aisle and heaving the sputtering thunderflashes onto their beds. Thunderflashes are long tubes of powder, something like a roman candle, designed to make a realistic bang for training purposes. Some of them even have a built-in whistle supposedly like a shell in flight. They are set off by striking a primer like an emery board. Groans, shouts and the smell of scorched blankets followed our attack and, come to think of it, we were lucky there was no fire or serious injury. The counterattack was not long in coming. Armed with brooms and other sundry weapons such as mops, squeegees and web belts, a howling mob backed us up the stairs and into our own dormitory. A couple of cadets with flailing brooms backed me into a corner.

"Hlynka, you hunky, you started this!" one of them shouted.

I never thought twice about using the bayonet. At that time we had the short spike type used on the Lee-Enfield. I always kept mine sharp, oiled and in reserve on the hip. With a quick and instinctive flick, having learned how to handle every kind of knife from my Finnish friend in the Coal Branch, I sent the bayonet flashing at him—I think his name was Reilly. Only by a startled jerk of his head, luckily the right way, did he save his life. As it was the heavy, square butt-end of the bayonet grazed his jaw line and opened up a dribble of blood. The bayonet shivered in the antique, dark woodwork behind him. The fight stopped in a gasping, hushed silence.

Nobody talked and no expulsion followed, although there was no doubt the word got around. I had high marks and they knew I wanted to make an army career, despite a background that was hardly typical of most officer candidates. On the other hand, it was perhaps for this reason that they made allowances while at the same time never letting me forget that they knew what had happened. They rode me hard that winter. Any kind of extra duty suitable for an upper-classman was imposed and I had to fight a truculence that I knew would end any chance of going into the forces if I allowed it to show through. But my marks suffered.

"Your chin strap must be too tight," snarled my history professor, an ex-major from the army historical section.

"It's cutting off the blood to your brain. If you don't smarten up, you'll end up as a salesman."

"Not the kind of commission I had in mind," I said and settled down to work. I took out my vengeance on the hockey rink, playing defence with every opportunity for use of hips, shoulders and the butt end of a stick. I kept some lecture notes in the penalty box and had plenty of time to read them.

When the cold winds slapping across our little peninsula were replaced by warm, spring air from the Gulf of Mexico, the hockey ended and they found extra duties for me on weekends, including the job of guard commander at Fort Frederick and its Martello Tower, a tourist attraction of sorts. It was on one of these occasions that I first saw Edith. The breeze off the harbour was whipping her long ash-blonde hair in swirls while she laughed uncontrollably at my antics parading the new guard. It is not easy to provide solemnity to an occasion when you are marching in two callow youths, attired in odd pillbox hats, to take over from two equally awkward and serious kids. She was with a Queen's Engineering man according to his windbreaker.

"Peanuts, popcorn," said the Queen's man, standing in my way.

I left my guard, standing rigid and looking at nothing, and thrust myself close to the other's eyeballs, while Edith stood so close to us that I could smell the fragrance of her hair. She listened intently for the repartee and must have been disappointed.

"Who let you out of your cage?" I muttered at him.

"Oh, let me get that down," exclaimed Edith.

I gave up and marched away with the old guard, thinking on the way back across the greening turf, of what I might have said. We met again at the graduation ball, where I had deliberately taken a well-known waitress from one of the awful cafes with which downtown Kingston abounds. I think everyone was somewhat amazed at how good Blanche looked in a long dress that hung precariously over her breasts. With exaggerated gallantry the boys gathered around and I found myself, for some reason, solo at the punch bowl, not unhappily hoisting a few and looking over the room. A cadet I didn't know well appeared with Edith at the punch bowl during a rock number he obviously couldn't handle. We nodded.

"Missee like a peanut?" I asked.

"Hold on," said the cadet, reddening.

"It's all right," she told him. "We've met. Introduce us."

A bit shaken by her logic, the cadet reluctantly exchanged our names.

"He throws knives," the cadet said.

Edith began to look interested. She was in a clinging, dark blue gown that set off her glowing shoulders and long, tawny hair brushed into smooth waves. I noticed what seemed to be a slight petulance detracting from well-formed lips. Spoiled and looking for kicks, I thought.

"Show me," she said, the grey eyes meaning it.

"Here?"

"I don't care." And she probably didn't.

"You'll have to come with me," I said, feeling tight in the throat.

"Wait a minute," said the other cadet.

"See you later, Alfred," Edith said cheerfully at the thought of something new. She took my arm. I took one backward look at my cinderella waitress, Blanche, her breasts almost ready to pop out, in a wild dance in the midst of a ring of admiring cadets. Edith led me outside into the warm spring night to a Jaguar which, in the pre-sports car era, opened my eyes. She threw me the keys.

"I know where there's a better party," she said.

Edith directed me east of town, past the Barriefield complex, to a metal, barn-shaped mailbox, where we turned into a narrow, gravelled driveway. The headlights of the Jag picked up a rabbit leaping ahead of us and then veering off into tall grass. The gravel trail ended at a stone arch and we drove into a cobblestoned courtyard to the door of a large, square mansion silhouetted against the moonlit lake below. The big stone house was in darkness, but I noticed other parked cars and heard the sound of rock and roll from a phonograph inside. As we got out of the car, I saw that the binds had been drawn on the windows; vertical slivers of light thinly outlined the windows. My hand in hers, we stepped into a large foyer with a black and white checkered floor and dark, wooden panelling rising up to a balcony and landing. About twelve young couples were dancing to the music, not noisily, but giggling and murmuring to each other furtively. There was gin and scotch and mix on a side-table, carefully protected by newspapers.

"What gives?" I asked.

"The owners don't know we're here," said Edith, her eyes shining. "We do it often."

"Who owns the place?"

"Somebody from Montreal; it's their summer place. I think Daddy knows him."

We poured ourselves gins and watched for awhile. Then we danced some, but I wasn't much satisfied because rock and roll in those days was the forerunner of the modern dance where there isn't much personal contact. Whatever happened to the dance as a means of establishing a tactile relationship with a girl? While everyone was taking a rest, someone asked Edith who the fink was in the monkey suit.

"Be careful," she said possessively, "He throws knives."

They insisted on a demonstration, so we set up a bread-board in the big kitchen pantry and I studded it with some lethal cutlery we found in the drawers. This seemed to inflame Edith.

"Have you seen the upstairs?" she asked, fingers tight on my wrist. We started up the wide staircase into the enticing, dampish gloom above.

"Cops!" called somebody from down below. There was a scramble for cars. As ours was the last one in and

220

nearest to the gate, we managed to get out before the O.P.P. car could get turned around in the courtyard and block the entrance. We drove away in a spurt of gravel, leaving most of the others to appear in magistrate's court the following week. They were mostly Queen's students.

Most men have some kind of oddball story on how they first met the woman they were destined to marry, but incidents of this kind are only the surface events, not explaining the curious chemistry that brings two people together. I don't know whether it was my animalistic knife-throwing that first attracted Edith, but I was infatuated with her cool assertiveness and lack of inhibition. We saw each other briefly before the university term packed up and we made love in her Jaguar awkwardly around the gear shift lever and other things. After graduation that year, I went to Korea and we lost touch until we ran into each other again in Ottawa where I was posted. Edith also had returned from overseas, sent home as an External Affairs secretary after a love affair with a French diplomat in Paris. On rebound, perhaps, we married.

Edith's parents, the Watsons, grudgingly condoned our marriage as an acceptable substitute for her affair with a foreign diplomat and the possible danger that she might marry a Montreal Jew or French-Canadian. Being an army officer qualified me as one who had crossed the barrier, even though they winced slightly for some years afterwards when they had to pronounce their daughter's married name to the people they knew. Mr. Watson was the sixth name in a firm of Montreal stockbrokers, where, it seemed, you became a partner if you sold a hundred dollars worth a year. He didn't speak French and regarded Westmount as an anchor of civilization in a barbaric camp of French, Jews and other foreigners who made up most of Montreal. Yet, he regarded Torontonians as bumpkins, spoke glowingly of Montreal as the only livable city in North America and voted for Duplessis, because at least you knew where you stood with him.

As Edith and I smoothed out our emotional troughs a little more over the years and the children came, we actually came to like each other more than we had at the start. We became really good friends, which I understand is a rarity and a priceless quality in marriage. Could any man ask for more?

"You all right?"

Ab Tremblay's hand was squeezing my shoulder, injured on our last trip. My head that had been wobbling loose, straightened in a hurry and I became aware of the engine noise and lakes slipping by below us. Ahead of me, the leather shoulders of Marc twitched as he looked around out of the windows. He was seemingly suspended alone in a glass capsule behind the blur of the propeller. I looked up at Tremblay and nodded. My head felt clearer after what must have been only a few minutes trance or doze.

"That it?" Ab asked in my ear, pointing down to the long, steel tower with its saucers on top.

"Looks like it," I shouted. "There should be an inlet to the left." Ab leaned over the pilot's shoulder, glanced at the map and pointed. He looked back at me and I stuck up my thumb. We began to tip and drift downwards.

When it comes to lakes in that part of the country there is only a fine distinction between those that might be labelled as "gloomy" and those that are somehow brighter. Much has to do with what is around the lake. Those that are crowded to the shoreline with ugly outcrops of granite and solid banks of coniferous trees, who in their mass have a blackish, blue or green tone, cannot throw off their forbidding demeanour even on the sunniest day. These are the ones where sunset and dusk throw long, black shadows marching up to the shores to blot out joy. Appreciation of them comes only on the few days when the temperature is in the eighties and nineties and coolness is prized above all else.

The brightness of other lakes comes from open spaces along the shore, perhaps even the occasional sandy beach and a mixture of evergreens and leafed trees whose foliage reflects light instead of soaking it up. During the spring or fall, their bare branches let through more sun and there is generally a more pastoral look about them compared to the stiff gloom of the stands of fir, pine and spruce. Lac Deschambault was one of the gloomy ones.

A yellow wing tipped into view as the plane throttled down and we skipped onto the water in a high spray. Marc taxied the plane into the long inlet surrounded by high banks of silvery gray granite, topped by solid masses of evergreens, some of which had apparently marched forward and tumbled at odd angles down the cliffs. No one that I knew of had ever lived on this side of the lake, the pressures of population not having reached the point where the other shores were so crowded that people would seek out such enveloping, dark solitude. There were no roads on this side of the lake.

The pilot eased the plane well into the protection of the inlet, turned us around facing outward and cut the motor. He heaved over the anchor and he and Ab eased themselves out onto the pontoons to undo the canoe. Feeling a bit ashamed at my own woolgathering, I at last got out of uniform and put on the heavy wool jacket.

"Hand down the rifles," said Ab. On the floor of the plane behind the seats I saw two short-barrelled, lever action Winchester 30-30's. They were passed out of the door to Tremblay along with two yellow boxes of ammunition. A cool, chill breeze came in through the open doorway causing the plane to rock gently. Stiffly, I got down onto the pontoon and stepped into the bow of the canoe where Ab was already sorting himself out in the stern.

"How long should I wait?" asked Marc.

"Until we bloody well get back," said Tremblay.

"What if someone comes?"

"Your only danger is from the flyboys who don't listen to instructions."

"There could be a boat, or someone shooting from up there," persisted Marc, looking sulky in his beard and long hair.

"Not likely," I said looking up.

"If there is, taxi around or take off and come back for us. Is there any way we could have Marc pick us up at the cottage?" Tremblay asked me.

"You're safest here, out of sight in deep water," I said. "I wouldn't want to take the risk of moving the plane over to the other side until we check it for logs or other junk."

"Is there a wharf at the cottage?"

"Yes."

"Let's take a flare and if it's clear, Marc could come over to pick us up." I agreed, and we shoved off rather shakily from the float. After bobbing around a bit uncertainly, Ab and I settled down in the canoe and he got the outboard started.

"This should wake up the whole damned neighbourhood," I said.

"Are we in any shape to paddle?" Ab demanded.

"No," I said and shut up.

It took us only a few minutes to make the mile and a half across the narrows to where Edith's parents had their cottage. There were no boats, no sound of other outboards you always hear somewhere on a lake, no voices, splashes or shouts carrying across the still water. The lake was like a tomb. Ahead, as the east shoreline, low and gravelled, came closer there was no sign of movement. The temperature was just above sixty-five; it was around six-thirty, and there was no smoke from any of the cottage chimneys.

When Edith's parents were young, they had built their cottage in the shallow bay. They had about three hundred feet of gravel beach with white birches, maples and some firs crowding up to the line where the soil ended. A thirty-foot dock had been built of plank cribs filled with rock and topped by a removable plank deck in sections that were taken in each fall and put back every spring when the ice subsided. Three small buoys marked the route of the plastic water pipe that went out deep into the lake. A small, gasoline-powered unit sucked up the water from the lake.

As our canoe bumped against the wharf, I listened. The pump motor was silent and the buoys swayed slowly in our small wake. A rowboat, half full of water, lay dormant at the wharf, its oars missing as if they had floated off. There was no sign of the aluminium outboard that the Watsons always had tied up there.

Swallowing the urge to run, I walked slowly, some distance apart from Ab, both of us squinting nervously and holding our carbines loaded and ready.

A dozen stone slabs, laid carefully many years ago, led us up through a screen of small poplars and willows towards the cottage. Before crossing the open ground to the building, we squatted down in the bush and watched in silence. A gravel driveway led in through the bush from the road that connected all the cottages along the east shoreline. There was no car on it or around the cottage. Ab tapped my shoulder and pointed. I saw the power line drooping and cut, lying across the driveway. I surveyed the cottage. We were at the front, facing a big picture window framed by weathered redwood siding. There was a steep roof to keep the snow moving off during the winter. Through the glass of the picture window, I could see the dim outlines of the big, stone fireplace on the opposite wall and the cream silhouette of a trilight lamp sitting on one of the end tables. The flowered drapes were pulled back to the sides. Beside the picture window was a short expanse of redwood siding and a smaller window for the master bedroom. The venetian blinds on the bedroom window were closed into a shiny, pale curtain. To the right we could see part of the back steps jutting out, and beside them, a garbage can tipped over, its contents scattered by raccoons or other animals. The debris looked as if it had been there for some time; the wrapping paper was limp and pounded into the ground by rain.

I reached over through branches and touched Ab. I made signs that I was going to circle around to the back door and go in. He nodded. Creaking and sore in every muscle, I made my way past him, crouched low in the bush until I came opposite to the back door. I paused and studied it. The outer screen door was closed and the inner solid, brown pine door was shut. Around us I could hear nothing except the occasional insect or bird venturing forth in the cool weather. My leg that had been peppered with steel splinters trembled uncertainly as I stood up slowly and waited some more. Ab Tremblay came around behind me and kneeled amid some thick maples to cover me.

I started loping towards the cottage. The short open space seemed like miles, and my boots clashed against the soft gravel surface. Up the familiar, weathered back steps I pulled open the screen door, which hummed on its coil spring. The inner door was not locked. I turned the knob, kicked it open and ran through the kitchen into the living room against the far wall and turned around fast, the carbine up at the hip. There was nothing except my breathing. I went to the door of the kitchen and waved Ab in. We didn't say anything, but went our separate ways to poke around. I went first to the bedroom that was always regarded as ours when we stayed there.

My jaw tightened as I looked around. Edith's white bikini was dry and stiff on a chair—she still had the figure to wear one. The closets contained some slacks, blouses and her favourite blue jeans. There were no dresses or suitcases. I checked the vanity. A few jars of this and that were around and not yet dried out. Most of the basic makeup had gone, including her sterling mirror, scissors and other implements. The bed was neatly made.

In the boys' room, I could not avoid a grin. Their bunk beds were unmade. On the upper one, which I assumed was John's, were rubber flippers, an eyepiece and a snorkel tube. Two sets of bathing trunks were stiff and dry over a chair. A *Popular Mechanics* magazine, undoubtedly Steven's, was open on the lower bunk. I looked for notes but found none.

"Not a clue," said Ab, appearing in the doorway and making me jump.

"They've left. But where to?"

"I don't think they went on their own," he said.

"What makes you say that?"

"Look at the kitchen floor," he said. He led me back to the kitchen. On the black and white linoleum we could see signs made by dried brown sand of a couple of large heel marks. Ab kneeled down and pointed to one that was particularly clear. It was a heel mark with a reverse horseshoe print outlined in the dry sand.

"Army boot," I said hoarsely.

"Afraid so," said Ab. "Maybe we should look around outside."

We went out, the screen door slamming behind us with a shattering crash. In the soft sand and gravel of the driveway we saw more footprints, blurred by rain but identifiable with hobnailed pockmarks and miniature horseshoes. A vehicle with heavy herringbone tires had been there. We didn't say a word as we walked out on opposite sides of the driveway to the road. We looked up and down and saw no signs of life. Head down and trying to think, I followed Ab back to the cottage.

"I'll look around over here," said Ab, moving over to the woodpile and ice shed. I just stood and stared blankly at the footprints.

"Alex," he called. "Come here."

His voice caused me to move quickly. I walked around past the shed to the other side of the cottage where Edith's father had cultivated a small patch of lawn for practising his putting. On one side of the patch of grass, now grown long and feathery, was an oblong mound of earth. At one end of it was a hastily-nailed cross about two feet high, and a crossbar where someone had written something with a marker pencil that had been blurred and washed into smudges by rain.

It was a grave, but who was in it?

18

At that point Ab Tremblay must have regretted the resurgent enthusiasm that had moved him to look me up again. In our semi-crocked state, we had both over-reached ourselves and were feeling the strain in our bruised tissues; mine compounded by a jittery anxiety. As far as I can recall, I ran for the icehouse where tools were hung by spikes on the wall inside the door and returned with a shovel, its blade caked with dry brown clay. Ab watched, horrified, as I lunged towards the grave.

"You can't do that," he said.

"Got to find out who it is."

"You can't do it!" he shouted, his distant religious background coming to the surface. Though he had done many things in the course of his army career, he came now to the barrier through which he couldn't allow us to pass. His wide, florid face had faded more than ever to a saggy, unhealthy beige. He stood in front of me shakily but grim.

"Alex, put down that shovel," he said.

We stared at each other and I could hear my own breath coming in scraping rasps. I put a foot forward towards the obscene mound of clay, but somehow Ab got a grip on the handle of the shovel. With straining muscles we rocked back and forth, the shovel horizontal, gripped by four hands. I pushed hard towards his injured shoulder and saw his eyes pop with pain. We teetered like two elk with horns locked. That I had a vulnerable spot hadn't occurred to me until Tremblay got his foot behind my injured leg, found a pressure point and moved the leverage. I let out a yell, tumbled backwards onto the soft turf and lay there glaring upward. Ab held the shovel at shoulder level, ready to use as a weapon. I knew he'd do it, too. Slowly I cooled off and began to shake a bit as I stared eye level at the rough cross, now slightly tilted because I had brushed against it. I got up on my knees feeling the cool dampness of the earth through the cloth, and carefully adjusted the cross to an upright position. Ab watched me, allowing the shovel to drop point down at his side. He held it loosely but was still wary as I got to my feet.

"We'll have to go into the village and find out," I said at last.

"You're nuts," said Ab. "We haven't time. And you know what happened before."

"Take off then," I said, except that wasn't exactly what I said. "I'll get back somehow."

Ab looked down the driveway through its narrow passageway in the bush to the gravel road beyond. Savagely he jabbed the shovel into the ground and picked up his carbine. I did the same and we looked at each other for a moment.

"How far is it to the village?" he asked.

"Five miles, but there's a general store and gas pumps a mile down the road. The Lalonde place."

"You know them?"

"Yes. For years."

He thought for awhile and looked up at the sky. Low, greasy-looking clouds were beginning to assemble and a chilly wind had started up. The first traces of dusk were beginning to seep through the bush.

"Let's go," he said.

I clapped him on his good shoulder and we started off on opposite sides of the driveway along the narrow, gravel road in the same way. There were small hay fields on the south side of the road, fringed with poplars and willows. The north side of the road was bush, interspersed by the occasional entrance leading to a cottage. I looked at the vaguely familiar names on signboards. Mostly English from Montreal. At the first curve, Ab went ahead and I crouched in the tall grass of the shallow ditch. He came back into view and waved. We went on in what seemed a menacing silence. After the curve the narrow road rose up in a sharp incline, its centre hump revealing chunks of granite poking through to provide any driver, not familiar with the road, a guessing game as to what might happen to his oil pan. This time I went forward, walking in the ditch close to the bushes. At the top of the rise I could look down a long curve that widened out at its base into a small, gravel platform.

Lalonde's general store sat by itself at the side of the road just before another narrow, gravelled grade from the south joined the one we were on. There didn't seem to be anything going on at the store. Two red, white and blue Esso pumps stood alone in the gravel apron. The store itself was a low, single storey frame building with two large windows at the front and an uncovered wooden porch where the locals sometimes sat out in good weather. I could see two unpainted kitchen chairs on the wooden deck. The store itself had been painted lime green and there were splashes of other colours where Coca Cola, Pepsi and some cigarette posters had been nailed up. There were no cars in sight, but I noticed a wispy film of light, blue smoke coming from the kitchen at the back. I looked at Ab and waved. When he got up to me we started our descent slowly down the long, gentle incline, keeping as far apart as we could get on either side of the road.

I remembered Lalonde—what was his first name?—as

a darting, little man with rimless glasses. He had mahogany, weathered skin and a bouncy repartee that eased any sense of exploitation the cottagers may have felt at the prices he charged for groceries. Because he knew them all and was the local handyman as well, he had always done well waylaying the summer folk before they made the effort of going into Notre Dame des Pistoles. His wife, bulky and fat, just managed to scrape up enough English to do business with the cottagers. He was the one who kept the business alive and when he came out to fix a sputtering water pump, he would always bring beer and groceries on the same trip. I think they had teenage kids who were away at schools, convents or colleges somewhere. Now I looked at the new blue and white flag flapping over the building and paused.

I crossed the road to Ab.

"I think we'd better go in fast," I said.

He nodded glumly. We continued together down the south side of the road keeping out of sight as long as we could. Where the bush cut back to form the clearing for the store, we stopped again at the edge and looked. The Lalondes' living quarters were an extension of the store, distinguished by a black, pointed roof. A large window at the back of the house marked the kitchen and I could see some kind of movement beyond the glass.

"Back or front?" I asked Tremblay.

"Front," said Tremblay. "They could see us from that window."

"Okay," I nodded.

We sprinted across the open space, clattered up onto the wooden porch and burst through the front door, setting off a jangling cacophony of bells. A customer entering at a normal pace only caused a slight ring, but we set off a chain reaction as the door swung back and forth on its spring. We looked around in the gloomy interior. There were counters on either side, running the length of the room. One side had a large, soft drink cooler, a beer

232

cooler and old-fashioned ice cream wells. The other side had a zinc-covered counter with a meat slicer, a glass case full of candy, and a clutter of cheeses, pickles and such things. The shelves behind seemed rather empty. Wooden kegs of nails, bolts, balls of twine and some miscellaneous cartons cluttered the centre aisle.

A curtain scraped back on brass rings and little Lalonde in woollen undershirt, braces and denim work pants, came in. He was chewing. He started to say something in French and then stopped. He squinted at me and started to back up.

"My family, Mr. Lalonde. What happened to them?" I asked, moving forward with the levelled carbine. Ab pushed past him into the back part of the store and I heard a torrent of French in his voice and that of a woman. I backed Lalonde through into the kitchen where his wife was staring goggle-eyed at Tremblay and his rifle. They had been seated at a linoleum-covered kitchen table which, I noticed, had food laid out for two. Lalonde backed against the big propane stove and stared at me.

"The Watsons," I said, seeing his failure to connect. I guess it had been three years since I had been there. "Where are they?"

"The Watsons?" He screwed his eyes and swallowed hard, the cords standing out in his neck.

"I'm Edith Watson's husband," I said a little more quietly. "Remember?"

He peered at me through thick rimless glasses and glanced across at Tremblay. He studied our rifles and then us again. After thinking it over, he said something in French to his wife. She replied quickly, nodding her head.

"We're in business," Tremblay said.

"I cannot remember your name," Lalonde said to me.

"Hlynka."

"Yes. You must come with me, Mr. . . . ."

"Hlynka."

"Yes. Let us go."

I looked across at Ab. He nodded and shrugged his shoulders. We had to take the chance. Lalonde started to slip into a jacket. Ab went through into the front part of the store and I heard a ripping sound as he tore out the phone. He also brought back two chunks of cheese and threw me one.

"That was not necessary, you know," Lalonde said. "We don't want no trouble."

"Never know these days," I said. "Where are we going?" I asked Ab.

"Ever heard of a family named McCarthy? On a farm near here?"

"I think they used to deliver cream and eggs," I nodded. "French-speaking Irish."

"My counterparts," said Ab with an unexpected bitterness.

"Why are we going there?"

"Our friend here says they know something," Ab said. "And I don't think he is going to lead us into a trap, are you?"

"No, no, no," said Lalonde, shaking his head like it was going to come off. "But we must hurry. There are patrols at night. Even your planes have not been able to stop that."

We went out behind the buildings to a two-car garage where Lalonde had a three-year-old, mud-splashed Buick in one stall and a light delivery truck in the other.

"That reminds me, I still owe you a pickup truck," I said to Ab as Lalonde backed out the Buick.

"You don't owe me anything."

"Next trip, we'll go and collect it for scrap."

Ab laughed and we both felt better. I got in front and Ab sat in the back seat, his rifle pointed at the back of the little man's fleshless head. He started to drive like a madman along the gravel road that curved south, away from the lake and the general store.

"What's been happening around here?" I asked Lalonde.

"Many things," he said. "It has been a very bad time."

"Who is in that grave at the Watsons' place?"

The little man stared ahead as we bounced along the narrow road.

"You will be told," he said in the voice of a man who feels he has already jeopardized himself too far. Ab put a big hand on my shoulder and pushed me back into the seat.

"Not now," he said quietly.

I subsided and watched our progress along the road with its fringe of bush and the hayfields broken by rocky knolls. We turned into a mud trail that led through a gap in a rail and stone fence. The postal box, tilted on a fence post, had the faded lettering "McCarthy" stencilled on it. Not many of the McCarthy clan spoke English any more. I remembered them as having an enormous family and little cash from a few cattle, hay and the dairy products they sold to the cottagers. You can't raise ten kids on a two-month economy. They lived in an unpainted two-storey stone and wood house with a sagging front porch and a yard cluttered with bits and pieces of neglected or dismembered machinery. The major piece of art was a rusting, twenty-year-old Ford, stripped of its tires and seated foolishly on blocks.

As the car slowed down in the muddy yard, Ab and I jumped out, scattering some chickens and a couple of patchy, yellow dogs who came yapping at us. We walked along on either side of the car, our rifles ready. Lalonde stopped at the porch steps and got out of the car. A big, black-haired man in blue denims came out of the door, a pump-action shotgun with polychoke cradled in his arm. He might be poor but he didn't stint on his guns. I remembered him vaguely as McCarthy, the cream and egg man. A series of white faces peered at us from various windows.

Lalonde sprinted up the stairs and spoke quickly to McCarthy in French.

"Holy Christ!" said Tremblay.

"What is it?" I snapped at him.

Tremblay lowered his rifle and grinned at me.

"I think you'll be glad you made this trip," he said. "Go on up."

After a moment's puzzled hesitation, I went slowly up the stairs and looked at McCarthy. He studied me, his shotgun still cradled, eyes black and glittering under oppressive eyebrows. Then his face cracked in an unshaven grin.

"You are the boy's father," he said in heavily-accented English.

"Boy?"

A lanky, teen-aged kid in dirty jeans shot out of the house and cannoned into me.

"Dad!" he said. It was John. My Johnny. I stood and wept, the long-stifled emotions and tensions breaking out at last. We both stood looking at each other sniffling, the vision of each blurred by tears. I placed my hands on his shoulders to make sure he was real.

At last I said, "You've grown a foot."

"It hasn't been that long, dad," he said, trying to be matter of fact. John looked a lot like me, except for his blue eyes. His hair was black and thick like mine and came back from the forehead in a peak. He had my high cheekbones and pointed chin, but Edith's shorter nose. At fourteen he was five-foot-nine and moving up fast.

"How are you?" I asked.

"I'm okay. The McCarthys have been great," he said. I saw his eyes slide to a McCarthy girl who must have been about his age and was sprouting breasts and thighs under blouse and tight jeans. Exile hadn't been too bad for him, I thought.

"Where's Mom? Where're the others?" I asked.

My heart sank when he told me, and some of my elation began to fade.

"They went away," he said. "I don't know where they are."

"How did you get here?"

"I ran away," John told me. "They didn't have time to catch me."

"Who didn't?"

"The soldiers," he said. "They were on the run so they didn't take much time."

"Who is in the grave at the cottage?"

He looked down at the floor. "Oh, that's grandfather," he said. "He wouldn't go with them and when one of the soldiers pushed him, he died."

"I see," I murmured and turned to look around. A fascinated audience of scruffy kids had gathered around, giggling among themselves in French. A cheerful-looking woman in a stained housedress looked on over their heads. Lalonde had darted back to the car where he fidgeted at an open door.

"Hurry," he said. "We must go."

"I'll get my jacket," said John, and went into the house followed by the budding, and now glum, McCarthy daughter. I turned to McCarthy.

"I'm in your debt," I told him. "When this is all over, I'll make it up to you."

"Forget it," said McCarthy solemnly. "I don't see you people ever coming back. It's too late now."

"What are you going to do?"

"We'll have to move. I can't live without the summer trade."

"If you ever get across the border, look me up," I said.

"We'll be staying on this side," he said. "This is my country."

"You can have anything you want at the cottage," I told him. It was a commentary on the local people that the cottage had not been touched—hard for them to break the habit of being custodians for their summer visitors.

With nothing more to say to each other, we shook hands and I went to the car. I thought of leaving him the carbine but decided we might still need it. John, after taking an inordinate amount of time to find his jacket, returned with the girl, her face tearstained. He said a few last words to her in French, hugged the other McCarthys one by one and folded himself into the back seat of the Buick. Lalonde drove out of the yard at a fast clip, scattering chickens and dogs in a flurry of squawks and yaps. The dusk was settling in but Lalonde didn't put on lights.

"Can you take us back to the cottage?" I asked him.

He nodded. "We heard the plane coming in."

"Any patrols at this time of night?" asked Tremblay.

"It's not them I'm afraid of," said Lalonde, showing emotion for the first time. "It's your goddam planes."

We lapsed into an uneasy silence. I looked at John, who, showing some unwelcome traits of his father, had sunk into a brooding study, his chin low on his chest. The girl back at the farm was on his mind, I guessed. I started to pry gently.

"When did the soldiers come?" I asked.

"Several days ago now," he said. "What day is this?"

I had to think. "Monday."

"It was last week then," he said. "About Wednesday, I'd say."

"What happened?"

"They came at night," he said, reluctant to discuss it. "In bad shape. They'd been on the run, hiding from the aircraft in the daytime. About seven of them came to our place in a small truck. Never seen guys so dirty and worn out."

"Why did they stop at the cottage?"

"For one thing, we had the lamps on. We were the only

ones left along the east shore by that time. Everybody else had left. The pressure was on."

"What kind of pressure?"

"Calls from the whiteshirts and the Q.P.P. They were always around asking questions. They cut off the phones and the power. We had to use Coleman lamps."

"Why did Mom and your grandparents stay on?"

"They kept telling me it was a lot safer than going back to Montreal but I didn't see why we couldn't have gone on down to Ottawa or something. Also, we didn't know where you were until we heard your name on the radio one night. Did you really capture a general?"

"They called him that," I said. "He was just a guy leading a mob of whiteshirts. Did the locals connect your mom with me?"

"No. She's known as a Watson and they never can remember our last name. Steve and I are known as the Watson boys around here."

"Did the soldiers hurt Mom?" I asked, an edge in my voice.

"No, they didn't seem to." He paused. "At least at the time. Steven and me were kept in our room and there was a lot of clumping around. Grandma and Mom cooked them a big meal, even though we were running short ourselves. Then we were hauled out. Mom and Grandma were standing there dressed with their raincoats on and suitcases packed. Grandpa was sitting at the kitchen table saying he wouldn't go. One of the soldiers got mad and pushed him. Grandpa looked startled and keeled over. It was pretty awful."

"Was your mom crying?"

"No. She was just terribly white. During the confusion of burying poor Grandpa, I slipped into the bush and hid till morning. They called and called, but didn't look for me very hard. About two in the morning they all drove off. When daylight came I went to the general store, because there wasn't any food left at the cottage. Mr. Lalonde took me over to the McCarthy place."

We were turning into the driveway at the cottage. Lalonde accepted our thanks nervously and drove off again as fast as he could. Ab went down to the dock and looked out across the darkened waters. The low flying clouds had brought on an early darkness but there was still some visibility because of light reflected off the lake.

"I'll try the flare," said Ab.

"I hope he's still there," I said.

The flare was a shattering burst of pink light in the gathering darkness. In the distance, the silence was broken by an engine coughing into life.

"He's coming," said Ab. "We'd better get lamps from the cottage."

We collected all the Colemans we could find in the cottage, six of them, pumped them up until their mantles glowed white, and placed them in a row at the end of the dock.

"He should have lots of draft," I said.

"It'll be all right," said Ab. "He'd better hurry before someone sees us."

We stood shivering a bit in the chill air and listening to the sound of the plane coming towards us. The lamps cast flashing lights far across the water, it seemed, and reflected highlights and sharp outlines on our faces. At last I turned to John. He had been holding out on me and he knew it.

"I don't see why they were taken along," I said to him.

He shuffled his feet, looking very much the awkward, uncertain teenager.

"I meant to tell you, dad," he said.

"Tell me what?"

"Well, the guy in charge of the soldiers, he was an officer, and he knows you." He thought briefly. "It almost seemed as if he had been looking for our place."

"Did you recognize him?"

"Yes, Dad." John's face looked miserable in the glare from the lamps. "He was the guy who used to be with you in South Africa; he was with us on the boat; the Frenchman . . . you know . . ."

"Rousseau?" I almost yelled.

"Yeah, Rousseau. That's the guy.

19

In the morning I awoke with something like wet cement clogging my sinuses and some kind of petrifying material in the muscles of my shoulders and legs. The nurse, her perpetual golden tan looking a bit flaky, listened to my voice as she came in at dawn with the inevitable thermometer. I sounded as if there was a clothes peg on my nose. She looked at me suspiciously, flipped the watch pinned to her bosom, and asked how come I had managed to catch a cold at a conference.

"It was the air-conditioning," I told her.

"Oh, sure," she said, pronouncing it "shirr" like most Canadian girls.

"Did you hear the prime minister last night?" she asked.

"What prime minister?"

"The new one." She looked at me sardonically, not believing the conference line, but the thermometer in my mouth prevented any more dialogue. "He sounds as if he means business," she went on. "He said that it was an insurrection and that it would be crushed. He quoted a lot of Lincoln."

It seemed as though I had been awake for half a day when the nurse reappeared at 8:30, a.m. that is.

"You're popular," she said with sarcasm. "A car's coming to pick you up at 0900."

"What time of day is that?"

"Oh, stop it," she said.

At nine a genuine black C.F.H.Q. Chev, equipped with the proper licence plates and a corporal driver, came to pick me up. He announced he was to take me to a meeting at C.F.H.Q. currently operating out of Uplands. I limped out to the car, collapsed into the back seat and tried to work myself up to a state of alertness. We took the National Capital Commission's new ring road, joining it at the old Montreal Road. The cloverleaf swept us past the neo-colonial, or Reader's Digest, architecture of Central Mortgage and Housing, its red brick exterior, funny little spires and weathered window frames looking a bit shabby. The road curved across St. Laurent Boulevard, leaving the green belt momentarily for a glimpse of Ottawa's other world of ugly small plants and businesses. We crossed over the Queensway and entered Riverside Drive. The neat landscaping of the N.C.C. resumed again with its seemingly inexhaustible supply of exotic flowers and shrubs. We passed under Bank Street and at Bronson took another half cloverleaf onto the airport road to Uplands.

The driver let me off at Number 11 Hangar, formerly the V.I.P. stopping place run by 412 Squadron. After much showing of I.D. cards and statements of intention to four security guards, I was reluctantly allowed to pass through. The lounge area had been converted by a series of beaverboard partitions, all freshly painted in standard green. The thin partitions were possibly only to provide an illusion of rank and privacy because it seemed everybody in the booths was yelling over phones to make himself heard. There were no doors on most of the cubicles and, as a signaller led me through the maze of cables strung out on the floor, I could see the inmates had some fringe benefits in that they had scrounged the armchairs and sofas from the lounge. White cardboard signs, hastily stencilled, identified my progress past cubicles into the far end of the lounge where there was an uninterrupted row of plywood doors, the improvised signs indicating their ascending place in the pecking order. Near the end of this row, a small stencilled piece of cardboard identified the office of Military Assistant/Chief Defence Staff (Lieut. Col. E. F. Mason). The runner stopped at the door and knocked. I knew there were only four other doors beyond, the Vice-Chief, his deputies and the Chief himself.

Ted Mason looked almost relaxed—in a wild sort of way. He was hemmed in by stacks of papers, clipboards, maps with grease-pencilled plastic coverings, and a Telex machine that was temporarily silent. He had hardly any room to move, but he looked happy. Two red spots stood out on his fleshless cheekbones on skin showing a blue tinge from a careless shaving job. His jacket was off, his sleeves rolled up and he had a slightly unkempt look because his crew cut had begun to grow out. He was on the phone and waved me to a magenta leatherette armchair occupied by several file folders. I picked up the folders, and finding no place to put them, held them on my lap. He finished his phone call, gave orders to the operator to place another call, and looked at me.

"You're looking fit," he said.

I shrugged my shoulders and tried not to wince. I decided to tell him.

"I got word last night that my son, John, is safe," I told him. "Some friends brought him out and he's with them at Hawkesbury; Ab Tremblay, he used to be with me on a couple of U.N. postings."

"Great," said Mason. "What about the rest of the family?"

"John tells me that Rousseau picked them up on his way through. Your planes didn't get them all."

"We know that," frowned Mason. "Why? Will they hold it over your head?"

"I don't know."

Mason sat down as if he had received a setback. He folded his hands and twitched his eyebrows.

"How do you feel about it?"

I paused, trying to figure out his line of questioning.

"I'm not sure," I said at last. "Possibly Rousseau thought he was taking them to a safer place or helping them in some way. Somehow I don't see him using them as hostages. I don't think he would harm them in any way."

"As long as they were in his hands."

"I can't see him turning them over to anyone. He didn't kill me when he had the chance."

Mason thought about it, then relaxed as much as he ever does; that is, he uncupped his tightly-clenched hands and sat back in the ancient, wooden swivel chair. He tipped far back on the old chair's weak springs and studied the black dots of the acoustic tile on the ceiling.

"You heard the P.M. last night?" he asked.

"No." It seemed to be the question of the day.

"You should have. He wants this thing stopped soonest. There are a lot of pressures from within and outside. It's been suggested from both sides of the border that it would be a good thing if the Seaway were opened up, especially before the wheat crop comes off." He paused. "As of today, all civilian flights have been ordered to go to Ottawa, Toronto or airports in the Maritimes. No more commercial traffic into Quebec. Second, we've been instructed to place a blockade across the St. Lawrence. We're moving D.E.'s up as far as Rivière du Loup and we expect to put a net across. Objective: to stop arms imports." His eyes sparkled. "The Quebec militia may have moved a 105 mm. battery up there, so it should be interesting. Recce is out trying to get some pictures, and we may have to put in an airstrike." He squeaked backwards in the chair. "So that brings you up to date."

"Not quite," I grinned.

"What do you think of it?"

I decided that this was no time to be political and, anyway, they would regard it as being out of character if I suddenly became circumspect.

"Okay as far as it goes. But all we're doing is broadcasting to the world that the Provisional Government has a border. I would have been inclined to take the other approach. Restore normal relations between Quebec and the rest of the country and back it up with guns. Continue the flights, trains, buses and ships, but under our control."

"We don't have the troops for that, Alex. That viewpoint was expressed by some, of course."

"I see." I waited.

"That's not all," said Mason, stating the obvious. "The P.M. wants us to go all out and finish it up on the ground. He's in a hell of a hurry."

"Bring back two brigades from overseas and you can clean it up in a week," I said.

For the first time, Mason looked a bit uncertain. He got up and stared through the venetian blinds, came back to his chair and brushed some files off his desk in the process. By the time he had picked them up and placed them precariously on another teetering pile, he had gathered his thoughts.

"We have been asked to try, without going that far," he said. "We are authorized to withdraw three companies of the Canadian Airborne from the Rhine and three companies of 2nd Queen's Own from Thailand. These elements are to be formed into a special assault battalion."

"Sounds like a good combination. The airborne boys are tough and Queen's Own have been in action. Is that all?"

He frowned. "I'm afraid so, for the time being."

"What are they supposed to do?"

246

"Hit the source and cut the country—or rather, the rebels—in two."

"That means Quebec City. Will it be airborne?"

"Yes. Not paratroops. In choppers." He held up a file and riffled through it. "We're working on a plan. The mobile forces now being built up around Montreal will strike overland for Trois Rivières and Quebec, combined with an attack across to the south shore of the St. Lawrence to get on top of the Seaway. The mobile force striking east will link up with the special battalion after it has taken Valcartier. We'll also be able to airlift reinforcements into Quebec."

"You don't have enough equipment to do an airborne job on Trois Rivières?"

"No. And an overland attack from the New Brunswick border is too risky with the forces we've got on hand."

"It's all very thin. Do you have estimates of militia strength at Valcartier?"

"It's fluid, with all kinds of comings and goings. They seem to be trying to form about four battalions."

I whistled.

"Valcartier will be hit hard with airstrikes," said Mason. "And some of them are bound to be drawn south by the activity around Montreal."

"You hope."

Mason became irritable.

"Professionals can do a lot of things that amateurs can't," he said. "You know that. I expected a better attitude from you."

"Why me?"

"You're it," he said, letting that make its way through my senses. "After much soul-searching and rather rancorous debate, the Chiefs have selected you to take over the special battalion." He waved his hand as I started to speak. "I know," said Mason. "Why wasn't someone else picked, like Sutton, or Moore, or Matthews from Thailand? Why pick someone who has been on peacekeeping?"

"You tell me," I said, using some aggression to cover up a sinking feeling.

"One thing you have shown," went on Mason, the compliments coming with difficulty, "is a remarkable capacity to carry out a crash program and to improvise. Third R.C.R. was well handled. You seem to have the drive and certain sense of deviousness in action that is needed to work up a scrub team."

"Thanks," I muttered.

"But no more solo efforts," he said. "Those were the subject of some discussion. In the future, leave interrogation procedures to the Intelligence people." He stood up again. "Now I think the Chiefs would like to have a word with you."

The sunshine coming through the venetian blinds left a pattern of shadowy ladders on the wallmaps. Mason was on the phone to see if our masters, two doors away, were ready to see us. It appeared that they were. I followed him a short distance through a small anteroom.

The Chief of Defence Forces liked to work in twilight. At least he had the venetian blinds drawn almost closed, giving the room a subdued coolness. The fluorescent lights in the ceiling were shut off. In his improvised headquarters, the Chief had his desk placed at an angle across a corner supplemented by a short conference table jutting at right angles to the desk. Chairs had been placed around the adjoining table, now occupied by the three Deputy Chiefs as well as the Vice-Chief (executive vice-president and odd jobs). General MacLennan himself sat behind his own desk at some distance from the others. He watched our progress into the room, beckoned Mason and myself to the two chairs at the end of the conference table and placed half-moon glasses over his beetling, sandy eyebrows. Even sitting down the Chief looked the part and so did the others, I noticed, as I glanced around in the rather dim light. I wondered once more if senior officers were in fact chosen for appearance, or if the commanding presence, well-developed, made senior officers of them in the first place. The Deputy Chief Operations had his arm in a sling and a large tape on his forehead. I remembered him vaguely from the raid on C.F.H.Q. He had been one of the officers Ted Mason had literally ordered to stay on the top floor.

"Colonel Hlynka," began MacLennan in his high tenor voice, "we think you have the stuff to put the special battalion together very quickly. Mind you, you are working with professionals who are already in good shape. It won't be like the Third R.C.R." He looked over his glasses. "The advance party is on its way to Sarcee and the airlift will commence in two days time. Within five days the six companies will be at Calgary. The Straths have cleared their barracks for you. My JetStar will take you out to-morrow. You will not be under brigade command, but will report directly to me through Colonel Mason. Any questions so far?"

"Sir, I'll probably think of them after I've left," I said, and everybody smiled thinly. "May I ask, why Sarcee?"

"Security," said General MacLennan. "We want you to do your training as far away from the scene as possible. We don't want any publicity on these forces coming back from overseas. Unfortunately, we can't give them leave, which may upset the troops a bit."

A bit, I thought. They would be enraged.

"I take it then, sir, that the C.A.R.'s are leaving their families in Europe?"

"That's correct. Their families will be told they are going on special exercises for two months."

"Is that the length of time I will have, sir?"

"We shall expect everything to be tidied up inside of a month."

To describe my reaction as being stunned would be an understatement.

"It would be the Queens Own troops who concern me,

sir," I said, after trying to be granite under a collective stare that raked me like a laser beam. "How long is it since they've had rotation?"

"There hasn't been any rotation," said MacLennan a bit testily. "The brigade has been in Thailand only six months."

"Perhaps Wainwright would be better, sir. Once the troops are turned loose on Calgary there won't be any security."

"You'll have to confine them, that's all," said MacLennan curtly. "Wainwright just can't handle them on this short notice."

"What about my officers and R.S.M., sir?" I asked.

"You can have your choice of adjutant, operations officer, I.O., and R.S.M., if you want," the Chief said reasonably. "The companies are being brought in with their regular establishments. All good men, you'll find. State your requirements to Colonel Mason."

"Very well, sir. Will I have support for training?"

The Deputy Chief Operations wrinkled the bandage on his forehead.

"We'll give you three Voyageurs for training and a CH-112 for your own use. We expect you will be airlifted to Gagetown when you are ready. Full airlift capacity will be assembled there for you," he said.

"I'd like to have an Iroquois for my command post when we're operational," I stated.

General MacLennan laughed, but there was an edge.

"Like the one you had at Dorval, eh? We'll see you get it."

"Thank you, sir. Are there any special instructions regarding my training syllabus?"

The Deputy Chief Plans, who had hitherto been following the conversation with a series of assenting nods, lifted his florid visage, blue veins testifying to many years of vast enjoyment in the Mess.

"Bunkers and house clearing," he rasped in a whiskey

bass. "The sappers have started pouring concrete at Sarcee. You'll have good mockups."

Again I was at a loss for words. If Valcartier and the Quebec airport were our objectives, why all this? Unless they had been heavily fortified, or unless . . . I decided to think about such matters later. This was not the time.

"No more questions at the moment, sir," I said quickly.

Everybody looked relieved and stood up to shake hands and wish good luck. The Chief came around the table, clasped my hand and peered at me in a commanding way.

"We're counting on you," he said. "The outcome of this whole business, and perhaps the future of our country may rest in your hands. I think, with your, er, origin and so on, this is quite significant. Remember, we're here to help you all we can."

It was a good act, but they just couldn't resist the condescension. I said I appreciated the opportunity and Mason and I left. In Mason's office, I told him I wanted R.S.M. Wilson and Captain Rhodes for my adjutant. I told him to get me a good operations officer from Thailand, who had been working with helicopters. I didn't care who they got for Intelligence Officer as long as he was fluent in French.

"The M.O. at Rockcliffe says you're all right," Mason said. "Don't worry, Alex, and don't overdo it at first."

"What do you mean, don't overdo it?" I said. "How else can it be done?"

"Down boy," said Mason. "Take it in your stride and you'll do fine."

I grinned and shrugged shoulders.

"It's quite a thing, isn't it?" I said. "The fate of the nation and all that . . ."

"You know the Old Man." Actually I didn't know the Old Man. "He lays it on thick sometimes." He fiddled with some files begging for attention. "I'll get Rhodes and R.S.M. Wilson pulled in from Dorval tonight, if I can.

The JetStar will be laid on for tomorrow. On one condition . . ."

I raised eyebrows.

"That you don't paint it yellow and head east," said Ted Mason with a smirk.

20

Against the prairie grass, already turning brown, the green field uniforms showed up as if they were redcoats at Bunker Hill. This worried me instinctively in my edgy drive for perfection, even though I knew it wouldn't matter much when we went into action two thousand miles way. At my back the land fell away in a long, downward slope, rising back up again into foothills. The mountains were a solid blue graph line with peaks and troughs like some kind of vast performance chart on a turquoise wall. From Point "M" they seemed close, but were at least sixty or seventy miles away. Down the slope in front of me and to my left, Echo Company, still wearing their C.A.R. patches, were well past their start line and beginning the involved approach to the two bunkers, newly-built and tucked in under the crest of the hill. In the distance I could hear the beat of helicopter engines and saw a Voyageur rise as it worked with Bravo Company.

It was like night and day compared to the struggles with a pickup unit like Third R.C.R. These professionals were in shape; they moved with economy, knew their weapons and their officers and N.C.O.'s were on top. The only problem was to get them used to working together and to keep the lid on the hairy Queen's Own, suddenly removed from the jungle to be set down within spitting distance of

Calgary and not allowed to go near it. I laid on a lot of night exercises for them.

Sarcee, I reflected, where I had spent my first summer as an officer cadet over twenty years ago. Currie Barracks in those days was a neat, rather small station. Narrow concrete roads meandered among evergreens to gleaming white buildings built in the thirties. We had been in wartime vintage barracks adjoining the circular driveway of the officers' Mess, a large, cool building with its flooring inlaid in V's and a stuffed buffalo head over the fireplace. At that time, before the Lord Strathconas had built their complex of barracks down where the weekend soldiers used to have their summer camps, we slogged up and down the cliffs overlooking the blue expanse of the Glenmore Reservoir, crossed Wolf's Head Creek and tried to find such exotic map references as Point "F" (the nearest one), Point "G" and other geographical nonentities. Occasionally a couple of Sarcee Indians on horseback would ride past a long line of us staggering along on foot, providing some kind of silent commentary on the old and the new. Where I had begun to learn of warfare, I now returned with the assignment of my career. I wondered if I could bring it off.

My operations officer was a Major Maclean, airlifted out of Thailand from 2nd Queen's Own, a tough, sandy-haired professional with five years liaison experience with the U.S. Army in southeast Asia, as well as being second-in-command of his battalion for the past six months. He was thin as a swagger stick and had that pale, yellowish look that jungle men sometimes get during the monsoon season. We were chatting about the propensity for one of the platoons to bunch up, when a CH-112 came in about six hundred feet above the hill. The small helicopter had the appearance of a dragonfly straining forward and blowing bubblegum.

"He requests permission to land, sir," said the signaller from my command vehicle parked behind us. I nodded and looked up at the solitary passenger silhouetted in the plexi-glass cockpit.

The pilot decided to be a hotshot and impress us with autorotation. We watched him disengage the motor and allow the rotor blades to windmill. The bird dropped towards the ground at 1,700 feet per minute. About sixty feet above the waving brown grass, he shoved the helicopter forward and upward in a curve, causing the blades to whirl more rapidly. With the extra lift, the bird paused momentarily before he shifted the pitch of the blades. The little machine sank easily onto the ground.

"Showoff," muttered Major Maclean.

The passenger was Ted Mason, who paused long enough to have a few words with the young pilot. We shook hands and I introduced him to Maclean. Knowing it wasn't a social call, I shifted uneasily while Mason, looking rumpled in summer greens too big for him, clutched an underarm briefcase and looked over the scene below us. I handed him my binoculars.

"How're they coming?" he asked.

"Very well," I said. "So far we've managed to avoid the rape of Calgary."

Mason was not amused. He was going to be brisk in front of my operations officer.

"Their cover isn't too good," he said.

"We should have good old-fashioned summer drill for prairie grass," I said.

"I'd like to see you in your office," he said.

Maclean and I exchanged glances and I told him to carry on. Reluctantly, I followed Mason back to the helicopter, which I always regarded as a frail and tenuous form of travel to be avoided whenever possible. The chastened young lieutenant at the controls played it straight, however, and we hopped over a couple of hills to the empty parade square at Sarcee Barracks. The place was practically deserted, all ranks out running around in the heather. I took Mason through the battalion orderly

room to my office, its walls still hung with Lord Strathcona insignia and photos. Mason closed the door behind
him and sat down. He zipped open the bulging briefcase.

"Normally we would probably call you in for this," he
said, holding an envelope tantalizingly in the air. He put
the envelope down on the desk and extracted my signature
in a black book before he would lift his thumb off. The
large white envelope was stencilled "Top Secret". I slit it
open and there was a standard brown envelope inside. I
pictured myself opening envelopes forever as they got
progressively smaller.

"In view of the time element, I was asked to deliver
it," Mason said, relaxing a bit now that the deed was done
and we were alone.

It was a cryptic Warning Order, the indication of an
oncoming operation. It was signed by the Chief, and re-
ferred to Special Battalion and how it was to make ready
for an operation to take place "in the near future". The
objective was the Citadel in Quebec City.

"The Citadel?" I said as calmly as I could. "Why not
Fort Henry or Louisburg? Are we after tourists?"

"Two weeks from Monday there will be some very
special tourists there," Mason said.

"Two weeks? You must be out of your mind." I glared
at Mason. "You knew this all the time."

"Look," said Mason. "I'm only supposed to deliver the
bloody order to you, but I personally think you should
know the whole bit."

I glanced at the order again.

"There's nothing in here about two weeks."

"No, but that's what it will be. Yukons will lift you to
Gagetown. From there you'll be airlifted to the objective
in choppers."

"Granting the need to wrap up this whole thing, it's still
ridiculous," I argued. "What's so special about Monday?"

"Our intelligence reports show conclusively there's a
top level conference scheduled to take place at the gover-

nor-general's residence in the Citadel. Attending will be the heads of the Provisional Government, including Lefebvre and Carpentier, and two military missions. The missions are from Cuba and China. Your job is to drop in on them."

"Oh." My thoughts were several jumps behind him. "You're sure about this?"

Mason sighed. "It's all documented. We've even got pictures of the Chinese. They slipped in by pairs, possibly by submarine. Some of them are in the Montreal area where it is assumed they are providing advice to the rebel commanders. The meeting in two weeks is where they will present their appreciations and recommendations on strategy and aid to the Provisional Government."

"You wouldn't have any of this evidence with you?"

"No. I don't think it concerns you." Doesn't concern me, I thought with bitter hilarity. They had better be right.

"Do you know why they selected the Citadel as a meeting place?" I asked.

"It seems logical. Easy to guard."

"Exactly."

"A drop-in on this scale won't be expected," Mason went on. "It's a chance to bag them all, finish the rebellion and make some propaganda yards about foreign intervention."

"In principle it sounds fine. How can we achieve surprise going across country from Gagetown? We'll have to stop and top up on fuel. You realize that?"

"This is being worked out now," Mason said. "To start with, we've stepped up jet passes around the area so they'll get used to air activity all the time. We've also arranged for sabotage of power and phone lines on the south shore a few hours before H-Hour. Airstrikes will be laid on in direct support of your assault group, and also to hit Valcartier and prevent reinforcements moving in from the camp. You'll be well supported."

"That sounds better," I nodded. "Got an airman for me?"

"Yes. He'll be in tomorrow. You'll have a squadron of CF-5's under your command." He dug into his briefcase and came out with a wad of maps, diagrams and photos. "Here's all the gen on the Citadel. Your I.O., Dawson, knows it intimately. He used to be with the Vandoos."

"I know."

After Mason had left to return to Ottawa in the Chief's JetStar, I spread out all the material he had brought. There were detailed specifications, diagrams, photos and sketches of every part of our objective.

The Citadel. La Citadelle. A sprawling redoubt, it had once been the anchor of Britain's 19th century Maginot Line along the Canadian frontier, interspersed with Martello Towers along the St. Lawrence to the next major pivotal point at Fort Henry, where the Lakes begin. Beyond that point, it was reasoned then, the wide open water would be fought for by the navy in mobile warfare. As late as the 1860's they were still working on the Citadel, and it was only in 1871, shortly after Confederation, that the last British troops had left the redoubt. By that time, Manifest Destiny was fading as the main thrust of American policy, mainly as a result of their own civil war; by the twentieth century they had more subtle methods—a cultural and economic tidal wave that bemused and sometimes hypnotized us.

As a seven-pointed maple leaf, its stem cut off by the cliffs of Cap Diamant on the south flank, the Citadel rose out of the ground at the north-eastern end of the Plains of Abraham. Except that they are now called "Parc des Champs-de-Bataille". An underground reservoir had hidden the actual terrain of the fateful firing squad confrontation between Montcalm and the young English general, whose name was gradually being erased from everything. The southwest wall of the redoubt formed part of the wall around the old city of Quebec. There was a dry moat and then stone walls thirty or more feet thick and reinforced ceilings covered by thriving green turf. The two northwestern points of the wall continued the outer defence perimeter, dominating the gentle slope that leads down to the Garrison Club and Rue St. Louis. The conference was to be held in the governor-general's quarters behind the south wall at the tip of Cap Diamant. These consisted of a three-storey, semi-detached structure, joined to the commandant's and officers' quarters, all built in 1830. This row formed the base of the rectangle looking across the square, which was bordered on the left by three long barrack blocks still used by the troops. The other end of the rectangle had a hole in it called Dalhousie Gate, taking one through a sort of tunnel to where the guides normally took over, carefully dividing tourists into English and French groups to hear completely different versions of what had happened in the neighborhood in 1759.

From 1693 to the twentieth century, the Citadel had been added to, subtracted from and remodelled as if it had been in the hands of a suburban housewife with an unlimited charge account at Eaton's and a subscription to Better Homes. Memories of the place were housed in a museum, a converted powder magazine of 1750 vintage, and in the honour roll of the chapel, another powder magazine, circa 1840. It made me mad to think of the rebels lolling around amid the history of our country and the tomb of a governor-general. I wondered if someone had gotten around to pulling down the Vimy Cross, the World War One memorial. Perhaps we should have brought back the Vandoos for this operation. The Citadel was their regimental home and, as far as I knew, not one Vandoo had joined the rebels, unless one counted J. J. Rousseau. But he had not been with any Vandoo battalion for some years.

I thought I would call an unofficial "O" group for that evening: Maclean, Rhodes, Dawson, but not the company commanders yet. Not really an "O" group; more like group therapy. I wondered when my air commander would get here.

The key question was how many Voyageur helicopters could be dredged up? Not more than twenty, I estimated. At twenty-five men per bird, we could lift three companies at a time, plus support and fuel carriers. Then they would either have to go back and pick up the three other companies, or we could bring in the Queen's Own by chopper and drop the three C.A.R. companies as paratroops onto the Plains, pardon me, *Champs*. If the winds weren't too strong, that is. Paratroops could also get fouled up in the helicopters if the timing wasn't exact.

I began to sweat, and got up to pace around. At last I took refuge in my many years of conditioning. I sat down and began to write out a check list and questions.

Objective, I wrote, is for Special Battalion to capture the Citadel, members of the Provisional Government and foreign military mission. Then what? I left times and dates open.

Enemy forces, I continued writing. Assorted militia units on guard duty at the Citadel, equipped with the same weapons we had. Perhaps some P.D.Q. Legionnaires with automatic weapons or sporting rifles. What support are they likely to have? Is the airstrike enough to neutralize militia units at Valcartier and prevent reinforcement? What is our policy re shooting up enemy forces on civilian streets?

Own forces. One Special Battalion, six companies with airlift capability and aerial firepower. Ask for one company aerial weapons platforms, Bell helicopters, 205 series with machine guns, rockets and grenade lauchers. Check on airlift capacity—need twenty or more Voyageurs. How many helicopters needed to carry fuel for the others? Indirect support: presumably one squadron of CF-5's with m.g.'s and rockets. Question: napalm—okay at Valcartier, but might make it difficult for troops to land at the Citadel. Question: how many Voyageurs can land at once inside the Citadel walls?

The next heading I wrote down was "Procedure". Embarkation points for us, I noted, would be Gagetown plus a refuelling stop somewhere near the New Brunswick-Quebec border. Where? Air support presumably from Chatham, New Brunswick, or possibly Ottawa. Could they make more than one pass?

Under "Procedure" I made a little box and slowly printed the letters P-L-A-N. When does the conference begin? I asked the lined pad. When will we be sure everybody has arrived? Calculate about fifteen minutes between the CF-5's airstrike and arrival of aerial platforms to provide covering fire for my first company. Phase Three: leading company will land within walls of Citadel and capture key points—we hope. How many other companies should land within the walls and how many outside, if any?

Battalion command post, I noted, a Bell Iroquois with myself, Major Maclean as operations officer, R.S.M. Wilson and a signaller. Dawson, the I.O., to follow with first assault force to identify V.I.P. prisoners as soon as possible. Attached units: a Unit Aid Station including a section from Field Ambulance with surgeon.

I thought about that for a while and wrote down some more headings: administration, communications, reorganization (Third Black Watch from Gagetown to follow up?) and some others. But I couldn't help thinking of the fine thread of minutes on which our lives and success depended. The airstrike should shake them up, and have some neutralizing effect, backed up by the aerial platforms coming in to keep heads down. And the poor bastards in the first company had to get inside the Citadel, pile out of those helicopters like civil servants at five o'clock, and lay on firepower and movement. Then the first section of helicopters, barely touching the ground anyway, would lift off and the second wave would drop down, their rotors kicking up dust and swirling away the smoke from the explosives and the burning insides of the stone buildings. And, while all this was going on, would the heads of the Provisional Government and the Chinese and Cuban liaison officers just sit there waiting for us?

From the window, I watched our CH-112 going through some more manoeuvres as he flopped down in a spectacular way onto the parade square.

Clown, I thought. I hope he's picked to go on this junket. It would serve him right.

21

West of Edmundston, the northwestern corner of New Brunswick is a wooded finger pointing into the rugged frontier country of northern Maine. Along the southern boundary of the finger is the Saint John River beginning its long journey through the province. The western tip of the finger, along the United States border, is marked by a long body of water called Glazier Lake. The last small settlement on the New Brunswick side is the town of Connors, reached by Highway 205. A gravelled road leads north out of Connors for a short distance and then peters out into a dirt track. The logistics planners had selected a site nearby for our helicopters to touch down on their way to our objective. From this point Quebec City was only about ninety miles away.

In a cold, drizzling rain the refuelling of our helicopters began. The tank trucks, leased commercial vehicles with Shell, Esso and Gulf logos deliberately left on, had made their way singly, their drivers in civvies. A sign imaginatively reading "Sunrise Camp—Private" directed the tankers and the other vehicles to the old logging road that snaked upwards through new growth of timber and down into open pasture land surrounded by low, wooded hills. A shallow-banked creek, brown in hue from its sandy bed, cut through the middle of the grassy plateau. A couple of sheds of silvery, bleached wood, and a pyramid of dark sawdust, marked the sawmill site which would be revived again when the second-growth timber was ready for cutting. Around the sheds a couple of service supply trucks had set up with hot coffee for the men, as the big, ungainly double-rotored Voyageurs sat down singly onto the grass.

I stood by my Iroquois command post, warmed my hands around a cup of coffee, and watched the proceedings. Behind me, a signals truck hummed and crackled with metallic voices. We were dangerously close both to the Quebec and Maine borders, and I worried that some stray aircraft or patrol would catch on. Up to this point the planning had gone reasonably well, I reflected. Frequent flights of aircraft and helicopters up and down the Saint John valley and across the Quebec border had, we hoped, blunted the senses of the local inhabitants to anything unusual. For days now the birds had been overhead singly and in pairs, establishing a pattern of flights that presumably would be dismissed as harmless and regular patrolling. This had to be done, for no one was sure what was happening to the New Brunswick French, the Acadians, and how they might react to the agitators from Quebec who were almost certainly in their midst. The patrols seemed a logical step that everyone in the area, in his own reference, could understand in one way or another.

"We could shorten this if the men stayed in the Voyageurs," said Maclean coming up to me, his boots muddy and his raincoat stained dark with the steady drizzle.

I looked at my watch.

"We're still all right," I said. "The airstrike is at 1015 and we're due in at 1030. I'd rather they had a chance to stretch and get something hot."

Maclean nodded, but jumped from one foot to the

other. He hugged his clipboard against his chest to keep it dry.

"Latest meteorological report. No change," he said.

"Too bad. It'll mean better cover, though."

"Seems odd, doing this halfway through the morning," said Maclean. "In the army everything usually begins at dawn."

"Timing of the bloody conference," I said. "We'll drop in during coffee break."

"I hope so," he said. I nodded and sipped at my coffee.

The ungainly CH-113's were scattered around the field like wounded birds, their rotors still and hanging low off the front power units as if they were broken wings. They squatted down in the turf, sterns settled and their bows up on fragile single wheels. In the drab surroundings, made almost threatening by the dark, wet stands of trees around us, the white and red maple leaf flags stencilled on the helicopters made a cheerful display. Around each bird stood a clump of men, their ponchos gleaming in the drizzle. The supply men were slipping from group to group in their jeeps with dixies of hot coffee. Unmilitary, white cups soon littered the ground in a plastic blizzard. The men were young, many scarred by pimples and acne-pits. The curious blank stare of youth covered their apprehensions. Officers and N.C.O.'s circulated quietly among them, even though every last weapon and piece of gear had been checked and rechecked before we had lifted off Gagetown. I had them travelling light. No helmets, only light peaked field caps. No packs, only waterbottles and one issue of cold rations scattered in their pockets. Rubber-soled boots for good traction. Two extra bando-liers of ammunition per man, four grenades each. All for a quick, fast-moving fire fight. I felt I had done all I could.

Above, a little L-19 Bird Dog spotter circled to talk in two more Voyageurs lumbering in at awkward angles over the hills. Three more to come and the entire force of twenty-five birds would be gathered after their two trips to bring in the complete battalion. Half the battalion would remain in this cold valley until the helicopters came back from the Citadel to pick them up. We had decided against paratroops, and seeing the rain slanting down, I was glad we had. When the last three birds had settled, the company commanders would make their way across the field to me to report in. Then we would be off. It seemed difficult to believe that history was just around the corner.

In the hectic two weeks leading up to this day, there had been no time for such contemplations. But the day before, when I was finally satisfied that the "O" group could report everything checked off and as ready as we were ever going to be in the time squeeze we were fighting, I had gone to the Mess and gulped my first drink in ten days. Gagetown's C.O., a relaxed, competent colonel who had turned the place upside down for us, almost shyly presented me with a parting gift. It was a collection of documents from the Quebec campaign in 1759.

"Just thought you'd like to know others had even worse problems," he murmured.

"Wolfe had all goddam summer," I said.

Later, in the quiet of my own quarters, when all was done and I was alone, I leafed through the book.

"My antagonist has wisely shut himself up in inaccessible entrenchments," Wolfe had written in his last letter to his mother, "so that I can't get at him without spilling a torrent of blood, and that perhaps to little purpose. The Marquis de Montcalm is at the head of a great number of bad soldiers." Not inaccessible any more, Wolfie, I thought. Not with air power. But he was right about the bad soldiers. Like his troops, ours were better than the enemy. No question about that. But Wolfe had some 4,500 troops. Our strength was 746 all ranks, and we had to take them in piecemeal.

I read Wolfe's orders to his soldiers on September 12th, 1759.

". . . A vigorous blow struck by the army at this juncture may determine the fate of Canada," he wrote. After outlining his orders, he went on to say: "The officers and men will remember what their country expects from them, and what a determined body of soldiers, inured to war, is capable of doing against five weak French battalions mingled with a disorderly peasantry."

A disorderly peasantry, I mused. The P.D.Q. Legionnaires with their white shirts and blue armbands. Were they the twentieth century version of the peasantry, or, with their ideology and tommy guns, were they a much more effective guerilla force? No matter what happened at the Citadel, it could take a long time to disarm and subdue the legionnaires. We had all seen what a few Black snipers could do in an American city. I foresaw a lot of bloody little scraps up and down the countryside unless the paramilitary arm of the Parti Democratique de Quebec could be disbanded completely. And in such guerilla actions, what would we accomplish? Had the spirit of independence gone too far for anyone to put the omelette back into the shell? Would Quebec become another Algeria, Cyprus, Nigeria or South Africa? It seemed that our century was one where moderate, reasonable men of goodwill were cowed and impotent before wild-eyed youngsters with machine guns, doing it all just for the hell of it. From 1917 on, this had been the story of our century.

I thought wryly of future historians somewhere collecting "Hlynka's Documents". What were his last words to his officers? A handshake and a good slug of scotch. There would be nothing inspirational in the stacks of memos, orders and messages of the past weeks. Only a virtually incomprehensible army jargon of strange initials organized into sterile numbered paragraphs.

FIRST HISTORIAN: What about Hlynka's personal letters? Surely, some measure of the man is shown there?

SECOND HISTORIAN: Mainly to banks, I'm afraid.

FIRST HISTORIAN: To banks? What else did he do on the night before the attack?

SECOND HISTORIAN: Had a bath and cut his toenails.

In the little time left for personal affairs, I had to arrange some kind of cash flow to Johnny at the Tremblay's in Hawkesbury. This was no easy task when my pay had dropped far behind my many moves. The chaos in records following the raid on C.F.H.Q. had not helped matters. I had written to my bank in London, Ontario. They wrote back saying there was only $2.56 left in my account and no subsequent pay cheques had been deposited. I had then written to my bank in Ottawa where I had opened an account, and they told the same story. The bank at London was then instructed to transfer the $2.56 to Ottawa and any subsequent pay cheques received. I wrote a letter of apology to the Tremblays.

The Wolfe documents did bring home one thing. I had not written any last message to Edith and Steven, wherever they might be. What could I write? That last night, I tried several times to compose a letter, but each time, I stopped in mid-sentence. It all sounded too camp. The words were parodies, and I gave up. This I rationalized into superstition. I was coming back and no doubt about it. If by any mischance of action I did die, Edith would know my feelings. There was no need to be dramatic about them. She would know.

Looking desperately uncomfortable and cold, my company commanders accompanied by their 2-I.C.'s, made their way up to me. Maclean and my I.O., Dawson, stood on either side in some kind of barbaric rite. Rhodes, the adjutant, was sitting inside the signals truck filling in forms. R.S.M. Wilson was off somewhere darting among his N.C.O.'s in his gadfly way. We conferred. They tried to show they were alert and on top. I listened and made comments. We passed monosyllables among us in our strange language. Their cap brims dripped and their clipboards were smeared. We did a lot of nodding. Maclean's rasping voice supplemented my own. Dawson said nothing. We moved our watches back an hour for Eastern Daylight. Our business completed, the company commanders picked their way across waterladen hummocks to their helicopters. Those who were not in the first wave marched their men off to the edge of the field to the shelter of the trees and watched us with pale faces as we made ready to lift off. I looked at my watch.

"Where the hell's Mr. Wilson?" I asked as we stood in the doorway of the Iroquois, its rotors beating spray out of the waving grass.

"Here he comes, sir," said Maclean.

Wilson, his poncho flapping in shiny, green wings, ran across to us and, ducking his head like all those do who have to walk under a helicopter's swirl, leaped aboard. We closed the door and lifted off in that curious slanting climb that always disturbs the helicopter passenger, no matter how many times he has flown in one. I had always admired the mechanical dexterity of helicopter pilots, and usually watched their movements knowing that I could never master them. One hand working the collective pitch lever and wrist working the throttle grip. Right hand on the control column and both feet on rudder pedals, they showed a degree of casual mastery that was beyond the skill of one who had difficulty double-clutching a sixty-hundredweight truck. We took our pilots for granted and felt safe as the ground fell away.

Looking back as we circled, I saw the Voyageurs lifting off, one by one. Taking our chances on the saboteur group fouling up phone and power lines on the south shore, we were to travel in formation. Maclean shouted in my ear.

"The CF-5's are on time," he said.

I nodded. As the Voyageurs rose out of the valley, sluggishly with their full fuel loads and cargo of men, we moved forward, slipping across Maine and the Little Black River to the finger of Lac de l'Est on the Quebec border. I wished the Government had agreed to let us follow the Saint John river in Maine instead of having to stay on our side of the border. To our left in the heavy, brooding overcast, we could see black hills, locally called mountains, sticking up and joining the clouds like fat typhoon funnels.

We moved into stringy cloud, splattering the windscreen and sideports with streams of water. Leaning over the pilot's shoulder, I peered into the shreds of grey mist and began to worry about control. I wondered whether to tell them to close up or to spread out and risk some losing their way.

"Tell them to close up," I said to Maclean. "They should be able to see each other. What's our airspeed?" I asked the pilot.

He pointed at the dial. "135, sir."

"Okay, tell them to close up," I said to Maclean.

Ducking my head, I went back and picked my way around the extra packs of food and ammunition on the floor. Near the closed hatch, R.S.M. Wilson was stripping and oiling his Sterling machine carbine for the millionth time. He had some kind of metal file and was working on the seer, for what purpose I didn't know. He looked up, his thin face calm in contrast to fingers fluttering over his weapon. In the noise of the helicopter we just nodded and grinned at each other.

Up front again, I saw a break in the clouds and glimpses of a paved highway. I looked at my map and assumed it was Route 24. We began to veer towards the St. Lawrence. The clouds were too low, so I ordered a lift in altitude and we got up into a fairly clear corridor between two layers. All birds reported in on course. Twenty minutes later I ordered us down under the clouds. We were coming to the point where we were over the hills and had to see.

Out of the cloud cover we came at 1,500 feet and

cranked up to 150 m.p.h. for the final run. The roads now were black or brown spinal cords joining together vertebrae of narrow fields, each one linked with a cluster of buildings at roadside, sometimes broadening into a group of buildings in a small village. They would hear us now, I thought, a beating of giant wings crashing into the stillness of the settlements, absorbed in their ancient rituals of work. I saw a panel truck dart to the side of a road and a man leap out. A small, red brick school disgorged tiny figures and a larger one in black. I hoped that the phone and power lines had been cut as promised.

Now we were coming up on Levis, and ahead of us, dullish green in the drizzle, was the St. Lawrence. The seminary at Levis, with its single pointed spire, slipped under us. We were beating in across the river looking straight at the windows of our objective: the grey walls and slanted roof of the governor-general's residence and officers' quarters, with eight chimney pots in line like refugees from a European city. The smoke, however, was coming from the three long barracks blocks inside the Citadel. These were known as the Armoury building, Mann's store (the mess hall) and a third unnamed, but now they were historical relics going up in black, oily smoke. I could clearly see flames reaching out of the upper windows. Looking up, I saw the last of the hump-backed CF-5's pulling up from its pass. More smoke oozed from holes and gaps around the inner perimeter, gathering in a low whirlpool over the parade square where the first wave was to land. On the horizon black smoke filled the sky in the direction of Valcartier.

Our timing was on. Heads were still down, I thought. There were no figures running around in confusion in the square, only one or two sprawled on the ground amid the smoke. I had expected more. Enough sight-seeing. We took up a tight circular course over Jebb's Redoubt, a tip of the maple leaf pointing towards a small street leading from the line of peaceful houses along the eastern side of the Citadel. We peered anxiously downwards. Maclean was talking to the squadron leader now spiralling high above us. The airman sounded exuberant and very young, his voice cracking. Looking at the oddly inactive scene below us, I wondered if we should have used napalm to ferret them out, but we had decided against it. Puddles of flaming gelatin wrongly placed could make it impossible for our own birds to land.

Now the single rotor weapons platforms (Bell 205's) came in right on our tails, dipping their noses low to sting. Ten thirty-two, I noted. From the tubes on the sides of their fuselages, each fired twelve rockets that skittered and probed for openings in the massive stone facings and searched out doorways and windows. The machine guns, mounted at their ports on either side, were ungainly levels hanging in space; now they sprayed at open windows below, striking sparks on stone, chipping off bits of granite. Spent and flattened slugs must have been ricochetting around the yard. A golden stream of spent brass casings tumbled to the ground. Expended, the weapons platforms tilted off towards the outside of the walls to land and set up a refuelling dump with the jerry cans packed inside them.

Maclean was talking quietly now into his mike, his eyes roving over the panorama below us. The first section of five Voyageurs came slipping up over the chimney pots, slightly distorted and surrealistic as seen through our rain-streaked ports. I looked down at my pilot who was sweating and working hard, juggling his controls to keep us almost stationary and hovering.

"Stand by to go in by the old detention barracks," I shouted at him, pointing. "As soon as number five is down we'll land. But we may have to lift off again."

He nodded, too absorbed to talk.

"Alpha Company, Red Leader, get those birds down," Maclean was saying. "Close up your formation; I say, close up your formation."

We watched, scarcely breathing. I glanced around as we rose and fell, suspended from the rotor grabbing at the uneven air currents coming up from the river. R.S.M. Wilson tapped my shoulder and pointed to the streets behind the first line of houses below us. I saw them, too. In the shelter of the buildings were people, standing in rows: men, women and children looking up at the show. There were blobs of faces peering up out of windows. As if we were putting on some kind of acrobatic display, they stood in the drizzle, pointing, gesturing and looking up.

"My God, the loud hailer!" I shouted, grabbing the mike. "What do I say?" I asked foolishly.

"Let me do it, sir," said Wilson. Over the sound of our thumping rotor, we could hear Wilson's voice echoing out over the rooftops in his fractured French. Added to the language problem, the loud-speakers filtered out any clarity in the human voice. It didn't have any noticeable effect. Except for a slight ripple of movement, the figures below stayed where they were. Some were now pointing directly at us, the origin of the disembodied voice from above.

The lead Voyageur was now coming in as close as he could get to Dalhousie gate, the others closed up and spaced carefully in a diamond formation above and behind. Their rotors caught the smoke from the buildings and twirled it around in whirlpools.

"Come on, get down," muttered Maclean, his jungle pallor muddy in the dim shadows of the cabin.

Another movement caught my eye. It was on the triangle of green turf on the northwestern redoubt opposite Dalhousie gate. And another similar flurry of activity on the wedge behind the refectory on the southern wall. And another at the far corner called "Bastion du Prince de Galles". They were moving. Green-clad figures swarming over their surface, peeling back the turf in rolls. Nets began to bob up in points. All along the high wall, figures were running.

"Do you see that, sir?" yelled Maclean.

I grabbed the microphone from him as the snouts of the guns rose out of the big gaps in the roof sod. There was no need for any more staring. I knew what they were as they came up quickly, men clambering around them. Already their commanders were standing and pointing beside the gun crews. The 20 millimetre rapid fire anti-aircraft guns moved muzzles and lined up with the helicopters now starting to settle sterns down above the level of the walls.

They had been waiting for us.

22

I began to remember. One of the reconnaissance photos coming across my desk some few days before had shown an arrow in black ink pointing to several white marks along one of the inner walls of the Citadel. A neatly-typed note had said: "New stonework. Note blocks stacked at base. Significance uncertain. No activity observed during overflights." And prior to that there had been an intelligence appreciation telling of heavy gunfire being heard at Valcartier. "Observer says it sounded like 20 mm. A.A.'s on range practice. Activity ceased and nothing further observed once daylight overflights commenced." Someone had written in the margin: "Where did they get them?" But there had been no answer.

So now we knew. Working at night, they had set up the gun mounts in the Citadel, carefully replacing everything by daybreak. All ready for us, now the guns were poking black clarinet barrels up out of the framework of turf and camouflage netting as soon as we made ourselves vulnerable at the crucial point of landing. None of our support fire had been directed at the pastoral sodding on the roofs.

It was a set up and my mind raced to figure a way out.

In a matter of seconds I was onto Support Group, the three weapons platforms down outside the walls, their crews hauling out jerry cans of fuel. Bunched up, I now realized, and in the circular parking lot, far too close to the southern tip of the redoubt.

"You see the guns?" I yelled at the lieutenant in charge, probably distorting my voice in the microphone. "Reload the pods. Get your m.g.'s on them now."

"Our fuel, sir," whined the lieutenant.

"Just get off the ground and start shooting. Even if you can only go ten feet, get those guns on the wall."

From around the helicopters, I could see the men leaping for the open ports. While watching them I got our air support upstairs.

"We're under fire," I told them. "Can you make another pass? Target is guns on Citadel walls."

"We've got five minutes and no ammunition," said the airman.

"Come on anyway," I snarled. "Go at them and keep their heads down. And find us another airstrike fast—napalm and rockets."

"See what I can do, sir," said the airman. "What kind of guns?"

"Twenty millimetre ack ack," I said.

"Christ." There was a moment's silence. "Okay, we're in. Tell your birds to stay clear."

I had just started to whistle up Alpha Company and get them off, when the world outside my plexi-glass cocoon erupted in sheets of fire and smoke. Off at the corner of the Citadel someone from the redoubt got at our aerial platforms with incendiaries just as their rotors were lifting them off. Number one, at no more than fifteen feet, blew up in a blast of orange and blue flame from the jerry cans of fuel packed in its innards. The second platform wobbled a short hop off the ground as flaming debris fell around it, and then it too opened up like a red tulip. Only seconds later, the third, its machine gunner striking sparks off the top of the granite wall, must have lost its pilot. It skidded forward along the asphalt roadway at the tip of the redoubt, and came down in a splash of vivid orange.

A three-pronged root of greasy smoke built a black parachute over them.

While seeing this on the periphery of my vision, I tried to raise Alpha Company and clear them from the landing zone. Just as they had strangely hesitated in their landing, now they hovered fatally before rising.

"Lift off, lift off!" I must have been shouting.

The first burst from the rapid-firing 20 mms., aiming almost horizontally and in danger of hitting each other, got our lead Voyageur which had been rising with maddening sluggishness on some kind of invisible string above Dalhousie gate. The bird broke in two behind its second porthole, spilling men and flame over the courtyard, where a millenium ago, tourists took snapshots of scarlet-clad, bearskin-topped guards.

"Red Leader Two, Red Leader Two. Turn back, turn back and return to R.V. Return to R.V. and await orders," I told the second flight of five helicopters now hovering uncertainly over the chimney pots in the Cap Diamant sector. Behind and above them I could see the big-bellied choppers beginning to lose their formation and drift out over the river.

"We could try further down the field, sir," the section leader, a captain, replied.

"Too exposed without support," I snapped. "Repeat. All sections return R.V. All sections return R.V. Clear the L.Z."

All sections acknowledged one by one. I only half heard them. Below me, number two bird, which had actually landed ahead of its section leader, had decided to fight it out. The men, a platoon of Queen's Own, came out into a blizzard of small arms fire at ground level from within the walls. The shooting gallery description is the only way to tell it. They were literally ripped apart as they scrambled across the open ground. At such close range the men within the granite walls got the rest of them, raking steel through the thin skins of the birds. At last, something reached the fuel and the Voyageur overflowed in a bright waterfall of colour. Behind them, now whirling upward off their carefully-sited L.Z.'s inside the Citadel, the other three birds of our first section were followed easily by the rising muzzles from the gun emplacements. I had never before seen helicopters taken apart at such close range. Bursts from the shells opened up the aluminium sausages with white-hot fragments that killed most of the men before they were spilled out into puddles of flaming turbofuel on the ground below them. Through all the deafening concussion of the guns, sucking up wind to press against the ears, and the roar of other explosions, I imagined I could hear the cries of the men. Possibly it was only illusion, yet I had clearly seen the open mouths of some as they clawed hopelessly at nothing in their plunge out of the ripped aluminium hulls.

Now, through the plateaus of smoke weaving into patterns in the turbulent air currents from cliffs and water, came the CF-5's. In line, as at an airshow, the jets ripped downward into the muzzles of the guns in a last toothless gesture before they had to return to their base for refuelling. It was a magnificent display of tight flying, snapping in so low that the gunners shrank and the men on the walls flopped down, some even rolling off the edges to become their only casualties thus far. As far as I know, the airmen did not lose a plane. Their intervention momentarily silenced the guns, as the relatively inexperienced militia men ducked. Hitting big, sluggish helicopters a stone's throw away was one thing, but trying to zero in on jets coming in to cut your hair was another.

Almost gently, Maclean was trying to say something to me. His eyes were shiny with tears.

"Shouldn't we go now, sir?" He shouted. "We can always come back."

"Come back?" I think I said stupidly.

Their heads now back up again, the gunners discovered our existence, weaving around in a useless course over

278

the old black cannons on the King's Bastion. I looked with academic interest at the muzzles of the 20 mm. guns bobbing around to set up a box pattern.

"Turn that thing off," I apparently said, jabbing at the radio.

Maclean slammed his hand on the pilot's shoulder.

"Down," he shouted in his ear. "Take it down behind the cliffs and follow the river."

The first airburst sent hot fragments flicking through the aluminium skin around us and clacking in deadly hailstones into the plexi-glass. Maclean looked down at jagged, burnt holes in the front of his green jacket and toppled forward onto the floor. My head cleared and I knelt beside him to unwrap a shell dressing. The next air burst thudded like a garbage can being kicked. It must have caught the edge of a rotor blade. The turbo engine squealed a siren of protest. Clumsy and ungainly, building up momentum as we fell, we whirled around and around helplessly on the stem of the rotor, as if it was taking revenge in its reversed role. We skidded back and forth on the floor in a pileup of bags, metal boxes and other junk. The pilot, strapped in, juggled the controls and swore in harsh, hysterical tones that somehow carried through to me as I slid around amid the debris. Then all motion stopped. I lay winded and gasping, pinned to the floor by a heavy bag of cold haversack rations. The pilot, a small, smooth-faced lieutenant, was first out of his bucket seat, pulling at my shoulders. R.S.M. Wilson crawled forward from somewhere at the rear; there were large patches of skin scraped off his chin and cheekbones. His nose was bleeding. I thought possibly my nose was broken and something pounded at my forehead. I dived across the pileup of gear to where Maclean was sprawled. When I turned him over, his eyes stared back and he was laughing. He was dead. Our signaller, strapped in beside the pilot, had either fainted or was knocked cold, his head lolling forward.

"Find the guns," I heard my voice croaking.

Wilson was already burrowing like a mad badger. He handed me a Sterling and grabbed one for himself. We each had two pouches of magazines on our belts anyway, and I fumbled at these to see if they were still there.

We had whirled off on our crazy fall over Governor's Walk, a promenade below the walls of the Citadel, brushed the low scrub along the cliff and had landed in a scraping howl of metal near the point where the two Champlain roads come together. We gathered outside the battered hulk of the chopper, our breathing raspy; we dabbed at our faces with handkerchiefs. The pilot, who was apparently unhurt, was dragging out the young signaller, his slack head marked by a rising, vicious lump.

"What do you say, Mr. Wilson?" I asked.

"I'm game, sir," he said.

I watched the lieutenant stretching out the signaller at the side of the road. They both looked pitifully young.

"You stay and look after him," I told the pilot. "If anybody comes, surrender."

The young lieutenant slapped his holster and began to stand up.

"And take that thing off," I said. "You've done all you can."

We heard the slugs zinging off the pavement before we caught the sounds of FN's firing from above. Several dark green figures were scrambling down the cliff above the Governor's Walk. From over near the ferry terminal we heard the intermittent bleat of car horns as if there was a wedding going on. Into view came two of the inevitably gaudy convertibles, tops down and packed with white-shirted legionnaires. Their voices, shouting to each other, could be heard in the stillness that now settled over the smoking Citadel. Without needing any words, Wilson and I headed for cover on the river side in a trough between the road and the C.N. railway tracks.

"If we could get one of those cars before the militia

gets down the cliff . . ." I muttered to Wilson.

Above us, the patrol from the Citadel was crossing Governor's Walk, stopping long enough to pop off some badly-aimed bursts in our direction.

"They haven't been taught how to shoot downhill," grunted Wilson with professional sorrow.

"Count your blessings," I said.

Now the first car had screeched to a stop only about a hundred feet away, and the kids in their white shirts and hunting rifles were jumping over the sides in the fluid, loosejointed way of the young. Except for the rifles, it could have been students arriving at a drive-in. I double checked my magazine to make sure it hadn't been bent and was feeding properly. With thumb and forefinger, I cocked the Sterling, made sure the "A" button was pressed down. Wilson started first with an expert light touch, spending only two slugs per man if he could. Two of the kids jumped and toppled backward before they could get over the side of the convertible. I got another one starting towards our unconscious signaller and the pilot who was now on the ground groping for the holster I had told him to take off. I caught the driver of the convertible in the chest, and he flung himself out of the open door in a last scream of pain. The other kid in the front seat was drilled neatly through the ear by Wilson and scattered brains all over the leopardine seat covers. One was left crouching behind the rear wheel. As we got up to go for the car, he started to run back towards the second convertible now coming up much more slowly. Wilson got him in the legs as he ran. The second car braked to avoid hitting him and the kids started to pile out. They still hadn't fired a shot.

I drove because Wilson was the better shot. He flipped the dead kid with no skull into the back along with the other two, crouched down with a grimace of distaste onto the slippery seat, and let go a long burst at the other gaudily-painted convertible. Our tires squealing on the wet pavement, we pulled away. We could hear the FN's echoing again from the cliffside. I wasn't sure where we were going, but thought we might take a chance on finding something at the Yacht Club a short distance along, and try for a run across to the south shore. There wasn't much hope for us on this side of the river unless we could break out into bush country.

With a sound like tearing canvas, the Starfighters came in low out of the overcast, a first flight of three, wingtips tight and their bombs arching forward towards the Citadel. I hoped they weren't nuclear because that was what the Starfighters were designed to carry. The first stick hit just inside the walls in a massive thunder of sound and smoke, but one fell short in the scrub below the crest. The hillside blew outwards in a volcano of grey rock. A huge chunk hit the side of our car with a bone-jarring clang. Wilson disappeared from sight. The world tipped upside down and I felt every tooth aching in the brief seconds of consciousness remaining as I hurtled outward.

Some time later, there was an impression of wet gravel pressing into my cheek. I must have moved, because a boot came into blurred view. It was muddy. Someone said something distantly in French. I felt my cheek pressing down again into the cool stones. Sharp, but at least cool. There was nothing more to remember, except the one thing. We had lost this fight, this twentieth century re-match on the Plains of Abraham. Me, the up-to-date technician, the green-clad, logical-minded, well-trained counterpart of James Wolfe now lay in a gravel gutter within the shadow of the Citadel, a crumby fixed-up tourist trap that had beaten the best we could send against it. Well, almost the best. A bad day, but I was too drained to care.

23

"Our first war criminal," said the dapper young man. "You're quite a catch, Colonel Hlynka."

From my hospital cot I sized him up. About thirty-five, immaculately groomed in a charcoal flannel suit, navy blue tie and a blue shirt with button-down collar. Only the twitch of his English style shoe at the end of a crossed leg showed any sign of tension. He had thick, black hair that had been razor-cut under a net and the pale features of so many young Quebecois, augmented by a straight nose and square jawline that made him look stronger than most of them. The eyes were deep brown and, under normal conditions, I would have said considerate in the traditions of the well-bred elite. He sat beside my cot in a white straight-backed hospital chair.

"Mercier," he said. "Director of the External Relations Division of the Security Bureau. You're looking much better."

The room was obviously a cell. There was my cot, the chair, a washbasin on the wall and a sidetable with shiny metal vessels in the odd shapes one finds in a hospital. The remainder of the room consisted of green-painted walls and a steel door containing a peephole. Near the ceiling there was a small window latticed by brassy metal strips.

"Don't let the title intimidate you," Mercier said. "These go with new governments. I'm glad to see you've snapped out of it."

"Snapped out of what?" I asked, feeling some energy flowing.

"Sodium amytal," he said. "Without it you'd probably still be out of your head. We're quite humane, you see."

It was hard for me to realize that I must have been in what is usually called shock. I thought I was too tough for anything like that.

"We got you quickly enough, before any patterns set in," went on Mercier in a smooth baritone. "Fortunately our patrol turned you over to me almost immediately and I recognized the symptoms. Other than that and some facial cuts you had no serious injuries. A miracle."

As if he shared in the pleasure of my return to the living, he offered a cigarette, a Gaulois made in Quebec. I took it, although I didn't like the damned things. I decided to smother any feelings of gratitude and prepare myself for the inevitable interrogation.

"Where is this place?"

"Temporarily, you are at the right of Wolfe's line," Mercier said without any sarcasm; but he was watching closely.

"The prison?"

He nodded. From our briefings, I remembered the stone jail set in the park about a mile from the Citadel. The battle lines in 1759 had extended beyond that point across where the four lanes of Grande Allée now pass. Mercier seemed gratified that my mind was working.

"What's this war criminal bit?" I asked.

"Come on, Colonel Hlynka. What else would you call someone who kicks prisoners out of a helicopter? You should never have let Sergeant Laliberté go. Then there is a certain suspicion about a forest fire deliberately set by saboteurs north of Montebello."

I said nothing. How did they plan to do it? Would there

be a trial, with television cameras, the international press corps and phoney judges? Or just a firing squad and a terse communique? Or both? I pulled myself up in bed and felt every muscle talk back. My face seemed to be pulled into odd shapes with pieces of elastoplast bandages in narrow strips. At least the tapes would prevent any kind of facial expression. Mercier sat easily, studying me and obviously in no hurry.

"I can smell smoke," I said at last.

"It's everywhere—even here in the basement," nodded Mercier. "Your friends made quite a mess of the Citadel." His jaw hardened. "We ended up losing almost as many men as you did."

"About how many is that?"

"Nearly eighty dead, each side."

"Then we're even," I grinned. He didn't like that very much.

"Not quite," said Mercier. "Your aerial invasion was called off. Your government doesn't have quite the stomach for a fight it thought it did. They have asked for talks."

I cursed them under my breath. Would I turn out to be some kind of showpiece in the negotiations: a propaganda pawn to be trotted out at some crucial stage for the benefit of international opinion?

"And Montreal?" I managed to sneer.

"Bogged down," said Mercier with a smirk. "In half-hearted street fighting and sniping. Your friend de Gruchy isn't very bright. He was drawn in."

He would be, I mused acidly. A few atrocities, some snipers seasoned by molotov cocktails, and de Gruchy would be suckered into the quicksands of narrow streets instead of barreling right through to Quebec. To give him his due, I thought charitably, he probably had political pressure to do a rescue job and restore order in the city. Or perhaps Montreal was a piece on the negotiation chessboard where the odds were in favour of the Provisional

Government. If they could prove effective control of large sections of the city, they might even achieve, at the very least, a free port status with United Nations troops in occupation. Our people in Ottawa couldn't afford to let that happen.

"Well, at least we broke up your conference," I said, probing.

"There was no conference," Mercier said. "You must have known."

"I suspected."

We looked at each other and finished our cigarettes.

"Ready for some food?" Mercier asked.

I grunted. He got up to go.

"We'll have more time for discussions later," he said. "I'm glad to see you are better."

He rapped at the peephole and a jail guard, in normal khaki uniform, opened the door for him. On his way out, Mercier paused and looked back.

"Nothing has been given to the press yet about any war criminal charges." He smiled. "I just thought you'd like to know."

After he had gone, I wondered why he had told me that. I looked up at the mesh-covered window. Outside it was night. I couldn't figure out what he meant. After a meal loaded with white bread and potatoes—a diet I recalled was sometimes given to mild shock cases—I fell into an uneasy doze, even though I was slept out. Nightmares swirled around me. Faces and more faces of J.J., Edith, Ab Tremblay, the girl Anna at Dorval, Budgy Tremaine, Wilson, Maclean, Rhodes, kept coming in on zoom images and fading out again. They were in full colour too, whatever the Freudian significance is of that. After a restless, sweaty night I woke up with the meshed window now a light grey rectangle. I got up and washed in the basin. A guard looked in and took me down the hall for the john, a shower and a shave with an electric shaver which he supplied. The cement floor was cold on my bare feet and breezes tickled my back through the vents in the hospital gown. By the time I had waded through a massive, starchy breakfast, my mind was clogged with genuine guilt feelings and an irritation at my own sloppy mentality. Unsuccessfully, I tried to justify my sins and omissions during the previous evening's conversation with Mercier and told myself that someone coming out of a slight mental mix-up might be conceded some allowances. I wondered how many days I had been shook up; not more than a couple at the most, I estimated. I waited impatiently for Mercier and cursed him for not leaving cigarettes. The grey light at the window had brightened considerably by the time he arrived.

Mercier threw a couple of packages of Players onto the night table.

"Your brand, I believe," he said. Not surprisingly he had on a different suit, navy blue wool, a pearl grey shirt and a dark tie with a thin, red stripe.

"My men," I opened, "when can I see them?"

"Don't worry. They're in good hands. We are not barbarians, you know." He had said something the same last night.

"What's the count of prisoners and casualties?"

He didn't need to consult any paper.

"You're entitled to know. Of a force of 139 all ranks in action at the Citadel, you had eighty-one dead, forty-nine wounded or injured, most of them seriously, and nine unhurt." He looked sympathetic. "I'm afraid a number of the wounded won't make it. Some of them fell out of the helicopters and the firefight inside the Citadel was at close range. I'll obtain a list of names, if you like."

I repeated, "When can I see them?"

Mercier laughed.

"A tour of inspection in a night gown? You wouldn't want to wear any of our uniforms, would you?"

"Look, a uniform is just work clothes as far as I'm concerned. Coveralls with baubles on them. Just get me some clothes."

"Does a uniform not have any meaning for you?" asked Mercier.

"Put a blue armband on summer greens, and what've you got?"

"Sedition?"

"You said it. I didn't."

"Does the uniform not stand for your own loyalties? Otherwise why did you almost get yourself killed in a foolish venture?"

"Not the uniform. It's the oath to our country. It's called Canada, just in case you didn't know."

"What is a country?"

"Look it up in Plato. If you want to hold dialogues, go find somebody else."

It didn't seem to bother him, although he did get up off the hardback chair and stretch. I thought he was going to leave, except that he sat down again.

"What do you think is going to happen?" Mercier asked.

"How should I know? You might have brought it off if you hadn't blocked the St. Lawrence, but that brings too many interests into play from the western farmers to the Americans. That was a boneheaded move."

He nodded. "It was a contentious issue in Council. There were those who said it would force everybody's hand."

"What was your stand?"

"I'm not on Council," he said.

"Even so. Where did you stand?"

"I was for blocking the St. Lawrence and the policy of establishing a border. It was the only way we could make our point."

"You have just used past tense."

"My poor English," said Mercier, who spoke English without an accent. He tried to change the subject. "For a soldier, you have had broad experience. It must be a comedown to fight in a dirty, hopeless little war at home after keeping peace in the world. I would think you're more of an internationalist."

"Don't forget," I said heavily, "The U.N. broke precedent on the South African caper. It moved in without the assent of the host country. What will you do if the U.N. moves in here?"

"We'd be delighted," smiled Mercier. "It would mean ultimate recognition for us." He leaned forward. "But you are an unusual soldier. After all that time with the U.N., how can you come home and fight a war of oppression against a people trying to do the very thing you've helped to safeguard in other countries?"

"To collect my pension," I said.

"No chance now, I'm afraid," said Mercier. "I can't believe you are that kind of mercenary. What would you have done if Quebec had consisted of some five million Ukrainians?"

"I'd move away," I said. "The place would be bedlam."

"Don't you comprehend us, at all? Our need to develop as a cultural entity, instead of being second class citizens in a loose, careless state that never could see that we were showing them the way to build a great nation. Instead, they sneered at us and kept us down." His nostrils twitched and he blew out smoke like a neat dragon.

"The only people who kept you down were yourselves," I said. "Your insufferable, unrealistic pride. Look at my people. We have practically given up our language; it's only a parlour tongue now. You have to compromise to build a new nation. My jobs in the U.N. were usually in places where somebody had too much pride, or too much dogma or just too much stubbornness. It always ends up the same way."

"Giving up your language and culture hasn't worked," he argued. "The descendants of your people, and all the others in the west, have little loyalty to Canada. They'd join the U.S. at the drop of a hat."

"They may have to now," I said bitterly. "As long as Quebec stayed in, they would too. But you people were the key to the whole thing."

"Where would you rather be? In the western provinces as part of the U.S. or here in Quebec?"

"A hypothetical question," I hedged.

"Come on. As a westerner where would you rather be? Or what about an Ontario linked to New York State and Ohio?"

"You've got better liquor laws in Quebec."

"Admit it. You would sooner be here."

"I won't admit it," I said hotly. "Your politicians deliberately set out to break up this country, and I'll never forgive you for that. After living for so long in some of the half-assed countries around this world, I realized that we had it made in Canada. We had a good place to live before you started acting like maniacs. Now it'll never be the same."

"That's the point," he went on unperturbed. "It never *will* be the same."

"Hell, you'll just be another banana republic," I said. "A nation of peasants living on french fries and pride."

His voice was still even and smooth. "You have always under-estimated us. We have the skills and discipline of the North American, but more imagination . . ."

"You have the imagination, all right."

"We have resources. And," he said, leaning forward, "we have guarantees of aid."

"Not from France any more," I said. "And China and Cuba can't even feed themselves. Russia is going to be cautious because you are smack inside the U.S. sphere of influence. Who?"

"The domestic problems of some of the countries you mentioned have no bearing on their ability to provide foreign aid."

"I gather there have been delegations," I said.

He smiled. "This is a strange interrogation—not the kind you are noted for. We did have a few local Chinese dress up to be properly photographed and reported, which your agents duly did. There have been delegations from our friends abroad, of course, but not around here."

"They still can't provide you with the capital to develop Quebec or whatever you're going to call it."

"No one can ignore our resources," said Mercier. "We have far more resources and know-how than many other colonies who are now successfully independent."

"Name one," I grunted. "And just what do you think the States is going to do about all this?"

Mercier laughed deeply. "Your government would go through the wall . . ."

"The roof," I corrected.

". . . if they knew that the States has been talking to us already."

"I'll bet they've been talking to you. When they seem to be tied up in Southeast Asia forever they won't tolerate any nonsense at their back door."

He snapped right back. "Colonel Hlynka, what would you do if the States intervened?"

"Me, personally?"

"Yes."

For a moment I was at a loss for words and just looked at him. Mercier savoured the hesitation and stubbed out his cigarette. He looked more satisfied than usual. Without another word he tapped on the steel door. The peephole blinked and the door was opened for him. I watched his silent departure. After he had gone, I told the guard I had to take a leak, but instead of taking me down the hall, he handed in a slop pail reeking with disinfectant.

"The service here is going downhill," I told him. "You'll lose your triple-A rating."

The guard shrugged and left. After having lunch, which made me think that probably Mercier was off at the Garrison Club or the Winter Club or some such place where he would have a three-hour sandwich with four wines and liqueurs, I paced around and tried to work out some leverage. Every time I talked to Mercier I wanted to ask about J. J. Rousseau. If I could somehow bring J.J. into this, I might then find out what happened to Edith. But in so doing, I could place myself in a position where Edith could be used against me—to obtain a confession or as a witness at a brightly-lit trial scene. On the other hand, if they were going to make an example of me anyway, with prison or a firing squad, I would want to see her again. A few minutes together might be our last. And, for someone carrying out an interrogation, Mercier was going at this business in an odd way. There was some other game behind his technique. What it was, I couldn't fathom at the moment.

Mercier didn't come back until the little window above me had turned dark blue and someone outside the cell had snapped on the ceiling light. I wished I had something to read to help ease my growing dependence on his company. That was the idea, I supposed. He came in briskly, trailing a slight aura of cognac, and opened up in French. I stared at him.

"Not a word?" he said.

"Nope. Only some high school grammar, long since forgotten."

"Of course," Mercier said sarcastically, "No bilingualism in the armed forces. You see?" There was an edge in his voice tonight.

"I was out of the country a great deal," I told him. "Most officers took the courses. Haven't you heard of the Royal 22nd?"

"Traitors," he said bitterly. "Lackeys."

"You're goddam lucky they weren't in the country," I said, and decided to continue the language kick he had started. "Where did you pick up such good English?"

"M.I.T.," he said. "I have my M.A. in economics. I was with the International Monetary Fund for a while."

"How did you ever end up in the Gestapo?"

"Please." He waved a manicured hand. "That is no concern of yours." But he couldn't help telling me. "My hobby was criminology and one thing led to another . . ."

"Congratulations," I said. "An honest cop in Quebec is a rare jewel."

He sighed and sat down on the stark chair.

"I am coming to the conclusion that you will never understand," he said, putting on a slightly mournful look. "Belonging to the movement; being part of all this, is for us a release of two hundred years of inhibition and restraint. It's like breathing fresh, cool air or swimming in a mountain lake."

"Not a good analogy," I said. "Swimming in a mountain lake drives your balls up to your throat."

He threw up his hands in a Gallic gesture that surprised me. Sometimes I forgot that he was, after all, French.

"You don't trust me?" he said after lighting another of his pungent cigarettes.

"I don't know."

"Try me."

I thought for a long time. The only sound in the room was when Mercier changed his position on the chair and recrossed his legs. Then I told him about Edith and J.J. Rousseau.

"Rousseau?" he said, showing his same casual control. "Ah, yes. I know who he is." He smiled. "One of our best officers. I shall make inquiries for you."

I said nothing and gulped down a tightness in my throat. Mercier got up to go, as if his job was done.

"You were right to trust me," he said.

After he had gone, I wondered. That night I didn't get much sleep.

24

In grey prison denims, I followed the two guards along the corridor, our footsteps echoing off the silent rows of steel doors. Up a stairway, we came to the main floor with birdcage cells stacked on top of each other, linked together by steel-railed catwalks. It must have been early in the morning because the prisoners were still locked inside and the low rumble of awakening male conversation sounded throughout the block in the same way it does in a barracks. They were awake, all right. In slow march, we paraded down the middle of the wide corridor separating the cells. Someone said something in French. In various stages of undress, men gathered at the barred doorways and a clatter began to mount in intensity. The rattling of doors started slowly and became deafening. Words changed into English and were now shouted.

"Let him in with us. We'll show him," a face called.

"Send us the war criminal!"

"We'll give him a trial."

"Shoot him now!"

Mixed with French and a lot more gutter English, the sound built up to an unholy rhythmic clash of the steel doors, cups and plates on steel bars, and stomping feet. It was enough to put a man back into shock.

I looked straight ahead and walked through the gauntlet

between my escort of grinning turnkeys. The realization that all of this was being staged occupied my mind more than the shattering thunder of the demonstration itself. The sudden quiet of passing from the uproar to a silent corridor, where the only sound was the muffled spatter of a typewriter, was even more unnerving. We came to an office occupied, temporarily at least, by Mercier. It was furnished in dark, wooden furniture, with a worn carpet on the floor and, like everything else, was permeated with the odour of disinfectant, wax and the sourness of mass cooking. Mercier was in a double-breasted black serge scored with a fine pinstripe, a white shirt and dark maroon tie. He didn't look so fresh this early in the morning. I blinked in the unaccustomed daylight, even though it was dulled by low clouds, and braced myself.

"I regret the disturbance," said Mercier. "But even for criminals, emotions run high at this time."

It was then I cursed myself for not following my first instinctive impression that he was a dangerous phoney.

"Are any of my men in this jail?" I asked.

"No."

"Then there are no other so-called war criminals?"

"The only other one, your R.S.M. Wilson, died when a bomb from your own planes fell short," said Mercier. "We would like to have had him too."

"When can I see a list of casualties and visit my men?" I repeated.

"Very soon, I hope," said Mercier. "Please be seated." I sat in a wooden office chair that had slippery, oiled arms. Here it comes, I thought, and I wasn't wrong. Mercier pointed to a typed document in front of him.

"If you sign this, you will be able to see your men, and I can pass along some good news. Also, if it still interests you, I will be able to guarantee your life," he said.

"What does it say?" I asked, "That I'm a fascist-imperialist-warmonger?"

For the first time, he began to look irritated and a

sharpness crept into his smooth baritone.

"It merely states the truth. Namely, that you take responsibility for the illegal execution of prisoners at Dorval Airport, specifically two privates of the Legion, who were hurled down from a helicopter, eight others, who were murdered in a washroom, and one officer who was executed while in your custody."

"He was a suicide," I said.

"That we don't believe. You will note, however, the way in which we have worded the document." He pushed it towards me; I reached over and slid it back to him.

"I said you could trust me and you can," Mercier flared. "If you take the trouble to read this, you'll see I have drafted it to save your life. Instead of saying you actually did these things, I have said that you take responsibility as the commanding officer. That's all."

"Look, Mercier, or whoever you are, I don't know what the hell you're talking about. The officer who was under guard by my men committed suicide. I don't know anything about the rest." I thought of one last bargaining point. "The best thing you can do is arrange for an exchange of prisoners and trade me for the brigadier we've got."

Mercier's mouth was prim and tight.

"Think again," he said.

"I have."

"Hlynka," he said omitting rank, "Your wife. We have her. And your son."

Out of the chair, I went across the desk for his throat, scattering papers, ashtrays, and a desk set. I don't think I even touched him. Someone grabbed my ankles and pulled back. I held onto the far edge of the desk. Mercier chopped viciously at my knuckles with the side of his hand. Something caught me a glancing blow on the head, jarring everything loose. The next time it must have connected in the right place, because I don't remember anything more about that room.

There was an eye from outer space. Faint lights from somewhere outside gave it shape and reflected its perimeter and the liquids in which it swam. It was joined by another eye, bright and glaring. Sluggishly, I recognized it as a pen flashlight, its narrow beam playing little white globs on my face. I shut my eyes again, too late. I heard a human grunt and something scrape on a metal slide. The eye and flashlight, having determined that I was now awake, disappeared.

So complete was the darkness, I wasn't sure whether or not I was actually conscious. I began to wonder if I had been blinded. A hand, painfully pulled around from where I had been lying on it, groped at my face and I could just see its faint blur about an inch from my eyes. I was curled up on some kind of cold, metal floor. I stood up carefully and felt my aching scalp touch the ceiling while my knees were still bent. By stretching out my arms, I could touch the walls. It was some kind of steel box. I wondered why I was so cold until I felt the welded seams under my bare feet. There was nothing else in the box but me. My bladder desperately needed emptying and I let it go in a noisy stream. The warm fluid momentarily cushioned the numbness in my feet. Then the urine ebbed away and I could hear the gurgling of a drain. I explored with a toe and found, in the centre of the floor, the grille of a small, round drainhole. Somebody must have been listening; the slide showed its rectangle of light again. The eye peered in, followed by its tiny beacon playing over me, stooped over in the black confines of the box. Another grunt and the slide squealed shut.

Something like a long, cold needle hit my back. I jumped, hitting my head on the top of the box, before I realized that it was a fine jet of icy water. My fingers felt out the small depression in the wall where the stream originated. I drank from it thirstily, although it was so fine and intense, it almost cut my tongue. Another cold jet of water cut at my belly. I rolled myself off into a corner and was hit by another fine jet from that direction. At last I gave up and stood wincing, shivering and cursing while about a dozen of these icy streams probed and cut at my skin between the goose pimples. I began to gasp for breath and hop from one foot to the other, until I slid downward, my back to a wall. One by one, the icy jets stopped, and I heard the water gurgle down the small drain in the floor. Now I knew why they had installed it, and wondered if this was some of the technical assistance the Provisional Government had received from its foreign friends—perhaps a modern-day version of the Chinese water torture? I was exhausted, trembling and gasping with pain and anger. I had dozed off, shivering and curled up, with hands between thighs for warmth, when it started again.

There must have been some kind of schedule. Through chattering teeth I counted to approximately 300 between the involuntary shower baths, about five minutes. As I grew weaker from hunger, cold and lack of sleep, the effects grew worse. I began to shake and vibrate and my teeth chattered against each other as I braced for the next volley. I began to think maybe I'd sign that paper, after all. It might be the only way to protect Edith and Steven, if they actually were prisoners or hostages. Sign anything they've got, hope for an end to the fighting and an exchange of prisoners. That is, if Mercier really meant it.

It is amazing, though, how resilient is the human ego. When they finally led me trembling and naked into the fluorescent lights of the hallway, I slowly felt an accumulated rage take over, flooding my responses just as surely as the icy jets of water had started to break them down. A sign of inexperience, I guessed. They hadn't left me there long enough, although there was no guarantee they wouldn't before they were finished. In some ways, I almost wished my physique was a little less tough and my psyche less inner-directed. I went into that room determined more than ever not to concede.

There was no Mercier this time. In a small room of barren, whitewashed walls and bright lights, a man sat on the edge of a table. It figured. A tableau of the third degree from the basement of a police station in the Bronx to its more advanced versions in Peking. If you can stay mad, I told myself, you'll be all right. Something else, farther down, told me to bend a little. Unfortunately, even with all the pain, humiliation and cold, it was still too far down. Perhaps I was destined to die of pneumonia in the cellar of this jail.

My interrogator was short, about five-feet-six, heavy in jaw and nose. He had a beer belly that stretched out his white P.D.Q. Legion tunic. The high collar cut into a fat neck. His navy blue shoulder boards had three stars on them, but I wasn't too sure of their rank structure, yet.

"We're bringing in Sergeant Laliberté," the man said in a hoarse voice. "He'll be here tomorrow. So why don't you save yourself more pain and discomfort?" His accent was so strong, I could hardly make out his English.

"Give him a promotion and I'll drop charges," I said.

The P.D.Q. man struck me across the face with a short, leather-covered swagger stick.

"The shower treatment will be stepped up," he said.

"I hope you've turned off the meter," I managed to say.

"Take him back," said the Legion officer.

I was led back. Whether or not the water treatment had cleared my head and improved my thinking, I didn't know. But I couldn't help noticing that he had not taken the obvious tack. If they actually had Edith and Steven, why weren't they using them directly to get me to sign? It's the first thing I would have done had I been in their shoes. Even though the searing jets of icy water left me shaking and gasping in the blackness of the cell, I had a glimmer of hope. It kept me sane. A routine developed, a dousing by the jets followed by short, violent interrogations in the traditional manner. Somehow, I managed to hold together throughout the day. Not once did the

299

grotesque little man in his tight tunic raise the subject of my family. This alone seemed to provide the inner warmth and strength to survive, for a while at least.

Whether it was a day later, or just hours, I never knew when they actually stopped. After awakening from a fitful, exhausted doze, curled up on the floor, I realized that the water treatment had not recurred for some time. I lay bunched up in a ball, vibrating like a tuning fork on the floor.

Some time later, a guard I didn't recognize stooped into the steel box, prodded my ribs and took me out again. This time we walked past the interrogation room, just as I was feeling a nerve in my chest, or my heart, starting to palpitate. Instead, I was taken to a large, empty ablution room, where I had previously done my showering and shaving. The guard pointed to the shower and turned on the water. Suspiciously, I put my hand under the water; it was hot. Even though I had felt I would never take a shower again, I basked in the heat of the warm spray. The guard gave me clean underwear and stood by while I wrestled with my beard and an electric razor. About three days, I estimated, judging from the wiry growth of my whiskers. Grey prison clothes again and we marched up the stairs and through the cell block. It was night. This time, there was no demonstration, only the faintly repulsive sounds of a large number of men asleep: slobbering intakes of breath, nostrils blowing wet snores and the ever-present click and grind of teeth mashing out images of the subconscious.

Mercier was again in the warden's office. It must have been getting warmer out, I thought. He had on a mixed-fabric, lightweight brown suit, a dark green tie with a faint yellow diagonal stripe and a button-down tan shirt.

"I'm finished with you, Hlynka," he opened. "I've run out of patience. This," he waved a paper, "is an order for your execution. The hell with a trial. You're not worth it. We'll just make an announcement."

My shakiness made it almost impossible to hold on, but somehow I did, and marvelled silently at my tough, peasant's heredity, or whatever it was.

"Make it a helicopter, if you don't mind," I said. "It'd take your firing squad all day to hit me."

His eyes were black and cold.

"That's it," he said. "The decision is final."

"If you're so humane, let me see my family."

"I'll think about it," Mercier said. He waved my dismissal immediately, and I began to wonder with a quavering chill, if he really meant it this time.

Back in my first cell with cot and washbasin, I almost felt at home again. Shortly after, a guard appeared with a bowl of thick, vegetable soup, wieners and beans and the kind of coffee that made me think a lot of army cooks must have ended up in jail. There were even cigarettes on the tray. Soon I rolled up in the warmth of the blankets and sank into an exhausted stupor. Most of the next day I slept, uninterrupted. The old routine was restored, with a morning trip to the ablution room for shower and shave. Three meals, but no human contact except the silent visits of the guard. I was too tired to try to open up any conversation with him.

On the third day, I felt restored in energy, but apprehensive and uneasy at being ignored. They hadn't even sent in a nurse or first aid man to replace the dirty peeling elastoplast strips on my face; I found clean bandages on my tray at one mealtime, and put them on myself. I felt as if I was waiting for something other than my own execution, but then, I suppose all condemned types just can't believe it will happen to them and have hope right up to the last minute.

The next morning I had dozed after breakfast and was awakened by the clash of steel-shod boots in the corridor. Here it is, I thought, and waited. The rhythmic beat of soldiers' heels went past my cell and stopped nearby. Next door, I heard a steel clang. After a shuffling start, the boots picked up their beat again and faded down the corridor. I had a companion. Presumably another war criminal; at least, he was some kind of military personage if he had a soldier escort rather than jail guards.

There was a long silence between us. After the evening meal, I kept out a spoon. When the window above had darkened, I tentatively knocked the spoon against the steel of our adjoining wall. After a long pause, I heard knuckles faintly replying. Then I drew a blank because I couldn't remember my morse code. The only way I could devise was the long way around: one tap for an "a", two taps for a "b", and so on. I tried to recall what Edmund Dantes had done. With suitable gaps between, I began to tap out the alphabet. There was some kind of reply with muffled knuckles. I tried to pick up the message by keeping an ear to the wall, but I couldn't make it out.

"I have a friend," I said to the guard when we were in the washroom the next morning. He shrugged and looked through me.

I noticed that they didn't take my cellmate out at all. Only silence until the following morning before breakfast. The small window was just beginning to show light when I heard the clash of army boots again. A clang marked the closing of the cell door and the boots retreated again with one man out of step. I wondered if it was the prisoner or one of his escorts with poor coordination. In prisons, I had heard, you could smell the tension when anything was going to happen, and now I sensed something indefinable. I paced the cell and used up my second last cigarette on a protesting empty stomach.

Outside the small window, apparently at ground level, I again heard the faint sound of boots in cadence. A voice called things distantly. Maybe they do shoot people around here, I said to myself. Even through the thick walls, the volley of shots was distinct enough. At least, my ear accurately picked up the heavy smack of FN's. Service rifles, I told myself with an ebbing drop in nerve.

In a surge of stored up panic, I hauled my bedside table to the outside wall of the cell. From the top of the table, after two attempts, I was able to leap up and grab onto the metal screen. The sharp strips cut painfully into my fingers.

The window glass was dusty and streaked, filtering out the pinkness of the growing light in the grey courtyard. I looked out at the backs of the firing squad, now standing with their FN's at "inspection arms" position, while an N.C.O. checked each weapon. These were not whiteshirts, but men in battledress green marked by blue and white armbands. They wore shiny, varnished American-style helmet liners. After the inspection, an order was given to shoulder arms and they marched off in single file.

As they moved away, parting a green curtain, I saw two men loading the body onto a cart near the base of the far wall of the exercise yard. Distantly, I could hear the rhythmic beat of the jail inmates having another demonstration on the bars of their cells. For or against the execution, I didn't know.

At that point, my fingers were cutting too painfully and I dropped down to the shaky little table. Despite their protest, I jumped up again, and wrapped the lacerated fingers around the wire mesh.

The cart was being pushed slowly across the courtyard by two jail guards, who were smoking and carrying on an animated conversation. Near my window, they turned their cart, with the whiteshirted body sprawled across it, head lolling over the side. Weaving loosely, the head stared back towards me, its mouth open and leaking blood from the corners. The stupid expression on the victim's face, and the dead eyes were not the way I had remembered them. But there was enough left of the unshaven, white features to recognize him.

It was Mercier.

25

As it flows past Quebec, the St. Lawrence forms an elliptical saucer, its width detracting from the height of the cliffs and ridges surrounding it. On the north bank, from the Anse au Foulon where Wolfe landed, to the city itself, the cliffs form an arrowhead rising over the harbour itself and Louise Basin. The other side of the river, on the south shore, forms the plateau on which the city of Levis is located. Further downstream, beyond the confusing melée of roads that take one down the heights and through Lower Town and along the north shore towards Montmorency, the cliffs rise again overlooking Isle d'Orleans. Among other things, it's a nice natural arrangement for gathering sound and bouncing it off in rolling echoes.

A fine echo chamber, I thought, as I listened to the explosions rumbling and reverberating in hollow waves. They seemed to originate where I reckoned the harbour would be, with its railway tracks and docks extending up into the St. Charles River. The explosions followed hard on each other in rapid succession in the form of a volley or barrage. I hauled myself up to the window again and tried to peer up into the sky where the high walls of the courtyard blocked the view. I could hear faintly the familiar, distinctive tearing of the engine blasts. The jets were back.

In the prison, there seemed to be a rush of activity. My breakfast was a chunk of white bread and lukewarm coffee, almost thrown into the cell by my silent guard. He looked at me sharply, started to say something, changed his mind and quickly slammed the door shut.

The bombing stopped and the thunder faded to a conclusion. I wondered if my Special Battalion, reinforced with more firepower, would be landing again. This possibility must have occurred to others, I realized. No lunch was delivered and I began to think perhaps I should start saving food and do some personal rationing. I rubbed a hand across my overnight stubble and, for the first time, thought seriously of making escape plans. In an atmosphere of panic and confusion, one might find possibilities.

That afternoon, I heard the whine of truck engines gearing down outside the window. Through practice I had improved the technique of leaping up to clutch at the mesh and had cut down the damage to my hands by ripping up a sheet into crude mitts. The jail population was being moved out. Cradling shotguns and old Lee-Enfields, the guards were loading them onto a fleet of civilian trucks, some with tarpaulins. I noticed that the prisoners were divided into two groups. The larger group had blue and white armbands on their prison denims and were making their own way to the trucks without much supervision. The armed guards seemed more concerned about the second group, linked together, wrist to wrist, by handcuffs. The dangerous ones, I guessed, or those who wouldn't volunteer for military service.

I dropped to the wobbly side table and to the floor. The prison might be cleared out if a landing was expected on the Parc des Champs but there was no indication of surrender if the convicts were being recruited for the white-shirts or the militia units. Somebody, somewhere, intended to continue fighting. The trucks moved out of the courtyard in blue clouds of exhaust and were replaced by others to take more of the convicts. At dusk, the jets snapped overhead, closer to the prison this time. More explosions echoed in the vast saucer of the basin. Nobody fed me. I did a lot of pacing.

When darkness came, my small window on the outside world reflected flickering lights from an orange sky. The city was being pasted. It wouldn't be long now, I thought. If the bombing was being continued at night, it could mean a buildup for something the next morning. Distantly, I heard sirens and automobile horns. The lights were not turned on in the cellblock. I lay on the bed and finished my last tasteless cigarette. Half-dozing, I heard the sound of army boots in the corridor outside. I was up on the side of the bed groping for my shoes. A flashlight shone in my face, its backwash reflecting highlights off a polished helmet liner and the young features under it. Another shiny helmet stood at his shoulder. An FN was slung from his shoulder and I could see he had on his full webbing. The inevitable blue and white cloth band moved on the arm with the flashlight.

"You are the colonel?" asked the youngster.

"That's right."

"Come with us."

If there was a panic about an expected attack, perhaps they had decided to clean up unfinished business, namely me, or any other prisoner marked for execution. I felt helpless and empty. We walked out of the cellblock to the exercise yard, the usual floodlights in darkness. This is it, I thought, and cast around for a way to plunge away into the night. Each man had a firm grasp on my upper arms and I regretted my lazy neglect of unarmed combat. According to the book, I should be able to do something like twirling them both ass over tea kettle, but I couldn't even recall the basic grips or movements.

Instead of putting me up against a wall, they pushed me into the back seat of a waiting car that was marked by a white door. Two men in peaked caps sat in the front. Quebec Provincial Police. One of the men in the front seat turned and handed over handcuffs. These were clamped on my wrists through a safety bar on the back of the front seat, making it just barely possible for me to sit back, squeezed between the two kids. When we started off, I noticed the headlights must have been painted over to provide a small slit of horizontal light. Blackout precautions.

Grande Allée was a nightmare of honking cars. Like Montreal must have been when violence broke out except, this time, it was the French moving out. A reverse situation, which somehow gave little satisfaction. A cop in white slicker manoeuvred us across the traffic onto de Salaberry. One of the cops in the front seat spoke French into his radio microphone, which presumably also cleared our way across Ste. Foy, backed up with streams of angry, scared civilians trying to get out.

Tires squealing, we shot up and down side streets that completely lost me, the cop sitting beside the driver carrying on a steady patter into the mike in harsh, guttural French while the radio spat back at him. There were no streetlights and most of the houses were in darkness. Ultimately, we found ourselves on a dual lane highway where Q.P.P. men were stopping every car and slapping black paint over the headlights. We shot on past the lineup and a convoy of trucks with scared-looking legionnaires scrunched up together in the backs. At one point, I managed to make out "Route 54" on a sign. We were heading north.

Beyond the end of the four-lane section, the driver took us onto the sideroad that goes through Stoneham. At the crossroads, an M.P. jockeyed us into the stream again and we followed the rear end of an army truck northwards into the darkness. In the front seat the radio at last fell silent. My escort said nothing; the two soldiers held their FN's, butts on the floor, on the side away from me. All four of them smoked but didn't offer me one. Despite the uncomfortable pull from my handcuffed wrists, I let my head loll and slept. There was some kind of holdup at the gates to Laurentide Park, involving a torrent of French and an M.P. who was checking credentials. We started up again and I slid off into the interrupted nap.

I awakened with French voices shouting to each other and our car weaving off onto the gravel shoulder of the road. A bright, glaring light lit the faces of the men around me.

"Flare," I said to myself.

The cop beside the driver leaned over and unlocked my handcuffs.

"Out," he said.

In the artificial daylight, we dodged out of the car for the ditch. Ahead I could see figures jumping from stopped trucks and cars. Another parachute flare opened up above the first. In the ditch we kept our faces pushed down into the tall reeds, but I could hear the beat of the choppers. The first helicopter let go its rockets, whooshing at an angle up the road beyond us. Explosions rocked the stillness of the forest. Smells of war—cordite, burning rubber and gasoline—drifted back in the soft night. Soon parachute flares weren't needed. The road was an orange beacon of flaming vehicles and the spilt gasoline soon caught the evergreens along the verges. A burning pathway pointed into the night. Voices shouted or screamed.

When the parachute flares had subsided, and only a distorted, jumping light remained, I slid slowly backwards into the willow bushes behind us. The two cops had already left, running down the road to a burning truck. My backwards crawl had taken me just past the boots of the two soldiers when another chopper started to beat up the road behind us. A rocket hit the ditch on the other side of the highway, showering us with turf and wooden splinters from the trees. I pushed backwards hard and rolled into the bush. Once clear of the road, I could head for the mountains behind us and they would never find me. But the forest around us was beginning to catch fire in large patches. I would have to take a chance on following the ditch for awhile.

Above us, the helicopters thumped and putted in a circle. Their rockets having gone, I guessed they would come back for some strafing with their .50 calibre mounts. I was right. The big, steel-jacketed slugs struck sparks off the pavement and it almost seemed the helicopters were coming in to land, they were so close. With all the conditioning and training so deeply ingrained, I still couldn't resist looking up at one of the birds almost directly overhead a few hundred feet above. It whirled by, tracers lining up its guns on the blazing convoy. In our flaming daylight I stopped to watch it go past.

The helicopter had a white star on its fuselage. A white star! A white star, for Christ's sake!

I don't know how long I stood there, looking up, oblivious to the snap of the rounds overhead and their soft whacks into ground or wood. The cold barrel of a pistol touched my cheek. It was one of the cops. I just looked at him.

"Americans?" I said.

He nodded. I shrugged and followed him meekly back to the car, which we found undamaged. Through a corridor of fiery trucks and a cathedral of burning trees, we pulled out into the southbound lane and slowly picked our way north, often driving at crazy angles along the side of the ditch. The smoke bit at us and we half smothered our faces in handkerchiefs. With M.P.'s waving us on, we managed to join up with a line of undamaged vehicles crawling along the highway. The helicopters came back.

Where from, I wondered, as my handcuffs were unlocked again.

In their sizzling arcs, the rockets ate up the convoy in front of us, balls of exploding gasoline spreading flame to the bush. We were crouched in some kind of gravel pit with a group of kids in green uniforms. I made out

Chaudière and Voltigeurs patches on their shoulders. As the choppers pulled off from their rocket runs to come back again, I looked around. A sergeant with a Sterling slung around his neck was just behind me. I couldn't take any more of this, I didn't give a damn who they were.

"Sergeant," I yelled, "do you speak English?"

"Yes, sir," he said automatically, I suppose, at the familiar tone of command in my voice.

"Those choppers are circling to come back," I said. "Let's get organized."

My two cops looked at me strangely.

"Come on," I said to them, and they followed me further down into the gravel pit.

"Sergeant, get these men standing up, their rifles on automatic," I said.

The sergeant, with a couple of corporals he rounded up, kicked the young militiamen to their feet. I showed him how to set them up for ack ack ground firing. The two kids with me joined them. I went down the line, checking the rifles and showing them how to hold them up and take a lead.

"Nobody's shot at them, so those birds are coming in too low," I told the sergeant. "Tell your men to aim half a length in front and fire in relays on your whistle. One blast for first relay, two blasts for second. Got it?"

"Yes, sir," said the sergeant, and rapped out his orders in staccato French.

By that time, the first chopper was over the highway, raking its .50's along the burning trucks. A single blast from the whistle and the first relay let off their FN's at automatic. They looked something like a firing party at a Wagnerian funeral, rifles up high on their shoulders, silhouetted against the fires on the road above. Nothing much happened with the first relay. The second group fired a little too soon, right at the nose of the second chopper. It veered off, obviously with a dead pilot, and at such a low altitude, it couldn't recover. Showing its white star, it tipped sideways and flew into the ground in a spray of flame.

I thought the kids in the gravel'pit would go mad. They yelled and whooped in French and in very unmilitary fashion, slapped the sergeant and myself on the back. The two Q.P.P. men gaped at me and then grinned.

When we started back up the road again I wasn't handcuffed. My escort even gave me cigarettes. Their English wasn't good enough to carry on any extended conversation, so after thanking me a hundred times, they lapsed into silence.

The attacks had stopped for the time being. It was dawn when we reached Jonquière, the southernmost of the grouping of modern towns located in the Saguenay basin. Chicoutimi, Arvida, Kenogami and others built on a base of hydro power and aluminium. Now we came into Jonquière along with a mass of bedraggled soldiery, whiteshirts and civilians. The journey from Quebec City normally wouldn't take more than two and a half hours. The Q.P.P. driver got instructions of some kind from an M.P. and we crawled into the town in the biggest traffic jam the place had probably ever seen. Women from some kind of auxiliary organization ran from the curb and passed in hot coffee. This we savored as we sat in the clogged streets, our weariness finally catching up. Through a suburban area, with its neat, ranch-style bungalows, we were funnelled into the narrow streets of the business district. The police car finally drew up at a four-storey hotel near the centre of town. A half dozen kids in green uniforms stood with FN's and bayonets around the doorway. As we went past them into the hotel, I saw their shoulder patches were Le Régiment du Saguenay.

Inside the hotel lobby, the cops turned me over to a lieutenant sitting at a desk that still had the name of the manager on it. There were officers and N.C.O.'s all over the place, most of them asleep in chairs or even on the floor. The lieutenant, who was from the Saguenays, had a big, black moustache and looked startled when the two cops shook hands with me. The two kids who had been my escort came to attention before they left, adding to the lieutenant's evident discomfort.

"Do you always charm your guards like that, Colonel?" he asked sarcastically.

"We aren't supposed to tip, are we?" I said.

He turned me over to a staff sergeant and then called back the Q.P.P. men and two privates, presumably to lecture them about fraternizing with the enemy.

In the hotel elevator, incongruously enough operated by an aging bellhop in a faded maroon jacket, the staff sergeant took me up to the fourth floor. Desks and chairs were crowded together on the shabby carpet in the corridor, most of them occupied by civilian women clacking out messages, memos and all the paperwork of a wartime headquarters. At a corner suite at the end of the hallway, an armed guard let us through the door, not without a long look at my dirty prison denims and the peeling bandaids on my face. The living room of the suite had been converted hastily into an office containing a battered desk in the middle of the room, surrounded by its regular furniture of a chesterfield and armchairs, brightly arrayed in garish slipcovers. My staff sergeant escort directed me to an armchair and left. I sank gratefully into it, too tired to get up and pry into the 1:50,000 scale maps stuck onto the walls in strips and marked with grease-pencilled circles and squares.

From an adjoining bedroom, J. J. Rousseau came into the room. He was wearing starched, knife-pressed field green with no rank badges or insignia except a carefully stitched blue and white armband. He was thin and tight-faced. We stared at each other coldly. I didn't get up; I think possibly I had half-expected to see him now that I had avoided execution as a war criminal and had managed to get this far. I wondered if he had intervened or what.

"Glad you made it, Alex," he said at last. "You look as though you've been through the wars."

I tried to keep my voice casual.

"What's all this about the Yanks coming in?" I asked.

"We'll come to that." He smiled. "I hear you helped us out."

"You can only take so much," I said. "However, your boys need a hell of a lot more training if they're going to be in that league."

"We realize that," he admitted wearily. "The Americans are expected in Quebec today or tomorrow. This is now army field headquarters. The government has gone to Chicoutimi."

"I knew this was bound to happen if you guys pushed this thing too far," I said. "What can you hope to do with the States in?"

"Let's get to that later," he said. "I expect you'd like to get cleaned up and see your family."

At that point I jumped up out of the chair and J.J. took a step backwards against his desk.

"Look," I said, "give it to me if you like, but don't hold them over my head."

J.J. looked genuinely surprised.

"What're you talking about?" he demanded. He thought for a moment. "The business down in Quebec. You'll have to tell us about that."

I gaped at him.

"Tell you about it?"

"Yes. We didn't know until we started getting a line on you."

"The war criminal bit?"

"There are no such charges that I am aware of. Certain things happen in wartime that are best forgotten. Think what they could do to me after Ottawa." We stared at each other like strangers for a while. At last J.J. spoke with a certain amount of sympathy in his voice. "Come on, get cleaned up and we'll go over to the house. I think Edith is making breakfast."

I was about to say I would go as I was, but one look in the big mirror on the far wall convinced me that the apparition staring back would only cause hysteria if it walked in on its family. In shaky anticipation, I had a shower, shaved with J.J.'s electric razor around the facial lacerations, and applied clean bandaids I found in his bathroom. I struggled into a clean field green uniform too small for me. On seeing the blue and white armband on the sleeve, I found some nail scissors in his medicine cabinet and snipped off the badge of rebellion. When I came back into the living room, where J.J. was busy on the phone, he scowled at the loose-hanging threads on the sleeve, but didn't say anything. After he handled a couple of incoming messages and turned them over to a staff officer, we left the hotel and got into a jeep in the parking lot at the back. To get out of the downtown section, still crammed with traffic, we had to drive part way along the sidewalks, scattering crowds of aimless whiteshirts and militia. We made our way a short distance through town to a pleasant, new-looking suburb with pine trees lining the streets. It all seemed very domestic and ordinary— J.J.'s casual and calm suggestion that I go and clean up and have breakfast with my family, as if we were just getting back from a fishing trip up north. I found myself going along with the atmosphere of normality as the only way I could keep my sanity after all I had been through. But I knew that J.J. never could be a friend again. He must have sensed this, too, because he drove in a preoccupied silence and with a grimness that was not typical of his usual buoyant attitude towards all things. Our little civil war had taken a lot out of both of us, I realized.

The jeep pulled up into a crushed stone driveway, gleaming white in the morning sun. The long, low bungalow had an attached garage, a picture window with the drapes pulled back and a clapboard siding exterior painted in lime green.

My son, Steven, was in the doorway. As always, he was quiet and composed, much like Edith in many ways with his tawny hair and grey eyes. He would only be embarrassed by intense emotion, so I swallowed back a trembling chin and clapped him on the shoulder.

"Boy, you have to wait a long time around here for breakfast," I said. It was the kind of opener he would appreciate.

"How are you, Dad?" I put an arm lightly on his shoulder after we solemnly shook hands.

"More to the point, how are you, your mother and grandma?"

"Oh, we're all fine. Any word of Johnny?"

"Yes, we got him out. Found him at the McCarthy farm —remember them? He's with old friends of ours, the Tremblays in Hawkesbury."

"Good," he said coolly.

Edith, in white blouse and tweed skirt covered by a small apron, came out of the kitchen like something out of the you-can-be-beautiful-while-you-cook section of Chatelaine. The sweet, hickory odour of bacon almost knocked me cold. I was shaking as she threw her arms around me. We just stood there for awhile sort of rocking. She put her fingers to the strips of bandaid on my face and the tears came to her eyes. When I looked up, I saw J.J. still standing there.

"Can't you get lost?" I snarled. "Come back in a couple of weeks and you can put me in the bag."

Edith and J.J. exchanged glances. Like all of us, she was showing the strain. Her normally rosy skin was a bit loose around the jawline; crow's feet and thin lines framed her light, grey eyes for the first time. She still looked warm, smooth and infinitely desirable to me, but I sensed a sort of emotional withdrawal on her part that caused me to step back and glare at them both.

"Even if I am a prisoner, you can give me an hour or two," I growled at J.J.

He chose his words carefully as if just learning English all over again. "You are not a prisoner in the usual sense. I'm afraid we have an appointment for you to see our Chief of Staff at eleven."

"Okay. Buzz off till then."

My former adjutant began to speak even more slowly, like someone being forced to say something he didn't want to. My inherent suspicion was aroused.

"Well, it's not quite that simple . . ." said J.J., brushing a nervous finger at his moustache.

"For Christ's sake, I'll give you my word."

J.J. couldn't say anything more. He looked almost beseechingly at Edith and then to me again. Edith turned to me, her eyes flowing and her freshness gone, as if a smoky film had dropped down between us. Like all women, she was much more practical about such matters.

"Alex, I don't know how to say this," Edith began. She paused, then the words came in a rush so fast that it took me a few seconds to digest what she was saying. Ultimately, they penetrated. I remember them clearly. She said: "Alex, you see, Paul and I are living together."

26

Their Chief of Staff had been so long in the Canadian Forces before his retirement that he looked completely Anglo-Saxon and would have fitted smoothly into any exclusive men's club environment in Toronto, New York or London. I had remembered his name: Drouin. He had done his share of peacekeeping with the U.N., had commanded 3rd Brigade for a time and then had gone to C.F.H.Q. as Director of Combat Development. As is typical of the army, on reaching the age when he was at the peak of his wisdom and knowledge, he was pensioned off. I didn't imagine he was receiving any pension now from the Canadian government. He was about 56, bald with a fringe of greying hair; he had a tanned, weathered face and a whitish moustache, obviously trimmed with nail scissors and a magnifying glass. He wore old summer greens, crossed by a shiny, leather Sam Browne. There were dark patches on his tunic from which his decorations and rank symbols had been removed.

I sat alone with him in his suite on the fourth floor of the hotel in Jonquière and tried to concentrate, not too successfully, on what he was saying.

"Have you been treated well here, Colonel Hlynka?"

"Yes, sir. Here I have been," I mumbled and looked down at my freshly-starched field greens.

"You have taken off our armband," he noted. "We are in an emotional time. If you don't wear it, somebody might shoot you."

I shrugged and looked sullenly past him. An emotional time was an understatement, as far as I was concerned, and I was hardly in any mood for a chat with a retired, treasonous general. I only half-listened to him, my mind still clogged with what had happened to my life and future on that deceptively quiet residential street only a couple of miles away.

After Edith had told me and had drawn away towards J.J., I could think of nothing better to say than to ask to be taken back immediately to the custody of the rebel forces and put into any kind of jail they wanted to find. I also told him, in front of Edith, that the first chance I had, I would kill him. Edith, almost incoherent, cried that it was her fault, that she had encouraged it when J.J. was in London on leave over a year ago, and that they had planned to do this, even if civil war had not broken out. Remember, she said, almost pleading, that he saved the lives of our family and brought them to safety at the risk of his own life and the men with him. Not being in any mood to listen to debating points, I had growled at J.J. to return me to the hotel.

Outside the house the silvery outer aluminium door had swung slowly on its hydraulic closer, reluctantly shutting off my life behind me. I stood alone in the clear sunshine. Down the road two little kids played on their tricycles along the curb. I looked back through the screen and dimly saw Edith standing at the kitchen door. Her arm was around Steven who had his cheek against her shoulder. In front of me J.J. sat in the jeep, staring stonily at the garage. Everyone seemed to have frozen into a wax-works display and I realized they were all waiting for me to move. I hung onto the black iron railing and came down the five steps like an old man. At the sidewalk, I stopped again and looked back, but this time could see nothing in the dim light behind the screen door. For some reason I studied the lawn. It was made up of oases of coarse, tufted grass trying vainly to reach each other across bands of thin, grey soil. There were quite a few dandelions.

A cool, dry hand touched my wrist and made me jump. Edith's mother had come around from the back of the house and now stood beside me. I looked down at her.

"Alex," she said.

"Mrs. Watson," I mumbled. "What's happening to us?"

In our years of marriage I had never been able to bring myself to call Mrs. Watson "mother" or anything like that, nor had such an endearment ever been encouraged. To me a mother was someone who cried in despair at us, who laughed and horsed around and sometimes even danced with us, who blew her top in squalls of sudden anger; a mother to me was someone who wore coveralls out to the henhouse and carried buckets of cream from the separator and presided over steaming vats of this and that over a wood stove. Or she wore a hunting jacket over a thin housedress, flapping in cold mountain air and carried an old wicker basket overflowing with heavy, soggy clothing to hang on a squeaking clothesline and hope that the coal dust and smoke was blowing the other way. Even now, living alone in the tiny frame house in Vancouver, she was probably steaming herself scarlet in the face, preserving sealer jars of pears, rhubarb or strawberries which no one would ever eat unless she gave them away to her neighbors.

The Watsons had occupied a specious, symmetrical enclave in Westmount, a gracious compound sheltered from the teeming world around them. When Edith had first "brought me home", as they say, I had stood transfixed in the high-ceilinged living room bemused by its sharp, glossy order. I had hesitated to walk across the wall-to-wall carpet, so carefully brushed in the same direction. It was a Wedgewood room, in blues and whites professionally blended with dots of colour from tiny, exquisite china figurines. An original painting by somebody famous hung over the mantle and had its own tubular light fixture at the base. I remembered Mrs. Watson had matched the room. Her trim, carefully dieted figure had been sheathed in a light, blue silk dress; her hair a moulded pattern of razored grey with a slight blue tinge; her fine features were unlined but pale, and she had blue eyes. A Wedgewood lady in a Wedgewood room, I had thought. In time she had more or less accepted me because, after all, the army was a respectable profession. I had really arrived when I achieved my three rings and reached lieutenant-colonel, mainly, I suspected, because she had a couple of civilian friends who still used "major" in front of their names. There was something to be said for a son-in-law who outranked them.

Now, Edith's mother was an old woman and, for the first time, I felt a tinge of kinship with her. Without weekly care, her hair had become frizzy and was a patchwork of fading brown and grey. Her face was brown-splotched and without regular dieting had become swollen and puffy as if starch had run riot in her system. Her eyes were surrounded by deep lines and circles. She wore a rumpled tweed skirt and a baggy cashmere cardigan.

"How can you stay here—with this?" I asked her bitterly.

"There is nothing else left, Alex," she said. "Where can I go? I have lost my home, my husband and now you."

I had never thought of myself as something she could lose, and was strangely touched.

"What made her do it?" I asked, still not able to bring myself to call her "mother".

"Edith was always wilful and spoiled," Mrs. Watson said. "She had a quality of restlessness about her which you only partly and temporarily held in check. But Alex," she said, her eyes searching mine, "she is still a good girl. I think she knows she has made a terrible mistake."

"I wouldn't know."

"It will take time for her pride . . ."

"Who's got time?"

"Alex, try to grow out of your bitterness. She needs help and kindness. That's what she saw in him," she said nodding toward J.J. who was staring at us from the jeep. We had turned away from him so that he couldn't catch our words.

"What are we to do now?" I muttered.

"I'll stay with her and keep talking to her and do what I can. For the first time, we are close to one another. Perhaps when things settle down a little more . . . Don't lose hope, Alex; don't ever do that." She tentatively touched my arm again with light, frightened fingers.

I looked down at her and saw the determination that must have had a good deal to do with her husband's success in the business world. Odd, I reflected, I had never noticed it before. I brought myself to squeeze her shoulder slightly.

"It's almost too much to ask," I said. "Maybe it's too much to ask of any of us now."

"You're strong, Alex," she said. "You'll make it."

J.J. turned on the jeep motor. We stood in silence for a moment. Mrs. Watson turned and walked towards the house and I started slowly along the sidewalk to the driveway. At the front door she turned and, with a shyness that was almost adolescent in gesture, waved to me. I raised a hand and made a conspiratorial nod. She was still standing on the step as we backed out onto the road.

On the way back in the jeep, I almost brought myself to asking J.J. why it had happened, but decided it was too risky to permit the emotional lid to come off. I was still a prisoner of some sort, if not a war criminal any longer. They might try to sugarcoat it all they liked, including so-called interviews with their Chief of Staff, but I knew the next stage would be an interrogation of some kind, followed possibly by offers to defect and, when I refused, prison again. I could see that one coming over the hill. So instead of asking J.J. anything, I let my head sag onto my chest and confined the questions to my own inner thoughts. I didn't know and perhaps never would. In all likelihood Edith and J.J. couldn't explain it themselves, either; life just doesn't provide pat answers. My only comfort from that bleak morning was the unexpected, brittle strength of Edith's mother. But that was only a glimmer in the darkness.

At the hotel J.J. wordlessly turned me over to a duty officer who took me to an anteroom where I was told to wait for my summons from the General. At eleven o'clock I was led to my appointment. The duty officer told me, not entirely hiding his envy, that J.J. had had a meteoric rise to become Deputy Chief of Staff.

"St. Hubert and Ottawa did that for him," the officer said maliciously.

Now their Chief was asking me: "Is there anything we can do for you?"

"Yes, sir," I said. "Just keep Captain Rousseau away from me."

"Colonel Rousseau in our organization," corrected the General. "Yes, he told me there might be some personal complications."

"He was right." There was silence and I shifted uneasily under the General's stare. At last I realized that I would have to ask the question. "I would like to know what's going to happen to me, sir."

"What happens will be up to you," said General Drouin. "We need good men."

I stood up.

"Let me make it clear, sir. I have no intention of joining you. Not after all that has happened."

He waved his hand.

"I don't expect you to. Sit down." I sat down. "I wanted to meet you and tell you officially that you are not a prisoner and that there are no charges against you. Naturally, we would welcome your assistance."

"In that case, sir, I must ask that I become a prisoner again."

"You don't seem to understand, Colonel Hlynka. That won't be necessary." He looked slightly exasperated. "Unfortunately, I haven't the time to brief you personally on the situation. However, I shall introduce you to someone who will." His carefully manicured hand lifted the intercom phone and he pushed down a lever. He spoke in English. "Colonel, could you come in for a moment?"

When Ted Mason burst through the door, energetically crashing the doorknob against the wall, I shot to my feet and glared at him. Except for the blue and white armband, he was wearing his regular greens, complete with rank and insignia. He looked brisk and alert and, judging by the stubble on his head, had even found time for a haircut.

"No wonder we don't fucking well win battles," I snarled.

Mason's grin of welcome faded and he shot a stricken glance at General Drouin, who stood up, icy and angry, suddenly dominating the room. His almost gentle manner had quickly disappeared.

"Colonel Hlynka, there is no need for that kind of talk."

"What am I supposed to say? I lost some damned good men at Quebec and Dorval."

"Jesus, Alex. Take it easy," said Mason.

"You've been with them all the time?" I shouted.

"No, no. Nothing like that," said Mason, obviously hurt. "He doesn't know, sir?" he asked the General.

"I'm afraid not, Colonel Mason. I think you had better enlighten him before I start losing my patience." General Drouin sat down, trembling slightly. I was feeling shaky too. "Perhaps he will come around after he is briefed."

"Don't count on it," I said.

"Come on, Alex," said Mason. "Let's go. We've got a lot of things to talk about."

"Forget it. Just put me back in the jug. I'll take your friend Mercier any day."

Mason looked blank. General Drouin had lost his patience.

"Don't waste too much time on him, Colonel Mason," he snapped. "We haven't got time for conversions. We can arrange to send him out."

Mason paused.

"He's an officer and he'll bloody well do what he's told, sir." He grinned slightly. "And he just happens to be a good man."

We were dismissed. Reluctantly, I followed Ted Mason through a series of busy rooms where French voices spoke on telephones and to each other in that rapid delivery that always sounds as if they are in a perpetual state of hysteria. We walked silently down the firestairs to the third floor where Mason occupied a corner suite. As we passed through the sitting room into the bedroom he used as his office, I noticed several other officers wearing their Canadian uniforms and badges. Mason closed his door and sat down behind a desk pushed into a corner of the room. The last time I had seen him he had also been operating out of confined space. He seemed to thrive on it.

"God knows things are touchy enough," he said in his best scolding manner. "All we need is for you to louse things up."

I started to say something.

"Shut up, sit down and listen," said Mason.

27

Ted Mason told me he was the liaison officer of the Canadian Forces to the Provisional Government and that he had a small staff of other officers to help in said enterprise. He repeated that it was a very touchy situation, but so far he had established a cool, correct working relationship with the rebels and he didn't want people like me around blowing their stacks when everyone was just a bit edgy anyway. If I could restrain myself just for awhile, he could put me to good use and it would all add to the considerable reputation I had already achieved at C.F.H.Q. as an officer with the ability to get things done no matter what the odds. I listened to the speech in disbelieving silence.

"You mean you haven't defected?" I managed to ask.

"Who me?" His pride was hurt. "You don't know anything that's going on?"

"How would I? I've just come off the war criminal circuit."

"Oh, that," said Mason, looking thoughtful. He tried to get up to pace, but his desk boxed him in the small space, so he sat down again and twitched.

"Would the Yanks have something to do with this? We were apparently shot up by their choppers last night."

"You're getting warm," Mason said. "In a nutshell our

job is to help both the Canadian government and the Provisional Government stall for time."

"And stalling for time means . . ."

"Stalling the Yanks. They've already occupied Quebec City and are moving out along the north shore of the St. Lawrence. Our little setback at the Citadel and all the political dilly-dallying that went on afterwards brought their patience to an end. It's kind of thin at the best of times and they sure as hell weren't about to put up with an unstable situation on their northern border."

I leaned toward Mason. "Does this so-called 'stalling' bit involve fighting the Yanks?"

"Well . . . Yes, it does. Not for long, we hope."

"You must all be out of your ever-loving skulls," I groaned.

"No we're not," said Mason primly. "We can't let them get away with it, y'know. We can't just let them walk in and occupy the St. Lawrence."

"How're you going to stop them?"

"Ever heard of the Viet Cong or the Pathet Lao?"

"Come on. You're talking about jungles thousands of miles away."

"We've got bush and darkness and the will to fight."

"Who has the will to fight? I've worked with Yanks throughout most of my military career. I like them; I respect them, and I'm not going to start fighting them now. Bring on some Chinese or Russians and I'll give it a whirl. But Yanks, not on your life."

Mason made a face. "I'm disappointed in you, Alex. This should appeal to your sense of the offbeat. You pride yourself in organizing impossible operations. Let's see what you can do. Or are you an amateur, after all?"

"I'm a professional, not a mercenary. There's a difference. You can't expect me to go out and organize a bunch of Frenchmen who cut down my own men just a few days ago."

"There aren't many of them around either," Mason

said. "That particular group got it when we sent in the Starfighters. You won't have anything to do with the legionnaires; they're no good in a situation like this. You'll be dealing with their top militia people or our own regulars."

"You're asking a lot, Ted," I said. "Maybe you'd better send me out and get someone else who doesn't have my memories."

"It didn't bother you last night when you set them up to shoot down that chopper," argued Mason. "Did you find that so hard to do?"

"Strictly spur of the moment stuff. I don't like anybody shooting at me, no matter who it is."

"Well?"

"Okay, so it's an intriguing idea. A nice little war game. Small Red Force takes on large Blue Force." I got up and rocked on my heels because there wasn't room to walk around much. "Listen, Ted, those bastards in Quebec had me tagged as a war criminal. They really gave it to me. I'd be just as happy to see the Yanks move in."

"It's not that simple, Alex. There's a lot more at stake than meets the eye."

"There must be, because nothing has met my eye yet that makes sense. Why the hell was I being held as a war criminal?"

"You weren't . . . officially," said Mason. "It was all the brainchild of this character, Fortier. Because of him and some others, the Provisional Government really got itself hung up in some nasty international intrigue. Of course, they should've anticipated that when they decided to separate. But such is fanaticism. Nobody in their bunch seemed to appreciate that once they had taken the step, they became a strategic prize, up for grabs in the power-plays of the major nations. That's exactly what happened, aided by some very subtle manoeuvring by people like Fortier. He took advantage of the desire of the Provisional Government to seek aid and support from abroad where-ever they could get it. Fortunately, their security men got to him in time and he was shot. But it may be too late for them now. All we can do is carry out our delaying action and fight for time."

"I don't know any Fortier. Would you mean Mercier?"

"Is that what he called himself to you?"

"Young, good-looking, well-dressed. He said he was from the Security Bureau and that I was to be tried as a war criminal."

Mason laughed. "War criminal? That must have been part of his scheme."

"What scheme?"

"Well," said Mason, snapping a yellow, wooden pencil in two. "When the Provisional Government sought outside aid, the only concrete offers, predictably enough, came from China and Cuba, followed somewhat later by rather vague assurances from the Soviet Union. It soon became evident, after innumerable meetings with the aid delegations, that there was a sharp difference of policy between the Soviet Union and China. Cuba was not a major factor in any case, except for guerilla-training personnel and its role as a funnel for weapons from the others."

"This is the 'it's-not-that-simple' lecture?" I asked.

"Do you want to hear this, or don't you?"

"Okay. Go ahead," I said wearily. "I haven't much to lose." Mason went ahead.

"In essence," he said, "China's position was that massive aid should be poured into Quebec to ensure that the new state could, in fact, survive against all comers. But China was dependent on Soviet logistical capabilities in the form of cargo-carrying submarines and jet transports to deliver the goods to Quebec. The Soviets, while professing complete support, apparently had seemed curiously vague about the details of aid. Only after some intensive work and listening by their Security Bureau, did the Quebec government begin to get an inkling of what the Soviets were trying to do. Stripped of a number of fringe

328

complications, the essential Soviet position was that the Provisional Government had no hope of survival. If the Canadians couldn't bring themselves to finish them off, the Americans would; and the Soviets had no desire to become involved directly or identified openly with a venture right on the U.S. border.

"There was, in the Soviet view, a way in which the situation could be exploited to their advantage. Soviet aid would trickle through to help beef up the Provisional Government's forces. If they could be made strong enough to make the Canadian government—which had shown considerable reluctance to come to grips with the insurrection—back off and reopen negotiations with Quebec, there would likely be one predictable result. American impatience would reach its limits and there would be intervention to prevent another Cuba on their borders. If this happened, and the U.S. became preoccupied in its own backyard, there might well be a weakening of the American effort in Southeast Asia, notably Thailand. Then the Soviets could hope that Thailand might end up like Viet Nam, a 'neutral' communist nation following a U.N.-supervised plebiscite."

"Worth a try," I nodded.

"It sure was," agreed Mason, his restless fingers busily straightening out their twentieth paperclip. "And, as a result, Quebec was caught in a fine squeeze play. The Soviet plan depended on being able to goad the Americans to interfere, while getting the Canadians to draw back. The Soviets were fortunate in that someone—we believe in the Fourth Department of the G.R.U.—had latched onto Fortier (or Mercier, as you knew him). Whether or not he had been an agent since his early days with the separatist movement, or whether he had recently been recruited, we don't know. We are not even sure whether Mercier was aware of the Soviet plan; in all likelihood he wasn't and thought he was doing his best for the new nation with Soviet support and advice. All we know is that his case officer or 'handler' from the Russian side was an engineer with the Soviet aid delegation at Quebec and that Mercier did what he was told.

"Mind you, it didn't take much persuasion to set up the hawks in the Provisional Government for a blockade of the Seaway, even though the implications of doing so were obvious to many. The doves on Council, who had advocated merely patrols and boarding of all shipping, plus collection of tolls in the name of the government, were outvoted on their 'open Seaway' policy. Until now, the Provisional Government has not been in the mood to listen to anyone's intelligent, moderate council. We think they bloody well will now; in fact, we foresee some changes in the Provisional Government.

"Anyway," went on Mason, shredding a memo pad with a paper knife, "when leadership in the Canadian government changed rather unexpectedly, Mercier and his handlers realized that something more had to be done. Again, they didn't have much difficulty in persuading the Provisional Government to go for a complicated plan to draw the Canadian Forces into a trap at the Citadel . . ."

"Don't tell Noah about the flood," I said.

"Well, it worked," said Mason frowning. He used a ballpoint pen to poke little blue holes in a sheet of paper. "Our intelligence fell down badly, Alex. And we owe you a great deal for sizing up the situation on the spot and withdrawing our forces before we had higher casualties. It took a lot of courage for you to do that. That's one of the reasons I asked General Drouin to trace you right after I arrived."

"You mean, I'm not to be court-martialled?" I asked sarcastically.

"Hardly," grinned Mason. He made a paper hat and tore it up. "We could have regrouped and followed through, you know. Their main body of militia at Valcartier was being pasted and could have been knocked off with a vigorous airborne landing. After the Starfighters had knocked out the Citadel, we could have walked in. We could have done it with the forces on hand, and we actually had air transport laid on, as you know, to take Third Black Watch into the airfield."

"Then, why . . ."

"Because while the hawks were in full cry in Quebec, the doves still held the balance in the Canadian government. And understandably so. We were plainly over-committed with troops overseas and there were a lot of ramifications in pulling them out to handle trouble at home. Secondly—and we can't blame them for this—there had always been an element in the Cabinet who wanted to avoid bloodshed in Quebec at all costs. Or, at least, if there was going to be any, we wouldn't start it. Those who had favoured a tougher line had their day at the Citadel. As soon as the first reports came in from the Citadel operation, the Cabinet agreed to the Starfighter strike, and then called off any more action. The Soviet appreciation of what then was likely to happen proved to be correct. When the Americans found out that the Canadian government had called off any further military action against Quebec, they then asked the prime minister what the hell he intended to do. I understand he gave them a rather snarky answer to the effect that the situation was being studied and they would be advised in due course. Understandably, the United States did not care very much for that answer. They kept pressing and got nowhere. Correctly or not, the Americans came to the conclusion that the Canadians were on the verge of recognizing the new government in Quebec. You didn't see them, of course, but about this time there were some obviously planted stories in the press speculating about the terms acceptable to Canada. The Quebec government, during all this, just sat tight and refused to clear the Seaway or permit normal rail and road traffic across its territory. They were riding high, and everyone was hysterical about their military victory. To keep things boiling, the hawks wanted to have

331

a war crimes trial with you as the star. Fortunately, they didn't get away with it."

"That's show business," I shrugged.

We were interrupted while Mason took an urgent phone call, in which he carried on a conversation of sorts in French laced with English nouns. He put down the receiver and started to circle all the dates on the calendar pad on his desk. He wanted to finish up our briefing, yet seemed anxious that I hear the whole story.

"After several more tries with the Canadian government," he went on, "the Americans lost patience. Evidently, they were unable to get the guarantees they justifiably expected from us. So they lost patience. And when the Yanks move, you know, they move!"

"They sure do," I agreed, echoing that peculiar admiration that Canadians have for American decisiveness.

"In no time flat," said Mason, "they had called an emergency session of the U.N. Security Council. Armed with documents, photos and transcripts of conversations —obviously provided by the C.I.A.—they accused the Chinese, the Soviets and the Cubans of interference and aggression in the affairs of Canada. Predictably enough, most of the Security Council walked out when Canada did. The Quebec government, of course, was not represented. Even though there wasn't a quorum left, those remaining passed a resolution calling for U.N. intervention based on the South African precedent. While everybody screamed 'illegal', the Yanks labelled two army divisions assembled at the Quebec border, a 'United Nations Emergency Force' and had them paint their helmets blue. These two divisions crossed the Quebec border a day ago, one towards Montreal and the other striking at Quebec City. They've had little trouble so far, except for sporadic sniping by whiteshirts. From the American viewpoint, they had to intervene and dress it up as best they could. In their eyes, this is worse even than Cuba."

"So we're up here with a government on the run and a

a disorganized rabble," I said without sympathy. "What happens now?"

"On the military side, the Americans landed a brigade on the Parc des Champs this morning. No resistance was made," said Mason. "On the political front, the Provisional Government has sent home the Soviet, Chinese and Cuban aid delegations. They have announced it today to establish their purity and to knock the props out from under the American excuse for intervention."

"So our bright boys in the Provisional Government have got themselves in a spot where they have no friends left," I sneered.

"They have one."

"Who?"

"Canada."

I stared.

"Canada has called for an emergency meeting of the Security Council and the General Assembly and has told the Provisional Government that they will provide all possible assistance to prevent a complete American take-over. The only way this can be done is with military assistance. All we can do is fight them to a standstill and try and mobilize world opinion against the Americans. It's another Dominican Republic situation, only on a much larger scale."

"So what are we doing?"

"I'm here, for one thing," said Mason without blushing. "We are sending in 'volunteers' in the usual twentieth century meaning of the word. All three battalions of the Vandoos are being flown in, regardless of our other international commitments. This morning three squadrons of CF-5's, without markings, flew into Bagotville. They are also flown by 'volunteers'. You don't believe all this?"

"No, it isn't that. I just don't see what you can do."

"Try to make the Americans change their mind. Give the Canadian government time to work with Quebec in working out a common proposal to restore stability that will be acceptable to the Americans and the U.N. It's not going to be easy until some more realistic people gain ascendancy in the Provisional Government. However, we are now optimistic that this will happen. General Drouin is insisting on it, for one thing. Lefebvre and Carpentier may not be in office very much longer. So on all counts, we must fight for time."

I stood up. "Well, thanks for the briefing, Ted. When can I get flown out and take my leave?"

Mason emptied an ashtray that had one butt in it and looked up with a scowl.

"I had hoped," he said heavily, "that I wasn't wasting my breath."

"Looks like you were. If there's any fighting to do, I'd sooner be with First Brigade in Thailand, thanks. You don't need me when you've got the Vandoos."

Mason suddenly got vicious and I sat down when I saw the look on his face. "Listen, Hlynka, we're not running a goddam conversion school here. We're fighting for the independence of Canada—the power to make decisions on our own soil without interference. We don't give a damn about the Provisional Government or who's jockeying for position in their funny little village council. We'll sort all that out afterwards. We're here to show the world that this is our territory and nobody else's. And the United Nations, the Yanks or nobody else is going to tell us how to handle our affairs. That's the issue, and if you can't see it you must be the thick-headed, plough-jockey that de Gruchy and some of the others think you are. Get the hell out of here, I've got things to do."

He picked up a sheaf of files and slammed them down in front of him. I didn't move for about five minutes. Mason never looked up.

"What about my seniority and pension?" I asked at last. "If I 'volunteer', do I go down to the bottom of the list, or what? And when the hell do I get paid?"

Mason looked up and smiled without humour.

"You'll be protected along with everyone else. Your name stays on the establishment and you're listed as being on special liaison duty. There's a per diem bonus arrangement. It's all kept in a special account in your name in Ottawa."

"I must have a bundle coming now," I grumbled. "If I ever get a chance to spend it." I thought of Edith and wondered who I would spend it on. Private school for the boys. I would send them to Upper Canada College in Toronto, or some such place, where they could meet some of the little bastards with connections who might do them some good in later life. They wouldn't have to start down at the end of the line the way I did. While I had been musing in this way, Mason had dug down into a desk drawer and had fished out a blue and white armband.

"If you wouldn't mind putting this on, Alex," he said. "We hope it won't be for long."

The armband lay in my hand like some kind of distasteful pelt from a small animal.

There was noise on the street and we opened the venetian blinds to look out. Below, truckloads of Vandoos were being cheered from crowded sidewalks. Tough and cocky, the professionals jumped down into the arms of the incredibly pretty women who always seem to appear at any kind of celebration in Quebec. Everybody was talking and laughing at the top of their lungs. Someone had an accordion and began to play it. I heard them starting to sing. They sang, *Il a gagné ses épaulettes* and their voices were taken up far down the street.

28

In the moonless dark, I sized up my pickup fighting patrol.
The N.C.O.'s and some of the officers weren't too bad,
but I worried about the kids and, besides, I had no way of
talking to them beyond some basic commands and simple
phrases I had learned the French for and in which I invariably got my tenses all mixed up. I hoped now that
they understood what they were to do and, more important, that they would do it when the moment came.

We had been in position in our ambush waiting for
three days. We were just south of, of all things, a place
called "Lac Petite Ha! Ha!" adjoining, naturally enough,
"Lac Ha! Ha!" itself. These are located on Route 56
where it dips into the eastern edge of Laurentides Park.
With the superstition of my ancestors, I hoped that there
was nothing symbolic in the names of those lakes, such as
somebody having a last laugh or the derision of the gods,
or anything like that.

All down the highway, the bridges had been blown days
before, and now we waited for the first U.S. recce patrol
to make its way over the Bailey bridges and reach us. We
were the screening force in front of the defence in depth
reaching back from the lakes to the little village of
Boileau. Here our firepower was dug in, stiffened by
permanent force elements who knew how to use such

336

things as 105 mm. howitzers and large-bore mortars.

Elements of the Third Battalion Vandoos also had set up their ENTAC anti-tank missiles. On the other side of the park, about forty miles away, a similar complex was dug in astride Route 54, appropriately enough, at a place called "Hell's Gate". Far to the south of us, combat teams from the Second Vandoos were slipping through the bush to hit the American infantry building up around St. Urbain. The U.S. forces obviously were planning a double strike up the two highways 54 and 56, to quickly finish off the little enclave that represented all that was left of the new nation so confidently launched only four months ago.

Because of my wild reputation, or something like that, they had given me a nice little sacrificial group of militiamen to specialize in fighting patrols, screening operations and such. For all of us, movement was slow because the Americans had air superiority during the day. However, our fighters kept their night helicopter sweeps to a minimum and it was in the darkness that we could get things done. But time was running out. American daytime airstrikes against our fields at La Tuque, Roberval and Bagotville were beginning to take their toll. It was only a matter of time, and we all knew it.

The forest clutched tightly against the gravel road, and even in the summer heat, a chill descended over us, lying covered with willow and pine branches. Further down the road, a two-man Carl Gustaf team was placed to hit the end of the line and another was half a mile north of us to hit the first vehicle. I worried about them having their drill tight enough so they could reload and get the other vehicles without standing up to cheer or some such gesture. I stewed about the two .50 calibre machine gun teams on either side of me and whether or not the others would remember to throw their grenades.

The sweet smell of cedars, pines and spruce enveloped us. It was so still, I heard a man across the road stifle a sneeze. I hoped they weren't going to get careless or impatient after two nights of this deadening, but tense, routine.

The whine of engines sounded far off in the night. The signaller beside me tapped my shoulder and I nodded. Crunching gravel under heavy tires, the armoured cars came slowly around a shallow curve, dim bulks of steel in the darkness. Except for the blown bridges and a few snipers, mostly whiteshirt freelancers, they hadn't run into anything yet. This was what we were counting on, and we hoped to hit them all along the road from St. Urbain up to the lakes.

So far we had been right. The armoured cars had their hatches open and their small running lights on. They had canvas sleeves over their guns to keep out the dust. The faint lights reflected off shiny, newly-painted blue helmets. Over the crunch of the wheels and their engines, we could hear the distant chatter of radio voices.

I wondered where they were from and what they thought about it all. I stared in fascination at the blurred, blue helmet sticking out of the cupola of the first vehicle as it whined past. Not so long ago, only a few months past, I had worn a blue helmet and had crouched in tall grass along a similar, narrow gravel road in the Transvaal. Then it had been a reverse situation. We had tracked down a raiding party of Afrikaaners, returning from some atrocities they had carried out in one of the Bantustan kraals. They had been in ordinary trucks, not armoured cars, I recalled, and we waited a day and a night before they came along. We had not counted on them being half-drunk, and they had fought back with a fury that left us no alternative but to raise our sights and shoot higher. Most of them had been killed or badly wounded. It had not been unlike lying here now amid the mosquitoes, the sharply-digging branches and the cool, thin air of the night. Just as then, I remembered the first whiff of dust and the exhaust fumes; the same tightening of belly muscles and the cold sweat on my upper lip; the same careful lifting of body to ease a leg that had gone into a tingling sleep.

In time it is sometimes difficult to accept what has actually taken place as reality. You wonder if certain intense and familiar experiences have ever really happened, or if what you see now is really there. I wasn't sure. Not positive at all. Not sure, that is, until I heard the crack of the rocket launcher far to my left. Soon the flames made the forest like daylight.

A. CANADIAN FORCES

—Disposition of Regular Force Units at the outbreak of the Civil War—

INFANTRY UNITS

Royal Canadian Regiment
— 1 Battalion: SEATO Thailand
— 2 Battalion: NATO Germany
Home station: Wolseley Barracks,
London, Ontario.

Princess Patricia's Canadian Light Infantry
— 1 Battalion: NATO Germany
— 2 Battalion: SEATO Thailand
Home station: Griesbach Barracks,
Edmonton, Alberta.

Royal 22nd Regiment
— 1 Battalion: NATO Germany
— 2 Battalion: United Nations, Viet Nam
(short-term assignment: supervision of elections).
— 3 Battalion (anti-tank): NATO Germany
Home station: Valcartier, Quebec.

Queen's Own Rifles of Canada
— 1 Battalion: United Nations, South Africa
— 2 Battalion: SEATO Thailand
Home station: Currie Barracks,
Calgary, Alberta.

The Black Watch (Royal Highland Regiment)
— 1 Battalion: SEATO Thailand
(reinforcement unit)
— 2 Battalion: United Nations, Greece.
Home station: Gagetown,
New Brunswick.

The Canadian Guards
- — 1 Battalion: Petawawa, Ontario
- — 2 Battalion: Picton, Ontario
  Home station: Petawawa.

The Canadian Airborne Regiment
- — NATO Germany
  Home station: St. Hubert, Quebec.

ARMOURED UNITS

(R.C.A.C.—Royal Canadian Armoured Corps)

Royal Canadian Dragoons
- — United Nations, South Africa
  Home station: Gagetown,
  New Brunswick.

Lord Strathcona's Horse
- — NATO Germany
  Home station: Sarcee Barracks, Calgary,
  Alberta.

8 Canadian Hussars (Princess Louise Dragoon Guards)
- — Camp Petawawa, Ontario
  Home station: Petawawa.

Fort Garry Horse
- — SEATO Thailand
  Home station: Petawawa.

ARTILLERY

1 Royal Canadian Horse Artillery
  NATO Germany
2 Royal Canadian Horse Artillery
  SEATO Thailand
3 Royal Canadian Horse Artillery
  Winnipeg, Manitoba
4 Royal Canadian Horse Artillery
  SEATO Thailand

B. CANADIAN FORCES

—Militia Units in Quebec at the time of the Civil War—

When the Civil War broke out there were approximately 8,000 volunteer, part-time soldiers in Canadian Forces Militia units in the Province of Quebec. Most of them were French-speaking and many joined the Armed Forces of the Provisional Government where they were reorganized into unnamed "Combat Teams". They became a significant factor in the heavy fighting during the last stages of the Civil War and the Intervention.

There were fourteen infantry battalions, three armoured units, three artillery units, two engineers and one signals unit in the Militia at the time of the outbreak. Their unit names and locations were as follows:

The Royal Canadian Hussars	Montreal
Le Régiment de Hull	Hull
27th Field Artillery Regiment	Cowansville
7th Field Battery RCA	Montreal
50th Field Battery RCA	Montreal
3rd Field Engineer Regiment	Westmount
9th Field Squadron RCE	Noranda
15th Independent Signal Squadron	Westmount
The Canadian Grenadier Guards	Montreal
3rd Battalion, The Black Watch (RHC)	Montreal
4 Battalion, Royal 22nd Regiment	Montreal
6 Battalion, Royal 22nd Regiment	St Hyacinthe
Les Fusiliers Mont Royal	Montreal
Le Régiment De Maisonneuve	Montreal
The Royal Montreal Regiment	Westmount
The Sherbrooke Regiment (RCAC)	Sherbrooke
Le Régiment de Trois Rivieres (RCAC)	Trois Rivieres
Les Voltigeurs de Québec	Quebec City

Les Fusiliers de Sherbrooke	Sherbrooke
Les Fusiliers du St Laurent	Rimouski & Riviere du Loup
Le Régiment de la Chaudière	Levis
Le Régiment de Joliette	Joliette
Le Régiment du Saguenay	Chicoutimi

C. THE QUEBEC LEGION

The Quebec Legion or the Parti Democratique de Quebec (P.D.Q.) Legion was a paramilitary arm of the Party organized originally as the youth branch of the Party. Later it was restructured on military lines and at the time of the Civil War was armed with light weapons, mainly sporting rifles or shotguns, some arms taken from armouries and automatic weapons delivered from Cuba and China. Control of the Legion remained at all times with the Party, oddly enough, even during the fighting, with the Youth Secretary of the Party. This was always a source of friction between the Chief of Staff of the Armed Forces of the Provisional Government (General Drouin) and the Party. While fairly effective during the civil disorders and the street fighting in Montreal, the Legion was not effective as a fighting force following the retreat to the Saguenay.

It is estimated that the Legion totalled about 65,000 at its peak, including leaders and ranks, most of whom were under 30.

Their "uniform" became a well-known trademark of the Civil War, and accounted for their unofficial name: "The Whiteshirts". They wore ordinary white shirts with a blue and white armband on the left sleeve. Some units wore blue sashes and blue woollen toques. Officers, or "leaders", wore high-necked, white tunics and navy blue breeches.

The Legion was organized into twelve "brigades" varying considerably in strength, depending on local support for the Party. Each "brigade" was headed by a "brigadier" with a rank-structure of majors and captains heading each local "company". Legion brigades therefore varied in strength from 2,000 to 10,000, depending on the density of population and Party support in its own area.

In a Party directive (No. 395) it was announced that the twelve brigades of the Legion would be named after the martyrs of 1839, all of whom were executed following the Second Rebellion of 1838 in Lower Canada (Quebec). Accordingly the Legion units were named as follows:

Joseph-Narcisse Cardinal Brigade, Amable Daunais Brigade, Pierre Théophile Decoigne Brigade, Chevalier de Lorimer Brigade, Joseph Duquette Brigade, François-Xavier Hamelin Brigade, Charles Hindenburg Brigade, Pierre-Rémi Narbonne Brigade, François Nicolas Brigade, Joseph Robert Brigade, Ambroise Sanguinet Brigade, Charles Sanguinet Brigade.

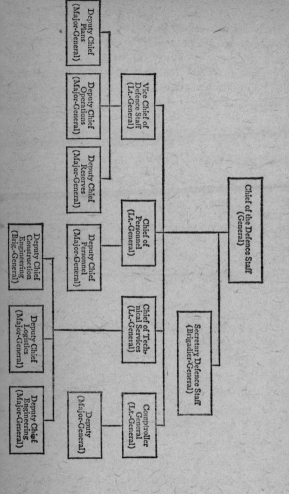

D. CANADIAN FORCES HEADQUARTERS
— *Organization Chart After Integration* —
Ottawa, Ontario.

Chief of the Defence Staff (General)

Vice Chief of Defence Staff (Lt.-General)
- Deputy Chief Plans (Major-General)
- Deputy Chief Operations (Major-General)
- Deputy Chief Reserves (Major-General)

Chief of Personnel (Lt.-General)
- Deputy Chief Personnel (Major-General)

Secretary Defence Staff (Brigadier-General)

Chief of Technical Services (Lt.-General)
- Deputy Chief Construction Engineering (Brig.-General)
- Deputy Chief Logistics (Major-General)
- Deputy Chief Engineering (Major-General)

Comptroller General (Lt.-General)
- Deputy (Major-General)

CANADIAN FORCES COMMANDERS

Mobile Command, (Lt.-General), St. Hubert, Quebec.

Maritime Command, (Major-General), Halifax, Nova Scotia.

Air Defence Command, (Major-General), North Bay, Ontario.

Training Command, (Major-General), Winnipeg, Manitoba.

Air Transport Command, (Major-General), Trenton, Ontario.

Materiel Command, (Major-General), Rockcliffe, (Ottawa), Ontario.

E. GLOSSARY OF TERMS

A.F.V. —Armoured Fighting Vehicle, an armoured car or tank, as distinct from "thin-skinned" vehicles such as trucks or jeeps.

Bird Dog (L-19) —Single-engined monoplane "spotter" aircraft used by Canadian Armed Forces as an artillery observation craft.

Buffalo (DHC-5) —DeHavilland turbo-prop troop transport used by Canadian Forces. Can airlift 41 fully-equipped troops, or 35 paratroopers, over 700 miles and return to base when equipped with long-range fuel tanks. Can take off with maximum loads in less than 400 yards. Operational crew: four.

Carl Gustaf launcher —Two-man, infantry anti-tank weapon; a portable rocket launcher.

C.D.S. —Chief Defence Staff: the general commanding the Canadian Armed Forces.

C.A.R. —Canadian Airborne Regiment, elite airborne unit formed in 1968.

C.F.H.Q. —Canadian Forces Headquarters, since 1971 located at Le Breton Flats, Ottawa, Ontario.

CF-5 —Canadian-adapted version of the Northrop F-5, two-engined, tactical jet fighter aircraft.

CH-112
(Hiller 12-E) —Small, two-man helicopter used for pilot training and reconnaissance.

C.S.M. —Company Sergeant Major, senior non-commissioned officer in a company.

D.E. —Destroyer escort, a naval vessel.

D.G.I. —Director General of Intelligence.

ENTAC —Missile-type anti-tank weapon mounted on light vehicles.

F.D.L. —Forward Defended Locality.

FN-(C1) —Standard NATO rifle used by Canadian Forces, 7.62 mm. or .308 calibre, semi-automatic. (Not used by U.S. Forces). Has replaced the old .303 Lee-Enfield.

FN-(C2) —Light machine gun, basically the FN rifle with a special barrel to handle automatic fire. This has replaced the Bren.

Hercules
(C-130) —Four-engined, turbo-prop transport used by Canadian Forces. Carries 80 paratroops or 90 regular troops.

I.O. —Intelligence Officer.

Iroquois
(CUH-1D) —Turbine-powered helicopter, carries a section of troops or six litter patients. Speeds from 120 to 130 m.p.h., normal range 293 miles.

Kriegsspiel —"War game" (Ger.) usually competitive military exercises on paper in the form of case studies.

L.Z. —Landing Zone.

MA/CDS —Military Assistant to the Chief Defence Staff, usually a lieutenant-colonel.

Militia —The volunteer reserve force to the Canadian Forces, part-time soldiers in greatly varying

347

stages of training and capability. At the time of the Civil War there were 239 Militia units in Canada, totalling approximately 26,000 men and women.

Mobile Command —Formed in 1965, it is the fighting core of the Canadian Armed Forces and has under command all Canadian operational land and tactical air units. Commanding officer is a Lieutenant-General, headquarters at St. Hubert, Quebec, near Montreal.

O.P.P. —Ontario Provincial Police.

P.M.Q. —Permanent Married Quarters, housing on a Forces base.

P.P.C.L.I. —Princess Patricia's Canadian Light Infantry, a Regular Force Regiment of two battalions.

Q.P.P. —Quebec Provincial Police.

R.C.E. —Royal Canadian Engineers.

Recce —Short form for reconnaissance, pronounced "recky".

R.I.N. —Rassemblement pour l'Indépendence Nationale, a Quebec separatist party of the late 1960's, later absorbed by the Parti Démocratique de Québec (P.D.Q.).

R.C.R. —Royal Canadian Regiment, a Regular Force Regiment of two battalions. Its third battalion, a militia unit known as 3rd Battalion, The Royal Regiment of Canada (London & Oxford Fusiliers) was mobilized at the outbreak of the Civil War.

R.M.C. —Royal Military College, Kingston, Ontario.

R.S.M. —Regimental Sergeant Major, senior N.C.O. in a battalion.

R.V.	—Rendezvous.
SEATO	—South-East Asia Treaty Organization.
Starfighter (CF-104)	—Fighter/bomber strike jet aircraft used by Canadian squadrons in NATO.
Sterling	—Sub-machine gun (or machine carbine), 9 mm. calibre, a somewhat better piece of plumbing than the old Sten.
T.O.E.T.'s	—Tests of Elementary Training.
Tutor (CL-41)	—Two-man, single-engined jet trainer.
U.A.S.	—Unit Aid Station, a first aid station. Used to be known as "Regimental Aid Post" (R.A.P.).
Vandoos	—Expression commonly used to designate the "Vingt-Deux's" the Royal 22nd Regiment, a Regular Force Regiment of three battalions, consisting mainly of French-speaking troops.
Voodoo (CF-101B)	—Long-range, two-man jet interceptor used by Canadian squadrons in North American Air Defence Command (NORAD).
Voyageur (CH-113A)	—Troop transport helicopter, twin-turbines, carries 25 fully-equipped troops or 5,000 pounds of cargo over a distance of 200 miles at speeds up to 150 m.p.h.